The unmarked pal
Evans turned sha
in protest. Foster flip₁
red roof beacon. The flashing crimson light played eerily on
leafless elms and denuded underbrush, giving the illusion of a
forest fire.

The lieutenant patted his .38 in its shoulder holster. The car
swerved. He braced one hand on the dashboard and reached
under the seat with the other for his shotgun. Shells were in his
jacket pocket. He loaded quickly.

Flashlight beams stabbed out. Shouts filled the winter night.
Foster's eyes stayed fixed dead ahead. His partner concentrated
on not hitting trees or colleagues.

A dark form huddled in the center of the path. Evans slowed
and swerved to avoid it. Headlights focused on a long gray
overcoat. A shattered gun stock lay across the man's spine. His
feet were lost in a tangle of brush beside the path. The head was
unrecognizable pulp.

In the beacon's blood-red glare, the killer loomed behind the
corpse.

Foster goggled.

Twice a man's height, thrice a man's breadth, a humanoid
thing hissed at them through rows of pointed, gleaming teeth.
Scarlet skin glistened as the advancing form stepped into the
headlight glow. The bulging loin-cloth affirmed its sex. The savage murders were well within this creature's capacity.

Black pebbling on the left flank marked where one shotgun
blast had hit. His right hand waved a thick, bloodied branch,
while the left circled the throat of a limp German shepherd.
Entrails dangled from the dog's torn belly.

"We're gonna need a bigger set of handcuffs," Evans
observed.

THE ONI

BY GORDON LINZNER

NEW YORK CITY

TUESDAY, DECEMBER 28, 1982

CHAPTER 1

Scritch.

    Scritch.

Scritch.

For one thousand three hundred and thirty-two years, his impenetrable coal-black eyes have seen nothing but more impenetrable darkness. He does not know the exact period of his imprisonment; only that it has been a very long time.

More vexing than this darkness is the virtual absence of sounds from the outside world. The iron encasement acts as an efficient damper. In the past millennium and a third, he has heard little beyond the desperate scrape of his bleeding fingernails as they worry the predetermined spot on the otherwise homogeneous interior surface of his prison; that, and the angry, bitter curses with which he passes the time when he must pause, not to rest but to let his nails grow out again.

It took centuries just to make a tangibly noticeable dent in the barrier, centuries during which he kept track of the site by marking it with his own viscous, sticky blood. Then hundreds of years more to deepen that first hairline scratch to its present groove.

He might breach the barrier tomorrow, or not for another thousand years. He has no clues by which to judge. His memory of the casing's thickness, glimpsed inattentively so long ago, is vague. He cannot recall its relationship to his present size, and layers could have been added after he was sealed within. Nor has he been inclined to speculation. Guesswork would not shorten his confinement by a single hour. Only the tedious wearing away of metal beneath his stinging and abraded fingertips could influence that. This task has been all to him. His waking hours—and he was not even sure he ever slept—held no other diversions.

Scritch.

Scritch.

Scri ….

In mid-stroke he was thrown off balance, tumbling heels over head over heels. Instinctively, he wrapped muscular arms over his face. The tips of his skullhorns pricked his forearm. He gnashed his pointed teeth, enraged by this interruption, as he was whenever such an event disturbed him. It held no terror for him. He assumed it was another earthquake, and long overdue, at that. He'd survived scores upon scores of quakes, including several before his confinement and even before his transformation, when he was as vulnerable as the inferiors over whom he'd ruled.

Disturbances rarely last more than a few minutes at a time, at most perhaps an hour. It seemed absurd to begrudge so brief a recess, considering the centuries he had been at his task. Nonetheless, he did begrudge it. He vented his anger in guttural curses as he rode out the upheaval curled into a fetal ball, rattling about the iron casing like a pebble in a New Year's noisemaker.

Whang!

Jing!

Clang!

These last vibrations, more forceful than the previous shock waves, threatened to shake loose the fangs in his massive jaws.

They also seemed to signal an end to the convulsions. He cautiously uncurled. His thick, horny skin was splotched with tender bruises, which he ignored. They would heal with unnatural swiftness. They always did.

He extended his right foot, gripping the concave metal with all three toes. The prison pitched abruptly. He tensed, ready to curl up again should the quake continue.

It did not. The iron casing had shifted in response to his own movement. It must have fallen, perhaps from a shelf, to land at an awkward angle. Or been set down so. It which case, there had been no earthquake.

Anger returned, a knot of fire in his belly. Someone had dared to toy with his prison! To toss it about like a fishing boat in a typhoon! To mock the power within! If only he were free, that rash fool would learn a lifelong lesson. Although his life would not be so very long.

On hands and knees, he began the familiar groping for his furrow, systematically running blunt fingertips along the metal interior. His only external clue to progress was the dubious one of gravity. Not this section. Nor that. Nor over here.

He stopped abruptly, neck muscles bunching in cords. The broad, flat nose snuffled once, twice, thrice. Trapped with the odor of his own sweat for so many years, he no longer detected it, but his sense of smell had not completely atrophied. His tongue, fat and dark and rough, lashed out as if to entice the heady aromatic mixture from the air like a snake's.

Grease. Varnish. Raw sewage. Saltwater tang. The faint hint of less-than-fresh fish. A mingling of less identifiable scents. More important than the nature of these olfactory stimuli was the question of their source. His outsized head swiveled slowly, dragging the torso after.

For the first time in more than thirteen centuries, a grin of hideous and undisguised pleasure twisted his grotesque features.

He could see the groove. The wall had been breached.

Dim light seeped through the hairline crack, less than the glow from a single candle but blindingly bright to the direct gaze of eyes long useless. His diligence had weakened the barrier at that spot, and the recent jolting saved him further months, perhaps years, with the application of the right amount of stress at the precise point. He could almost forgive whomever had treated the shell with such disrespect. If it had been his nature to forgive.

He pressed thick lips to the opening and filled long-empty lungs with comparatively fresh air from without. The sensation further fired his anxiety to escape. Blunt, powerful fingers forced their way into the narrow gap, pressing the sides outward. Muscles bulged on forearms and upper arms, shoulders and back, as increasingly better leverage permitted them to come into play.

With a sharp hiss, he drew back his right hand. From where the knife-like edge of cast iron had pressed into his palm welled a line of thick black ichor, vivid against his brick-red skin. Tears of agony seared his cheeks. He should have realized. The iron had not lost its power to hold him with the passage of centuries; why should it lose the ability to harm him?

Scowling, he used the three fingers of his left hand to press the gaping wound closed, clamping it for the minute or so required for his flesh to heal. Waiting, he bent to peer through the hole. His pupil-less eyes were adjusting to the faint glow. The view was monopolized by dark, coarse-grained wood. The side of a clothing chest, he supposed, or a section of molding. He did not greatly care. His immediate concern was the size of the opening.

It could now accommodate his limbs and even his great skull, but not his chest and shoulders. He flexed his right palm, examining the bright strip of red scar tissue only slightly less dull than the surrounding skin. Its movement was stiff. Exercise would remedy that. He grimaced. If he tried to further stretch the gap, he risked another and potentially deadlier injury. On the verge of his liberation, he might unwittingly accomplish what his captors had failed to do. The irony did not appeal to him.

There was a better way.

He wedged himself into the gap as far as possible, careful of the keen edges. The metal shell grew warm beneath his touch. Mass—his mass—converted to heat energy. Little conversion was required, fortunately, for he was already near the lower limit where too much mass would be lost for him to regain it. The iron became no hotter than if it had been held in a mortal's hand for five minutes. The sides of the opening seemed to retreat. He struggled further. Suddenly, as though his body were greased, it slid forward to tumble onto a hard, wooden surface.

Free!

He rocked on his back, grasping three-toed feet in three-fingered hands, chortling exultantly. Huge splinters gouged his flesh. He reveled in the sensation of real wood. Not iron! Wood!

Free!

His capering carried him away from the shell that had held him captive. As the first flush of triumph faded, he took in his new surroundings. He was on the next-to-lowest step of a steep stairway in a narrow room. The cabin of a boat, for it pitched and rolled beneath him. Still, the water seemed calm, gently lapping alongside. In harbor rather than at sea.

He was not alone on board. Now that his ears were no longer filled with his own gleeful gloating, he heard other voices. The syllables were meaningless, but the throats undoubtedly human. Two of them. Male and female.

The pair were at a berth on the starboard side. The man, whose back was to him, wore oddly-cut clothing that lacked the rich, flowing lines he was used to. The woman, similarly clothed, faced him, her features partially hidden by the shoulder of the man who was bent over her partly supine form.

Only her too-narrow nose and rounded eyes, reminiscent of certain primitive tribes, were visible. She was too occupied to notice his tiny form. Her hand shot toward her companion's face. The other caught it and twisted her arm. She cried out.

His thick lips writhed with remembered pleasures. The world had not changed so very much in his absence. The scene confirmed what his ears conveyed. Although the words were ugly gibberish, the urgent tone of the man's voice and the protest in the woman's told a familiar tale.

At some point in this ageless drama, however, his prison had been disrespectfully treated. This had hastened his freedom, but the crime was inexcusable. Discipline must be enforced.

Further, as the struggle progressed, his own appetites began returning. They demanded appeasement. It was not his nature to question his urges.

Instead, he satisfied them.

The cabin cooled. Heat energy was sucked from the iron shell, the metal fixtures, the single dim overhead lamp, the wood paneling and stairs, even the very air, and was rapidly converted into mass. When he stood as tall as the man beside the berth, he noticed the heavy brass railing along the port side of the companionway. He grasped it. The metal was icy beneath his blunt fingers. It grew colder yet as he wrenched it from the wall. The retaining bolts rattled down the steps and along the keel.

He hefted the railing in one hand. It felt solid and well-balanced. A good weapon.

The cabin temperature continued to drop.

The woman saw him first. She stopped struggling and her eyes went wide. The man leaned forward, pressing his advantage.

A towering shape blocked the light. Its shadow engulfed the berth and darkened the bulkhead beyond. The man stiffened, mouth suddenly dry, and turned to look.

He didn't give the mortal time to duck.

CHAPTER 2

"Aieeee!"

The scream awakened Andrew Kura suddenly and completely. It reverberated through the shadowy, barren loft. It caused him to lurch awkwardly erect in the narrow cot, one elbow digging at the ribs of the woman who lay beside him. Sweat coated the upper half of his body.

After a moment he realized, with a shudder, that the scream had come from his own throat, ripped from it as though by barbed hooks.

Kura stripped the blankets from his naked body. He swung his legs over the side of the cot and sat up. The glow of the electric heater reflected off the sheen of his perspiration; his hairless chest crimson. That, too, agitated him. He clasped his shaking hands together and pressed them between his knees to stop the violent trembling. Air whistled through the gap in his front teeth as he sucked great, rapid gusts into his lungs. Blood pounded in his ears.

The woman stretched her cramped legs into the space where his had lain. She rolled over to look up at his back. Highlighted by the shadows of the heater's faint illumination, its muscles jerked and contracted in an eerie dance.

"What the shit was that?" she demanded. "A delayed orgasm?"

Kura shook his head. He had to swallow twice before he could speak.

"I don't know, Jen. A nightmare. The granddaddy of all nightmares. Jesus." He licked his lips obsessively until a trickle of saliva touched his chin. "Christ. I need a smoke." He bent forward, almost double, fumbling beneath the cot for the half-empty pack he'd dropped there earlier.

Jen slid to the foot of the cot and sat up cross-legged. It was disconcerting to talk to a pair of buttocks—although, she reflected impishly, this was not the first time she'd thought of Kura in those terms. She kept the blanket wrapped about her shoulders, but not from modesty, for she was unconcerned with the exposure of her apple-sized breasts. No matter what Kura claimed, this vast loft was *cold*, even on this unseasonably warm winter night. Cracked windows, ill-fitting doors, spaces between shrinking, ancient floorboards meant perpetual drafts that were invariably dank. Jen also noticed that Kura always wound up on the side of the cot near the heater.

She reached out to touch his shoulder where a muscle seemed to form a hard knot.

Kura jerked forward. His knees banged the rough wooden floor. He spun, crouching, and gripped the metal rod along the cot's edge. The flesh beneath his fingernails was white. In the orange aura of the heater, his wide, dark eyes gleamed ferally, like those of a trapped tiger.

"Sorry, I'm sure!" Jen snapped. She drew back her hand as if burned and tossed her shoulder-length red hair, which looked almost black in this light. Kura looked away from her. He shook his head, trying to clear it. The cigarette pack in his right hand was mashed against the bedding. He pried his fingers loose enough to hold out the pack to her.

"Want one?"

"You know I don't smoke, Andy. And I wish you wouldn't. Not around me. Kill yourself if you like but don't drag the rest of the world along."

As usual, Kura did not hear the lecture. His shaking hands drew out a cigarette torn in the middle, where a golden thread of tobacco poked through. He reached under the cot again to come up with a red and black matchbook.

"What kind of nightmare?" asked Jen, her tone softening.

Kura suddenly realized that his bare rump rested on an icy, splinter-laden floor. He hauled himself onto the cot beside her. His reply was slow.

"There was a presence of some kind, ancient and powerful and utterly evil. It seemed tied to me in some way but didn't *want* me, unaware on the most basic level that I even existed. I tried to escape before it became aware of my presence. Then something else, another force, compelled me to approach it. I remember a blinding pain, as though I was being torn apart from within ... but that wasn't *me* it was happening to! Then there was a strangled cry ..."

"That's where I came in," Jen interrupted.

"No. You heard my reply." Kura tore a match from the cardboard book and tried to light it. Without success.

Jen pushed a loose strand of red hair behind her ear. "You were probably reliving your birth trauma. I went through similar changes in the six months I did Primal Therapy, before I decided it was bullshit."

"It wasn't that kind of cry, Jen. It was ... Never mind. It'll sound stupid."

Jen sniffed. "You might as well finish it, Andy. Better not hold it in."

Kura shrugged and shuddered. "It was a plea for help. Or justice. Something like that."

"Those exact words?"

"No words. Nothing intelligible. Just an impression, from the tone."

Jen felt a draft on her belly. She pulled the blanket closed in front. She took a long deep breath, let it escape slowly. "You're right, Andy. It sounds stupid. You'd better give up comic books for a while."

"I don't read comic books." He coaxed a flame from the next-to-last match.

"Don't kid me, Andy. I saw that box in the corner, full of issues of *Tarmak the Tyrant-Fighter, The Blue Streak, The Thrasher, Doc Justice and His League of...*"

"A commercial artist lived here before. Must belong to him." Kura lost interest in the conversation. He could not light his cigarette. The match flame wavered in his hand; he nearly singed his eyebrows. Cursing, he blew out the match and dropped both it and the cigarette to the bare floor, amid a half-dozen discarded, unstruck matches. His heel ground the cigarette to a heap of shredded leaves.

Jen studied his pudgy frame with concern. "You are bad off, aren't you? Andy, tell me the truth. Are you tripping?"

He shook his head violently. "Haven't dropped LSD in ten or fifteen years. These last twelve months I couldn't even afford it. As you know."

"Could be a flashback and you're reliving an old trip. That was the big hazard in dropping acid."

"I know what those are like. This was different. More vivid."

"Aren't hallucinations usually vivid?"

"Not in the same way. It's the difference between being somewhere and, I don't know, not being somewhere else."

Jen smiled encouragingly. "Well, you seem to be your normal self again. You're not making any sense at all." She touched his shoulder again, barely scraping the skin with her fingernails. His muscles twitched under the slight pressure, but he did not pull away. Instead, he placed his hand over hers, pressing it for a moment before letting go.

Jen was shocked by the heavy moisture on her palm from the brief contact.

"Lie down," she urged. "Get some sleep. In the morning you'll have forgotten the whole thing."

Kura shivered. "I can't sleep. I'm too keyed up."

Jen bit her lower lip. Her expression was that of an impending martyr. "All right, Andy. I'm still sore from the last time, but if anyone ever needed to release tension, it's you, right now." Her hand crept across his hip.

He stopped it with a touch. "No."

"No?"

He lay down, stretching the full length of the cot. She turned to make room. Gently, he pulled her down alongside. "No. Just ... hold me."

Jen's eyes dilated and she laughed sharply. "Are you serious? Killer Kura, the terror of a thousand bedrooms? Handy Andy, any time, any place? You want to be cuddled?"

Any other time he'd have risen to the bait.

"Please, Jen. That's all."

"It's *your* reputation." She whipped the blanket around, stirring the chilled air, to cover them both.. One arm slid about Kura's shoulders, the other across his chest. His thin layer of flab felt as tight as a drumhead. With a sob, Kura rolled up against Jen. He buried his face in her small breasts. His cheeks were as damp as his back.

Tears? wondered Jen.

"It's okay, Andy. You'll be all right. Want me to sing a lullaby?"

He shook his head. His tangle of short-cropped hair tickled her chin and throat. Jen stifled a giggle. Slowly, the tension in Kura's body melted away. She began relaxing, herself.

After a quarter of an hour, Kura felt the woman's limbs weigh more heavily on him. Her breathing changed to a soft, whistling snore. He moved carefully, working himself free, trying not to wake her.

There would be no sleep tonight for Andrew Kura. The nightmare still waited for him. He could feel it. He glanced at the luminous dial of his wrist-watch, then stared straight up at a ceiling rafter.

Less than seven hours to morning.

CHAPTER 3

Homicide.

That was the single word painted on the frosted glass panel of the first door to the left of the third floor landing. Lieutenant Amos Foster noticed it because a detective first grade noticed everything. His habitual alertness made his associates outside the police force—civilians—uneasy around the thick-set man. Foster had grown as accustomed to this situation as a stable human being could. His childhood had provided plenty of experience in being alone.

So he noticed the word, and the gilt room number above, but he could have found the squad room with his deep set eyes shut. Five days a week, forty-eight weeks out of the year, Amos Foster climbed the too-wide marble steps and walked the seven paces to this door. He'd been doing so for close to eleven years.

He turned the knob and pushed.

"Damn," came clear and soft from his right as he entered. A detective second grade sat at her desk, one hand still on the telephone receiver she'd just replaced, the other grasping a slip on which she'd taken down some information. The paper crinkled. Her back was to Foster. He slipped off his raincoat noiselessly.

"Damn. Damn. Damn." She folded the slip and stuffed it into her blazer pocket.

Foster grinned as he leaned into her line of sight. His light brown complexion seemed to glow with mischief. "Your Christmas spirit didn't last long, Sergeant Davis. I'll admit this balmy weather isn't very Christmas-y, but it's starting to blow a little. We should get some of Denver's blizzard before the year's out."

Davis swiveled around, accidentally—perhaps—slapping Foster's flat, wide nose with a raven curl. "Lieutenant. You're early, aren't you? I haven't seen Sergeant Evans yet."

"A little early. I want to start some overdue paperwork before my shift begins." He pointed at the blazer pocket. The yellow slip didn't match the maroon trim. "If that call was urgent, you'd have told me to go to hell and been gone by now."

"Seconds don't exactly count, but it's urgent enough. At the worst possible time, too." Davis sighed. "I know I shouldn't bitch. This is what I'm here for. It's my job. But I've been warming this chair for the past six hours, playing with my toes and clearing my desk, and now, at ten to midnight, ten lousy minutes before I go off duty and start my week's vacation, some green foot-patrolman on a Riverside Park beat trips over a body!" She yanked her blue down-lined jacket off the coatrack and struggled into it. "Don's been looking forward to this ski trip for weeks. You should have seen his eyes light up when he heard about the storm in Colorado. He'll never believe I was the only homicide detective free to take the call."

"Why not?" asked Foster. He scanned the squad-room. Most of the desks were empty, their detectives out on call. At the rest, plainclothesmen were taking statements from nervous civilians, including one who verged on hysteria. A lot of people were obviously not happy with what Santa Claus had brought them.

Davis shrugged and her shoulders slumped. "You're right. He will. Only, in a way, that makes it worse. Don's been acting funny lately." Her lips thinned. "I don't think he wants to wait another four years to have the baby, after all."

Foster nodded. He'd lost track years ago of the number of colleagues who'd lost spouses and lovers to the strain of police work. He'd recently broken up with the latest in a string of girlfriends, himself. The most stable marriage in the department was that of his own partner, Joe Evans, and even that relationship was a little frayed at the edges. Sergeant Davis had been married for just under a year, and although Foster did not work closely with her he'd seen danger signs as far back as Labor Day. She was a hard-working, dedicated officer. Foster doubted she would have a husband next Christmas.

Still, you don't push someone off a ledge if there's a rope handy. Foster thrust his right hand, palm up, under Davis' nose. His fingers waggled.

"Lucky for you I was here to take the call."

It took a moment for the offer to penetrate the sergeant's self-pity. Then her eyes brightened. "Amos, would you? I can't tell you how much it would ·mean." She reached for the slip. Her fingers froze at the pocket's lip. "No, that's not fair. You worked over Christmas."

"And got holiday pay for it, and no family to disappoint. Are you going to give me the slip, or do Joe and I have to cruise the whole park looking for stiffs?"

Conscience salved, Davis handed over the paper. "You'd never find it that way. Dead woman on a houseboat, at the boat basin off Seventy-Ninth Street. A neighbor heard screams, threw on a bathrobe and reached the shoreside telephone just as the regular beat man strolled by. He investigated. Says it's messy."

"Murders usually are. That told you he was green?"

"That and the catch in his voice. Oh, damn."

"What?"

"I gave him my name."

Foster laughed. "You don't think a rookie at a murder scene will remember *that* on top of everything he's *supposed* to remember? He'll probably forget your voice was female. If he doesn't, I'll have Joe do his falsetto. Your shift is over, Davis. Punch out and go home before I ask Captain Matherson to throw you out!"

Davis quickly cleared her few items left on her desk into the top center drawer. "I owe you one, Amos."

"Don't think I won't call you on it, either," he growled. He slipped the raincoat on again. "I'm going downstairs to pick up a uniform to go with me. If you run into Joe on the way out, tell him to meet me."

"Sure thing." Suddenly, Davis grasped Foster's arm, leaned upward, and pecked a kiss on his milk-chocolate cheek. "Sorry about your unfinished paperwork."

Foster shrugged, stepping backwards through the doorway. "Doesn't matter. Like most cops, I hate paperwork."

NIHON (ANCIENT JAPAN)

649 A.D.

CHAPTER 4

TWELFTH MONTH. SEVENTH DAY.

The tiny province of Imuri consists of a narrow valley that crouches like a borrowed cat between towering mountain ranges, far north of the Kanto plain, on the main island of Honshu. Seventh-century Japan is politically fragmented by scores of warring clans and scheming lords. Even by those standards, Imuri is notable for its isolation.

Credit for this distinction goes not alone to the single ill-tended path that twists more or less southeast from these highlands to the northern shore of Lake Biwa, whence better routes can lead the bold traveler to the Emperor's court in Yamato province. Nor is it due solely to the familiar dangers of attack by bandits, or dispossessed Ainu barbarians, or the armies of neighboring lords hungry for territory but unable to penetrate Imuri's rough surroundings in sufficient force to conquer. The almost total insularity of the province is primarily attributable to the fierce cruelty, lustful ambition, and oppressive rule of one man: Lord Uto, absolute master of the secluded valley and its inhabitants.

Yet not, it seems, master of inexorable nature.

Lord Uto is dying.

A panel slides aside, without sound, to admit a visitor to the lord's presence. The despot's private quarters are large, second only to the audience chamber at the opposite end of the residence. The atmosphere here is thick with stale air, greasy smoke from the oil lamps that line the walls, and a tangible mixture of anticipation and dread. Sandalwood from burning censers at the room's four corners cannot wholly disguise the odor of physical corruption.

More than a score of men, the loyalest of Uto's retainers and a much greater number than this room is designed to accommodate even with all the shoji screens removed, are gathered here. Their combined body heat takes the edge off the winter chill that seeps from the garden through the thin paper walls, but white fog still hovers near lips and nostrils. These men are warriors, and so they do not complain of the cold, though every one of them prefers active duty to standing guard. Some, not all, heads turn to the opening door; some, not all, hands brush icy sword hilts, only to drop away empty as eyes confirm the newcomer's identity.

"Move aside, you dung-eaters!" roars the dying Lord Uto, interpreting the motion of those standing nearest his deathbed. "Why should I summon the priest, if not to see and speak with him?"

Sandals shuffle on polished wood as the retainers, uniformly garbed in saffron kami-shimo, hurry to obey. Even now, prostrate on his thick chodai straw mattress, helpless as a crab with its claws torn off, his body wasted by disease, Uto inspires fear with the mere hint of his displeasure. The yellow sea circling him ripples and parts, forming a corridor from the sick man to his guest. Without raising his head, Lord Uto stares stonily along its length.

There stands the priest Monaga, a thin-faced, balding man, come to answer the nobleman's call, clad in nothing more elaborate than the much-patched drab gray kimono he always wears, its lower half darkly stained where he'd knelt that morning in the snow, tending the sacred sakaki tree on the grounds of his humble shrine. Monaga's terror is lessened only slightly by the knowledge that of all those who dared defy the lord, he alone has been suffered to live.

Does Lord Uto intend to correct that oversight before his death?

A tug at his sleeve reminds Monaga of Hoke, the boy who brought him here and now stands at his side. Not yet ten years old, Hoke has the watery, fearful eyes of a broken, aged peasant, highlighted by close-cropped wiry hair. Six years earlier, in the same month that then-Empress Kogyuku moved her residence to the village of Asuka, Uto dispatched his wife and son to the Imperial Court and sold his concubines to a brothel in Naniwa. Thereafter he demanded from his subjects, in addition to the regular annual taxes, a male child to add to his household each summer. Under a less savage ruler, such duty could be advantageous, even enjoyable; but the fate of Uto's chosen youth by the start of the following summer is a mystery. Rumors are horrifying; the truth worse. Hoke was taken from his family two weeks before illness struck the lord. In the months since, his duties as pillow boy have been light. Yet the strain already evident in the boy's face tears at the priest's heart.

Hoke starts down the human corridor, stops, turns pleadingly to Monaga. The priest follows slowly. The cold of the raised wooden floor seeps through his thin cotton tabi. By special dispensation, Uto's bodyguards are permitted to wear sandals here today, but Monaga must tread the floorboards in his white, toe-divided socks. He does not relish this meeting, but Hoke's instructions were explicit. Bring the priest, or perform self-strangulation before the torii, the gateway of the shrine. How can Monaga refuse?

Lord Uto's ebon eyes, as usual unnaturally bright, pull the priest forward. The lord's tight smile, never pleasant, is doubly unnerving with the flesh drawn taut over his skull. Uto lifts his head a finger's-width from the makura. The padding on the wooden pillow is stained black from fever-sweat. The topmost of several layers of expensive Chinese silk sheets, drawn to his chin but leaving his right arm free, is more ominously spotted.

The priest kneels beside the deathbed, and waits.

"My old nemesis come to see me off, eh?" Uto's dry chuckle degenerates to a cough. A crimson droplet stains his lip. The retainer nearest his head stoops to wipe it clean with a silk cloth already stiff and discolored with dried blood.

Monaga glances at Hoke, who stands rigidly beside him. The look is not returned.

"I had little choice. As you well know." Monaga's voice does not waver. He has lived with this fear for many years.

"You always had a choice, priest. You always chose wrong. Your ridiculous consistency saved your life, you know. It allowed me to despise you."

"Then perhaps it was not so ridiculous." Monaga rises. Blood pounds in his ears. "If I am here simply to endure more of your taunts, I see no purpose in staying."

"I think you will stay," replies Lord Uto.

Monaga turns. Retainers close ranks behind him. Those he can see rest hands on swordhilts. The slap of flesh on metal resounds menacingly in the crowded chamber.

The priest shrugs. He kneels again, scowling. "I do not see what you can gain by this. You cannot expect to make amends at this late hour, Lord Uto. You led a life of unconscionable evil, even denying your ancestors the worship and respect that is their due. You would need several lifetimes to undo it all. Imuri is the only province in all the islands from which the territorial kami have fled in revulsion from your rule."

"Yet, deprived of your gods, you still tend the shrine."

"Someone must remember. The spirits will one day return."

"After my death, you imply." Uto chuckles again. "How obvious you are, priest. How thoroughly tactless in your attempts at diplomacy. It would have been amusing to offer your services to the Emperor for one of the trade delegations to China, if I'd dared to let you leave Imuri. I wonder how long you'd have lasted among those barbarians."

Monaga's response is an eloquent silence.

"Enough pleasantries," Uto continues. "You may have nothing better to do than plug leaks in your dilapidated shrine, but I have some serious dying at hand. I called you here today, priest, to bear witness to a particular desire of mine, one which my retainers may conveniently forget after my death. You are the most trustworthy man in Imuri. That is the second reason for your survival. I can depend on you to arrange my funeral according to my wishes."

"Surely that is for your son to attend to."

Uto's mouth twists. His pale cheeks color slightly. "At this moment, Jiko paces my courtyard, anxious for the moment he can close my eyes in fulfillment of his filial duty—and incidentally claim his inheritance. If the warriors in this room were not so loyal—that is to say, if they did not fear my wrath more than Jiko's—he might long ago have found it in his heart to shorten my suffering." Again the unpleasant smile. "I taught him well. No, priest. You are the only man I can depend on. In lieu of the full burial ceremony, my remains are to be cremated."

Monaga tenses. His fingers brush the shaku, the tapering wooden slab in his belt that is a symbol of his priesthood, in instinctive distaste for Uto's apostasy. "I see. You turn your back on the worship of your ancestors, only to embrace the foreign Buddhist teachings."

"Those Buddhists will put you out of work one day, priest. More than one emperor has been converted to their teachings. You would do well to incorporate their wisdom into your own lore."

"I know something of their superstitions," Monaga says flatly.

Lord Uto lifts a thin eyebrow. "Pity you never mentioned that before. We might have had some interesting discussions."

"Not so very interesting."

The eyebrow lowers. "Nonetheless, I insist on this unorthodox arrangement. There are full instructions in the compartment of my pillow. You will see that they are carried out exactly. Else my restless spirit will haunt Imuri for generations." He pauses to discharge a wad of phlegm. Hoke opens a drawer at the back of the wooden pillow and removes a roll of rice-paper. He hands it to the priest.

"If it appeases your scruples," Uto adds, "I assure you that I expect no heavenly reward from this request."

Monaga shifts the weight on his knees, which are starting to stiffen. "I do not like it. But I do not like anything about you, Lord Uto."

"Then you will do as I wish." It was not a question.

Monaga thrusts the rolled paper into his sleeve. "It seems little enough to ask, and can harm no one … except yourself, and I doubt you can blacken your soul much further."

Lord Uto's hard black eyes drift from the priest's face to Hoke's. His withered hand rises to stroke the boy's buttock.

Hoke endures the caress stoically, but trembles at the lord's next words.

"Naturally, I should like my pillow boy to accompany me in my final journey."

Monaga grasps the boy's shoulders and pulls him out of Uto's reach. Hoke gasps in horror at the priest's breach of hierarchical respect. Punishment for such is worse than simple death. He struggles to return to his master's side so that none can accuse him of sharing in the disobedient act. The chamber echoes with the snicking of long swords being drawn from their scabbards.

"You press too hard, Lord Uto," Monaga says, aware—as in previous confrontations—that each word may be his last. "Will you continue your foulnesses even after death?"

At that, Uto roars with laughter. His thin arm falls to his side atop the covers. Another coughing fit cuts him short. Blood trickles down his chin. It is hastily removed. A fresh silk cloth is sent for.

Breathing easily again, Lord Uto signals his retainers to sheath their blades.

"So close, priest," he mutters. "So close."

"It does not take a physician to see your end is near," Monaga replies.

Lord Uto shakes his head. "I can restrain myself, priest, when it suits me to do so. Do not be concerned for Hoke. I bequeath him, with the rest of my possessions, to my son ... for as long as Jiko can hold on to him. Just attend to my cremation as instructed."

"I will do what I can."

"You will do as I say."

Monaga licks his lips. "Agreed. May I leave now?"

"Of course. There's nothing here of interest to keep you. Anyone can die. It's as easy as twisting a baby's arm. Hoke will keep me company to the end. Right, lad?"

The boy wriggles free of the priest's grip and kneels at the head of his master's straw sleeping mat. Monaga offers a smile of compassion, but Hoke dares not meet his eyes. It is ironic that Uto's deathbed is attended by a kidnapped peasant boy because the lord cannot trust his own son, even in the presence of a score and more armed bodyguards—warriors whose allegiance transfers to Jiko at the moment his father dies.

With a sigh, the priest gets to his feet. None of the warriors offers to help. He wishes that his staff had not been confiscated at the gate, as a potential weapon.

The retainers fall back, forming a path for Monaga. He turns to the door and starts walking.

"Priest." Uto's voice is empty of blood and tears.

Monaga stops but does not look back.

"Pass by the courtyard on your way out. Tell Jiko I won't delay his chance to close my eyes much longer. Blood is only blood, and my death *must* be natural."

The priest bobs his head once, in acknowledgment, and hastens from the chamber. He feels more disquieted than seems warranted. He is inured to the presence of death and familiar with the lord's inhumanity. Uto's parting words express a perfectly understandable desire.

Why, then, does their memory form a small, hard knot in his empty stomach?

CHAPTER 5

Amid the bamboo huts of the village overlooked by the late Lord Uto's residence, a short whistle trills. To the uninitiated, it sounds not unlike a nightingale. Light sleepers toss on their beds of loose straw, giving no thought to the bird's unseasonal visit. Certain villagers, however, have been sitting in darkness for more than an hour, awaiting this signal.

For a moment, stillness. Then a cloaked figure steps into the narrow, shadowed road, shielding the glow of his paper lantern with his body. Two huts away, the action is repeated. And again; now three shapes are abroad this bitter eve, crunching frost beneath the wooden clogs called geta. Then five, clutching tattered double-lined cloaks over goose-fleshed bodies. Seven, snuffling as the crisp night air steals from their nostrils the stench of family and livestock huddling for warmth in single-room dwellings. Finally, ten sets of teeth clacking in the cold despite their owners' efforts.

Farmers are not trained like warriors to endure without flinching. Yet their hardships are often greater.

The ten converge on the only structure in the village from which a dim light shows through the cracks in its walls: the sake shop. Oiwa, its proprietor, greets them wordlessly at the door. Palsy of the hands put an end to Oiwa's farming days, but does not interfere with his qualities as a host—nor with his duties as village headman, which consists primarily of agreeing without protest to the lord's demands.

The peasants kneel, or crouch, or sit cross-legged in a rough circle around the feeble warmth of the irori—the hearth—in the center of the main room. Wood smoke stings the eyes of those seated nearest, who nonetheless keep to their places.

Oiwa latches the door shut with a length of bamboo pole. He rubs his aching fingers together and speaks to his guests.

"A cold night, my friends. Never mind. Hot rice wine will prepare us for our work, and more is warming to take the chill off afterwards. If one of you will assist me?" He points to a chipped porcelain jar resting on a trivet at the edge of the fire.

Cups are distributed. The youngest of the group, a newlywed named Echi, pours for Oiwa. Steam rises from the liquid. Lips smack politely.

"Well and good," growls burly Kujo, at the third filling of the cups. "I want to know why we must construct that bastard's funeral platform. Let the eta build it! It is *their* duty!" His lips twist at the mention of those despised outcasts, mostly Ainu half-breeds, who scrape minimal livings from begging and tasks no self-respecting person would stoop to. Even their hovels are isolated from the village proper.

"That is why we meet in secret," Oiwa replied. "I regret there was no opportunity this afternoon to fully explain. The eta will, rightly, transport the corpse, but Monaga says it was Lord Uto's will that the platform be built by clean hands."

"We have only the priest's word for that," Kujo answers sourly. "Suppose he only wants to teach us a lesson? All know he is displeased that so few of us worship at his shrine."

Oiwa's scowl is invisible in the darkened room, but his eyes glow bright with anger. "This is unworthy, Kujo. Monaga knows our situation. We haven't enough to feed our families properly, much less to spare for sacrifices. Did not he himself announce that the kami of the shrine had fled Imuri, making such sacrifices pointless? He knew what that admission would mean."

Kujo grunts as though slapped. "Huh! I only bring up the possibility. Did I say it was so? I am the last man to accuse our priest of ungenerosity. Still, with the old lord dead, where is the need to comply with his whim?"

"Would you prefer his spirit haunt our valley? Would you welcome a visit from the footless shade of Lord Uto?"

At that, a deep groan echoes in the room. Several of the farmers look uneasily around. Some reach for short, crude knives hidden beneath kimonos. Young Echi leaps to his feet and points a shaking finger at the blackest corner of the room.

"Hai! Something moved there! Not dead two hours, and already he returns!"

Oiwa laughs gently. The others, realizing who the groaner must be, gradually join in. Flickering hearth light plays across Echi's features, rendering his initial distress and increasing discomfort plainly visible.

The shopkeeper takes pity on the young man, and explains. "It's only poor Beni. His agitation has been growing all day, as though fed by the waning of Lord Uto's life."

Echi looks as if his head had been set on fire, and well he should. Everyone in Imuri knows of Beni and his bitter tragedy. The farmer had been a widower for less than a year when Lord Uto chose his only son as the first of the notorious series of pillow boys ending with Hoke. Like most of those boys, Beni's son was not permitted to leave the lord's palace. He was never seen again. One night, the following spring, Beni claimed he'd heard a scream that could only have come from his son's throat. Of course, this was his imagination. Uto's residence is too far from the village for any peasant to hear what goes on within, not even when the wind blows from that direction. Beni's neighbors deny hearing anything that night.

A fortnight later, Lord Uto chose a second pillow boy.

Many times since has Beni heard that scream, in monstrous dreams so vivid he wakes bathed in sweat on the coldest winter nights, such as this one. Villagers could barely keep him from attacking Lord Uto on sight. That rash action would not only have cost Beni his head—a price which, privately, a few impatient neighbors would have gladly paid—but would have earned punishment for the whole province, followed by stiffer taxes. The inhabitants could not imagine anything crueler than Uto's usual governance, and had no desire to learn.

Thereafter, whenever Lord Uto passed through the village, Beni's neighbors got him too drunk to stand and tied him to a post in the sake shop for safety. Lord Uto never noticed Beni's absence from the crowds which gathered, with some urging from his retainers' blades, to honor him. He knew few of his

subjects by sight or name. Fewer still survived his notice for long.
"How was I to know?" Echi protests. "Of all people, Beni is
least likely to bemoan the tyrant's passing."

Oiwa sighs indulgently. "Lord Uto took with him Beni's last
opportunity for revenge. This dawn, I found Beni swinging a
mattock like a sword, glaring upward at the lord's residence. He
obviously hoped to deny his tormentor a natural death. I lured
him to a bowl of wine and kept him here all day."

Kujo claps his meaty hands in approval. "Quite right,
headman. In fact, we should keep him confined until after the
funeral. He might cause a scene. Once he realizes nothing can be
done, he'll settle down. Most of the time he's lucid and taciturn."

A tall thin man on Kujo's left thrusts his head forward.
Shadows play eerily on his pock-marked face as he speaks. "Yes,
Beni will understand. After all, it's the last time we'll have to do
it."

"We hope," comes a whisper from behind.

"Kujo speaks wisely," Oiwa says. "We don't want our new
lord to get a poor impression. Jiko may prove a kinder ruler than
his father."

"He could hardly be less so," snaps the pock-pitted man.

Echi laughs. "Perhaps he'll let us keep our anus hairs at tax
time!"

A ripple of amusement passes through the group. Oiwa
turns a stern eye on each man, stifling them in turn. He steps
into the irori's glow. His face is drained of blood.

"Fools!" he hisses. "You go too far! Already you forget the
prudence so painfully learned under the late Lord Uto."

Echi rubs the back of his neck nervously. "Come, Oiwa! You
wouldn't cross a stone bridge without tapping it like a blind
man. Uto is dead. What good would it do a spy lurking beyond
your shutters to carry tales to his corpse?"

Echi points to a barred window behind the aged shopkeeper.
The others follow his finger suspiciously. The shop grows quiet.
Ears strain to detect the faint crunch of a sandal on the time-
frosted ground, the brush of a sleeve against the bamboo wall,
the snag of cloth on a splinter.

Straw rustles as Beni rolls onto his back. He belches.

The spell is broken. Several held breaths are expelled. Oiwa sighs, disgusted that his admonition should even be necessary. "If the bird had not sung out, it wouldn't have been shot," he reminds them softly. "Lord Jiko has spent most of his life at the Imperial Court. He will have even greater need of spies than did his father. We knew, or suspected, who Uto's informers were. Jiko will surely have found fresh worms in the lion's belly."

Echi opens his mouth, shuts it again. The group is properly chastised. Oiwa's claw-like hand removes the empty sake jar.

"Enough wine for now," the shopkeeper says. "More than enough talk. It grows late. There are ropes and knives, if any here have come unequipped to cut and tie bamboo."

Without haste, Oiwa leads his fellows from the shop and over frozen mud trails that lead to the clearing chosen for the cremation. Echi, as youngest, brings up the rear. Thanks to Oiwa's outburst of common sense, he found the discussion unproductive. As a novice spy, of course, Echi does not really expect useful results at once. He considers his pretended fear of drunken Beni a clever bit of misdirection to keep suspicion from clinging to him. He worries, though, because the most damaging words spoken this evening are his own, meant to draw out others. Suppose one of them is *also* in Lord Jiko's pay, and reports Echi?

Well, he shrugs, it can't be helped. There will be other chances. Surely a hint of the shrewd mind behind Oiwa's bland features will be worth something to the new lord. Jiko knows already of the conspiracy regarding Beni. He cares nothing for the old farmer, but if the peasants can keep *that* from his father, what further plots might they hatch? No small concern for a man who has just assumed lordship over the tiny province.

His mind whirling with these thoughts and others, Echi straggles at the end of the line. More than once he comes out of his reverie alone on the forest path, fair game for any mischievous long-nosed tengu or malevolent ghost that might haunt these woods. Then he runs, clogs slapping, cloak streaming, puffs of human fog pouring from his mouth, until he reaches his companions.

If Echi's lagging is noticed, it goes unmentioned.

CHAPTER 6

EIGHTH DAY.

Smoke from the pyre rises almost vertically against the dawn-pink sky, fanned by the slightest of icy Siberian breezes, to meld with the gray overcast. The blaze's hungry crackling echoes in the clearing. A fat snowflake flutters in front of Monaga, tickling the priest's nose. He stifles an urge to sneeze. Succeeding, he finds the new Lord Jiko studying him with amusement.

"Not restraining a tear for your old associate, are you, priest?"

Jiko's voice is pitched higher than his father's, but carries no less authority. The young man's features are soft, mirroring those of his deceased mother as Monaga remembers her, but the black, over-bright eyes are his father's legacy.

Jiko is an unknown quantity. He was exiled to the Imperial Court at the onset of his adolescence, followed the Emperor Kotoku when the court was moved to Naniwa, but was recalled three days earlier from the port city. Monaga hears the Emperor is a wise and gentle ruler despite his Buddhist leanings. His example should be more of an influence on Jiko's policies than his father's. So Monaga hopes.

The priest phrases his reply carefully. "These are not fit sentiments for one such as I, Lord Jiko, but I know of no man whose death better becomes him than your father."

Jiko's smile is almost as unpleasant as Uto's had been. "You speak boldly to the bereaved, knowing that I now hold the power of life and death over all in Imuri."

Despite his qualms, Monaga pressed the point. Fear for

his own life is not sufficient to still his tongue. He has spent too many years in terror of one man—Uto—to so soon dread another.

"You loved your father as little as his subjects did."

Jiko stands stiffly in his ceremonial kimono of crimson silk. His eyes dart to and fro, although his head does not move. He sees no one in earshot. The funeral is poorly attended. The new lord is too disinterested to compel anyone's presence. Monaga, Lord Jiko, and the boy Hoke, whom the new lord keeps by his side constantly, form an island of three. Jiko's bodyguards stand two dozen paces behind, alert but relaxed. It is unlikely that anyone, even the drunken Beni, will attempt the life of the new lord and risk social chaos, certainly not before his policies are announced. Jiko has wisely avoided mixing with his father's cliques these past few days, preferring his own counsel and the safety of uncertainty.

"Not much more. I'll grant you, priest," Jiko replies through tight lips. "Quote me, however, and your head will crown a road post."

"Threats are unnecessary." Monaga will not risk his life to speak publicly of matters already common knowledge. "Nor are they in keeping with a new, more humane regime."

The unspoken question hangs between the two men, thick as the storm clouds passing overhead. Jiko stares at the wooden platform supporting his father's body. A beam burns through. Bamboo creaks and gives way with a loud pop. The corpse rolls into the flames. Most improper. Jiko decides to have the headman, Oiwa, executed for supervising such poor carpentry. Although the young lord had ordered that quality be sacrificed for speed while complying with Uto's instructions, examples must be set. Besides, this morning he'd learned that Oiwa is too sly to be relied on. This mishap will allow Jiko to choose a more malleable headman.

He turns his head. Monaga's eyes meet his. The priest must be answered or he may think Jiko weak.

"I have several reforms planned. The procedure for collecting the rice tax, for instance, needs revising."

"Yes. The current rate is ruinous."

Jiko's eyebrows knit in puzzlement. He shrugs. They speak at cross purposes. "I must first raise a new residence, of course. My father's house is tainted by his death. I must stay there for now, as there is no other suitable dwelling, but the sooner the villagers erect my new home, the better. As a priest, you understand the necessity."

Reluctantly, Monaga nods. The peasants will, in fact, grumble if Jiko does not construct a new residence, as tradition demands. "The village shrine is also in need of repairs."

Jiko looks sharply at the priest, eyes glittering. "What of it? Did you not remind my father on his deathbed that the territorial kami had fled Imuri? The people worship their own ancestral spirits at their home shrines. What use is a communal one?"

Monaga's lips twitch. He told no one that detail of his last conversation with Lord Uto. Jiko already has a network of informers culled in part from the ranks of those retainers who'd kept vigil during Uto's last hours. Monaga's eyes fall on impassive Hoke who stares intently into the flames. Perhaps the information comes from a closer source, he muses.

"The kami may return." It is almost a whisper.

Jiko grunts. "Time enough then to consider repairs."

Monaga swallows the retort that comes to his tongue. He does not wish to antagonize the new lord so soon. The people of Imuri suffered greatly under Lord Uto, and the priest does not want to jeopardize any opportunity, however slight, to ease their lot by influencing the son.

Jiko's grip tightens on Hoke's shoulder. His other hand cups the child's chin and kneads the smooth cheeks between thumb and forefinger. Hoke is forced to look up. His lips shape a parody of a smile.

"A long day ahead, eh, Hoke?" says the new lord. "I think we have earned a rest. Help me examine my sleeping quarters."

Monaga's jaw muscles ache from the effort to remain silent. His gaze fastens on the blazing bamboo frame. The structure caves in on itself.

Flames surge high. A great black cloud rises to the heavens.

Lord Jiko's bodyguards follow their new master from the field. Monaga remains alone at the pyre. He approaches, feeling its heat through his thin gray cotton kimono. There is no comfort in that warmth.

It is a raw morning. More snowflakes fall, hissing, to be consumed in the fire, but the storm clouds move swiftly. Most of the snow will fall to the east, beyond the mountain range.

Air undulates above the scorched ground, giving the impression that something moves amid the crumbling cinders.

Monaga tries to pray to Amaterasu. Words do not come. Even Lord Uto's ashes seem to radiate evil. There is too much hatred here. With a sigh, the priest steps back to brush airborne soot from his garment.

He starts the long, slow walk to his hillside shrine.

Harsh gusts of wind tug at his rough clothing as if on purpose. Monaga shivers for the entire distance. His bones are chilled long before he reaches his tiny shelter on the shrine's grounds.

CHAPTER 7

The sky is clear but moonless. Starlight alone brightens the empty clearing. The flames were permitted to die of their own accord and the cremation site remains undisturbed—as Lord Uto desired. A thin crust of fresh snow borders the pyre. The flakes ceased falling before the center grew too cool to melt them.

No guard stands watch here in the cold black night. No one cares now if Uto's final resting place is desecrated, not even Lord Jiko, provided the desecrator is too discreet to boast.

Beni the rice farmer pulls his thin rags closely about his frail body. His fingers are stiff with cold, but his numbness is not due to frostbite. Beni is drunk again, this time of his own volition. He barely remembers Kujo shaking him awake in the afternoon, does not recall whether or not he saw his old friend Oiwa. Likely not. Oiwa would never be so careless as to let Beni stumble out of his shop with a full jar of cold sake hidden in the folds of his soiled kimono. Neighbors see him, nod and go their ways. No longer need they tie poor Beni down.

He scurries across the open ground, crunching paper-thin frost under his wooden geta. A sharp wind stings his ears and tugs uneven strands of hair before his eyes. His bladder is swollen near to bursting; he walks with a straddling gait. Not yet. Not yet.

Upright sticks of charred bamboo surround the spot where, that morning, the hated Lord Uto's corpse was cremated. Beni feels a warm, anticipatory trickle down his thigh. He bends almost double and groans with the effort to hold back.

Eyes watering, Beni races the last few paces. He stops at the edge of the pyre, lifts his kimono, and loosens his loincloth. His sigh of pleasure sounds through the clearing as he relieves himself on Lord Uto's remains.

The golden stream steams in the frigid air. Beni's knees tremble with the joy of release. His free hand grasps a jagged, blackened bamboo pole for support. He ignores the charred splinters jabbing his palm.

Never has the farmer known such a satisfying piss.

Drained at last, Beni staggers back. He sinks to his knees, jolting against the rock-hard ground. Happy tears dampen his face. Now his son's spirit can rest.

The urine droplets start to freeze. Ashes shift as they expand. A mudslide spills down the tallest of the heaps.

Something digs itself out.

Beni does not see it. If he did, he would think it a worm. A tiny red worm, perhaps tricked by the heat of Beni's elimination into believing in an early spring. Then three tiny worms. No; a single, three-headed serpent.

Not that, either.

It is a hand with three fat, stubby fingers, pushing through the moist gray flakes. A hand that, on first emerging, is no larger than the tip of Beni's thumb.

It waxes quickly. The air grows colder.

Beni's cheeks feel stiff. His tears are freezing. He wipes the half-formed icicles free with his sleeve. When he looks up again, a man's form stands silhouetted in the center of the pyre.

Beni is not concerned that he did not hear the stranger approach. He knows how dulled are his senses. He greets the newcomer gleefully.

"So! I am not the only one come to pay respect to Lord Uto. Do not let me inhibit you, friend. There isn't piss enough in the world to drown that murderous bastard!"

The stranger's voice is deep and sluggish. "Do I know you, peasant?"

The farmer laughs. He claps a hand to his straw hat to keep it from falling off. "All Imuri knows Beni. All Honshu shall know what I did tonight. I will be put to death, but that no longer matters. And you? My memory is fuddled by too much sake and the night too dark for my old eyes."

The other takes a deep breath. His lungs sound like bellows. "That's the trouble with having many enemies. You never get to know them all."

"Eh?" Beni struggles to his feet. The temperature has dropped dramatically in the last few minutes. He squints in the starlight at the outline before him. The torso is as thick and broad as a sumo wrestler's, but not even a sumo could support so massive a skull. And there, growing from the forehead … are those horns?

Beni's fear comes out as rage. "Take off that mask! You should be ashamed, frightening harmless old men!"

The stranger steps forth. He grins. Teeth catch and reflect the faint starlight. They form a row of razor-sharp points as long as Beni's forearm.

"I take no shame from *my* pleasures, Beni."

Distorted though the stranger's face is, Beni suddenly recognizes it.

The farmer turns to flee. His muscles are stiff. He stumbles. His ankles are grasped. In the blink of an eye, he dangles head down, so far from the ground that his fingers cannot touch the boulder they scrabble for. His body spins until he again faces his demonic assailant. The latter, incredibly, stands taller now, twice a man's height.

Beni pleads for mercy. The words are snatched from his dry lips as his body whips violently through the night air. His vertebrae pop. The pain is too great for screaming. The agony ends when Beni's head splits like a ripe melon on the frozen, rocky soil.

The killer swings the limp corpse over his head and smashes it to the ground again. And again. And once more. Finally, in disgust, he hurls Beni across the clearing. The incident has been diverting but unproductive. He wants a weapon that will last throughout a good fight. A peasant's broken body will not suffice.

He shambles toward a dense stand of pines. Their branches are invitingly thick and solid. Conveniently, the trees lie in a direct line to the lord's residence.

CHAPTER 8

Torches burn bright orange, with little visible smoke, along the perimeter of Lord Jiko's residence. Warriors stand stoic guard, seemingly unaware of freezing wind and wearying muscles. They are taught to endure these minor discomforts without complaint. A soldier's greatest concern on such a night is that his two swords—one long, one short—are not made brittle or damaged by frost. Many of the guards tuck their weapons beneath their outer garments, pressed against warm flesh. This will slow them if any enemy attacks, but not by much. Anyway, no attack is expected tonight. The warriors are posted as a matter of maintaining discipline.

Inside the residence it is not much warmer, for wind slips around and through the paper walls, penetrating every room. Lord Jiko crouches over the irori in his chamber and blows on his fingers.

Double-lined blankets are draped over his back. It seems to him that the city dwellings in Naniwa are better insulated than these rural ones, though perhaps they are simply more crowded.

A door panel slides open. Hoke enters, along with a fresh gust of icy wind. With a twist of his bare foot, the boy closes the panel behind him. Being in Lord Uto's service has developed his acrobatic skills. Both hands are occupied with a lacquer tray on which two newly-heated jugs of sake are balanced. Each jug boasts a painted stork, a symbol of long life.

"How did you go—by way of Pekche, Silla, and Imna?" growls the new lord, naming the three kingdoms of the Korean peninsula that juts from the China-dominated mainland.

Permanent envoys of these kingdoms reside in Naniwa. Jiko saw them many times at state functions. He never bothered speaking to them.

Hoke shakes his head. His body shivers as well, partly due to his passage along the unheated corridor. His sole garment is an unlined cotton kimono. The room's only light, aside from the glow of Jiko's wood-hearth, comes from a pair of pine-resin candles that shed little heat.

Jiko's scowl reverses as he sees Hoke's burden. "Come here, lad. I thirst. Have a cup yourself. All the better if you are relaxed, eh?"

The words slur. This is far from the first jug of potent wine consumed by Jiko since the cremation.

Hoke kneels by his lord and places the tray on the floor. He touches a jar to his forehead, a sign of respect, before refilling Jiko's cup. "I am here to do your will."

"Damned right you are." Jiko's free hand gropes at the boy's garment. His fingers are like icicles; the nails scrape young skin like dagger points.

A scream from outside rends the night.

Jiko leaps to his feet, bowling the boy over. He snatches up his sword, kept within arm's reach at all times. Hoke scuttles across the planks to a corner he hopes will put him safely out of the way. The new lord yanks open the door panel. A paper section tears. In the corridor, a warrior darts past with sword drawn.

"Guard!" snaps Lord Jiko.

The soldier stops as though jerked short at a tether's end. He turns and bows. Forehead touches floorboard. "I beg pardon for disturbing my lord!"

"Yes, yes. What was that shout?"

"I was just going to find out, Lord Jiko. An intruder, obviously."

"Obviously," Jiko mimics. "Attend to it at once. I want a full report in the morning. And post two guards outside my chamber immediately. I do not wish to be further disturbed."

"At once. Lord Jiko." The warrior prostrates himself, careful not to damage his exposed blade but heedless of scraped knees and elbows. Jiko acknowledges the honor with a grunt. He waves a hand, dismissing the soldier to complete his errands.

Jiko returns to his irori. Unseeing eyes stare into the fire, as they had earlier stared at his father's cremation. His mind is troubled. He does not notice Hoke drawing a shoji screen in front of the torn panel. He is barely aware of the slight weight when the boy slips a blanket back on his shoulders.

Who dares invade the lord's residence tonight? Who would *want* to? The lordship has no other claimants; Jiko's father had thoroughly eliminated his own rivals. A local uprising would more likely have taken place during Uto's prolonged illness. A neighboring province's army? Then runners should have warned him. He'd ordered a double set of lookouts on every road. Some fanatical religious sect angered by his blasphemous act of sleeping in a dead man's house? A minor indiscretion compared to the sacrileges his father indulged in.

Pah! It must be high spirits among the villagers. Some fools bold with drink. A few heads dripping on road posts tomorrow will remind the people that although shrimp may dance they do not leave the river. Burly Kujo's head will lead the row. The new headman cannot be well-suited for his duties if he permits such outrages.

A plain matter with a plain solution.

Why, then, does his heart pound so?

"Lord?" Hoke slips his hand under Jiko's blanket. Small, blunt fingers tickle a hairless thigh.

"Not now, Hoke. Drink your sake."

The boy withdraws and lifts a shaking cup to his lips. Some warm drops spill on his kimono. He fears lest he has somehow offended the young noble who holds Hoke's life in his hands.

Further screams overwhelm the pair's reflection. Metal crashes and clatters. Wooden planks vibrate under their buttocks. Jiko's throat goes dry. A cup of sake rests in his left hand, but he does not drink. The longsword's hilt feels slick against his clammy right palm.

Groans rise and fade. For a long moment the residence is unnaturally quiet. Lord Jiko strains his ears.

A plank creaks in the corridor beyond his chamber. He turns toward the sound.

A crimson fist as large as his head rends the wall panel before his dilating eyes. Lord Jiko tenses. His cup falls. Warm wine stains the polished wood and drips through cracks to the cold earth underneath.

Two more panels crash inward in a single motion. The final breach is made. In the flickering shadows cast by Jiko's irori and the pine-resin candles stands a creature of enormous breadth, squat and thick-limbed, a thing out of nightmares. One three-fingered hand grips a heavy, bloodstained pine bough.

"By the gods!" gasps Jiko.

"By the demons," comes a bass response. "Don't you recognize me, *Lord* Jiko?"

The invader kicks over the screen and steps nearer the irori's glow. An oversized jaw, razor-sharp teeth, flattened nose and pig-like ebon eyes distort the face into a parody of humanity. A demon, beyond a doubt, and with a most unpleasant grin.

Unpleasant and familiar.

Jiko struggles to his feet by bracing himself on Hoke's cowering, huddled form. "What do you wish here?"

"Only what is mine. Of course, that includes a great deal." The demon flourishes his gore-encrusted branch. "A poor son you are, Jiko. The retainers recognized me after suitable persuasion. Even this ignorant farm boy knows me."

It is true. Hoke remembers well those too-bright, ebon eyes. Like a hunted fox, the boy dashes to his previous corner. He curls into a tight ball and covers his eyes.

However: kowai mono mitasa—what one dreads, one must see. Two fingers separate so Hoke can watch.

Jiko staggers backwards. He kicks over a sake jug. "You … no! It's not possible! You can't be my father!"

"Cruel words, Jiko. You hurt me. How would you punish your son if *he* denied you?"

Jiko slides his blade from its scabbard. The demon's makeshift club cuts the air.

Crack!

The blow's force snaps a bone in his forearm, and Jiko gasps his agony. However, it is not his sword arm. He slashes at the apparition.

The demon moves quickly for its bulk. The pine branch falls again. Jiko's sword drops from nerveless fingers, clangs against the irori's metal frame, and bounces silently onto a discarded blanket.

The club strikes a final time, crushing the top of the young man's head, driving bone fragments into the brain. Blood spurts from eye-sockets and nostrils. Lord Jiko is dead before his body thuds on the polished planks.

Behind the mask of his fingers, Hoke's eyes are wide with fear. The winner of the brief, one-sided contest turns slowly toward him. That awful grin returns. The inhuman face is spattered with fresh gore.

"Now, my boy," the demon says. "Where were we?"

NEW YORK CITY

WEDNESDAY, DECEMBER 29, 1982

CHAPTER 9

The full-figured middle-aged woman was the last passenger to debark the Boston-to-New York shuttle at LaGuardia Airport. Above the navy-blue collar of her coat, her face was unnaturally pale, its almost translucent skin contrasting with her rich brown hair. Her mouth sagged as though the jaw muscles were too weary to hold it shut. Despite an antiseptic mouthwash, she still tasted sour breath. She crossed the carpeted corridor in short, deliberate steps, making sure that one leg would support her full weight before she moved the other. The sound, if not the sense, of announcements over the terminal's public address system cut through the buzz in her ears. When she turned her head, she did so slowly, so the vertigo would not return.

Her name was Francine Cooper.

Matching Mrs. Cooper's stride was a stewardess half her age, whose crimson tailored uniform and fresh-scrubbed complexion pointed up Cooper's haggardness. The younger woman's left hand was near the other's right elbow, ready to support if necessary but not impatiently insisting. Cooper's mental haze had cleared enough for her to appreciate this courtesy. She made a conscious effort to memorize the name tag, and a silent promise to write a letter of praise to the airline.

When the stewardess tried to steer her to a lounge area, however, she hung back, shaking her head.

"You don't want to lie down for a few minutes?"

Cooper tried to smile. Her thin lips twitched into a grimace. She gave up the effort. "I'd rather not. I'll be fine now. Sorry to have been a bother."

"No bother. That's what I'm here for. You needn't feel embarrassed. Even Dramamine doesn't work for everyone."

"It's not fair," Cooper protested, "to get airsick when you're over forty."

It wasn't motion that had made her ill, though. After the visit at dawn from a Boston police detective and a hurried confirming phone call to New York, Francine Cooper had had a dozen details to attend to: checking flight times, calling a cab, advising her answering service, cancelling appointments, extending deadlines, making preliminary arrangements long distance with a New York crematorium. Her conscious mind locked into neutral, but inertia kept her going. Once aboard the airplane, with an hour or so ahead of her in which she could do nothing more, Cooper felt the full sense of her loss like a blow to the stomach.

The stewardess didn't know this, of course. She nodded solemnly. "Some things one never outgrows, unfortunately. Well. If you're sure you're all right, I have to get back to my station."

"I'm fine." Her memory slipped; she looked at the name tag again. "Thank you, Brenda."

"No problem. If you want to freshen up, those stairs lead to the rest rooms. Have a good day, Mrs. Cooper."

Cooper fixed her gaze on those steps for a moment, missing Brenda's departure. A knot of passengers from another flight stampeded down the corridor, filling it with babble and shoe-scuffles. They split around her, reforming the herd once past without a pause.

Cooper brushed a strand of hair away from her eyes. She turned to stare past glass walls. A DC-10 started to taxi toward the runways. If she looked half as bad as she felt, Cooper did not want to face a washroom mirror yet.

She was ready to look for a cab to Manhattan when the man walked up to her.

He was half a head taller than she, with thinning hair, deep set eyes, and skin the color of a manila envelope. His raincoat hung open, revealing an ill-fitting sports jacket and a loosely-knotted tie of some indeterminate dark shade.

"Mrs. Cooper? Francine Cooper?"

His voice was low but clear, even against the backdrop of roaring jets. The question, by its tone, was a statement.

"Should I know you? I'm not meeting anyone."

He flipped open his card case in a smooth, practiced move. The gold badge glittered in the hazy light from outside. When he put the case away, Cooper saw the black holster at his shoulder. "Lieutenant Amos Foster, Detective First Class, N.Y.P.D. We spoke this morning. You made it clear that we were to expect you. My car is waiting." He nodded at her oversized purse. "Do we stop for luggage?"

Cooper noticed with mild surprise that the detective was already leading her down the corridor at a brisk clip. His touch was so assured she hadn't noticed it. "I didn't bring any, Lieutenant. I'm only here for a few hours."

"Good. That's something, anyway."

Cooper decided she did not like Amos Foster. She did not like his acid tongue, his brusque attitude, or his habit of alternately making eye contact and looking everywhere but at her when he spoke. No further words were exchanged until Foster sat behind the wheel of the unmarked car, Cooper beside him, and they sped toward the Midtown Tunnel.

"This won't be pleasant," Foster growled.

"I know what to expect, Lieutenant. Freelance researchers have taken me into morgues. The nasty part is that it's Lynda who's dead, and the shock of that hit me right after the shuttle left Logan. I won't get hysterical."

Foster spared her a sharp glance. Abruptly he swerved into the next lane, accelerated past the Nova in front of them and slipped back into place.

"I hate when they crawl like that," he muttered. "What I meant to say, Mrs. Cooper, is that *this* is unpleasant for me. I should be tracking your daughter's killer, not playing chauffeur to her grieving mother."

Cooper's cheeks colored. "You didn't have to pick me up, Lieutenant. I'd planned to take a cab."

Foster watched the asphalt disappear under the hood of his car. "We haven't the slightest doubt of your daughter's identity, you know. The photo wired to Boston for your verification was a formality. There's no need for you to view the body personally."

"I haven't seen my daughter since last Christmas. I was tied up on a project until yesterday. We'd planned on New Year's for my annual visit." Manhattan's skyline loomed before them. Cooper turned sideways, bracing a hand on the dashboard. "I just want to see her for the last time, all right?"

"The body will be released to you, shipped up to Boston if you want," Foster snapped. "We had to reschedule the autopsy. You would have arrived in the middle of it. Don't tell me *that* wouldn't bother you!"

Cooper stared out the side window. Leafless trees lined the shoulders of the expressway. Gasoline fumes mixed with the stale smell of sweat and gun oil. Her stomach churned, but held nothing more for her to lose. She lowered the window halfway. Cold air blew her dark, straggling hair, drying perspiration she hadn't realized was beading her forehead.

"Lieutenant," she said at last, "exactly how did my daughter die?"

Foster's scowl deepened. "What did they tell you in Boston?"

"Assault. Internal hemorrhage. It doesn't take Sherlock Holmes to deduce rape." She took a deep breath. Her fingers intertwined in her lap.

"That's about it," Foster said.

"Lieutenant."

"It's not police policy to discuss an active investigation with civilians." He paused. "Especially reporters."

Cooper's jaw tightened. "That's a cheap shot and you know it. As a researcher I do background, not news. I am not writing up a lurid sex murder. I'm Lynda's mother."

Foster said nothing.

"I'll find out eventually."

Foster sighed. "Hell. The worst of it will be in the afternoon papers, anyway. The opinion of the Medical Examiner at the scene was that the victim had been violated by a foreign object of unknown origin, capable of inflicting internal damage." He let that sink in. "We won't know if she was actually raped until the autopsy and lab reports are completed. From my experience with this kind of crime, I'd guess she wasn't."

"Jesus."

"Yeah."

Cooper chewed her lower lip. "It's hard to imagine, *really* understand, how often something this … awful … happens. You must see more of it than anyone."

Foster shrugged. "You get used to it. You can get used to anything."

"How do youcatch someone who commits such a pointless crime?"

"Not entirely pointless. We think we know the motive." Foster freed one hand to knead bunched muscles in his thick neck. "You sure you want more?"

"I'll get it anyway."

"I bet you will. Your daughter's body was found on a vandalized houseboat moored at the Seventy-Ninth Street Boat Basin on the West Side. The vessel is registered to a small-time dealer named Gary Cross. Cross has disappeared which makes him our prime suspect, though it may not be that simple."

"You said … dealer?"

"We found three kilos of cocaine under a deck plank. Cross has a record, so we knew we should look. Your daughter was not a known associate but our files aren't complete. My theory is that Cross got ambitious and the competition decided to make him an example. It was your daughter's bad luck that she chose to connect with him last night."

Cooper stiffened. "You're saying Lynda was an addict?"

"I'll remind you, this is all off the record. To be frank, she didn't look like one, but the autopsy will tell us if she used drugs. Even if she didn't, she could still be involved, either just starting to get hooked or maybe distributing the stuff for Cross."

"That's even more ridiculous," Cooper declared.

"You would say that, naturally. It's still a good reason for her being with Cross."

"You'll find you're mistaken, Lieutenant."

Foster shrugged again. "I might, if we were interested enough in her relationship with Cross to check it out. We aren't. Not yet. I figure Cross for the real target. What the squad is doing now—what I should also be doing—is checking out everyone who might know where Cross is hiding, and anyone with a motive for wanting him out of the way. There's quite a list."

"Won't you even try to prove Lynda was an innocent bystander?"

Foster sighed. "Mrs. Cooper, this city is short on manpower as it is. Which do you think should take priority: locating a killer before he strikes again, or proving that a dead girl was as wholesome as apple pie? Especially when our time is taken up by visiting relatives."

"You keep throwing that up, Lieutenant," Cooper said icily. "And I told you you didn't have to meet me at the airport."

"No," he replied softly. "I didn't."

Silence filled the car as it plunged into the Queens Midtown Tunnel.

CHAPTER 10

Homicide detective Sergeant Joseph Evans rested an elbow on the roof of the unmarked patrol car he'd signed out. His heel scraped the pebbled curbing, dislodging a grease-glued gum wrapper. The green paper strip fluttered into the gutter. The sergeant's hands sank deep into the pockets of an unbuttoned smoke-gray overcoat, his one concession to a day of drizzle. His necktie flapped over the lapel.

New York winters could not pale Evans's ruddy face, which set off the turquoise of his bulging, shifting eyes. A long chin weighted the corners of his mouth into a perpetual frown. The detective was unaware of this attribute, which contributed to his high success rate in interrogation.

This coming June would mark the twentieth year of his solid if unspectacular career, but Evans gave little thought to early retirement. This was not ambition; he knew his limitations. He'd never rise above his present rank, and actually felt he'd done well for an undirected college drop-out who'd joined the force primarily to escape the military draft. At that time, Evans was one of the few people aware of how serious the Viet Nam involvement was, and how easily it could worsen. Evans was not cowardly, but he despised senseless waste. For the same reason, he'd failed to meet the requirements for a college degree. He'd been delighted to discover real purpose in police work. What he did made a difference in people's lives. Not always, not even most of the time, but often enough to satisfy him.

It was for Liz's sake that Evans considered retiring at all. In their early years of marriage, his wife had accepted the risks of his profession. Recently, however, as it became obvious they would never have children, Liz had grown increasingly dependent on her husband. Evans admitted he'd been lucky the past two decades. His most serious on-duty injury was a minor knife wound, requiring a tetanus shot, a few stitches and a night in the hospital. Liz Evans bore that bravely, even cheerfully, but that was eight years ago.

Liz did not nag. She never mentioned the subject. But sizing up people was part of Evans's job. Facial expressions and odd phrases in her conversation told him that a decision to quit and enjoy his pension would not be unwelcome.

A strand of curly brown hair fell in front of his eyes. He patted it back into place. He was overdue for a trim. After the holidays he'd take care of it.

A slim black patrolman, sweating in his winter blues, hurried down the precinct house steps. His heels clicked sharply on the stone. He waved to Evans.

Took long enough, Evans grumbled silently. Probably had to polish his shield. Well, he could've refused when the desk sergeant offered him a rookie. Evans grunted, opened the car door, and motioned the patrolman to the street side.

"You drive," said Evans. He slid in, coattail tucked between the seat of his pants and the icy plastic seat cover.

The patrolman turned the ignition key. The engine groaned to life. The uniformed man flashed a quick, nervous grin.

"I'll let it warm up."

Evans nodded. He rolled his window halfway down. In his own uniform days, Evans had had a partner nearly suffocated by a faulty exhaust. Since then, the detective never took for granted the ability of any patrol cars, marked or unmarked, to properly vent carbon monoxide fumes. Intellectually, he accepted the event as a freak accident, but to die that way would be stupidly wasteful.

"My name's Sam Carver." Carver looked to Evans for conversational encouragement.

The detective watched the street in the constant search that becomes second nature. "The desk sergeant told me, Carver."

"I recognized you right off. I know every detective working out of this precinct, by sight, anyway."

Evans's lips pursed in what might have been a smile. "He also said you were a little green."

"Not so green, sir. I've got two felony arrests to my record."

Evans rubbed his long chin, hiding his grin. "This should be a piece of cake for you, then. Carver. Routine. We're picking up a man for questioning."

"About the houseboat murder?"

Evans grunted again. He didn't feel like talking. He and Foster had established a rapport over the years that made speech almost superfluous, and he hadn't talked shop with a civilian since that damned reporter quoted him at length and turned a good bust into a mistrial. He was out of the habit. That wasn't a good enough reason to cut Carver, though. Evans remembered his own rookie days, when *he* was eager to make points.

"That's right. The boat belongs to a penny-ante pusher named Gary Cross. We want to talk to anyone to knows where he might be hiding—if he's still alive—or who might be gunning for him. Most of the squad is rounding up known dealers on the West Side. One or more of them should know something."

Carver's fingers drummed on the steering wheel. "Known dealers? You know who's selling junk?"

"We keep active files on them."

"Then why don't you put them all away?"

Evans settled back. The seat cover squilched beneath him. He rubbed his neck on the headrest and released a languid yawn. "No, you're not green. Not much. You're talking nickel-and-dime operators, Carver. Say we bust them. Say we even get convictions on every one. How long are they off the streets? Two years? Three?"

"That's three years the streets are clean," Carver spat back. This sort of thing had been mentioned at the academy but had sounded so bizarre he'd given it little credence. Let drug dealers run free? Carver's best friend in high school had overdosed on heroin on his fifteenth birthday. If the pusher who'd sold that junk had been locked up in the Tombs, that kid would still be alive, maybe a lawyer or a baseball player, instead of ashes on a plastic mantelpiece in a rent-controlled apartment. Carver's fingers tightened on the steering wheel. The flesh beneath his nails turned white.

Evans noted this.

"It doesn't work that way, Carver. Sure, those guys are off the street, but new talent takes their place. We start from scratch, rebuilding our files. I don't like it myself, but it's more practical to have a line on who's doing what when something big comes along.

Carver rubbed damp palms on his blue slacks. "Like a homicide? You wait until someone gets killed?"

Evans shook his head. "Usually it's Narcotics, looking for a line on a bigger supplier."

Carver stared straight ahead, returning his hands to the steering wheel. "And who's the scumbag we're picking up?"

Evans now regretted getting drawn into conversation. Carver was too much on edge. He still possessed self-control, though. The sergeant shrugged. The kid had to learn sometime.

"He uses the name Eric Fuchsia. Damned if I know why. Lives with a fortyish secretary in her apartment on West Eighty-Ninth, between Broadway and Amsterdam. Been with her about two years, off and on. She's clean, if not too bright. His yellow sheet's what you'd expect. We don't know his current source, but Narcotics has some candidates."

"You working with Narcotics on this one?"

"Not yet. Not until we tie the killing to drugs with more than a theory."

"This Fuchsia, he's dangerous? Armed?" Carver's nostrils flared.

"Never carries anything deadlier than a homemade nightstick. That could be the murder weapon, but it's unlikely. We don't have an excuse to enter with guns blazing, if that's what you're after. We're only asking questions. Foster's orders."

Carver was visibly dissatisfied. "You partner with Foster a lot, don't you?"

"We work well together."

The patrolman licked his lips. "How come you asked for a uniform this morning?"

Evans watched the intersection ahead where a taxi was

illegally blocking a crosswalk to pick up a fare. An insolent edge was creeping into Carver's voice which the sergeant did not care for. Had Academy discipline deteriorated since his day, or was middle age making him overly sensitive?

"The dead girl's mother flew down to view the body. Foster went to LaGuardia to meet her."

Carver looked at Evans with widening eyes. The sergeant did not care for unspoken innuendo.

"She wasn't expected," Evans continued. "Most of the squad was already out. If we were close to a break, or making collars, he probably would've sent one of you instead. Not that it's any of your damned business."

"Shit, I know that," said Carver. A grin split his face. "He'd never have made Lieutenant if he was yellow all the way through."

Evans sat up straight. He glared at the rookie. His cheeks grew hot. Menace clung to his words.

"That's not funny, Patrolman Carver."

Carver's grin disappeared. He avoided Evans's eyes.

"Just a little joke I heard in the locker room, Sergeant. It doesn't mean anything."

"I guess it doesn't, to you," Evans growled. "That's the trouble. Who said it? No, forget that. I don't want names. Just spread the word that if I ever hear a remark like that from anyone, I'll have that officer transferred to Flushing Meadows. That's me. God help you if Foster hears it."

"Shit," hissed Carver.

"Speak up, Patrolman Carver."

"I said shit, damn it. You got no call to come down that hard on me. This ain't no suntan I'm wearing. Foster'd be the first to understand. Maybe he'd chew your ass, but not mine. He's a brother. Half a bro', anyway."

Evans glared again at the man beside him. "I'd almost like to see you try him."

"And I'd like to hear how you talk about him to your white buddies!"

"You'd better shut your mouth, Carver, while you've still got a shield. I'm a hair's-breadth away from putting you on report.

If you think Foster's being mulatto makes him only half a man, that's your problem. I only wish you were the only clown with that problem. I don't care how screwed up you are, but you'd goddamn better keep it to yourself. Amos Foster is a good cop, a good friend, and a hell of a better human being than you'll ever be." Evans took a deep breath and let it out slowly. "That motor's plenty warm. Move out."

Carver had a scathing reply on his tongue. He swallowed it. He'd already pushed too hard, and it wasn't important. Not at the moment.

The man in blue jerked his steering wheel to the left and pulled out, tires squealing. A courier, riding his bike down the street in the wrong direction, scrambled onto the sidewalk in a hurry.

CHAPTER 11

Brakes screeched on glistening asphalt. Francine Cooper's eyes opened wide. She thrust out a hand to brace against the bullet-proof Plexiglas separating her from the thick-necked cabbie. Her left elbow bounced off the padded door panel as the taxi skewed into the one empty parking space on the block, next to a fire hydrant. The piercing blast of a cherry-red Ford Pinto's horn swelled up from behind, peaking quickly and fading as the car raced past to run the changing light at Broadway.

The cabbie made a remark Cooper didn't quite catch. She suspected she didn't want to. She glanced at the meter and counted out enough bills to provide a generous tip for the privilege of still living. Wordlessly, Cooper stuffed the money through the narrow slot in the Plexiglas and slid across the cracked, pseudo-leather seat to exit on the curb side. It was a relief to be free of the vehicle's stale and bitter atmosphere. She'd barely had time to close the door when the cab shot east again with a shuddering rattle.

Cooper did not follow its progress. She stepped up onto the sidewalk, pausing next to the hydrant. Her gaze focused on the three brass numerals over the doorway of the building before her. It was a number she'd seen most often as a return address. Not often enough. Never again.

Her eyes lowered to the rough surface of the stoop leading to that door. Although the day was overcast and drizzling, bits of quartz in the sandstone glittered wetly, almost hypnotically.

The wire-photo that the Boston police had shown Cooper could not convey the ghastliness of Lynda's bruised, swollen face. The reproduction quality wasn't very good, and of course the Medical Examiner here in New York had the photos taken with colored filters and at an angle that minimized the damage. As she'd stood beside the narrow, glass-enclosed elevator that carried bodies from the basement storage area or autopsy rooms to permit viewing, the shock Cooper thought she'd purged on the shuttle flight threatened again to numb her mind. Irritation at Lieutenant Foster's abrasiveness helped her deny those emotions then, but the reaction set in when she stepped out past the blue and white glazed brick facade of the building. Subliminally aware that no helpful Brenda would walk her through mental oblivion this time. Cooper compensated by becoming over-sensitized to her surroundings. Like a legendary evil spirit who could be kept outside a home by placing a sieve over the keyhole because of its compulsion to count each hole—impossible to do before sun rise banished it— Cooper adopted immoderate vigilance. Every detail imprinted itself, from the number of cracks in the sidewalk to the brand names on discarded candy wrappers. That was why her eyes were tightly shut as the cab had sped up Eighth Avenue, though the driving would have been reason enough. Sensory overload would have paralyzed her before they'd passed Times Square, let alone reached West Seventieth Street, where she now stood.

A damp gust swept down the block-and-a-half from the Hudson River, slashing rain against her face. Cooper took the hint. She sucked cool air into her lungs. Her feet moved forward. Her right hand grasped the clammy bannister. Fingertips probed age-pits clotted with countless layers of rustproof paint. Her low heels scraped the sandstone steps as she climbed, barely audible over the two-way traffic on Broadway.

How many times had Lynda climbed these steps? How often had the railing that now shook under Cooper's grip borne her daughter's weight? Had Lynda ever sensed the texture and mood that threatened to overwhelm her mother? Had she noticed them at all?

More questions flowed, unbidden. Would Lynda be alive today if they had met at Christmas as originally planned instead of putting it off until New Year's so Cooper could meet her deadline? When she had taken a self-defense course five years earlier, should she have more firmly insisted that Lynda attend sessions with her? Was there something she should have done, or shouldn't have done, that would have kept Lynda in Boston with her?

Put those thoughts out of your mind right now, Cooper, she ordered. No one could have foreseen this tragedy. There was no reason why *you* should have. It might have happened anyway. If not here, somewhere else, some other time. If not Lynda, some other child. Guilt feelings were completely irrational.

And nonetheless real.

Cooper halted at the door to the vestibule. Its glass panel was rain-streaked. She rubbed a thumb on the rough-grained facade beside the jamb. A sandstone fleck slid into her palm. She watched it roll haltingly along her lifeline.

A window rumbled open. A head thrust out. The face was a pasty, pulpy mass framed by a blue-flowered kerchief. Tiny emeralds were pushed into the dough for eyes. A dull pink thing flicked in and out about where a mouth should be—passably a tongue.

The sandstone grain dropped to the stoop. Cooper stared at the apparition. A croaking baritone addressed her.

"Lookin' for some'un?"

Cooper was rarely at a loss for words, but the abrupt greeting, after her hellish morning, left her gaping.

"Speak up or move on. No loiterin' here."

"I—your room—top front—I was told—"

The face crumpled enigmatically. "Agency don't waste time, do they?"

"Are you the, er, landlady?"

"Landlady? Landlady?" The voice went up an octave. "I *run* this place."

"Oh. The superintendent."

The head came out further. A wad of spit landed just beyond the buttock-tall gate that defined the property line. The woman in the window might have a neck, but the high collar of her violet bathrobe kept it a secret.

"Not one of those, neither. A super's a big-bellied slob in a torn shirt, can't even speak the language proper. I'm a concierge."

The emeralds glinted. "Know what a concierge is?"

French for nosy super, Cooper thought. "Yes, I do. Could I see ... ?"

"See what? Did I say there was a vacant room?"

"I don't want ..." Cooper changed tactics in midsentence. She was in no mood to argue or barter. She unsnapped her purse and took a bill from her wallet. Folded twice, it showed only the number twenty clearly. She held the bribe up to give the concierge a better view.

"I don't take money from people in the street."

Cooper's lips drew back. "In that case ..."

"Step inside the vestibule. When I buzz, push the inside door. Hard. Sometimes it sticks. Get in fast and shut it good. Don't want no junkies sneakin' in with you."

Cooper turned her head, checking for hordes of addicts. Across the street, a heavy-set woman fumbled with a black umbrella that had two ribs as she pulled a creaking grocery cart up the slope. At the southeast corner, a truck driver unloaded cases of Scotch for a liquor store. The block was otherwise deserted.

The window rattled shut. Cooper entered as instructed. The door lock was released electrically, with a sound like a raven's death cry. Then she was inside.

Cooper stood in an entrance hall lined with green or maybe blue wallpaper, in a flower print or perhaps an abstract pattern. It was too faded to be sure, in the dim light. An aroma of lilac seemed to come from everywhere except the gothic vase on the narrow hall table, where dingy plastic roses sprouted.

The concierge's door opened noiselessly, betrayed by the murmur of her television set. Leathery fingers rasped Cooper's, plucking the bill from her hand. A violet bathrobe filled the crack of the opening. By peering over the stout wearer's head, Cooper could have glimpsed the living quarters, but that would be obvious and she wasn't interested. The television volume rose for a commercial.

A key slid into Cooper's fingers, in place of the money. It was an old-fashioned key, long and thin; a child could pick the lock this fit, if he or she dared slip past the guardian ogre. The metal was smooth with age and handling. Time treated people less kindly.

"Top floor front," the concierge croaked. "You can't miss it. I'm up and down these stairs enough as it is, and there's nothing I can tell you up there that you can't see for yourself."

"That will be fine, Miss … ?"

The concierge tapped the gold ring on her left hand against her thickly-varnished door. "Knock if you want the room. Else leave the key on the table. My time's valuable."

Cooper glanced at the narrow stairway with its thin green carpet and dark oak bannister. "You're apparently under a wrong impression, Mrs … ?"

The television voices died as the door closed with a snap.

The hallway seemed very warm after the dampness outside. Cooper unbuttoned her coat before starting upstairs. A score of envelopes was stacked on the hall table at the far side of the vase. The vestibule contained no individual mailboxes; all was delivered to the concierge, and tenants were expected to sort out their own correspondence. Opposite the table was a calf-high wastebasket containing a single piece of junk mail, torn in half, showing the addressee. Few tenants, if any, would have picked up mail at this hour. It must have been for the concierge. As soon as she read the name, Cooper remembered it from one of Lynda's first letters home.

"Barclay," she finished softly.

She went up the stairs slowly. The bannister was sturdy, inspiring confidence. The steps, in contrast, groaned as she trod the threadbare runner. A yellowing but neatly-lettered sign on the first landing read "First Floor." Mrs. Barclay tried to run a European building.

CHAPTER 12

Faint, pungent odors of urine and sweat and boiled vegetables permeated another stairwell, in a tenement on West Eighty-Ninth Street. Wood splintered and crackled under the heavy heels of the two policemen as they mounted uncarpeted steps.

A fluorescent bulb on the fourth floor landing had burnt out, leaving a broad black scar on the colorless wallpaper above the fixture. The landing was gloomy, but not pitch dark. Winter sun seeped through overcast skies to the rooftop skylight at the next and final landing, so that bannister and railings were dimly visible. The top landing needed no artificial illumination by day.

"Maybe I should hide here," said Carver in an acid tone. He still smarted from Evans's lecture. "If I cover the whites of my eyes, I'll be invisible."

Evans pinned his gold shield to his coat lapel "Like to live dangerously, Carver?"

"I can joke about my own skin, can't I?"

"While you've got one. If you think it's funny."

The patrolman moved past the detective to the final flight of stairs. Evans tugged his elbow with one hand, used his other to rap solidly on the door of the front apartment.

Carver pulled free. "You said Fuchsia lived on the top floor."

"Uh huh. Did you happen to notice the fire escape out front, as well?"

"Sure I saw it ..."

A woman's voice, muffled by the door, responded to the detective's knock. "¿Que?"

"Police," said Evans. "We need your help."

Evans counted the clicks that followed. Four locks on a door he could kick off its hinges in twenty seconds. It opened the width of a palm, and an indigo eye set in swarthy flesh peered over the taut chain. It took in the two badges that caught and reflected the meager sunlight overhead.

"Official business," Evans added. "We're in a hurry."

The door shut. Carver stepped forward to pound on it.

Evans stopped him with a gesture. The chain slid noisily in its bracket. The door swung inward to admit both men.

Evans pointed Carver across the living room to the window opening onto the fire escape. Then he herded the woman and two pre-school children into the kitchen, assuring them of safety and even adding a few words on the advantage of peepholes over chains. When he returned, Carver was half out the window. The patrolman's right hand rested on his gun butt, and the holster guard was released.

The weapon could be drawn at a moment's notice.

"Get your hand away from that," Evans whispered. "What good does it do, my telling her nothing's going to happen, when you're fooling with your gun?"

"I might need it."

"A good cop rarely does. This little melodrama is just a precaution. For all we know, Gary Cross is staying with friend Eric. Covering the escape route will keep either of them from going shy on us. That's all. Now, count to twenty to give me time to get upstairs. Don't show yourself before, or you might scare someone into bolting before I'm ready."

"That much I figured out myself." Carver's fingers circled the slick bare metal of the fire escape framework. Drizzle spotted his uniform. "I'm not stupid, despite what you think of me."

"I don't think anything of you, as a cop. I haven't seen you in action. Yet."

Evans waved to the woman and her children on his way out. He left the door ajar. Carver heard the detective's dull, distant tread on the final flight of stairs.

Carver licked his lips. "One." His foot was poised for the first step of his own ascent. "Two." A cold wind whipped up his uniform's pants legs. "Three." He'd show that smart-ass detective how good a cop he was.

"Four."

The apartment walls were papered with life-sized posters of nude and semi-nude movie stars and starlets. In the center of the room, facing away from the windows with their bleak view of the tenements across the narrow street, Eric Fuchsia lay in bed, shivering under half a dozen blankets. Rock blared from the stereo speakers atop the bar that doubled as a headboard. A couple of folding chairs and a parson's table completed the furnishings. Fuchsia usually had to move in a hurry and had learned the hard way to travel light. The secretary he'd been balling, the woman whose name was on the lease and who signed the rent check, was learning the same lesson. He'd already hocked most of her stuff.

The apartment door trembled under heavy blows. Fuchsia blinked.

"Police, Eric!" came a voice from the hall. "Open it!"

Fuchsia's sweating body tensed. He must have been set up. The dude who'd provided his latest stash had turned him in. How else would the cops know Fuchsia had the flu and couldn't get out to distribute the junk to his street dealers? He didn't know himself he'd be sick until he woke up at three that morning, shaking and vomiting. And that dumb bitch gone to Detroit, visiting her parents for Christmas week, just when he needed her!

He sank further under the blankets, trying to remember if he'd touched anything the supplier might've fooled with.

"We know you're in there, Eric. Don't make us break down the door."

Bluff. They couldn't know he was home. He always kept the stereo on full volume to discourage burglars. You couldn't be too careful in this neighborhood. If he stayed quiet, the cops couldn't be sure. Let them break in! He'd claim he was asleep and didn't hear them. That might earn him a mistrial.

Then he sneezed.

The pounding redoubled. Hinges groaned. "Now, Eric!"

Cursing, Fuchsia leapt out of bed and pulled on the shorts puddled on the floor alongside. There was enough junk in the bathroom to put him away for twenty years; far too much to flush it all before they busted in. "I'm coming!" he shouted. "Let me get my pants on!"

"You don't need pants, Eric. You've got three seconds to open this door, keeping your hands in sight. One."

Right. He didn't need pants. Fuchsia grabbed a knee-length raccoon coat from the closet, jammed his feet into cracked leather slippers, and raced to the window.

Sam Carver crouched on the fire escape, gun in hand. He grinned at the dealer, touching the brim of his uniform cap in mock salute. The grin broadened as the officer glanced at the posters papering the wall.

"Two."

Fuchsia dropped the coat to scoop up his homemade nightstick from behind the radiator. He heaved it through the window.

Carver staggered back. His gun arm rose to fend off flying glass shards. The stick bounced off his shoulder. He heard it clatter on the sidewalk below.

"Three!"

Behind Fuchsia, the apartment door splintered. The cheap lock popped loose, thudding on the linoleum.

Fuchsia clambered out the window. He was lucky the cop's fingers hadn't been on the trigger. Jagged glass gashed his leg; he didn't have time to notice or worry about it. Carver blocked the way down. The officer's shoes slipped on the wet grillwork, but he kept his balance and he still held the gun.

Fuchsia went for the roof. Cold rain stung his skin.

"Son of a bitch!" Carver screamed. His footing was steady now, but his lower back throbbed where it had banged against the railing. Crimson peppered his face and hand where flying glass had bitten. Eyes watering—from rage, he thought—Carver hauled himself after the criminal. Evans shouted at him from inside the apartment, but the wind whipped his words away.

"I'll get him!" Carver yelled back.

Weakened by flu, Fuchsia stumbled over one of the eaves.

Flesh scraped from his knees and palms. He rose on shaking legs. In shorts and slippers, he found the chilling damp overwhelmed other sensations. He did not feel blood pumping from the severed artery in his right calf, was unaware of the sticky red trail he left on the way to the adjoining roof. His only thought was that, with a good head start, he could reach another fire escape and descend to Eighty-Ninth Street. It would be better to go down through another building, but he couldn't spare the time to look for a roof trap that wasn't bolted shut.

If only there was some decent cover up here!

Carver was panting as his free hand grabbed the looped top of the fire escape. He heaved himself up and over. Fuchsia's blurry silhouette wove ahead of him, he couldn't tell how far. Rain cut down on visibility, though it didn't feel as if it was coming down that hard and he didn't remember reports of fog.

Faces appeared at the windows of taller surrounding buildings. Carver did not see those at all.

Fuchsia tripped, smashing one knee on gravel-strewn tarpaper and gasping for air. Sweat and rain turned to ice on his flesh. He looked back. The blue uniform came up fast. He'd cornered himself. The next building after this was four stories higher and separated from this one by a wide, garbage-filled alley.

"Police! Freeze!" shouted Carver. The patrolman took a two-handed shooting stance, feet spread. "Or I'll blow your balls off!" He fired a warning shot straight up, then lowered the revolver barrel chest-high.

Fuchsia spat something thick and yellow into the alley. It struck with a sucking noise. No miracle escapes today. He struggled to his feet, raising his hands. It was over.

Behind Carver, the roof trapdoor on Fuchsia's building popped open. The patrolman swung his head at the sound. Evans thrust his long face out into the drizzle.

"Don't shoot, Carver!" the detective said. "He can't go anywhere!"

The rookie's ears were buzzing. He recognized Evans's voice, felt relieved that his back was covered. But the sergeant must have seen something that Carver couldn't, because the patrolman heard only one word distinctly.

Shoot.

The bullet caught Fuchsia high on the left thigh. The pusher twisted sideways at the impact. His right leg, the slashed one, folded under him. His arms flapped wildly for support. One hand slid along the lubricous rooftop and over the lip.

Fuchsia toppled head first into the alley, five stories below. His scream was horribly brief.

Carver felt locked in position, legs apart, gun stretched out before him. His limbs refused to move. His throat burned. He'd never killed a human being. He hadn't *wanted* to kill this one; just stop him.

Evans walked up behind him deliberately, making sure Carver heard his footsteps. He reached the patrolman's side and gently pried the revolver from stiff but unresisting fingers. Evans slipped the .38 into his raincoat pocket.

"What ... ?" rasped Carver. His arms sank to his sides.

Evans walked to the edge of the second roof and peered down into the alley. He turned away with a grimace.

Onlookers in the neighboring buildings shouted angry abuse. A hurled bottle exploded with a loud pop somewhere; it never had a chance of hitting either policeman. Evans realized that the longer they stayed in view of the outraged community, the more likelihood there was of a riot. Last night, in Miami, police had shot an unarmed juvenile, and *that* city was already erupting in violence. The cancer spread too easily.

"Jesus, Carver," he said when he stood before the patrolman. "You didn't have to kill him."

"It was a warning shot," Carver mumbled. "A warning. I wasn't trying to hit him."

Evans shook his head. "Internal Affairs will eat this one up. Christ! Don't tell me you thought he was going for a weapon in his fucking underwear! He even threw away his stick!"

Carver swallowed, hard. His face glittered with moisture. He raised a hand to clear his vision.

Evans got a close look then. Suddenly, he yanked Carver's arm aside.

"Don't rub your eyes!"

"Blurry," Carver muttered.

"I know. They're probably full of glass splinters. We have to get you to a hospital." Still gripping Carver's arm, Evans led him to the roof trap. "I'll go down the ladder first. You follow. I'll watch that you don't miss your footing. And don't even think about touching your eyes! Understand?"

Carver nodded. He licked his lips, tasting salt.

Welling up from the street came the wail of sirens, replying to a 911 call. Evans was grateful that someone, at least, was doing something more productive than littering.

Carver knelt by the open trap. His fingers trembled over the metal-edged lip. His uniform clung to his back. Rain dripped down his neck. That object just ahead, slowly sinking—that had to be Sergeant Evans. For all that Carver could see, it might have been a dying vine, or the Loch Ness monster.

"I guess this wouldn't have happened to Lieutenant Foster," Carver said gloomily. His lips thinned.

Whup-whup-whup echoed from the direction of Broadway, growing swiftly louder. Evans paused, looking up into Carver's bleeding face. He sensed the patrolman was fumbling to form an apology, something he rarely did.

"Fucking right it wouldn't have happened to Amos," the sergeant growled. "The lieutenant would've been in charge, and I'd be the one taking a faceful of window on the fire escape. You want to snap it up? That's okay, I've got your leg. I hear an ambulance whooping away down there, and you need it more than Fuchsia."

CHAPTER 13

Mrs. Barclay had a touch of the fantastic or surreal about her that had briefly drawn Cooper from her languor, but she began to regress as she crossed the first floor landing. The remaining three flights took hours, it seemed, and when Cooper did reach the top floor she felt as exhausted as if she'd run up. Passing certain doors, she'd heard muffled scrapes and taps and, once, a rush of water. Not every tenant was at work today. Still, although stairs and floorboards creaked beneath her tread, no one looked out to question her.

She stood before the door to Lynda's room, breathing deeply, gripping the key with bloodless fingers. Her hand crept forward, dragging the arm's dead weight.

The key slid in easily but refused to turn. Cooper jerked her hand away as if the metal was electrified. The building had apparently decided to make her feel unwelcome.

Her lips curled with impatience. That she should even consider that notion! "Pull yourself together, woman," she whispered. "You've a reputation for being level-headed. You didn't earn it by fantasizing."

She experimented, jiggling the key in place. When she withdrew it the thickness of a fingernail, the key practically turned in the lock by itself. Age had worn down the metal tip, The serrations had overshot the pin-tumblers of the lock.

Cooper gripped the doorknob, noting with annoyance her whitening knuckles. To let such a small thing fluster her, even for a moment, was further indication of the overwrought state she'd been trying to deny. Was she trying to do too much too soon? Should she have checked into a hotel and come here tomorrow?

Then she'd have been alone with her thoughts for the entire day.

To hell with that.

Cooper turned the knob. The door swung inward with a faint squeak.

Hazy sunlight poured through the south-facing windows. It reminded Cooper of her first glimpse of the glass-enclosed elevator in the middle of the room at the Medical Examiner's building, before Lynda's body rose into view. She rushed forward to close the Venetian blinds. Then she opened a window. The southern exposure combined with radiator steam to make the room unbearably hot on this drizzling but unseasonably warm winter day.

Cool, damp air rushed in. Cooper let it push her back until her calves found the edge of the bed. She sat. Plastic buttons on the unpadded mattress dug into her rump. For no good reason, she clutched her purse against her stomach with both arms.

An empty armoire stood at the foot of the bed, doors flung wide, drawers half open. Even the drawer of the night table, which Cooper could reach with her left hand if she dared to let go of her purse, stuck out far enough to bare its yellowed paper lining. The waste basket was also immaculate. Perhaps Lynda Cooper had never lived in this room, after all. Perhaps she'd never existed.

Occupied or not, furnished rooms seem emptier than unfurnished apartments. The difference was between a failed promise and one yet to be fulfilled.

There was nothing here for Francine Cooper.

She wanted to leave. She tried to stand. Instead, she slumped forward, catching her chin in her palm, bracing elbows on knees. Her eyes focused on the relatively brilliant thin white lines between the slats of the ill-fitting blinds. Incredible that the cloud-shrouded sun should still be so high in the sky, after everything that's happened on this brief winter day: the dawn visit from the Boston detectives, the travel arrangements, the shuttle flight, meeting Lieutenant Foster at LaGuardia Airport, the muted voices and antiseptic smell of the building on First Avenue....

Yet Cooper had had to see for herself. She'd had to.

CHAPTER 14

As a rookie beat patrolman, before he'd even cracked open a book in preparation for the test for Detective Third Grade, Joseph Evans practiced, for half an hour a day, a stride of two feet, give or take half an inch. It had been an experiment in self-discipline, and he was proud of the ability, although he naturally verified the measurement whenever possible before it went into his report. Foster wouldn't let him get away without a check, even if Evans had wanted to.

Sergeant Evans paced the otherwise empty waiting room. It was too early for regular visiting hours. The distance between walls was eighteen feet one way, ten feet the other.

"Sergeant Evans?"

Evans stopped and turned in mid-stride. At the entrance to the room stood a tall, white-smocked man with a doctor's ID badge pinned over his heart or where most people thought the heart was. The detective glared without passion or resentment. The doctor repeated himself.

"You *are* Detective Evans, aren't you?"

Evans pointed to the shield still pinned to his lapel. The other man shrugged, slightly embarrassed.

"You're not the same doctor who's looking after my man in uniform," Evans rumbled.

"No. A specialist is attending Patrolman Carver. My name is Asprin, William G., and if you don't make a joke we'll get along better. I've heard them all. The nurse at reception told me you'd be here."

A jest sprang at once to the sergeant's mind, made all but irresistible by the doctor's plea for restraint. As an officer of the law, however, Evans was disciplined in more matters than leg-stride. He choked it back, substituting terseness.

"So?"

Doctor Asprin rubbed the smooth skin atop his skull. The prolonged but inevitable balding process had begun early, in his last year of medical school. Impatient with it, Asprin shaved his head. His schedule and priorities, however, did not permit daily attention to this bit of grooming, and the lower third of his physiognomy more often than not boasted a fine growth of shadowy stubble. Today was no exception.

"I'd like to ask a favor of you, Sergeant. It shouldn't be too much trouble, since you're here anyway, waiting for word on your partner."

"Not my partner."

Asprin blinked. "Colleague, then."

"What kind of favor?"

The doctor looked at the sagging couch. He'd prefer to make his request sitting down. The detective was just as clearly in no mood to be seated. Asprin cleared his throat.

"Last night—actually, early this morning—the Emergency Room admitted an apparent mugging victim in critical condition. I specialize in head injuries; he became my patient. Naturally, our staff called the local precinct house to report the crime …"

"Probable crime," Evans growled. His neck itched. He saw where Asprin was heading and he didn't want to go along.

The doctor nodded. "As you say. We were told a unit would stop by to take statements as soon as one became available. I realize that this is not a high priority matter. In fact, the desk sergeant was advised that the man was unable to speak coherently and would not be able to do so for some hours. Still, it's been almost twelve hours since his admission. I can't stay here all day."

Evans studied a spot on his tie. When he looked up, he was scowling.

"You want me to take a look."

"If you could, and sign a form to prove that we *did* report the incident, in case something more comes of it. The patient is starting to come around a little. You might get a few words out of him before we renew the sedation."

Evans put a thick hand to his chin. Bad enough he'd have to file a carefully-worded report on the Fuchsia shooting, a report Captain Matherson would want yesterday and which would be scrutinized by the police commissioner, the mayor, and anyone else who felt New York might become another Miami. If Evans looked at Doctor Asprin's alleged mugging victim, he'd be stuck with enough paperwork to keep him off the streets through another shift and possibly up to New Year's Eve.

"Our squads have been pretty busy during that time, Doctor," the detective began. "You've heard of last night's homicide in Riverside Park? Everyone available is combing the area or picking up suspects. Don't worry. I'll call in and cut a team loose for you."

Asprin's face fell. He worried his lower lip. "That'll take another hour or two."

"Maybe not," Evans said, his tone belying the optimistic words.

"All right, if that's the best you can do. Annie'll have a fit about my coming home late again, but..."

"That's Mrs. Asprin?"

The doctor nodded. "I suppose I'll manage to calm her down. I usually do."

"Sure. A doctor's wife has to expect this sort of thing." Just like a cop's wife, Evans mused. He could almost hear Liz saying that. "Hell. What time are you due home?"

"Half an hour ago."

"This really belongs to Street Crime. I'm Homicide."

Doctor Asprin rubbed his stubbled chin. "He's in pretty bad shape, Sergeant. It's more than possible that, in a matter of hours, the man *will* fall under your jurisdiction."

Evans grimaced. The balance was tipped. "I'll regret this. You'll owe me, Doctor William G. Asprin. Lead on." At least, the detective thought, it would keep his mind off Carver for a few minutes.

CHAPTER 15

Doctor Edwin Bailey's office was on the ground floor of the Medical Examiner's building, a short distance from the cubicles in which clerks and typists dealt with records of thirty thousand autopsies a year. The clacking of typewriter keys drifted in through the open door.

Not a large office, but comfortable and tidy except to the left of Bailey's desk, where Amos Foster leaned back in his chair so that the front legs cleared the floor by a hand's breadth. His long fingers picked apart his empty coffee container. His eyebrows shifted in dubious time with his atonal humming. He appeared oblivious to the white Styrofoam scraps that clung to his sweater or bounced off the stained gray envelope in his lap before they scattered across the tile floor.

"Christ, Amos, are you still here? I thought you'd left with the mother!"

Like his office, Ed Bailey was a small, neat man, with a fine-clipped moustache and eyes of so light a blue they were nearly transparent. He entered the room and slid smoothly behind his desk, noting Foster's artificial snowfall with a curl of the lip. His white hair was damp from the post-autopsy shower.

"She didn't care for my company," Foster explained.

"I hope you don't think that I do."

Foster fingered the gray envelope. "I walked over to the Forensic Lab to see what they'd found so far. Thought you might have something for me to take back, too."

Bailey removed a sharpened pencil from his desk drawer, ostensibly to write a memorandum. Actually, he'd picked it up in order to throw it down again in disgust. He did so.

"The M in M.E. doesn't stand for Miracle-worker, Amos. My assistants are still closing up the girl. It'll take hours to work up tests on what I removed. I just popped in here to use my phone to cancel a lunch date, before I go up to the lab on the fifth floor."

Foster tossed what was left of his cup into the wastebasket. "You can give me a preliminary, Ed. You know I won't hold you to early guesswork. Hell, let me feel as if I'm doing something! My squad is busting its collective ass digging for leads, while I cool my heels in airports and morgues."

"Our basement is full of cooling heels, Amos." Bailey sat back in his padded swivel chair, bracing one foot on the edge of the desk. He'd give the lieutenant what he wanted—there was no reason not to—but not without a little struggle. Just because he played cards with Foster one or two times a month didn't mean the detective should be spoiled.

Foster recognized the game, but he didn't want to play.

"That's not funny, Ed."

Bailey swallowed his half-formed smile. "You and Joe are usually my best audience. Where's your professional detachment?"

Foster looked past Bailey's ear, at a shelf of thick brown medical books. "These are the ones I hate, Ed. Messy. Vicious. There's no excuse for such brutality. It's ... amateurish."

"Gary Cross would be such an amateur. You said that nothing in his record indicated a violent streak. Maybe he's just starting."

"I also told you I didn't buy that version. I think the muscle was directed *at* Cross. I'm more certain now. The trail of blood found on the dock groups as A-negative. Cross's type. Not Lynda Cooper's."

"She fought back. He lost his temper."

"Maybe. But if I'm right about new talent moving in, and this is a sample of their style, I want a line on them fast." He sucked in a deep breath. "I hope it's that simple. I'm scared to death the killer might be a *real* psycho."

Bailey lifted an eyebrow. He'd seen the detective upset before, but not quite in this way, not since the first autopsy Foster had witnessed. And the lieutenant hadn't opened up this much then. Bailey wasn't sure how to deal with the situation. He tried changing the subject.

"Mrs. Cooper get to you?"

"Of course not." Foster frowned thoughtfully. "I don't know. Maybe. Damn it, I *have* to look at broken bodies! Why would anyone else *want* to, especially … ?" He glanced down at the Styrofoam flakes on his sweater for the first time, and brushed them off. "I assume the girl was raped?"

"Probably." Bailey relaxed. Foster was back in control, a policeman with a job to do.

"You're a big help."

Bailey showed his palms helplessly. "Indications of sexual intercourse are ambiguous here. The vaginal swabs taken at the scene of the crime fluoresce under ultraviolet light, which is indicative of seminal stains but not conclusive. So far, the acid phosphatase tests are negative. I'll run new ones with the autopsy samples. We could not locate or identify any spermatozoa, not even fragments. Unusual, but not impossible. No luck on blood grouping, either, but about twenty percent of all men have seminal fluid free of blood-group substances."

Foster finished picking his sweater clean. He shifted in his chair. His frown deepened.

"Just tell me what I don't know, without the explanations."

Bailey straightened. He clasped his hands atop the desk. "Samples of dried urine from the boat cabin *do* contain blood-group substances. They type out as A-negative."

"I've got that, too. What about drugs?"

"From scrapings? Give me a break, Amos!"

"I mean the girl."

"Oh, her. No, she seems clean, though I won't swear to that until all the tests are in. No needle marks, no observable damage to nasal membranes. If she used anything, it must've been pills."

Foster's loose-leaf notebook was in his hands. He took close notes. "Last night, the medical inspector said cause of death was internal hemorrhage."

Bailey rubbed a thumbnail along his moustache. "No question about it. The lower intestinal wall was perforated, along with everything in the way. We're still looking for clues to the nature of the weapon. There are no visible splinters or glass fragments."

Foster leaned forward, replacing his notebook in his jacket pocket. "A brass railing was found next to the highway overpass in the park."

"And it was smeared with A-negative blood with nary a drop of Type O, which is what the Cooper girl was. One doesn't wash away the other. The most I'll grant you is that the rail could have been used to break her jaw. The metal is so smooth, though, that there are no indentations in her flesh to connect the two."

Foster grunted. A cramp was forming in his right leg. He twisted and bent to knead it. The leg bothered him on and off in damp weather, ever since half a score of shotgun pellets were dug out of the calf muscles seven years ago. X-rays to the contrary, Foster suspected one or more pellets, or fragments of same, had eluded the surgeon's knife.

"Deductions?" asked the lieutenant.

Bailey smiled. "Don't expect me to do *all* your work. I shouldn't even be discussing that aspect of the case."

"Sorry. You're right. I usually talk things over with my partner, but Joe's been out on call all morning."

"Apology accepted. I can say this about your killer: he's extremely strong. That rail is heavy, and the girl was struck with considerable force."

"Cross doesn't have that kind of build."

Bailey's smile widened a trifle. "I know. I was playing devil's advocate before. I promise you, Amos, as soon as I get anything, a scrap of skin, a stray hair, that doesn't belong to Cooper or Cross, I'll let you know."

"I'll appreciate it. Might even let you win a hand next week." Foster lurched to his feet. Three more white flakes, hidden in the folds of his sweater, drifted to the floor. He shrugged. He'd peel off the cardigan in the car, anyway. The day was warm, but this building felt chilly to Foster no matter what the outside was like.

With the gray envelope tucked in his raincoat pocket and

his hand on the doorjamb, Foster looked back at the man behind the desk.

"You don't care for my drug war theory, do you, Ed?"

Bailey shook his head. "It sucks, Amos. Too complicated. Personally, and off the record, I think it's a lunatic. A Son of Sam who prefers something more personal than a .45 bullet."

Foster's throat tightened. "I can't wed myself to that. If it's true, my people are wasting their time. All we can do is wait for him to strike again and hope we get lucky. The newspapers will blow it up out of proportion, and that will only encourage him."

Bailey threw up his hands in resignation as his desk phone started ringing. "So go with the drug gangs. Maybe you're right. You have to start somewhere. Excuse me." He picked up the receiver in the middle of the second ring.

Foster glanced at his watch. "Joe ought to be back at the station now. I'll ask him what he thinks."

Bailey waved him back. "Find out now. He's on the phone. Asked for you."

The lieutenant leapt forward and clasped the receiver to his ear, almost bowling over the pathologist. Evans wouldn't take the trouble of tracking him here unless it was important.

Bailey gleaned nothing from Foster's grunts and terse, single-word responses. He feigned disinterest, but his eyes betrayed him. Abruptly, without even a goodbye, the detective slammed the receiver in its cradle and shot out the doorway.

"Hey, fair's fair!" Bailey shouted to the hallway. "Throw me a bone!"

Foster stuck his head back in the office. He was all smiles and shiny eyes. "Joe's found Cross at Roosevelt Hospital. Says he might be able to give us some answers."

"That's nice," murmured Bailey as the detective's face vanished again. He retrieved his pencil and placed it carefully in the desk drawer. "Answers are always nice."

CHAPTER 16

"You want the room, or what?"

Cooper blinked, coming out of her trance. As she turned, red streaks flashed before her eyes from staring at the daylight coming through the blinds.

She'd left the door standing open. Mrs. Barclay stood on the threshold, violet bathrobe flapping in the dank breeze from the window, flabby arms crossed at her shapeless bosom.

"I beg your pardon?"

"You've been up here over an hour. I came to check, make sure you hadn't walked off with the key."

Cooper shivered. The room's oppressive heat had leached out the open window. It seemed cooler in the room than outside.

The tightness of Cooper's pale face did not go unobserved by Mrs. Barclay. Few things did.

"You feel all right?" The bright green eyes flitted to the closet-sized bathroom. "You ain't been sick, have you? You'll have to clean it up yourself. I don't do that even for those what pay their rent, which you haven't, yet. Assuming I decide you're okay."

Mental fog dispelled under the concierge's assault. Cooper was torn between laughter and indignation. Her lips quivered as the emotions reached an uneasy truce.

"No," she replied. "I just haven't eaten today."

"One of those, eh?" Mrs. Barclay swept into the room, lilac scenting her wake, to shut the window with a bang.

"Did I miss something?" Cooper asked.

The concierge applied ample buttocks to the windowsill. The light from behind shadowed her face, adding depth to the features, making her look more human.

"Get this straight, girlie. I don't give credit. Rent is by the week, in advance. No exceptions." Her arms flapped limply during the speech, ending entwined under her breasts.

With the foot of the bed for support, Cooper stood. Her eyes took in the whole room before meeting Mrs. Barclay's stern, suspicious expression with a blank stare.

"There's nothing here. No personal belongings."

"You want to make it homey, that's your business. No permanent changes, and don't clutter." The pale tongue flicked. "You're sorta old to be breaking into show biz, aren't you?"

Cooper's eyes dilated. The conversation was starting to make some sense. "Do you get many would-be actresses?"

"Neighborhood's lousy with 'em."

"You thought Lynda was one?"

The concierge's cheeks caved inward, glowing crimson. Her hands curled into thick fleshy fists. "I'll be damned. First time in twenty years a reporter's conned me. After I drag my ass up those crummy stairs, too.

"I'm not a reporter, Mrs. Barclay."

"Bullshit. How do you know my name?"

"I'm Lynda's mother. From Boston." Cooper fumbled with the catch of her purse.

"And I'm Bo Derek's twin sister!" Mrs. Barclay glowered. "Don't bother trying a bigger bribe, Miss Snoop! I've half a mind to make you eat your twenty. Morbid bastards, you newshounds. What you did to Mr. Barclay, God rest his rotten soul! Running a few numbers doesn't make him a god-fath …

Cooper stuffed a Massachusetts driver's license into the puffy right hand and forcibly raised it to the concierge's line of sight. Mrs. Barclay tilted her head, letting light fall on the photograph. Moving lips read the name. She looked up.

"Why didn't you say so?" she grumbled.

Cooper took back the license. "I didn't have much chance."

"Could've saved us both a climb. Your daughter's things are in the basement. Figured someone would send for 'em. Didn't 'spect you'd come in person."

"People don't expect much these days. Understandably."

"Needn't be bitter. Want some tea? Look like you need it."

"Did you know my daughter well, Mrs. Barclay? Had she any unusual … habits?" Cooper dared not say drugs, partly for fear of planting suspicion where there might be no ground for it.

The concierge shook her head. "I don't pry, Mrs. Cooper. Lynda paid her rent on time and didn't make a racket. I asked her not to type after ten at night, that's all. She stayed in her room a lot, went downtown couple times a week and brought back large envelopes."

"She did freelance copy-editing. Did she ever mention me?"

"On the lease application. That's what I showed the cops, for next of kin. Quiet girl. Stayed out late maybe one night a week. Kept to herself. Maybe too much. You know?"

Cooper's legs felt weak again. "Like her mother. Odd. When she was growing up, I only saw the differences."

Mrs. Barclay took Cooper's arm and steered her to the door. Her touch was unexpectedly gentle.

"Come along. Hot cup of jasmine will settle you."

"Yes. I *would* like something." She resisted the tugging to study the room once more. "What did Lynda pay for this?"

"Fifty a week. Includes utilities. Fair price for the area. There's nothing due, if that's what you think. Lynda always paid for her week first thing Monday morning."

"Is a traveler's check all right?"

The emerald eyes narrowed puzzled. "Eh?"

"A personal check on my Boston account would be an imposition on you, and I need the little cash I have on hand."

Mrs. Barclay's lips vibrated indignantly. "No charge for packing and storing the poor girl's things. Had to be done."

"Not that. You said payment in advance. I haven't booked a hotel room. I hadn't intended staying in New York more than a few hours. This room is just as convenient as the Waldorf, and much more appropriate."

"You want to rent this room?"

"Is there a problem? Another tenant?"

"No. Not yet. Ah … how long?"

"No later than the end of the week, I hope."

"Well ... the room *is* already paid for, but ..."

"I'd rather pay my own way than live off my daughter's leftovers. Also, I'll need your telephone to re-arrange my affairs in Boston. I'll reimburse the long distance costs."

Mrs. Barclay sniffed diffidently. The sudden transformation of Francine Cooper from bereaved mother to efficient career woman seemed, to her, neither natural nor healthy.

"I discourage short-term tenants as a rule."

Cooper paused uncertainly, traveler's check in hand. The uncertainty persuaded Mrs. Barclay to give in.

"Under the circumstances, I can't refuse. You sure this is smart, though? Lynda's passing was not, forgive me, easy. It's not fashionable to believe in ghosts, but ... my late husband, whose last years were so unbearable, came back one night to tell me of the torment of dying." The concierge's jaws clamped tightly shut in anticipation of derision.

Cooper did not laugh. "In a way, Mrs. Barclay, that's just what I want... to unearth Lynda's ghost. Not so literally, though. One or two points, which the police have no interest in, are very important to me."

The concierge frowned. "I wouldn't fool with the cops, Mrs. Cooper."

Cooper smiled thinly. Her skin prickled with a strange exhilaration at her decision to stay in New York. "Personal matters only, I assure you. Maybe I'll learn what I want to know by going through Lynda's things."

"After tea," Mrs. Barclay said firmly. She clamped a thick hand on the woman's elbow, and checked that the door was locked before they started downstairs.

CHAPTER 17

Allison Zebar, public relations staffer at the American Museum of Natural History, groaned as she hunched over yet another bulging file carton. Her calves grew stiffer by the minute, each ready to develop a massive charley horse. Long fingers, scarred by paper cuts, flipped through yellowed photographs and meticulous inventory lists—and, alas, many that were less than meticulous. Decades of dust dulled her shoulder length silver-blonde hair and clogged her snub nose. She sneezed a lot. Her eyes burned from reading too many fading words penned by now dead explorers who wrote on camelback, or by the unsteady glow of a whale-oil lamp that could not thaw frostbitten fingers, in ink that froze on the nib. Shadowy lighting didn't help. Why hadn't the museum installed decent overhead fluorescents in this storage area?

"Allison! Come see this!"

The cracking voice belonged to Warren Harrison, a squat teddy bear of a man in his early twenties. Harrison normally worked on exhibit maintenance, but today Zebar dragooned him and a pair of model-builders to supplement the three people from her own section for this scavenger hunt. They weren't enough. Tomorrow she would raid the other departments in earnest. She had plenty of favors outstanding with most of the department heads, and it was time to collect on some.

Zebar sneezed as she slowly stood up. Her leg muscles screamed silently, overwhelmed by the throb in her lower back. She took a quick personal inventory. Three fingernails had broken, one to the quick. She sucked on a freshly bleeding paper cut. A pearly button had vanished from the midriff of her ruffled blouse, and would no doubt turn up fifty years hence as part of another forgotten collection, perhaps even put on display. Her knee-length aquamarine cotton shirt, chosen from the back of her closet to take advantage of the recent balmy weather, was streaked and stained and ready for the dry cleaner months before its time. One nylon stocking received a gaping run from splinters on a crate that had arrived thirty years earlier from a country that, politically, no longer existed; the crate had never been opened, and probably never would be.

Another promise for tomorrow: to dress properly for this grungy task.

Zebar stepped over the open carton, grateful for flat-heeled shoes. She threaded her way around a wobbling metal shelf, past the giant clamshell, turning right at a dull brown meteorite the size (and shape, if you looked hard enough) of a St. Bernard, to get to where Warren Harrison was conducting a similar search. At least, that's what she'd told him to do.

"Found something?" she asked.

Harrison nodded. The top of his head was level with her chin and his pudgy frame made him seem even shorter. His body seemed to pull him down. One day a huge pancake Harrison would enter the dioramas by sliding under the glass.

He held a black metal object half again as long as his arm and perhaps three fingers wide, tapering at the tip. He wheezed for approval.

Zebar considered it dubiously. "What is it?"

"A sword. Heavy bastard, too. Feels like solid iron."

Zebar turned her head and sneezed. "So?"

"It's out of the same lot as that busted hilt. I guess that hilt was a spare."

The lines in Zebar's forehead deepened; mild puzzlement became annoyance. "Is *this* what you've been doing all this time, Warren? Rooting around for that? For crying out loud, we *know* the mutilated hilt belongs to the museum. It's the only piece we *could* identify and document immediately!"

Harrison pouted, his lower lips trembling. "I thought you'd be interested, that's all. I wasn't looking for it. I just sort of tripped over the crate it was in, and felt I ought to take a look inside."

"There's no need to open crates," Zebar snapped. "We're looking for records, not artifacts." She took the proffered weapon. Its weight dragged her arms down. For comfort, she rested the blade against her shoulder, point up.

Harrison thrust his hands behind his back. He looked at his dust-caked Adidas. "It seemed like a good idea at the time." He met Zebar's eyes defensively. "Give me a break. I don't know what I'm doing. This isn't my job. I'm supposed to be touching up backgrounds in Akeley Hall this week. The African veldt is getting dingy."

Zebar shrugged and nodded. Harrison might be a whiner, but he had a point. *She* didn't know how best to go about this task, either. If there was a 'best' way.

"I apologize, Warren. Of course you're right, and I know how you feel. I planned to write some year-end press releases today, and instead I'm burrowing around amid dinosaur bones. I shouldn't have taken it out on you."

Harrison accepted the apology with an awkward nod. He turned away, avoiding eye contact. It was embarrassing to have someone older, and in a higher position, defer to him. Even though she had been in the wrong.

"That's okay."

Zebar suddenly sneezed again. The sword leapt, and fell back heavily on her shoulder. An eddy of dust now seemed to swirl around her ... or was it just the haze of her watery eyes? She had a distinct impression of moving air, although she did not actually *feel* a breeze.

"Do you notice a draft, Warren?"

The young man shook his shaggy head. "Not now. There was one before, when I picked up that sword."

Zebar looked around the cluttered storage room. Her snub nose crinkled, as if trying to smell the air flow. Strands of silver-blonde hair clung wetly to her neck, tickling her. If there was a draft, its cooling effect was nil.

"Probably freak currents, set up by our own movements. Or maybe I'm hallucinating. I need oxygen. Moreover, I need food. Let's knock off for lunch. The files aren't going to walk away on us."

Unconsciously, Harrison patted his abdomen. "That's something I know how to do." He started forward, then paused. "What about the police?"

"What about them?"

"You said the detective that came this morning promised that the lieutenant in charge of the case would talk to you later today. Suppose you're out when he comes?"

Zebar clucked her tongue. "Well, he's not going to arrest me, Warren. Even police lieutenants eat sometimes. Anyway, I'm only going as far as the cafeteria. He'll be able to find me there."

Harrison screwed up his face. The tip of his tongue popped out. "How can you eat that stuff?"

Because I usually buy the packaged yogurt, Zebar thought. As a publicist, though, she had to avoid reflecting negatively on Museum management, and in any case it was more fun to bait Harrison. "It's not bad, if you stick to the right things. It's cheaper than that place across the street where you hang out."

"Worth the difference. I can have a different brand of beer every day of the month, including Sundays, and still leave some untried."

Zebar sneezed again. She rubbed her nose. This was getting to be annoying. "I hate beer. By the way, Warren, if you get a chance, try to scrounge a couple of surgical masks out of one of the research labs."

"What's in it for me?"

"Reduced risk of emphysema. Not having to eat in the cafeteria. Also, I'll let you off an hour early."

"Consider it done."

Smiling, Zebar followed as Harrison cut a swath to the door. There they parted. The cafeteria was in the basement, but Zebar headed upstairs first. She wanted to clean off some of the crud clinging to her skin. When she reached her office, she realized that she still carried the heavy iron sword. It was an uncharacteristically absent-minded act, but she shrugged it off. Dragging the weapon onto the elevator, up to the fifth floor, simply to rest it in one of less cluttered corners of her tiny office, seemed like a good idea at the time.

CHAPTER 18

Amos Foster clipped the gold shield to the lapel of his sports jacket and eased out of the car. His raincoat remained crumpled on the passenger side of the front seat. What Foster most disliked about winter, and inclement weather in general, was the need for outer clothing. Coats and sweaters impeded his mobility and, therefore, his effectiveness as a detective. The drizzle that had started in the late morning had let up before he'd walked out of 520 First Avenue, and the unseasonable warmth made him consider stripping off the cardigan as well. Crossing a few yards of asphalt to the hospital's side entrance, shorn of the raincoat's protection, seemed a feasible risk.

If a nor'easter blew up in the next half hour, he'd borrow his partner's coat.

Even the parking lot smells antiseptic, Foster mused as he sidled between a pair of ambulances.

His soles scuffed wet gravel. On consideration, he decided that observation was not accurate. The odor filling his nostrils had clung to his clothes from the office of the Medical Examiner. He hadn't noticed it earlier because he'd driven with the side window wide open, the breeze whipping past, taking advantage of rain-cleansed fresh air, a rare commodity in New York City.

Joe Evans waited behind a glass door, watching his superior approach. At the last moment, the sergeant pushed the door open. Foster had to back down a step to avoid being struck by the blue edge.

"Hey!" the lieutenant protested.

"That's for taking so long. I expected you twenty seconds ago."

"Banter later, Joe. What happened to Fuchsia?"

"Got shot, fell off the roof. That was after he'd blinded Carver, my backup in uniform, by smashing a window. Almost."

Evans started down a long, yellow-green corridor as he spoke. Foster kept pace.

"Almost?" asked Foster.

"Eyes heal fast. When they heal at all."

The lieutenant grunted. This was more than Evans had given him over the telephone, but not everything, not by a long shot. No matter. Evans wouldn't leave out any details that Foster had to know at that moment. If, later, the senior detective hungered for the full story, Evans would show him the full report before it went to Captain Matherson. In fact, Joe would probably insist he read it first.

"Why did Fuchsia run?"

Evans shook his head. "Probably holding. I've got a couple of third-grades tossing his apartment."

"Even so, if he'd already told you where to find Cross ... ?"

The hall ended abruptly in a sharp turn and a pair of high elevator doors, their dark brown paint marred by waist-high scratches. The wide doors whooshed apart before Evans pressed the up button. A clean-shaven intern shot out of the cab, pushing a rattling, unoccupied gurney. The two detectives flattened against opposite walls.

"Jersey driver," muttered Evans.

The doors were closing, but the sergeant was quicker. He gripped and held one door until the machinery admitted defeat and opened wide again. Evans was practiced at this. He rode the West Side IRT every day.

"Fuchsia told us zilch," he said, selecting a floor button. "I found Cross through dumb luck, the detective's best friend. There I was, lolling around the waiting room, having a good time at the taxpayer's expense, when I'm asked to look at a probable mugging victim. Lo and behold, a belated Christmas present!"

Foster shook his head in mock amazement. "If the public only knew how crimes are *really* solved."

The elevator jerked to a stop. Foster and Evans stepped out

into a corridor indistinguishable from the one they'd left except for an increased number of doors, and the nurse's station before them. Evans waved to a stout woman in white as they passed the post unchallenged.

"Has Cross made a statement?" asked Foster.

"Nothing printable. Or even intelligible. He's only begun trying to speak within the last ten or fifteen minutes. He collapsed last night at the emergency desk, bleeding all over the nice new tiles. He has to be kept sedated, for pain, but Asprin will allow us a few trenchant questions."

Foster couldn't let that pass. "Roosevelt sedates its patients with aspirin? I didn't think the city was *that* broke!"

Evans grinned. "William G. Asprin. Cross is his patient."

"You're kidding."

A right turn, and the homicide detectives almost ran down the tall, shaven-headed doctor coming out of a private room. "At last," the latter said. He nodded at Evans and met the lieutenant's searching gaze.

Evans skipped the introductions. Everyone knew each other's name. "How's our patient?"

Asprin rubbed his pate. "Theoretically he should still be unconscious but, as you know, he's coming out of it sooner than the initial dosage should permit. He must have a tolerance for the drug."

"Our files show he's a user," Foster said, "but not a heavy one."

"I thought that might be it. There were no track marks or other overt signs, so we haven't tested for that. Yet. We've been too busy keeping him alive."

The lieutenant found a clean page in his notebook. "Who brought him in? Cabbie? Good Samaritan?"

"No one," the doctor replied. "He walked in under his own steam, just. Considering the extent of his injury, though, I'm amazed he could hobble half a block, let alone the mile from the boat basin Sergeant Evans mentioned."

Foster let that pass. An unlikely feat of willpower, but not impossible. His squad had already checked for cabs picking up any passengers, bloodied or not, near the section of Riverside

Park around the time of the murder, without result. Something else bothered the detective.

"We had an APB issued on Cross, Doctor. Your people must have gotten a copy. Why didn't you identify him when you called the precinct?"

"Because we couldn't identify him, Lieutenant. He had no wallet or ID, although we found three hundred-dollar bills in a double pocket in his jeans."

"I figure," Evans interrupted, "that someone rolled the poor fish while he was dragging his ass down West End or Amsterdam."

Asprin nodded in agreement. "This neighborhood gets worse every year. Only magazine editors and real estate promoters insist it's undergoing a renaissance. That's why I moved to Katonah. To anticipate your next question, Lieutenant, I couldn't match the description, either. There isn't much to match, as you'll see."

Doctor Asprin leaned back against the door, pushing it open. The detectives entered, Evans taking the lead.

The doctor had a point, Foster conceded. A trained observer might identify the man lying stiffly on the bed by the shape of his ear, the cheekbone angle, the eyebrow slant, a dozen minor details. Sergeant Evans was such an observer. Even so, if he hadn't had the mug shot on his mind he could easily have failed to recognize Gary Cross.

The overwhelming impression was of whiteness. From the neck down. Cross was motionless beneath pristine sheets. Less than a quarter of the dealer's face, on the left side, remained unbandaged. The flesh was so pale Foster had to look closely to tell where the thick, swathing gauze began. The colorless scheme was shattered by the spectral blue of Cross's good eye, lined with red when it snapped open as the three men circled the bed. Several thin brown threads also seeped through the bandages at his right temple.

"Dressing needs changing again," Asprin observed. "I'll tell the head nurse on the way out."

Foster placed a visitor's chair flush against the left side of the bed. This placed him squarely within Cross's line of sight.

A bottle half-filled with faintly yellow fluid hung at the head of the bed, dangling plastic tubes that vanished beneath the gauze where his nostrils would be. Foster felt a sympathetic pang in his sinuses. He ignored it.

"Gary Cross. Can you hear me?"

The eye's pupil rolled toward the detective. The lid blinked once.

"Good. I'm Detective-Lieutenant Amos Foster of the NYPD. On the other side is Detective-Sergeant Joseph Evans. We have some questions. We need answers." Foster spoke slowly, softly, clearly. "Feel like talking?"

Cross's lips twitched. "Naw tew pirrs."

"Residue of the local anesthetic," Asprin explained. "Just a slight numbness. We didn't have to wire a broken jaw or anything like that. Most of the damage was confined to the upper skull."

Foster nodded, keeping his eyes on Cross. He reached between his knees and turned the chair sideways, so that his legs pressed against the cool metal bedframe. He leaned forward, bending his right ear to the injured man's lips. A faint, cloying odor wafted from the bandages.

"I didn't catch that, Cross."

A tongue like a swollen, badly bruised maggot plopped out, moistening cracked lips. Cross repeated himself. His voice was weak, his enunciation exaggerated. This time he made himself clear.

"Not. To. Pigs."

Foster straightened and exchanged a weary look with his partner.

"It's nice to be appreciated," said Evans.

Foster grimaced.

"Listen carefully, Mr. Cross. My name is Amos Foster. I am a Detective First Grade, with Homicide. Not, I repeat, *not* Narcotics. At the moment, I don't give a shit if you've got a warehouse in Newark full of junk, unless it has something to do with your being here. I want only one thing. I want the man who did this to you. You'd like that, too, wouldn't you?"

The blue eye flickered. The left cheek developed a tic. Stiff, dry lips trembled. Cross was remembering.

"No. Man. Did. This."

Evans raised an eyebrow. "He's accusing Ulysses?"

"Cut the clowning, Joe."

"All right. If it wasn't a man, maybe the Cooper girl cracked his skull. Self-defense."

Foster shook his head. Neither Cross nor the girl could have inflicted so much damage on each other. The detective noticed the tubes swaying slightly. Cross was shaking his head, too.

"Describe your assailant, Cross. Was there more than one?"

Cross's mouth quivered.

"I want the bastard, Cross. I want him bad."

The tic faded. "Like to. See that."

The man's voice was stronger now. Foster did not have to strain for each word. He arranged himself more comfortably on the chair. Perspiration beaded in the nape of his neck, dripping cold under his collar. His muscles sagged from missed sleep. That lone, near-vacant eye pulled at him.

Something extraordinary was eating Cross. Foster understood the dealer's initial defiant attitude, as well as the suddenness with which it was dropped. You had to establish the rules before you played the game. Gary Cross *wanted* to help get his would-be killer off the streets. Foster knew when someone wanted to cooperate. Yet Cross still held back.

"Maybe you'd like the bully-boy who danced on your head to drop by and finish the job," Foster pressed. "Maybe I wouldn't lose any sleep if he did. If it was only you. Technically, you don't even belong to us in Homicide. You're alive. The girl wasn't so lucky."

The pupil of the eye became a pinpoint. "Dead?"

"Dead. If you hinder our investigation, you're aiding the killer. You'll be an accessory."

"Shit," said Cross. His eye shifted, evading Foster's hard stare but making his head ache. He closed the eye and took as deep a breath as he could manage. His chest shuddered beneath stiff sheets.

"Give me something, Cross," the detective urged. "Anything. A name. A description. Even a guess."

Bandages rasped on the starched pillowcase as Cross turned his head to face the detective squarely. "I saw. No. Won't believe."

"Try me. Wednesdays and Fridays I'm gullible."

Cross lay still for a long moment with his eyes closed. Foster feared he'd fallen asleep, that the pain-killers had caught up with him again. His hand reached forward to shake Cross awake again, despite Doctor Asprin's warning glare. The fingertips brushed Cross's shoulder.

The injured man's lips moved sluggishly.

"Big. Red."

"Not Big Red Torgeson," Evans blurted. "He's still in Dannemora."

Cross shook his head violently. When he reopened the eye, red overwhelmed the blue; more blood vessels had shattered. Doctor Asprin leaned past Evans to grip Cross's head in both hands, holding it still. Both the tubing and the stitches were temporary, but if Cross pulled them loose in his precarious condition the additional blood loss would kill him.

"Big!" Cross shouted. "Huge. Bright red skin."

"Indians," whispered Evans.

Foster ignored the jibe. Naturally, the killer would be splattered with blood. Neatness was not among his virtues, to judge by the job he'd done on Lynda Cooper.

"I need specifics. Cross. You know the routine. Hair and eye color. Height and weight. Distinguishing marks."

Saliva trickled from the corner of Cross's mouth, staining the gauze over his chin. He coughed half a dozen times. Foster could have sworn that Cross was trying to laugh.

"Distinguishing. Oh yeah. Fangs. Little horns. Pointy ears. Claws. Can't miss 'im."

Foster sat back in his chair. The metal backrest was not kind to his shoulder blades. "Is he hallucinating, Doctor?"

Asprin peered into the patient's eye. Cautiously, he loosed his grip on the man's head. Cross lay still. The doctor stood erect.

"It's possible, Lieutenant. He's going under again. A more natural sleep this time, I hope. If there's a particularly vital question you need answered, I suggest you ask it now."

One question? Foster had scores. Or would have, if he could drag enough information out of Cross to build on. The lieutenant's fingers drummed on his thigh as he sorted his priorities.

"He's slipping," Asprin warned. "Better hurry."

Foster bent forward abruptly. His flat nose scraped the top layer of bandages. His voice was taut.

"The girl, Cross. Lynda Cooper. What was she to you?"

"Girl? Nothing."

"She's dead, Cross. You can't hurt her."

"Too bad. Like to. Not that way. Tease. Changed her mind. Too late then."

"She wasn't a customer? Didn't work for you?"

The lips became fixed, with that unhealthy tongue protruding. The eye gained a hard, sardonic light. Then the lid shut, and stayed shut. Asprin pushed the tongue tip in, wiped his fingers on his white shirt. A frown deepened on his face as he examined the dressing.

Foster rose slowly, stretching, stifling a yawn. "When can I talk to him again, Doctor?"

Asprin shook his head, moving back from the bed. "Let's step out into the hall, Lieutenant."

A passing pair of candy-stripers stared indiscreetly at the gold badges as the detectives left Cross's room. Once out of earshot, they whispered eagerly to each other. Evans smiled after them. Doctor Asprin seemed not to notice.

The doctor spoke uneasily. "Lieutenant, x-rays indicate that some bone slivers have penetrated the brain. I can't tell the extend of the damage at present. Obviously Cross can talk and hear and think with a degree of clarity. We haven't tested all of his motor responses. In fact, we dare not. Those slivers could shift any time. Just being where they are, they exert pressure that can build up fatally. He received some emergency surgery on arrival, but he needs a major operation." Asprin cleared his throat. "An expensive operation."

Foster rubbed first the bridge of his nose, then his right temple. A ten minute nap would do wonders, but he didn't want to borrow a bed here. The one in his own apartment was far more inviting; it was already beaten into his shape.

"I get your drift, Doctor. Don't worry. Gary Cross is a key witness in a murder case. I think I can get the city to pick up the tab."

Asprin's face grew ruddy. "It's not for my benefit, although I'll be the one to perform the operation, tomorrow or the next day. It's that the hospital facilities are so expensive ..."

"What isn't?" growled Foster.

Asprin acknowledged the point with a nod and a shrug. "Another thing. In all honesty, I can't promise a successful operation. Going in after the bone will do further damage. Cross could become comatose, a vegetable. Or he could die."

"What can you promise, Doctor?"

"Only that, without an operation, Gary Cross *will* die."

"Aw. I thought aspirin cured everything."

The doctor's face went blank. Foster sucked in his lower lip. "My apologies, Doctor. It was a poor time to make a joke, especially one you probably hear every day."

"Joke?"

Foster's eyes narrowed by a hair. "About your name."

"Oh. I see. Asprin cures everything." The doctor glanced past the lieutenant, fixing Evans in his gaze. "I see. No, I don't recall any. Clever. Ah, Sergeant Evans said I could leave after you'd spoken to Cross. My wife's waiting for me."

"Sure, Doctor," Evans said quickly. "We've got your home number if we need you."

A startled Amos Foster watched the bald man hasten down the hall, shoulders quivering. Then he turned to his partner.

"That was a good line, Amos," Evans said, smirking. "Maybe the doctor can use it on his business card."

"Damn you, Joe. You set that up with him."

"Of course I did." The smirk faded. "Although it seemed funnier before that grim interrogation. You waited too long."

"I was preoccupied." Foster turned the corner and headed toward the elevator. "I need some air."

It was Evan's turn to keep pace. "One thing I don't get, Amos. Of all the details we need to learn from Cross, why did you throw away that last question?"

"I was rushed. Couldn't think of anything else."

"This morning you told me her background was irrelevant."

Foster shrugged. "To our case it is."

"Ah." Evans turned smug. "Of course, you saw the mother this morning. Well, even Fearless Foster is entitled to go soft once in a while."

"That's got nothing to do with it."

"Bullshit. I know you, Amos. I'll bet you gave Ma Cooper a hard time for pulling you away from the investigation, and now you're feeling guilty."

Foster stopped a few paces short of the elevator. He laid a thick hand on his partner's shoulder. "She might call from Boston to ask how the case is going. She's that kind of lady. At least we'll have something to tell her."

"Sure."

Foster looked at his partner through narrowed eyelids, and sighed. "Maybe I should team up with someone who doesn't know me so goddamn well. You can partner with that uniform you were with today."

Evans gasped in less-than-mock horror. "Carver? Preserve me from trigger-happy rookies! And you didn't hear that adjective from my lips."

Foster grunted. Usually this sort of banter was an invaluable aid in facing their often grisly job. He couldn't keep it up today. "You'll have to break in a new partner someday, Joe. They'll kick me out years before they get around to you."

"Not if I retire first."

The lieutenant snorted. "That's Liz talking. You aren't that sensible. You'll stick it out."

"I might surprise you."

"Don't. I hate surprises."

Evans jabbed the button for a down elevator. His response was muted.

"I know."

CHAPTER 19

His waking lacked transition. One moment, black and dreamless sleep; the next, senses alert, eyes wide and darting. Sunlight pierced the thinning cloud cover to touch the recess in which he'd taken refuge out of instinct—*not* fear. Its orange glow suffused the stone wall of the pedestrian underpass. Traffic rumbled on the highway above, thunder announcing a storm that never struck.

He hadn't meant to sleep here. He'd only wanted a vantage point from which to observe his new subjects before he declared his regime. Were he mortal, such a lapse might seem a sign of weakness. He knew better. He remembered that in the last weeks before his treacherous imprisonment, his attention span had grown shorter. Naturally; fewer things of the world were worthy of his regard. He suspected, but could not know, that there had been similar gaps in concentration during the centuries of darkness.

No matter. For surveillance of this new world, sunrise was soon enough.

He gouged a handhold in the mortar behind him and peered past the cut stone's edge.

The shrouded sun was low, half visible across the river. There, steep cliffs apparently were topped by a multitude of ostentatious shrines. He'd put an end to that nonsense soon enough.

His gaze lowered to take in the large but motley and ill-designed fishing fleet. At night, emerging from its midst, he'd been more impressed. Now he felt scorn for the clumsy vessels. Scorn—and puzzlement. Why were those boats still moored at dawn? Villagers must eat. For that matter, where were the fisherfolk? Was this a festival day?

Ah! One approached. The clothes were strange, but the bright colors and leisurely pace identified the man as one of the privileged class. This, despite the lack of even one sword, let alone two, and a proper entourage. Had swords been banned? Gods knew why! If they had, a large bodyguard could be dispensed with, but some token force should have been maintained, for prestige.

Scuffling echoed in the tunnel. He turned to the source. Two people in dark blue, single piece outfits ran side by side. No; more of a jerky walk. He drew back unseen as they passed, barely containing his contempt. What poor messengers this village had! If those were the swiftest runners available, he would have little trouble deposing the lax lord of this province!

And what was this? The runner passing nearest him was female! Pacing beside the male instead of respectfully behind!

This province was indeed decadent!

He itched then and there to show himself, and barely restrained the urge. Something more formal was preferable. He wished to announce himself the new lord to the greatest number of inhabitants, the entire population if possible, at one time. That would be far more effective.

Again, though, where were they? If the inhabitants of a fishing village did not congregate at the docks at dawn, when and where *did* they assemble?

He looked to the boats again. His lips writhed.

The sun was gone!

He remembered now. He *had* seen the pale gray light that slowly washed the black from the sky ... a light that had come from his back! The setting, not the rising, sun had broken his slumber. He'd slept the entire day!

He recalled, too, the score of people who'd rushed on the dock minutes after he'd left it. They'd arrived in strange, low pannikans whose carriers were swift, strong, and invisible. They'd also brought flashing lights and whirring noise-makers to chase away evil spirits. He'd smiled at that. Some things did not change.

He scowled. He should have recalled all this immediately on waking. The thousand years and more spent at a single-minded task had obviously dulled his memory.

How much else had he forgotten of last night's events?

He reconsidered his timetable for conquest. The people of this village bore watching a while longer. They seemed to possess a degree of sorcerous knowledge, and his ignorance of their ways might make him look a fool. That impression would vanish once he'd demonstrated his power, but it was better not to appear foolish at all.

He settled back in his niche to brood.

CHAPTER 20

The plate glass window fronting Eighty-Eight's was thickly painted over with amber curlicues, blocking the glow of streetlamps and traffic on Broadway. In the shadows just inside the window stood the low upright for which the bar was named. It was unattended, the pianist not due for two hours. In dubious compensation, the room vibrated from the thrumming of a jukebox at one end of the bar and the bubbling electronic sound effects of the Donkey Kong game next to it.

Francine Cooper came to a full stop at the threshold, letting her eyes adjust to the dimness, and her ears, as best they could, to the decibel level. This was not the sort of place where she'd have guessed Lynda would hang out, but the matchbook bearing the bar's logo—packed away with a box of scented candles—was the only substantial clue among her belongings to the young woman's New York social life. Lynda's letters home each month had rarely touched on her leisure activities. Her mother never noticed that. Perhaps Lynda had known she wouldn't.

Cooper's gaze wandered over chessboard-sized tables that cluttered two-thirds of the room in rows barely a hand's-breadth apart. A bearded man near the piano picked at a salad while he worked on a crossword puzzle—apparently by sonar. Two thin, dark women at a table near the kitchen door spooned sour cream into their chili with lackluster motions. One had an order pad dangling from her jeans' back pocket. A third waitress, paler and on duty, moved from table to table lighting finger-thick candles whose glow barely extended past the colored glass holders. A pair of secretarial types sat at the end of the bar nearest the juke box, alternately sipping martinis while they ignored the skinny young man feeding an endless supply of quarters into the video game. Not a promising clientele.

Cooper zeroed in on a stool at the more peaceful end of the bar, where a busboy had left a tray of freshly-washed glasses. The bartender, a burly man with crew-cut hair and only half of his right ear, waited for her to sit. Then he put away the glass he'd been pretending to wipe while he'd eavesdropped on the secretaries with his eyes, and moved fluidly to her.

"What's your pleasure?"

Cooper didn't catch the words, but the intent was plain.

"Scotch! On the rocks!"

At the shout, a waitress glanced up from her chili, but returned quickly and wordlessly to her dinner. She would not get to eat again until after midnight.

The bartender smiled sympathetically at Cooper's discomfort. He leaned toward her conspiratorially.

"No need to yell. I read lips. I have to. When I work here, I turn this thing off." He tilted his head. His good ear was plugged with the plastic bulb of a hearing aid.

Cooper smiled back.

Watching the gold liquid spill over cracked ice, Cooper became aware of a knot in her stomach. Discounting two of Mrs. Barclay's crumbling tea biscuits, she'd had no solid food for almost twenty-four hours. Whiskey on an empty stomach was a bad idea, particularly in these surroundings and more particularly after the day she'd had. Cooper inclined her head at the tables arrayed behind her.

"I see you serve food."

The man shrugged. "Have to. Not an elaborate menu, by any means. Hamburgers, fried chicken, chili, salads, quiche, things like that. There's a blackboard against that wall with daily specials, but you have to practically stand on top of it to read it." He pointed to the Scotch glass. "I can have this brought to your table."

Cooper shook her head. "Those tables inspire claustrophobia in me. Can I eat at the bar?"

He scratched his forehead, just below the hairline. His eyes darted left and right. He shrugged. "Why not? It's slow now.

Won't pick up until Rusty comes in. Shouldn't bother anyone."

"Rusty?"

"The ivory-tickler." He waggled his fingers on top of the bar. "Show tunes, mostly."

"Oh. Well. I'd like a hamburger. Make it two."

The bartender signaled to the candle-lighter and conveyed Cooper's order. He also conveyed something else. On the way to the kitchen, the pale young woman detoured by the jukebox and cut its volume in half. The secretaries, being perceptive predators, turned as one to sneer at Cooper. Then they picked up their martinis and moved to a table in front of the jukebox speaker.

"Better?" the bartender asked Cooper.

"Much. Thank you. I thought my ears would start bleeding."

The bartender rubbed at a dry spot with his rag. "You have a nice voice."

Cooper toyed with the ice in her drink, clinking it against the glass with her swizzle stick. "How can you tell?"

His grin was sheepish. "Oh, I turn it up when there's something worth listening to."

"I see." She sipped Scotch, collecting her thoughts. The alcohol made her cheeks flush.

"I've embarrassed you," the bartender observed. "I'm sorry. I'll leave you alone, if you want. It's just, well, you're not Eighty-Eight's usual customer. *Some* nice lookers come in, but they're half my age, with brains the size of gherkins. Not only are you attractive, but your face has character. You're smart too, or I've wasted twenty years behind bar counters learning to size people up."

Cooper swallowed a deep gulp of air tinged with greasiness that seeped from the kitchen. Getting picked up in an Upper West Side singles bar was the furthest thing from her mind this night, but it was flattering, and she didn't want to cut short a conversation with the one person on Eighty-Eight's staff most likely to have noticed Lynda. The situation called for careful handling. She hoped her wits were up to it.

"That's all right, ah …

"The name's Jack."

"Cooper. Francine Cooper. It's sweet of you to say those things, Jack, but …

"I know it sounds like a line, Frannie, but I mean it."

Her voice took on a hard edge before she realized it. "Fran, if you must shorten it. Not, for God's sake, Frannie."

Jack the bartender straightened, taking his elbows off the bar. "Sure, Fran. Okay. I'm not trying to rush you."

Another sip of Scotch warmed her throat. Easy, lady, she told herself. How could he know?

"A matter of personal preference, Jack. No reflection on you." She clinked the ice. "May I ask you something?"

Jack checked the room. No new customers. No old ones going dry. "Whatever you like, Fran."

"Do you work here every night?"

Jack relaxed. Her interest was a favorable sign. "Mostly. Especially now, during the holidays. The married guys want to be home with their families. Since I live alone …"

He left it hanging, trying to take his next cue from her eyes.

Cooper placed her purse on top of the bar and took out her wallet. Jack felt a smile of qualified triumph flit across his face. He figured he was going to get her phone number, at the least.

Instead, Cooper opened the wallet at the photograph wings and turned to a snapshot of a pert, dark-haired young woman wearing a scarlet cap and gown.

"Did you ever see this woman in here?"

"Shit." Jack threw his bar rag on the slatted wooden floor, in disgust. "You're good, lady. I'd have never pegged you for a cop."

"I'm not with the police."

"Great. If you're private, I don't have to talk to you." He picked up the rag and started to walk away.

Cooper shook her head, amazed at how poorly she'd handled that. She should have started by telling Jack the whole story. Sudden revelations were dramatic, but childish.

"Still wrong, Jack. The answer is important only to me, for personal reasons. I'm not working for anyone, and I'm not going to pass my information to anyone else without a damned good reason."

Jack's fingers hovered at the volume control of his hearing aid. He turned back and leaned over the bar until his forehead nearly touched Cooper's.

"Let me tell you something, lady. I hear lots of stories in this job. Most are bullshit. That doesn't matter. I treat them as confidences, and I don't pry. Did I ask what someone of your age and class was doing in this kiddie park? You want to tell me, that's your business. If not … people have a right to privacy."

"One more picture," Cooper urged, flipping over the graduation pose. "Two people. My daughter and myself."

Jack looked in spite of himself. He pulled the wallet across the polished bartop with a faint squeak. The family resemblance was more striking with two flat images to compare. He closed the wallet and handed it back to Cooper. He still wasn't entirely pleased.

"What exactly do you want?"

"I don't know. That's why I'm asking questions."

"Such as?"

"Would you consider her a regular here?"

Jack shrugged. "If I don't talk to you, someone else will. No secret there. I see her here maybe once every other week. Quiet girl, always alone, usually carrying a book or an envelope stuffed with papers. Vodka martini. Rarely more than one. She's one of the few customers who actually seems to listen when Rusty plays."

"Always alone? No friends or acquaintances I could talk to?" Jack's eyes narrowed. His thick shoulders rose. "If your little girl ran away from home, Francine, she's old enough to take care of herself. My advice to you is stop looking. She'll find you when she's ready. Otherwise, ask the police. Eighty-Eight's isn't a missing person's bureau."

Cooper grimaced. "In a more flippant mood, I'd argue that last point. No, Jack, the police know where Lynda is. They told me. I saw her this morning."

"Any place I know?"

"The City Morgue."

Jack's mouth filled with cotton. He stared down at the

polished wood, ran a hand over his crew cut. He fumbled for the right words.

The pale waitress saved him, sliding Cooper's hamburgers between them. "I hope medium is okay. You didn't say how you wanted it, so I figured medium, but, Jeez, you'd be surprised how some customers bitch when ..."

"Medium's fine," Cooper assured her. "Thank you."

Jack saw a way to make amends. He crooked a finger at the waitress. "Stop for a moment, Angie, and take a look at this photograph, will you?"

Cooper opened the wallet to the graduation picture again.

"Jeez, I got silverware to put out." Angie sighed and tilted her head forward. Strands of light brown hair trailed over the bar. "Yeah?"

"You recognize her?" Jack prompted.

"Who wants to know?"

"Her mother."

Angie looked up at Cooper. She curled a lip thick-caked with carmine lipstick. "Jeez, I got an old lady just like you. Always spying."

Jack snatched at Angie's wrist and shook his head. "The girl's dead, Angie."

"Oh." She pulled her wrist free and pushed her hair back behind her ears. "Jeez, Jack, why didn't you say so? Jeez, I'm sorry, lady."

"So am I." Cooper left the wallet on the bar and picked up a hamburger. Hot juice trickled from the bun and down along her thumb. Suddenly Cooper no longer felt hungry, although she didn't want to put the burger back down, either.

"Fran, here," Jack continued, "I mean Mrs. Cooper, wanted to talk to her daughter's friends. Personal stuff, you know. I'm stuck back here most of the night, but you're on the floor, Angie. Did she hang out with anyone in particular?"

"Her name is Lynda," Cooper added. "Was."

"Yeah, she looked like a Lynda. Scorpio, right?"

Cooper inclined her head noncommittally. Lynda had been born in March.

"Jeez, I can't tell you much. She was pretty strange. Not to be insulting, or anything. A loner, I mean. Sometimes she'd seem to respond to a come-on line, but usually she deliberately scared guys away. Not that I blame her, Jeez, the creeps we get. Couple months back there was this guy, she had to drop an ice cube down his open-front shirt. That's why last night was so weird."

Cooper forced herself to take a bite of hamburger. She swallowed the meat without tasting it. Jack, unbidden, refilled the Scotch glass.

"Weird in what way?" Cooper asked.

"That she left with Gary Cross. Jeez, what a scuzzo … !"

Angie's hand flew to her mouth. "My God, did Cross kill her?"

Cooper shook her head. "The police don't consider it likely. You really didn't know? There was a headline in the afternoon paper."

"That rag? Never touch it. Jeez, not that anyone would care if that creep did buy some heavy trouble. I mean Cross. Jeez, I hope you don't think …"

I know who you meant, Angie. I also know that Cross was a drug pusher. You don't have to soft-pedal any details."

"Mrs. Cooper isn't interested in scum like Gary Cross," Jack growled.

"Actually, I am, Jack. The police think Lynda was simply in the way at a bad time. They don't care whether she was involved in drugs or not, or how deeply. I do. There are many things a mother might not know about her child—certainly there are things I don't know about Lynda—but I can't persuade myself she used anything stronger than alcohol, and that only in moderation."

A strand of hair had crawled back in front of Angie's face. She tugged it into place. "Jeez, no. She looked super-straight to me."

Cooper smiled. "I appreciate that, whether you mean it or not. Tell me about Cross. Did he have a regular job, or did his entire income come from drugs?"

The waitress made a dent in her chin with an uneven fingernail. "Every couple of months he'd brag about some steady job. It always turned out less impressive after he was sacked. Jeez, let me think. He was doorman at that new apartment building on Seventieth around March ... busboy at McDonald's for about two hours ... spent half the summer as janitor at the museum ...

Cooper realized with a sudden, mild shock that her hands were empty. Apparently *some* part of her was ravenously hungry. She reached for the second hamburger.

"Which museum? New York has hundreds."

"The big one across from the park. With the dinosaurs and stuff."

"Natural History," Jack translated.

Cooper chewed on that along with her ground beef. One piece of information Amos Foster had grudgingly allowed her was that certain curios found at the murder scene had been turned over to certain officials at a certain museum for identification. He hadn't said which museum, and she hadn't cared ... then. After all, it was only after her trance in Lynda's former room that Cooper was inspired to check out those details the police weren't interested in. So. Suppose Cross picked up a patina of arcane knowledge from his brief museum tenure. That might have been enough to intrigue her daughter. Cooper could more readily believe Lynda's suffering a lapse of discretion than a sudden craving for drugs.

Yet belief was not proof. The doubt that Foster's assured attitude had planted in her mind remained. Before she could fit Cross into the picture she was building, she had to learn more about him. No point seeking the man in person; Foster was doing that. Nor did she need to. As a professional researcher, Cooper often assembled profiles from several sources—such as Cross's former employers.

While Cooper reasoned this out, Angie slipped off to wait on a newly-arrived couple. When the Bostonian looked down, her plate held only crumbs and red juice. She wiped her greasy fingers with a paper napkin.

"I must have been hungrier than I thought."

"Looks that way," Jack replied.

Cooper hadn't realized she'd spoken aloud. She flashed a smile to cover her embarrassment. "Excuse it, Jack. I wasn't thinking. Rather, I was thinking of something else."

"Natural enough."

She reached for the wallet, still on the counter. "I need some sleep. Can I get the check?"

Jack signaled Angie across the dim dining area, then turned back to Cooper. "It'll be here in a minute."

"You've been a big help, Jack."

"Sure. Any time. I suppose Mr. Cooper is checking out Lynda's other haunts?"

Cooper was tempted to let Jack's assumption stand, but that seemed unfair. It wasn't just a matter of forgoing a pointless argument over astrological superstitions. "Mr. Cooper died seventeen years ago, Jack, in a war no one wants to be reminded of."

"Put my foot in it again. Sorry."

The hell you are, Cooper thought, seeing the glint return to his eyes. But she kept silent. Why deflate the poor guy's balloon?

"If there's anything else I can do for you," Jack went on confidently, "you know where to find me."

"I'll let you know," she promised.

Angie dropped the check beside the empty Scotch glass and vanished before Cooper had a chance to thank her, too. Instead, she over-tipped. She felt much better as she slid from the bar stool, and not merely because of booze and food. She'd collected some bits of information that hadn't been sifted through Lieutenant Foster's overdeveloped sense of discretion, and was already forming a plan of attack. She knew exactly where to start tomorrow.

CHAPTER 21

Gary Cross lay in the same unnatural alignment that, two hours earlier, the orderly assigned to preserve Cross's body from bed-rash had left him in: on his back, legs together, feet pointing straight up, top sheet drawn to his armpits, arms straight along his sides, head centered on the pillow. Cross looked depleted, like a rag doll with the stuffing removed so recently it had not yet lost its shape.

A perspiration drop beaded on Cross's forehead, a finger's width over the templemost end of his exposed eyebrow. When it grew too heavy to cling there any longer, it dipped toward the hollow around his eye, then swung away sharply, leaving a faint moist trail on the side of his face and skimming the top of his ear. It was soaked up by a thatch of black, matted hair. A second drop formed, in the center of the forehead. It touched an edge of stiff gauze bandage and was absorbed.

A shred at a time, the stuffing seemed to be put back.

Cross felt himself float in a gray, featureless world—floating because there was no place to stand. Lighting was diffuse; it had no particular source. He accepted this passively. He did not bother to look around. One patch of gray was like another.

Almost.

Something moved. Cross neither saw nor felt nor heard it. He *perceived* it. The wind that was not a wind. An ethereal force that nonetheless had carried him off the docks of the boat basin and out of the twisting asphalt paths in Riverside Park, along West Seventy-Second Street and down Amsterdam Avenue. Weakened by shock, half paralyzed from trauma, Cross could not resist, although the intangible touch revolted him and it seemed that his own two legs were doing all the work. Once, for a brief moment, their grip loosened ...

(They?)

... and he collapsed against the long, high concrete wall that backed Lincoln Center. Something flashed. A knife. Rough hands tore at his pockets. Then the mugger was gone, and Cross was on his feet again, walking jerkily on to Ninth Avenue and Fifty-Eighth Street and up the ramp to the brick-faced emergency entrance to Roosevelt Hospital.

Cross whimpered as the black tide of sedation receded. An image coalesced: that brunette with the nice tits. Lynn something. He'd seen her in Eighty-Eight's before, but never been able to catch her eye. Last night, though, he saw her with a paperback on Incan culture, and he reeled her in with a hint about his collection of ancient pottery. Actually, he had only one piece among a motley of artifacts assembled over a brief period, opportunely. Furthermore, the piece was Mayan, not Incan, and the girl let him know it at once. He didn't see that it made much difference.

The look on her face when she realized she'd been conned on board his houseboat! If Cross didn't know women so well, he'd have thought she really was surprised. That was part of the game, of course, as was the struggle she put up. When she tried to brain him with that chunk of iron, though, and he had to take it away and toss it across the cabin, Cross began having second thoughts.

His hand got under her plaid shirt.

And the thing attacked him.

Cross's skin glinted with a coating of sweat. It drenched the bandages and diluted the clots that criss-crossed the right side of his face. His breathing grew rapid and shallow. More air. More!

Relax, something told him. That was past. He was safe now.

The panting eased, but the mind became wary. That soothing interior voice was not his. He did not think in those terms.

The bloodshot, pale blue eyes snapped open. A nightlight near the head of his bed cast long shadows in the hospital room. Antiseptic odors stung his nostrils-. Circulating air dried his exposed flesh, cooling it. His fingers twitched along his thighs. There was a window to his left, beyond which the lights of New York City glowed and winked.

He must rest. He must heal. He was not of the blood but he had, unknowingly, been for a time a conservator of the relic. If he let them, they would help.

His cracked lips tightened. Fear angered him. These were *not* his thoughts. *They* had put them in his mind.

They were in this room. They. It. The force that brought him here. The force he would have resisted last night, out of horror, had he had will and consciousness then to do so.

They communicated in images, not words, so Cross could understand them. But he did not *understand* them. He'd been uneasy with the police detective who'd questioned him that afternoon, but at least Amos Foster was a comprehensible part of Cross's world. This was not. It terrified him.

"Leave me alone!" he shouted. The bottles to which he was attached by plastic tubes rattled in their racks.

Be calm. You don't know what you ask.

"No! Get out of my head!" His hand bunched into white-knuckled fists. "I don't want you! Go away!"

The soft-heeled tread of the night nurse echoed in the hall. The door to Cross's room swung wide. The woman in white crossed the threshold. As she did, Cross felt the others, the force, whatever they or it might be, withdraw. He smiled stiffly. He'd achieved a pyrrhic victory of will. His single good eye drooped shut, for the last time. Only his anguish remained, joining that of other victims.

Doctor Asprin would not be operating again on him.

The kami could not aid those who denied them.

CHAPTER 22

R ichard Alexander Jones was pissed off.
Ask him why. If he felt like answering—he probably wouldn't—he might mention the dirty look he got for smoking in a crowded subway car. The sister who slapped his face after a friendly little feel. The lousy rain that forced him to dodge from doorway to doorway. The two hundred dollars of prime weed he'd had to dump in the river last night, less than twenty minutes after scoring it off his connection at the Seventy-Third Street baseball field, because half a dozen cop cars suddenly tore along the paths of Riverside Park. And they weren't even after him, not then. Word on the street, though, was that a pair of pigs had nosed around his tenement apartment that afternoon. Good thing his momma didn't know shit.

Richard Alexander Jones could always find reasons to be pissed off. He never realized that most of his anger was directed at himself, for letting the outside world get to him. In the lower reaches of his mind, where he rarely looked, Jones pictured himself as the ineffectual, much-abused David Roberts, alter ego of Jones's favorite comic book character, the Thrasher. Unlike Jones, Roberts didn't have to take shit off of anyone for long. Pushed too far, Roberts metamorphosed into a blue-skinned giant who existed only to destroy. Somehow, only bad guys bought it in the comics, but the implication was that the Thrasher didn't care who he wasted.

That was why Jones liked the Thrasher. That was why, at the age of twenty-three, Jones still had not outgrown spray painting the initials R A J on subway cars, inside and out, whenever he had a chance. That was why he ignored "No Smoking" signs, and why he shouldered a Sony stereo tape deck twice the size of his head, with its speakers blasting at full volume as he bounced along Broadway or West End Avenue or Riverside Drive. He didn't care, and he damned well wanted to let the world know it!

Tonight, in particular, those cocksuckers with their houseboats moored off Seventy-Ninth Street were going to hear that Jones didn't care. He didn't know what they'd done to bring so many cops into the park late last night, but it had cost him good grass and some credibility with certain steady customers. The boat people didn't worry about what changes Jones had had to go through, but they would tonight. He would take over the wooden bench in front of the wire gate that led to the docks, with his speakers pointed at the Hudson River. A fresh package of batteries nestled in a pocket of his down jacket, just to be sure. Those fuckers would watch their step next time. Believe it.

He patted another pocket, which bulged with a trio of disco tape cassettes. Richard Alexander Jones did not fuss with the AM/FM radio built into his Sony. Too much talk. He never listened to news, and so knew nothing of the murder. Even if he had, it wouldn't occur to him that the killing might explain why Riverside Park was nowhere near as crowded this evening as it usually was. Consumed by his anger, Jones did not notice the emptiness. He stalked the asphalt paths on long legs, glaring sullenly at the sharp shadows cast by the vapor streetlamps. He was a man with a mission.

Before him yawned the pedestrian passage beneath the Henry Hudson Parkway. Beyond lay the river, and the boat basin. Peering through the tunnel, Jones could see houseboats bobbing on the choppy, ill-smelling waters. Three electric light sockets were set in the roof of the underpass. None of them held functioning bulbs. That didn't bother Richard Alexander Jones. It didn't even surprise him. He'd broken those bulbs himself two nights earlier. More proof that he didn't care.

He stepped into the murky tunnel.

Stubby fingers dug ant-sized indentations in the stone of the recess. Razor-sharp teeth ground together. Pointed ears and, yes, even the skull-horns throbbed with pain.

The first distant sound could have been of a battle, perhaps between warriors and beasts. Then it came nearer, growing more senseless even as it gained definition. At last, the unholy cacophony echoed through the underpass. This was the music of the Egg of Chaos itself! The hell of the Buddhists could not have included such torment. As a creature dedicated to despoiling, he ought to have found it a welcome, comforting sound … but even pure evil demands some semblance of order.

No mortal would create that clamorous horror. Of that, he was certain. Perhaps he'd set a precedent, those many years before, and one of his demon-kin already ruled this village. That might explain the decadence of its inhabitants.

The rival must be challenged.

He pushed off from the rough mortar at his back, flying from his hiding-place—a crack between stones set below eye-level of most villagers. As he tumbled through the air, his body rapidly filled out, drawing mass from energy. Mud at the side of the path hardened, its water content freezing. The stone wall shone white with frost. His unshod feet cracked the hard, slick blacktop in the center of the tunnel, landing with all three toes of each extended for traction. Already he had as much height as when he was mortal.

Yet the one who'd entered this cave, bringing discord, was a head taller. These villagers had that edge over the peasants and warriors he'd known. No matter. He was not finished growing …

It took Richard Alexander Jones two long strides to react and halt. Lights along the Hudson melted before his eyes, as if a thick fog had suddenly poured down the river. His skin tingled with cold. His rubber soles braked hard on the asphalt, and he stood enveloped by the tunnel's blackness. The only illumination came from the faint red dot that showed his 'box' was turned on, and that was worse than useless.

Another fucking blackout!

Then Jones grinned. The Broadway stores would be ripe for picking. He spun on one heel, eager not to miss out on the looting.

The lights along the path he'd walked down still shone.

Jones's ears pricked up. Heavy panting, each exhalation a growl, came deep and harsh and loud enough to cut through the disco beat. Hot, fetid air stroked the back of his neck. Jones's own breathing quickened. Sliding one foot after the other, he was out of the short tunnel before he realized it, before his head had fully turned back to the river … and whatever lay between.

What kind of animal could be loose in Riverside Park?

Sweat beaded on Jones's forehead at the guttural howl that came next, a howl with an unmistakable tone of command.

A thousand years of absolute darkness developed one's night vision enormously. The tunnel gloom was as daylight. A poor sort of oni this was! Skin burnt nearly black, that was all right, but the frame so thin, even with a padded tunic! This demon-lord would not make a respectable scarecrow!

He issued formal challenge. The common villagers had abandoned the Imperial tongue for a peculiarly unrhythmic speech pattern, but surely their ruler had not sunk so low!

Alas! After a moment's hesitation, the dark-skinned demon *did* reply in that same gibberish.

He felt cheated. This was no contest. The other had not even understood the challenge.

Now that the other stood outside the tunnel, however, the cacophony no longer seemed to come from everywhere. Its source was a black-and-silver box that the dark one carried on one shoulder—a box which, though roomier, might serve the same purpose as the iron artifact from which he'd escaped but twenty-four hours earlier.

He snorted, annoyed at himself. A child could have seen the truth of it!

As the Ainu barbarians were paler than civilized folk, so too might there be darker races. Darker, but no less mortal. This one had captured his demon-kin, no doubt tricking the unfortunate as he himself had been unfairly deceived. Worse, the mortal displayed his catch in a thoroughly humiliating manner. Small wonder the prisoner roared!

Disrespect for one's betters called for severe punishment.

The thing entered a bright circle cast by the vapor lamp. Jones's jaw sagged. He recognized it! This creature had brick-red skin instead of blue, three fingers to a hand instead of four, and the face was rounder, with flatter features, than the familiar vulture-like profile. Yet the overall shape and overwhelming size were close enough for these minor discrepancies to be discounted.

Richard Alexander Jones's grip on reality was flexible.

"Holy shit! The Thrasher!"

The creature towered over Jones. Fingers as thick as Jones's arm wrenched the tape deck from him.

The thing stared at the box, mumbling at it, and then set it on the brown, patchy grass beside the path, speakers face down. Muffled, the noise level lowered, almost as if in approval.

Baleful ebon eyes locked on Jones's terrified frame.

"Hey, Thrasher, I'm on your side! You want to smash someone? Hell, I know hundreds of people who deserve to be put down. Thousands. You and me, we'll clean up this fucking city!"

An enormous hand wrapped around the lower half of Jones's face, stifling his prattle as the nostrils pinched together. He gasped for air. The red flesh felt unnaturally hot; the three fingers seemed to burn his cheeks to the bone. Jones was spun around and forced to his knees, with no more effort than if he were a doll. The other massive hand pulled off the down jacket, ripping seams apart.

Jones worked his lips against the confining hand. If only he could speak! He was clean tonight, but he always knew where to get good junk. That had to be what the Thrasher was looking for.

The jeans split, pooling around Jones's knees. His penis shriveled in the dank air, and he realized his undershorts had been torn off in the same motion.

The Thrasher couldn't be … could he?

Jones struggled, trying to crawl to the leafless bushes. If he could work loose and plunge into the undergrowth, maybe the Thrasher wouldn't follow.

For a second, Jones thought he had a chance. The hand on his face seemed to slip. He sucked in a lungful of moist air. Then the grip retightened. Jones could not even exhale. He was forced down further. His forehead cracked against blacktop.

Paralysis engulfed him. He moaned as the creature's searing flesh touched his buttocks. Jones's sphincter muscles tensed. No use. His muffled scream came a moment later. Jones thought he was being ripped in half.

As lack of air ended his life, Jones felt a final wave of impotent anger. The fucking comics never said Thrasher was gay.

He let the corpse fall. It sprawled half on the path, half on hard brown soil. His lips twisted like mating worms.

Much more satisfying than last night! He'd always preferred male to female partners, though not to the exclusion of the latter. This time he'd remembered to shrink to human proportions before consummation and thereby prolonged the pleasure. This one still perished during the act, but since he'd controlled the event he was better able to enjoy the sensation of the death shudder.

He retied his loincloth and stifled a yawn. He felt drained, almost drowsy. Just like the night before. He was long unused to so much activity. A short nap would settle that, but not yet. His task was not complete. There remained the fellow demon captured by the dead one.

He picked up the box. The chaotic noise grew loud again. This prison seemed flimsy compared to his own. A weak colleague, to be held thus. Still, the box's material was unfamiliar. Perhaps it had magical properties akin to that of his iron shell. Or the interior was thinly lined with iron. He was a poor judge of mass; nearly everything felt light to him.

He scowled. Tampering with magic was dangerous. Furthermore, he recalled his own overwhelming rage when he'd escaped. Could he expect gratitude from another like himself? Even tolerance?

No. He tired with disconcerting ease, for which the expenditure of his energies in sex might or might not be responsible. Contend with another for this village? It was *his* village now, his province, too. Why risk all in a gesture of kinship?

He could, and would, do this much: spare his fellow further public shame.

Ignoring the screeches, he carried the box through the underpass and to the edge of the black, swift-flowing river, north of the boat basin. The box sank quickly, with barely a splash. He could tell that the demon appreciated this small favor, for the protests ended abruptly.

In the sudden silence, he heard footsteps. He turned. An elderly man was scurrying southward, away from him. He cursed. The old fool had seen the hiding place. Increasing his mass once more, he snapped off a thick tree limb and followed, taking one step to every three of his quarry's. Those rheumy eyes would spy out no more secrets, that tongue reveal none already seen.

That done, he sought out another underpass, climbed into another rugged niche, and slept.

NIHON (ANCIENT JAPAN)

650 A.D.

CHAPTER 23

Twelfth month. Tenth day.

The door to the audience chamber slides silently aside. Here, the acrid odor permeating the residence is at its strongest. The assault on the senses is almost physical. Steeling himself, Monaga crosses the threshold. Retainers line both sides of the chamber. A wide, clear space remains for the priest to traverse.

Monaga stiffens when he sees the dark form sitting on the dais, in the place reserved for the lord of Imuri. He sinks to one knee—not out of respect, but in horror. His voice, a whisper, carries throughout the silent room.

"It is true, then. Yesterday's rumors are not just the barkings of dogs. You *have* returned to plague Imuri, in the form of an oni, a demon out of Buddhist hell." The priest rises, with an effort. "The shape seems apt punishment for your evil."

Lord Uto throws back his horned head and laughs. His saffron-garbed retainers, disciplined warriors capable of slicing open their own bellies without a murmur, flinch at the grating crackle.

"How like you, priest, to see my transformation a penalty. In fact, I prefer this to my previous body. Much more powerful and intimidating!"

Uto towers over Ashika, his new chief bodyguard, who sits to the left of the lord in lieu of a sword-bearer. Uto has given up the sword. He favors the cruder elemental satisfaction of the wooden club. Ashika is there for show alone. Bodyguards normally hide behind a screen. Demons are not as easy to kill as men. Ashika fidgets; his left knee shifts the width of an eyebrow. For him, that is a major breach of personal discipline. He keeps his gaze fixed forward, unwilling to meet his lord's awful ebon eyes.

Monaga urges his feet forward, shuffling along the hardwood floor. Lord Uto dominates the chamber as never before. The reborn nemesis has skin of scabrous red, rough as sand and deeply scored. His loincloth, his only garment, is fashioned from the kimono worn by Jiko at his funeral. The groin bulges obscenely.

"You may believe that now," Monaga says, halting before the dais. "You'll soon miss your human side."

"Hai! Did you not call me the most inhuman of lords?"

"An Expression."

"Foolish priest!" roars Lord Uto. "You look at the heavens from the bottom of a well. *Your* aid made my reincarnation possible! *You* were the focus of my hatred, keeping the will alive when the flesh failed. I *chose* this! At my request, you arranged the ritual that freed my spirit for rebirth. With a customary burial, my body would have taken years to decompose. Years that even my deep hatred might not endure."

Monaga cries in anguish. He falls to his knees. His hands cover his face. The truth of Uto's words douses him like cold water. Certain Buddhists claim that evil personages *can* be reborn as oni. Monaga knew this and yet he had forgotten, so rare was the event, so profound his own distaste for the superstitions of the foreign religion.

Uto stands. Floor planks shiver beneath his weight. His hairless skull, topped by horns, scrapes the rafters. A tree branch crusted with gore appears in his right hand. The room remains as still as if sprinkled with water.

"You have served your purpose, priest. Time at last that you die."

Seated on the oni's right, previously hidden from Monaga's view by the creature's bulk, is Hoke the pillow boy. Hoke's eyes widen at the unexpected death sentence. Since the day he was taken from his father's house, the boy has been treated as an object by Lord Uto and his staff, and as a living corpse by the few villagers he encounters. Monaga alone treats Hoke as a human being, despite the unpleasant summons he delivered three days past, a summons which it now appears will lead to the priest's execution. Unseen by Uto, the boy leans forward. His tongue darts over dry lips. Words of protest form a knot in his throat, threatening to spill out in an incomprehensible and unstoppable rush.

Yet Hoke has no real influence over Lord Uto, did not have before his transformation, and certainly does not now. He can speak, and Monaga will still die. He simply will not die alone. The protruding stake is always hammered down. The boy speaks only with his eyes. No one notices.

The club poises above the priest's bowed head. Monaga lifts an arm before his angular face, an instinctive but futile attempt to ward off the death blow. Realizing this, he lets the arm fall. His body sags within his drab kimono.

"Yes, slay me. Life is too bitter to bear, knowing I am responsible for a monster."

Uto clumsily checks his swing, knocking over a glowing brazier. Two retainers hasten to smother the flames.

"Eh? You wish to die?"

"I welcome death. I burn with shame for my foolishness."

Uto growls indecisively. He stamps his foot. Paper panels jar loose from wall frames. The club drops, scarring the dais.

"Then I shall not deliver you." Uto leans forward with his unpleasant grin. "You really suffer, priest?"

Monaga nods, avoiding the oni's too-bright eyes. The priest speaks truly enough; if Uto the oni continues, Monaga takes no joy in living. Neither, though, is death desirable. Alive, Monaga can work to thwart Lord Uto's evil, alleviate the villagers' sufferings and, most important, seek a way to defeat the demon and restore the natural balance. Lord Uto will not find it easy to re-establish his old life. Monaga remembers enough of Buddhist legends to guess that certain aspects of demonic vitality will interfere. Already, the dull-wittedness for which oni are notorious is affecting the lord. The mortal Uto would not fall for the simple ploy of a condemned man begging for death. The club is another oni preference. Their propensity for cave-dwelling will soon make this residence unbearable to the demon Uto.

The lord sits heavily. He slaps his knee. Floorboards tremble. "I want a daily audience with you, priest. Let us say, at dawn. I will see the agony in your face as I describe my latest accomplishments and future plans. I will watch you age as I read the pain in your heart. Mark me, priest. From this moment, suicide is forbidden you. Slay yourself, and a hundred villagers die as well. That includes suspicious accidents, eh?" The oni chuckles. "To be certain, I will enact the penalty no matter what your manner of death. Watch your health, priest."

Monaga's fists shake in rage at his sides.

"Monster!"

"Demon," Uto corrects. "You are dismissed." He looks over the gathered retainers. With his bellow, it is hardly necessary to raise his voice. "All are dismissed. Today's audience is done."

Monaga takes a deep breath, lets it out slowly. He backs toward the door, between rows of warriors.

The oni turns to his right. "Come, Hoke. We still have to make up for time lost during my illness."

Monaga stops in mid-stride. His face turns ashen.

"Lord Uto, I beg you! You'll rip that child in half!"

Uto snarls at him.

"You were dismissed, priest! What I do or do not do is none of your concern. If Hoke is companionable, his safety is assured. For now."

As he speaks, the oni seems to rapidly drift back, and for one impossible moment he seems to have moved further off than the rear of the chamber allows. Monaga's mind suddenly deciphers the illusion. He remembers that an oni can change size at will, from no larger than a rice grain to more than double a warrior's height. Lord Uto is a little taller than his mortal form when he takes Hoke's proffered hand to lead the boy to his bedchamber.

Monaga wipes his forehead with a sleeve. The chamber is now uncomfortably warm.

Saffron-garbed retainers close about the priest and escort him to the gate. Their expressions seem too impassive. Veins protrude with the strain of maintaining discipline under these conditions. At the entrance to the residence, Monaga retrieves his priestly staff. He fingers it in thoughtful silence.

CHAPTER 24

It is the hour of the rat.

In a small, screened area at the rear of the sake shop, six men wearing saffron kami-shimo sit with heels bracing haunches, so close that knee brushes trousered knee. The irori's flame gives little light and less heat. Long swords rest in scabbards lying across their laps.

During Lord Uto's mortal reign, these same men were feared and shunned by villagers. Tonight they are made welcome, even though discovery of their purpose means death to all who give them aid.

Two silhouettes flicker against one of the shoji screens, illuminated from behind by a paper lantern. None of the six move; they already face this panel, anticipating. Shadowed faces betray no emotion, though each man feels the tension in the tightening of his vertebrae. No one breathes until the screen moves aside. In its place stands Kujo, the shop's new owner, and Ashika, Lord Uto's bodyguard.

"Shall I heat sake?" asks the burly ex-farmer, now reluctant village headman.

Ashika notices that Kujo keeps his trembling hands hidden in his kimono sleeves. A brave man, for a peasant. The bodyguard presses a Chinese coin into a secreted palm.

"You have done too much already, Kujo. Go to your sleeping mat. For your sake, and your family's, you should know as little as possible of this meeting."

The headman bows, more grateful for the opportunity to leave than for the money, and backs away. Ashika watches narrowly as the screen is replaced. Beyond, the light from Kujo's lantern fades as the shopkeeper makes his way to the living quarters. Still Ashika lets long moments pass in silence.

The bodyguard's throat *is* dry, but sake will not quench that thirst. He will not indulge in ritual tonight. Nor is this amenity the least tradition he plans to violate.

"Is this all?" Ashika asks at last. "We seven?"

Bald Mateo answers. "We had to be circumspect. Some who might have joined us were baffled by over-subtle approaches."

"Otomi wished to come," adds young Ichiro, "but he had watch tonight. To change his duty would have aroused suspicion."

Ashika sits. His back is to the screen by which he entered. "We may be enough. Perhaps it is better there are so few; all the fewer will find self-strangulation necessary."

"Must we suicide afterwards?" Ichiro asks nervously.

Ashika scowls. "When trusted retainers turn against their lord, honor demands no less."

Ichiro bows his head. Long, stringy black hair falls across his face.

"I mean no disrespect, Ashika. Only ..."

"Yes?"

"When Uto ... was like other men, even then, his cruelty and rapaciousness were such that we'd not have been blamed for turning against him. Surely it is unnatural for men to follow a demon!"

"Unnatural, yes, but whatever his shape, Uto is our lord. We have sworn fealty to him. His transformation cannot wipe out the blackness of our conspiring to assassinate him."

"In a sense," Ichiro continues bleakly, "he already *is* dead."

Mateo snorts. "The choosy man ends up grasping garbage, Ichiro. If you join us, you must accept the consequences. You cannot have it both ways!"

Ichiro touches forehead to floor, in apology. "Forgive me, comrade. The enormity of our crime addles my wits."

Ashika's iron tone softens slightly. "All people live in fear, Ichiro. Only those who recognize their terror can master it. If we must eat poison, let us lick the dish." His ice-gray eyes pass over the other five warriors. "More to the point, *can* we assassinate Lord Uto? Can a demon be slain by mortals without the aid of sorcery?"

"I believe so," Mateo replies slowly. "I know something of demon-lore. I received my education at a Buddhist monastery, although I did not forsake the Way of the Gods. An oni is a creature of remarkable vitality and strange powers, but he is not unkillable. The elemental touch of iron is supposed to be efficacious. I trust the blade of every man here is forged, to some degree, of iron?"

"My blade is good steel!" Ichiro states with pride.

"Which contains iron," responds Ashika drily. "For your sake, for all our sakes, I hope it proves enough."

The rest of the night is devoted to careful examination of their plans, to insure that no ant hole remains to collapse the embankment of their intrigue.

CHAPTER 25

Fourteenth day.

Lord Uto is dissatisfied with his tree-limb club. The bark is bruised, discolored, missing in chunks. Twigs jut unevenly and splinter at every use. Such a weapon is good enough for an ordinary demon, but not for the lord of Imuri province. So, after a perfunctory dawn audience with the pathetic Monaga, Lord Uto stumbles into the armory and begins to rummage.

An hour of clattering, cursing, and casting aside finally brings to light a handsomely-wrought double-headed axe with a handle that is longer than most men are tall. Rust scales cling to the blades. Uto tests it on his makeshift club. A single, clean cut is sufficient. The edges remain keen.

Uto's mouth writhes into the familiar, disconcerting grin. Well and good, but chopping firewood is not enough. One does not often battle a forest.

He must test this weapon properly, and at once, for Uto the oni has even less patience than did Uto the man.

A stroll to the village will serve his purposes neatly. The first dozen peasants to cross his path shall have the honor of losing their heads in this experiment. Warriors often enjoy this method of trying new blades. It is understandably unpopular with the lower classes.

Lord Uto steps from the armory, his free hand raised to shield his eyes from the winter sun.

Ashika and his fellows launch their attack from a bamboo grove a few paces outside the entrance gate of the residence. Dressed in white to blend with the previous night's fresh snowfall, they startle the oni. Uto has almost forgotten he ever had a bodyguard.

With speed and skill, Ashika presses his advantage. Despite his bulk, the oni moves swiftly when he must. He twists his brick-red torso as Ashika thrusts at the abdomen. The weapon strikes a mortal blow—but Lord Uto is no longer mortal. The blade turns aside, scraping horny hide without penetrating. Ashika staggers, off balance.

Uto's axe descends.

Ashika rolls forward in the snow until he is too near Uto's feet for an axe-blow. A pair of warriors racing to their leader's aid are less fortunate. A honed edge takes off one's sword arm at the shoulder. The flat of the blade swings back to crush the other's skull. The snow steams with crimson.

Ashika rises up on one knee, preparing to stab again. The demon kicks his side. Ribs snap like rotten twigs. Ashika lands on his back, still managing to retain his sword.

The axe rises.

Uto is distracted by a pricking at his back, like the bite of a mosquito. He kicks snow in Ashika's face, then turns, swinging the axe level with his waist. Two heads roll into a ditch beside the road, one severed neatly, the other accompanied by a neck and part of one shoulder.

Over half their number slain with but two strokes! Were Ashika less disciplined, he would give up now in despair. The conspiracy is doomed. Their deaths accomplish nothing but dishonor. Yet they must follow through to the end. The die is cast. Uto would not pardon them, anyway.

"Hai-eee!" shouts Mateo. He rushes forward, sunlight glinting from his polished skull. He must distract Uto until Ashika regains his footing.

Ashika's side is aflame as he stumbles erect. He watches as Mateo's blade, like his own, is turned aside by the thick red skin. Lord Uto's axe swings, cutting the air. Mateo, though, is prepared for his failure. His stocky legs carry him beyond the oni's reach. Ashika waits for Mateo to charge again. Perhaps if they attack Lord Uto from two sides at once…

Mateo sinks to his knees without a sound. His chest sags

forward, horribly, impossibly. He seems to be folding like a sheet of paper. Lord Uto did strike true, before the bald warrior could elude him. Mateo's spine is sliced through, his torso cut so deep that only skin and muscle keeps it together. Too late, Mateo's dead legs carry him beyond that fatal range.

And what of Ichiro? Has the youngest conspirator fled in the face of disaster?

No! Even as Lord Uto turns once more on his bodyguard, Ashika sees a white hillock rise from the snowy ground. Ichiro is the only conspirator clever enough to keep using his kimono's camouflage. The young man leaps to his feet within a hand's breadth of the foul monster, and with both hands thrusts his blade upward to the creature's heart!

Ashika plunges forward, sword raised, to help deliver the final blow.

Ichiro staggers back, eyes wide with shock. His hands are locked about the cold, slick hilt. The blade is jagged, snapped in half.

Lord Uto grins. His free hand extracts the sword tip from his gut. A thin thread of black ichor seeps from the wound, dries, and flakes off. The cut is healed.

The axe divides Ichiro from head to crotch. As the two halves fall, the oni spins about. He slices through Ashika's thrusting blade before it can touch him.

The awful grin widens. A three-toed foot again smashes into Ashika, pinning the bodyguard to the blood-spattered ground. Uto digs down with his heel. More bones snap. Ashika cries out in pain.

"Fools," Lord Uto says. His breath hangs thick and grayish-white in the cold air. "But it was a good test, eh, Ashika? You've saved me a walk."

Sweat drips from the dying man's face, freezing to icicles. "You ... unholy ... argghh!"

"You're quite right," Uto says, black eyes glittering. "I should check that this exercise has not dulled my edge."

He cuts through Ashika's right wrist.

Then the left.

The right ankle.

The left.

Lord Uto takes his time with the leader of the rebellion, killing him piecemeal, slicing a bit from each limb in turn. So much blood from one man! The traitor still dies too quickly to suit the oni.

The sun reaches its zenith. Six heads bask in its faint warmth, atop tall road posts where all can see. To make sure that all *do* see, Lord Uto orders the entire village to march past the display. Twice.

The seventh skull, that of young Ichiro, is cloven and will not stay in place. It sags. It drips. Finally, it tumbles into a ditch by the road, where it becomes the plaything of a stray dog pack. In lieu, Ichiro's broken corpse is displayed in the village square.

That evening, the scent of death still hangs heavy in Imuri province.

Burly Kujo slips out of his sake shop. The road is empty. The villagers have retired earlier than usual. No guard is posted over the corpse in the square. Surely no one will be foolish enough to interfere with Lord Uto's exhibit.

Foolish? The word doesn't begin to describe how Kujo feels. Nevertheless, a man can take only so much horror, so much abuse, without striking back in some way. He studies the shuttered doors and windows facing the square. No eyes peer from them. Village eyes have seen enough this day.

Kujo moves quickly through the darkness. He shoulders the broken body, staggering under its awkward weight. Avoiding the road, moving through harvested fields, Kujo carries Ichiro's remains to a nearby bamboo groove. There he digs a shallow grave in the rock-hard earth.

From his hidden post on the thatch roof of his own home, the farmer Echi watches this with interest. After, he hurries to Lord Uto's residence. As his reward, he is allowed to live.

Headman Kujo is dragged from his bed. He faces the demonic ruler with sullen resignation. Uto orders him boiled alive. Keeping the flame low, the lord's retainers afford their master over an hour of amusement before the headman expires.

CHAPTER 26

Fifteenth day.

The villagers are in shock. If Uto's own warriors cannot slay him from ambush, who can?

Several elders gather at the sake shop to comfort Kujo's widow and discuss, in low tones, the problem. One patriarch, bolder than the others, finally mentions Emperor Kotoku.

"If the Son of Heaven knew this hell-spawn ruled Imuri, he would not permit it!"

Heads bow in hesitant agreement.

"It is rumored," says another, encouraged, "that the present emperor is sensitive to his subjects' needs. If we send a petition explaining the situation."

Three young men are chosen as runners to carry petitions to the imperial court in Naniwa. The village scribe begins the first copy at once. The rest of the peasants quickly disperse, to avoid the appearance of conspiracy.

Lord Uto sits alone in his audience chamber. A deep scowl etches his face. It is not accurate to say that his dull, inhuman mind is developing a plan by which he can usurp the imperial throne, strip the emperor of his divinity, and become absolute ruler of the islands. At the moment, Lord Uto only begins to perceive the possibility. Is not a living demon as proper an object of awe and worship as a mere descendant of the gods?

This line of reasoning can not escape Emperor Kotoku himself, once that worthy learns of the transformation of the lord of Imuri province. As he must, eventually.

The oni growls and scratches a scabrous kneecap. How will an emperor who is trying to bring the warring clans and provinces of Nihon together under his rule react to such a threat? The same way Lord Uto will. Strike first. Strike hard.

Lord Uto slaps the floor with the palm of a hand. The polished wood is deeply scored already from his steely nails, and the boards badly warped from his ponderous weight. He is not yet ready to challenge the man in Naniwa. He needs time to consolidate his lands, reaffirm his rule, conquer a few neighboring provinces, and accustom himself to his new abilities. He has much to learn about being an oni. He does not understand, for instance, his recent compulsion to rip up the planking in his bedchamber and dig a pit in the dirt below. Why should walls of stone and soil suddenly seem more comfortable than those of wood and paper?

Lord Uto is pondering this need for secrecy when Echi arrives to tell him of the runners.

CHAPTER 27

Sixteenth day.

The first runner is met by Lord Uto himself.
Half of the body is buried on the right bank of a local stream, the other half on the left. Years later, people swear that the murmur of rushing water is actually the groaning of this unfortunate crying to be made whole in death.

Three of Uto's warriors, more loyal or less brave than Ashika and his six comrades, corner the second runner. They permit him to commit suicide. When the weathered rope snaps too soon, the senior warrior lends him another. Lord Uto later condemns the lender to be crushed under a pile of rocks, along with his family, for aiding a traitor. His two companions are beheaded. Lord Uto is merciful in his impatience.

These slayings outrage the warrior class, though no one dares to protest in Uto's presence. Privately, the soldiers agree that Ashika struck too soon. Now he would have found many willing arms. Alas. That brave man's example remains fresh, his head still nailed to a bloodstained road post, attracting the first insects of approaching spring. No leader steps forward to take his place.

CHAPTER 28

Seventeenth day.

The third runner is captured and brought alive to the audience chamber of Lord Uto.

The oni interrogates him personally, starting with the fingers of the right hand. He has grown more skilled with his axe since playing this game with Ashika. A dozen irons are kept heated on a blazing irori, to cauterize each wound as new slices are removed. The ebon eyes sparkle.

The peasant has the soul of a warrior. Feeling his will weaken, he bites off his own tongue to keep from speaking. He soon chokes to death, swallowing his own blood. Lord Uto continues hacking, unaware he is tormenting a corpse. His aides are too terrified to point this out.

Finally, in disgust. Lord Uto tramples the torso beneath his callused feet.

This last runner was seized while running *toward* Imuri. Even an oni's sluggish wits deduce that capture came too late. The man never intended to reach Naniwa himself. The petition he bore must be in the hands of a runner in the next province. It will certainly pass through other hands before it reaches the Imperial Palace.

There is no chance of intercepting it now.

What the emperor actually can or will do on receiving the petition, Lord Uto cannot guess. As Supreme High Priest of the Eight Islands, however, as well as a Buddhist convert, the Son of Heaven possesses the resources to make Uto's lordship disagreeable.

Lord Uto orders his retainers to leave him in solitude and take what is left of the runner to be displayed in the village square. The bloodstains on the polished planks will not wash clean. Well, leave them, then! Another reminder to Imuri mortals of the penalty for betraying their demonic ruler.

Uto douses the irori's fire with a slap of his enormous hand. Flames do not scorch the rough-scarred palm. With a growl, he retires to his cavern den, carved from the frozen earth beneath his bedchamber with his own thick, blunt fingers.

There Lord Uto sits and broods and plans.

CHAPTER 29

Twentieth day.

Monaga decides to greet this dawn from the hillside shrine he tends, rather than shiver in the shadow of the oni's residence, begging admission. He stands on the low wooden steps that lead to the inner shrine. The sky is deep blue, a promise of good weather—for today, anyway. A crisp, dry wind swirls powdery snow laid down the previous evening. Monaga breathes deep. Tangy air fills his lungs. It feels good; almost good enough for him to put aside his qualms at disobeying Lord Uto's command.

This defiance is not arrived at lightly. If the priest is to be of any help to the people of Imuri, he must test limits, learn how far the demon-lord will let out his tether. The timing seems propitious. For the past three days, Monaga has presented himself at the residence and been denied admission. On the first day, Lord Uto was occupied with matters of state. After that, not even an attempt at an excuse. Likely the original order is forgotten. Oni are not noted for long memories.

In any case, Lord Uto knows where to find him should he feel a desire to gloat.

A step creaks when he shifts his weight. Monaga moves back to view the building. It is a small shrine in the Shinmei style. From chigi to chigi—the curved projecting beams at either end— only three katsuogi, short logs, are necessary to hold the steep-pitched thatch roof in place. The doors of the inner compartment are kept closed and locked, housing the shintai, the sacred symbol. For this shrine, as for many others, the shintai is a mirror.

The mirror is cracked. This happened the day Lord Uto took power over his father's cooling corpse—poisoned, it is believed, though none would say so aloud. This crack is the sign by which Monaga knows that territorial kami no longer dwell in Imuri province.

Monaga shakes his head vigorously, as though to dislodge memories and misgivings. A corner of the pitched roof sags. Warped cypress boards bend outward. In spots, the thatch is thin enough to admit sunlight at noon. The shrine is several years overdue for its ritual rebuilding. Small wonder the kami left, if this is the best home Imuri can offer them.

The priest takes a pine branch out of his sleeve. It serves as a brush to clear snow from the sando, the approach to the shrine. Walking slowly, bending frequently, Monaga clears a narrow strip in the center of the dirt path. When he accidentally dislodges some small stones strewn on the path, he carefully replaces them. He does not consider the futility of his caretaking, or the infrequent visits of worshippers. This is his responsibility. He performs his duties.

At the bend in the sando, Monaga comes to the temizuya, the open pavilion where worshippers perform ritual ablutions. One does not approach the kami in an impure state. The night before, Monaga used one of the wooden dippers to break the ice topping the water in the stone basin. Now it is newly frozen over. Monaga again uses a dipper in this non-ritualistic fashion, and pauses to warm his hands in his armpits. When he can flex his fingers, he continues clearing the approach.

Now the torii is in view—the entrance to the shrine compound. A simple structure of unfinished wood, formed of two pillars and two crossbeams, the torii marks the gateway between the mundane world without and that of the kami within, between the secular and the spiritual. Strung between the pillars, parallel to the crossbeams, is a tattered straw rope called a shimenawa, which symbolically indicates a place of sanctity.

Beneath this rope, in the center of the torii, just where he'd stood almost a fortnight earlier, is the boy Hoke.

The priest puts aside his pine branch. Hoke's dark, lusterless eyes meet his, drawing him forward as flame draws the summer insects. The boy seems an embodiment of enduring sorrow.

"You're getting thin, lad," Monaga observes. "You should eat more."

"My master feeds on the misery of others. His diet leaves poor table scraps."

The priest is surprised at Hoke's eloquence. Yet, under what previous circumstances had they this opportunity to speak freely? On his last visit to the shrine, the boy was preoccupied with fulfilling his mission so he would not have to kill himself. No time for small talk then. Good. This summons is not serious if the demon forgoes such threats.

"All right, Hoke, I suppose I'm as ready now as I can be to face Lord Uto." He steps through the torii, passing the boy. He walks three paces, but hears only his own pair of sandals crunching snow. He turns.

Hoke stands beneath the torii, shaking his head.

"My Lord Uto has withdrawn from society. No one has seen him for days. I am not even called to share his bed. He dug a pit beneath the floorboards of his bedchamber and refuses to come out, even for state business."

Monaga raises an eyebrow and rubs a thick-boned hand across his long chin.

"That sounds encouraging. A repugnance for human company is a common oni trait. I dared not hope it would develop so soon. Perhaps he will shortly abdicate and join his demonic cousins in the remote mountains."

Hoke rubs his hands together with more vigor than warming one's fingers requires.

"His mood is foul and growing fouler. If you are right, and my master becomes dissatisfied with Imuri, I fear the people will suffer. Those Lord Uto cannot rule, he slays."

Monaga sighs. Hope is extinguished too swiftly to stave off his internal chill. "I feared as much, myself, but chose not to think of it."

"Who can say? He confides in no one, trusts only myself and that no more than he must." The boy shrugs. His indifference seems callous, but Monaga knows that no mind can dwell on great horror for long. Not if it is to remain sane.

"Then Lord Uto does not wish to see me this morning?"

"He does not. I do."

Monaga points to a boulder beside the path, on the mundane side of the torii. The stone is worn smooth by the buttocks of worshippers who needed to recover from the steep climb before they entered sacred ground. It has eroded very little since the day Lord Uto began his reign. The two sit side by side. A breeze flits among surrounding pines. The boy trembles.

"What troubles you, Hoke?"

"I have great fear." His fingers clutch the priest's arm.

"With good cause."

"Please, take me where he cannot reach me. Take me to the Imperial Palace in Naniwa."

Monaga's eyes widen. "The emperor's court?"

"There are rumors in the village of a petition sent to the emperor. He is wise and beneficent and will surely take action. Perhaps he will send Prince Naka for Lord Uto's head. What I know of the fiend's household may be useful to the prince."

For a peasant boy, Monaga muses, you are well informed. Of course, Uto's network of spies reports to him at all hours. The lad is bound to overhear things. The priest is less sure of the benevolence of Emperor Kotoku, who cut down the trees of the shrine of Iki-kuni-dama. Still, Kotoku continues to perform the ancient rituals, to appease the populace, and he is slowly but aggressively extending imperial influence throughout the islands. He would not wish a demon in power over even so small and inaccessible a province as Imuri.

"Uto has forbidden my leaving," Monaga points out.

"He forgets that you exist; have I not said so? If you are worried, leave a message promising to return. He honors your word. Say you're visiting a sick colleague."

Monaga shakes his head. "He will take his anger out on the villagers. He knows I can spread word of his cruelty."

"What does that matter, in view of the petition? You can forswear to be silent. Likely he will not even notice you have left."

Still the priest hesitates.

"He will be suspicious if we vanish together."

"He no longer cares about me, either. His desires turn more and more on violence for its own sake. My life is in danger."

Whose is not? wonders Monaga. He frowns. Hoke has an unexpected, and disturbing, well of persuasive words.

"I will take you as far as the Ise shrines. It is safe enough there."

The boy grimaces. "I thank you, but no. It must be the capital!" Hoke presses the priest's weathered hand with his own smooth palm. "Naniwa is not much beyond Ise. If you do not aid me, I will journey alone."

Monaga grasps the boy's shoulders and studies his grim child-face. Hoke is as inexpressive as if he were born of the fork of a tree. Only the flaring of his nostrils betrays the volcano below the youthful surface. Some greater terror eats at the child's insides, something he will not speak of. Monaga must discover what it is, but now is not the proper time.

"We leave at sunset. Meet me here."

Hoke bows gratefully, striking his forehead on the priest's bony knee. He looks up again suddenly, his lower lip caught in his teeth. He grips the older man's arm once more.

"Day is better."

"We would be seen."

"And ulterior motives therefore less suspected. Please. We must leave as soon as possible. I know the patrol schedule. We can avoid Lord Uto's men."

A strangely commanding tone for one of tender years and lowly class. Monaga again scrutinizes the lad, searching for something he does not know, something he does not find. No matter. The priest is committed, whatever his misgivings.

Monaga rises and walked to the torii. He unties the straw rope from one of the pillars.

"I usually replace the shimenawa on New Year's Day, but I had better attend to it now. Can you wait *that* long, at least?"

Hoke bows, oblivious to the gentle sarcasm.

CHAPTER 30

650 A.D. First month. First day.

In Naniwa, the imperial chariot arrives at the Palace of Ajifu.
Here, Emperor Kotoku views the ceremonies of the New Year's
celebrations. Plays and poetry competitions, dances and proces-
sions and sporting events that range from wrestling to kite-fly-
ing—these are the matters that occupy the court today.

"I ruined two pairs of sandals on the road from Lake Biwa!" the
runner protests. He waves a sealed paper under the gatekeeper's
nose. "I bruised and froze my toes on the cobbles of your streets,
searching for the emperor!" He pauses to gulp crisp morning air;
he has not yet recovered his breath.

The guards shrugs. "The emperor's orders are explicit. No
state business until our New Year's festivities are concluded. You
should have realized as much."

"I realize that even my calluses are blistered."

"Nevertheless, you must wait. Afterwards, you may visit the
emperor's residence properly, and add this petition from … where
did you say?"

"Imuri province."

"Izumi?"

"No, Imuri."

"Don't know it. Anyway, *then* you can add this petition of
yours to the others presented in the past few days. I promise you,
our emperor personally reads every petition brought to him."

The runner sighs and tucks the message up his sleeve. "Very
well. I had better find lodgings. Can you recommend … ?"

The guard is not unsympathetic. Prior to his appointment as

gatekeeper, he had been a court messenger. He gestures the runner to approach and unlocks the gate.

"You seem a man of honor," he says, "so I'll do this much for you. Ajifu is overrun with court servants, and no man, not even the Son of Heaven, knows them all. You're welcome to join us menials in our celebrations, but you must promise not to bring up this matter of a petition. Save it for later, as I said."

The runner is not an Imuri native. He is ignorant of the petition's content. Why should he object to such a promise? Besides, he's earned a holiday.

In Nikko, a small mountain village, strange wild men burst into house after house, roaring and yelping and leaping into the air so that their rags and strips of fur flap in every direction. Children shriek and run, for they are the favorite prey of these madmen. At last, the apparitions are appeased with bean cakes and sake, and their disguises are put aside.

A middle-aged priest and a boy stagger through the brisk dawn down Nikko's main road. At first, they are mistaken for fellow celebrants. Their cloaks are rent, their packs about to fall apart. A gray strip of cloth circles the older man's balding skull, and a swollen bruise mars his companion's cheek.

They do not wear costumes. They are challenged.

"It seems a miracle that we have come this far," Monaga replies to the headman's pointed questions. "I never knew so many hazards existed between Imuri and Nikko. I shudder to think what may lie ahead."

"More details, if you please," the headman orders. He slips a badger pelt from his back. A few moments earlier, he'd been leading the 'madmen' of Nikko on riotous rampage.

"Extraordinary luck we've had! Once, we stumbled into a bandit camp in a pine forest, apparently within an hour of a dispute that left broken skulls and shards of bone and no survivors … unless, of course, they fled. Again, we strayed into an Ainu village that was completely deserted save for the corpse of an aboriginal woman who'd been raped and then strangled until her cheeks were as blue as the moustache tattooed over her lips."

"Nothing less than they deserve," the headman comments,

remembering a recent Ainu raid on Nikko's rice crop.

"In any case, their misfortune allowed us to replenish our food supplies. Then, we were nearly buried alive in an avalanche caused by an earthquake. How it was that we awoke at the foot of a mountain, stiff and sore but only slightly injured, I cannot even guess. Hoke refuses to discuss the incident."

Monaga ruffles the boy's hair. Hoke's face is bland.

"Come, come, what is all this?" demands Yaku, the village priest, as he pushes through the gathering crowd. "These visitors need food and rest! Don't keep them jabbering in the cold!"

The headman reddens, apologizing immediately.

The hospitality of the people of Nikko is matched only by the beauty of the local scenery—particularly the waterfall. Baths and hot meals are quickly arranged. A portion of the day's offerings to the gods, which are not slight, is set aside for the travelers, that they might later buy what they need when they meet less generous folk. Monaga and Hoke are named guests of honor and given favored spots from which to watch the traditional fertility dance held at the village shrine. After days of hardship, Monaga welcomes such a respite.

Hoke, who has known few truly carefree days in his short life and should thus be even more pleased at the fuss, balks at further delay.

"We must reach Naniwa as soon as possible!"

Monaga rubs his aching calves, avoiding a tender purple blotch as large as a rice bowl where a falling boulder nearly crushed his leg.

"I don't understand you, Hoke. Any other boy your age would jump at a few hours' holiday!"

"And a priest with the welfare of his people at heart would not let himself be diverted from his duty!"

"Here, now! Some respect!" snaps Yaku. He enters the room set aside for the wanderers, bearing bowls of hot miso soup.

Monaga raises a disparaging hand. "It's all right, Yaku. The boy has suffered much. If his manners are a bit rough, well, whose would not be under the circumstances?"

"You know best." The slant of his eyebrow indicates Yaku's true feelings are otherwise. He puts down the soup bowls. "I will have your clothing cleaned while you bathe. Meanwhile, you will of course receive fresh kimonos."

Monaga nods as Yaku reaches for their packs. "You are too gener—"

"No!" Hoke flings himself across his pathetically small pack. "No one touches my things!"

Yaku glares at the boy. He turns to Monaga. "Really!"

Monaga shakes his head. "Look at him, Yaku. That isn't greed in his eyes, nor malice. It's terror! Indulge him, for my sake. He's lost more than you can imagine!"

Yaku scowls, but nods brusquely. Not trusting his tongue, he leaves without another word. The travelers are alone again.

"Now, you listen to me, boy," Monaga says sternly. "I grow weary of making your excuses. The people of Nikko are extending their most gracious hospitality to us …"

"I didn't ask for it!" Hoke clutches his pack tight against his chest. Hair falls raggedly before his eyes, which take on an almost feral glow. "You can't say I did!"

"Nor did I, so you needn't look at me that way. Still, we cannot refuse it. I share your desire for haste. By this time, the petition must surely be in the emperor's hands. However, we have been pressing ourselves hard. Another week like the last will kill me, if I don't rest. It is only one day. We leave at dawn, refreshed. I guarantee that with our strength renewed we'll soon make up for lost time. In the meantime, try not to act like an ungrateful eta!"

Hoke's eyes remain fixed on the priest. They seem to glitter as they fill with tears. He nods, unable to speak. Several minutes pass before he lets go of his pack.

"Hoke?" asks the priest. "Is there something you wish to tell me?"

The boy does not move. Monaga suspects that he is very close to learning Hoke's secret, but he is too weary to press him now. Morning may tell another story.

Morning *will* tell another story, in a way Monaga does not anticipate. That evening, as he helps Yaku with the ritual ablutions, the priest from Imuri collapses. Within an hour, fever is upon him.

The travelers will not leave Nikko at dawn, after all.

CHAPTER 31

Ninth day.

The governor of Anato, a province on Honshu's southwest tip, sits unattended in an open pavilion at the center of his garden. He taps an ivory penholder against his thick lower lip.

The governor is a heavy-set, sour-faced man with pitted cheeks. Half of his body hair makes up his full eyebrows. Once a middling-strong sumo wrestler, the governor each day feels more keenly the burden of muscles atrophying to flab. His digestion also suffers. His household affords a variety of foods beyond the imagining of most inhabitants of the Country of Eight Islands, yet his diet is as bland as that of the meanest eta. Essentially a good man, the governor tries not to take out his internal discomforts on the people of Anato. This is easier on some days than on others.

The big man has sat here all morning, composing a flattering poem he hopes to read during his visit next month to the imperial court in Naniwa. Invitations to the emperor's palace do not come often, partly because of his own dour demeanor, an aspect of his personality too ingrained to change. Since the decline of the Soga clan, land reform proceeds quickly, especially when former Soga supporters are involved. Like many old officials, the governor is distantly related to that family—another factor in his casual ostracism—and so he is particularly anxious to win Emperor Kotoku's favor.

The poem is nearly complete. A single line remains to be written. The perfect phrase finally coalesces in the governor's mind. He wets his brush with ink, touches it to the rice-paper.

"Hai!"

A shrill greeting shatters the garden's tranquility, driving the closing line from his thoughts.

The governor cleans his brush and lays it down gently, resisting an urge to hurl it at the intruder. The ivory handle would only crack against Bokuden's thick skull.

For of course it is Bokuden who stands grinning on the steps of the pavilion. Few people are privileged to enter the governor's presence unannounced and unaccompanied by at least one guard, and of those few only Bokuden regularly abuses the privilege. His ragged hunting outfit drips mud and less pleasant things on the polished wood. His pipestem-thin arms never wholly rest.

The governor sighs. His great belly quivers. "I trust you have not come about a new loan, Bokuden. I warned you when I forgave your past debts at the New Year's festivities that I would not …"

"I remember, Governor," Bokuden interrupts, bobbing his bony skull. For a nobleman's nephew, Bokuden has little sense of decorum … perhaps because he *is* a nobleman's nephew. "I welcome this opportunity to again thank you for that generous gesture, although I fully intended...

"It was no more than tradition required." And, the governor adds silently, a scandal-hating uncle with connections in the new emperor's court. Naturally the governor does not refer aloud to the bargaining that led to his imperial invitation. Even Bokuden does not violate protocol that far. Inwardly, however, the governor grimaces. A new loan is precisely what Bokuden wants. By this time, the young man ought to have guessed what the rest of Anato knows: the uncle will not intercede on his nephew's behalf again.

"Yet I feel obliged to your honorable self," Bokuden replies. "I have prayed since then for an opportunity to repay you. Today, while I hunted on Mount Wonoyama, the gods answered those prayers."

The governor cannot repress a scowl. Bokuden's ploy is subtler than usual; the stakes must be higher. Although he senses the trap, the former wrestler is intrigued.

Bokuden claps his hands thrice. Before the third clap's echo fades, two bearers appear. A bamboo cage dangles between them from a crosspiece resting on their shoulders. They halt at arm's length from the pavilion steps. A beak stabs out to peck at the ropes that bind the cage bars together. The winged captive emits a high-pitched squawk.

The governor's suspicion-narrowed eyes open wide. He heaves himself onto his feet, heedless of the act's indignity, and waddles past Bokuden down the steps. Standing before the cage, he reaches out a thick hand. The bird attacks the swollen finger as if it were a juicy worm. The governor jerks back. He sucks at the wound contemplatively.

"This pheasant's feathers," he mutters, "are pure white."

"As the snows of Fuji," Bokuden adds with shameless pride. "An auspicious omen, is it not?"

The governor grunts. Auspicious for Bokuden, anyway, who has had the sense to recognize superstitious significance in a naturally blanched creature. For himself, the governor realizes he has already erred in revealing his fascination with the oddity.

"Perhaps," he says. "How much do you ask?"

Bokuden staggers as though shocked. He may even *be* shocked, but the governor doubts that.

"This is a gift of gratitude," Bokuden protests.

Beneath his voluminous kimono, the governor's shoulders sag. This *will* be expensive. He can refuse the gift, of course. That would free him from further obligation. It would also be inexcusably rude. The news would precede him to Naniwa and cast a pall over his visit … assuming Bokuden's uncle did not have the invitation rescinded.

On the other hand, this pheasant is impressively handsome. The governor admires its beauty and singularity. He is not much swayed by its alleged function as a favorable omen, but many of his countrymen are … including Emperor Kotoku, at least publicly. The emperor's new programs were meeting with resistance. He could capitalize on such a sign that the gods favor his reign.

"I accept your gift, Bokuden," the governor says, stroking

his double chin. "You honor my house."

"Your acceptance honors mine." Bokuden gestures to the bearers. They lower the cage to the ground, balance the crosspiece atop it, and depart, unburdened, as swiftly as they came.

Bokuden turns to follow. At the foot of the pavilion steps, he stops and turns again.

The governor waits uneagerly.

"There is one minor difficulty," Bokuden begins.

The governor nods, almost imperceptibly.

"When I went hunting on Wonoyama, it was with no thought of bringing back live game. Consequently, I have incurred unforeseen expenses. These have jeopardized certain plans of mine for establishing...

The governor climbs up into the open pavilion again. He picks up his unfinished poem and tears a blank strip of paper from the bottom. He reaches for his brush.

"How much, Bokuden? That's all I need to know. No. Don't even tell me that. Take this to my treasurer. He will satisfy your needs."

Bokuden snatches at the ragged paper. Fresh ink smears his fingers. In the time it takes him to read the scrawled instructions, the governor pushes past to stand again before the pheasant's cage, meditating on the living whiteness. No point in addressing further words to that broad, indifferent back. Bokuden hurries from the garden before the governor can change his mind.

CHAPTER 32

Tenth day.

Hoke pauses at the foot of Nikko's most glorious water-fall. Its silvery beauty makes little impression on his half-glazed eyes, but the boy lacks a better goal. He perches on a smooth rock no bigger than himself. Because the low end happens to face the falls, he does also. Icy spray spatters his forehead, where droplets cling to furrows. Hoke shivers, although his borrowed kimono is double-lined with soft red cotton and the air hints of spring, inducing anxious trees to shoot green buds from branch-tips.

To Nikko's inhabitants, the boy could as well be a ghost. He is seen frequently, but almost always at a distance. Few even hear his voice. Such willful aloofness seems particularly unhealthy in a child, but for the sake of the priest who accompanies the boy, and who lies deathly ill in the sanctuary of the local shrine, the villagers respect Hoke's desire. If not respect, then tolerate.

Hoke does not dislike these people. Given a choice, he would readily join their activities, work and play alike. They demonstrate a joyful pride unimaginable in Imuri. Since he cannot stay, however, Hoke dares not form attachments. The sooner he leaves Nikko, the easier it will be.

The delay caused by Monaga's illness grows worrisome each day. Not for the first time, Hoke contemplates leaving the priest in the hands of these good folk. The plan is unworkable for several reasons. A lone peasant boy has little chance of penetrating the imperial court. A new mentor will hardly be as tractable and understanding as Monaga, whose very priesthood carries influence. Hoke would have to reveal too much to a strange companion, with possibly fatal results.

Should Monaga not recover, of course, Hoke will have no other choice.

The boy wipes a damp cheek with his sleeve. He prefers not to dwell on that thought. He concentrates on rushing waters.

Footsteps rasp faintly on the path behind him. Hoke stiffens; even his sphincter tenses. He draws the kimono tighter about his thin body, huddling against the cool stone. Why did he wear red today?

The footsteps stop. Their maker stands to Hoke's left. With an effort, the boy shifts his eyes to look.

And releases a pent breath. It is only Yaku. The faint odor of sandalwood should have told Hoke this, as soon as the priest was no longer downwind.

"So here you are," Yaku grumbles. His deep voice acts as counterpoint to the soprano laughter of the stream at the base of the falls. Spray forms dark spots on his ivory-colored kimono.

"Obviously," the boy replies, hiding his relief.

"I was told you walked this path."

Hoke shrugs. His gaze returns to the cascading waters.

Yaku taps his staff softly but impatiently on the stone. "You were not at breakfast."

"I was not hungry."

Yaku scowls. "So you left the sanctuary without a word. Knowing how my colleague and your protector, Monaga, worries about you. His life is already in the balance."

Hoke swallows, clearing his throat. "The way you speak, my protector may soon be past all worrying."

Yaku's right hand clenches the staff. Knuckles whiten. He pauses for a long, deep breath before he speaks again.

"Perhaps I sound that way," he admits grudgingly. "Of late, I sense a gloom deeper than any I have known. The kami are restless. However, I have good news this morning. Monaga's fever has broken."

Hoke's shoulders rise the width of a finger. Almost, his shining eyes turn to the Nikko priest. He stops himself. Hopes have been dashed too often in his few years for him to raise them again on such slim evidence. His voice remains flat.

"You said as much five days ago. Then, the fever returned with the setting sun, worse than before."

"You presume to question me?" Yaku chokes back further angry words. He is bound by his promise to Monaga, though the vow galls. How great a spirit the Imuri priest must have, to endure such insolence!

Swallowing his rage, Yaku confesses, "I was premature. This time I waited to be sure. There has been no fever since dawn yesterday."

The boy chews his lower lip. "You did not mention this."

"I did not wish to disappoint you again. Monaga is recovering. With proper rest, he will soon be able to travel."

Hoke leaps from the stone. His feet jar on the hard ground. He stares up at the priest anxiously. From this angle, Yaku's expression seems even severer than usual. "Today?"

Yaku glares. "Is that all you care about? Is Nikko so unpleasant?"

"How long?" the boy insists.

Yaku shakes his head in resignation. What can one do against such single-mindedness? "Two or three days. Four at the most. At present, he can barely stand unaided. He wishes to see you, though why he should is beyond me."

Hoke's jaw works violently. He cannot, will not speak.

Yaku takes this as a sign his comment has struck home. Contrite for hurting the boy, the priest recalls his secondary purpose for pursuing Hoke today.

"This brooding is not good for you, lad. With your patience sorely tried, you might welcome a diverting task."

Hoke's lips thin. "No."

"You have not heard..."

"I will not be involved in village life. Every day you try to talk me into joining some communal effort. Do you wonder that I skipped breakfast today?"

"All Nikko knows your preferences," Yaku replies sourly. "I have a solitary undertaking in mind. A message to be delivered to the provincial governor, on behalf of the village."

Hoke snorts. "Some idle flattery, I suppose, or the dedication of a new hovel in his name. I recognize make-work when I see it. No thanks, priest." He starts to mount the stone again, and halts with one knee raised. "What *is* a provincial governor?"

"I thought you knew everything. He's a sort of lord. Ours, in fact, was lord of this province, prior to the new imperial regime. I'd forgotten that Imuri, being small and remote, has so far eluded the emperor's land reforms. Our governor resides a day's journey from here, beyond that mountain. You walk as far as your pacings about Nikko."

Hoke considers this information as he considers everything … warily.

"There is a small element of risk," Yaku adds, "but, again, no more than you already take in your daily, solitary walks."

"How so?"

"That is the nature of the message. It seems that bandits have resolved this year to exercise greater boldness, or perhaps the Ainu grow uneasy. In the past week, while you've wandered oblivious to others' words and deeds, five corpses were discovered on nearby roads. Two of the dead were residents of Nikko. You must have seen the funerals. We are petitioning the governor to increase his patrols in this area."

Color drains from Hoke's face. His knees weaken. His palms turn clammy, and not alone from the touch of the cold damp rock. "How… how did they die?"

"It is not proper for a child your age to hear …"

"How did they die?" Hoke grasps the priest's flowing sleeve and pulls violently. The material rips. Losing his grip, the boy staggers back until his spine presses the rock.

Yaku glowers at the torn cloth. Before him, unrepentant, stands a pale, shivering child with cold eyes and thin lips. What does one do with such a boy? Cast him into the falls, out of frustration. Clutch him to your bosom, out of pity.

Yaku does neither.

"All were bludgeoned to death." He sniffs haughtily. "Will you take the message? A boy may pass unseen where a man cannot."

Hoke shakes his head. His very stance radiates refusal.

Yaku sniffs again. "Very well. I thought to do you a favor.

Frankly, I feel better relying on one of the farmers."

Hoke's eyes dart right and left. The surrounding forest appears free of lurking shadows, though one can never be wholly sure. He licks his lips. His voice comes low, barely discernible over the waterfall's roar.

"Your messenger must be extremely careful. It would be best if you did not dispatch him until Monaga and I have left."

Yaku's eyes widen at this unasked-for advice. "You arrogant little ... I dare not say more. Do what you wish."

The boy turns once more to watch the falling waters splash and leap, the stream froth and surge. Sunlight flashes on the surface, mesmerizingly. It is his only escape.

Yaku stares at the small, stiff form for a long moment. He fingers the torn kimono sleeve. An old garment, easily sewn. An unintentional act. Yaku is shamed that he has come so close to anger more than once during the brief exchange. Hoke is not just strange; he is disquieting. Perhaps the boy is right. The sooner the strangers from Imuri leave, the better. For Nikko as well as themselves.

CHAPTER 33

Twenty-ninth day.

A sampan skims the waters of Lake Biwa, propelled by the sculling of its single oarsman who stands at the stern. His passengers are willing to help, but neither priest nor boy is used to strenuous rowing. Instead, they rest in the center of the boat. Hoke peers over the sampan's side, his chin on the bamboo frame, watching the western shore creep by. Monaga lies on his back. One hand shields his eyes from the sun. The wobbling, sideways motion of the vessel makes him uneasy. He hopes today he can keep down the bit of fish that was his supper.

His soft moans carry over the lake.

The oarsman is a gangling fisherman named Toki. Toki's personality swings from taciturn to verbose. The former, Monaga thinks, seems a pose he cannot long maintain, although the latter is a dangerous trait for one of his low class. However, Hoke's personality is puzzle enough for the priest to grapple with.

Toki draws back the oar and spares a sympathetic look for his elder passenger. "Be grateful, priest, that we voyage this month, instead of next."

"I know. The Hira hurricanes." Monaga sighs. A dozen times, at least, Toki has recounted the legend of the unfortunate girl who rowed the lake every night to visit her lover, the lighthouse keeper. When the keeper, fearing she might be a sorceress, deliberately left the fire out one night, the girl became lost, frustrated, and angry. She threw herself into the lake, cursing her lover with her dying breath. At once, a hurricane blew up, demolishing lighthouse and keeper. Since then, at the same time every year, the storms return to Lake Biwa.

"Exactly," Toki confirms. "You couldn't get me out on this lake then for all your threats."

The oarsman's jaw snaps shut on that bitter note. Hoke turns from inspecting the shoreline to glare at Toki with cold, fathomless eyes. A forceful oar-stroke hastens the boat with a jerk.

Monaga observes the strain in Hoke's face, but cannot think how to interpret it.

"You invited us aboard, Toki," the priest states, disregarding his abused stomach. "All but kidnapped us. We made no threats."

"Did I say you did?" Toki's voice is a shade too loud. "I did not. I never said I'd been threatened, only that *if* I had been ..." The sentence trails off. He falls into one of his silent moods.

Hoke looks shoreward again.

At least, Monaga muses, they are spared another telling of *that* legend. Actually, Toki is a fairly good storyteller with too limited a repertoire. If the oarsman's tales pulled Hoke out of his sullen introspection, Monaga would willingly listen again and again. They do not. The lad seems unimpressed by the knowledge that the lake was formed in the fifth year of Emperor Korei's reign, by the same earthquake that created glorious Mount Fuji. He is so indifferent to the existence of the Dragon King's palace at the bottom of the lake that he does not even look for the shining dome of its roof. He yawns at the adventures of the artist-priest who, because of his great skill and goodness, was permitted to explore the lake in the shape of a golden carp, and of the equally skilled painter Kwashin Koji, rumored to have sailed off into one of his own paintings of Lake Biwa. Pointing out the famous eight fair views for Hoke is a waste of time.

Monaga feels less easy every moment, and the erratic motion of the sampan becomes the least of his distresses.

Suddenly, Hoke leans forward, jabbing a finger towards shore. The shift in weight causes the boat to rock even more.

"Misasagi!" he exclaims, staring wide-eyed at the succession of conical earth mounds.

Monaga rises on one elbow to see for himself. The effort costs him; he tastes bitter bile at the back of his throat. No matter. The boy is finally taking an interest in something outside of himself.

"Yes, Hoke," Monaga says. "Each one marks the burial spot of a high-place noble, if not an emperor."

"Then we are but a few miles north of Otau!" Hoke turns to the oarsman. "Aren't we?"

Toki nods, but with the bouncing of the boat this is impossible to detect. "True, lad. By afternoon we'll be out of the lake waters and on the Uji River, which runs into the Yodo River, which will take us to Naniwa." He licks his lips, tasting cold freshwater spray mingled with his own perspiration. "The current will be with us. We'll make good time. Believe me, I'm as anxious to be rid of you as you are to arrive!" Toki falls silent once more, staring straight ahead.

Monaga lies back on the rough bamboo deck. He closes his eyes and rubs his temples. A frown tugs at his mouth. He wonders, not for the first time, if luck alone led to their meeting Toki, who'd landed to repair his curious, arrow-shaped fish traps, on Lake Biwa's northern shore. If so, was it good luck or bad?

He wonders even more where a peasant boy from a remote province learned so much of Nihon's geography.

CHAPTER 34

Second month. First day.

Toki's sampan glides into sight of the harbor shortly after dawn. These waters are rougher than those of Lake Biwa but, considering their rough-and-tumble time on the rivers, Monaga now hardly feels the mild yaw caused by the tide. Already the boards of the Naniwa docks quiver with activity, though trading does not reach its peak until later in the year, when the Sea of Japan is less treacherous to cross. Chinese and Korean tongues vie with native dialects, the latter almost as exotic as the former. Merchants disparage the newly-arrived wares, prior to bidding on them. Pimps circulate among fresh-landed sailors, praising whichever brothel pays them. Dock-workers curse and shout and jockey for employment unloading the wealthiest vessels, but there are no fights. Not yet. The day is young, and many choice openings may still be had, particularly as certain imperial reforms of dock hiring practices go into effect. A sharp westerly breeze chills the air, yet those thick-muscled stalwarts just hired strip to their loincloths for their arduous work.

Monaga and Hoke both gape open-mouthed, while Toki maneuvers his tiny boat to a narrow space at the end of a pier. The priest recalls visiting several cities during his apprenticeship, but the reality is all the more striking for the gloss of decades-old memories. Hoke, despite a fund of inexplicable knowledge, finds the scene beyond his imaginings, piercing his dark moodiness. There! Beyond the bustle of the docks! Buildings rise two and even three stories high!

Imuri may be ruled by terror, but it is still a sleepy, slow-paced province.

The sampan's port side scrapes along a thick, weather-beaten piling and thuds to a halt by the hempen rope ladder that dangles from the dock. Iron weights secure this ladder's legs to the harbor bed, and are meant to hold it steady—but hemp fibers stretch, knots tighten, tides play havoc with water depth, and salt water corrodes. Hoke clambers like a monkey up the yielding rungs. When the rope swerves under his weight, he leans into the twist, using its inertia to aid his ascent. Monaga follows cautiously. One thick-veined hand does not lose its grip until the next hold is secure.

At the top, Hoke flips his child's body past the overhanging boards in a single, smooth motion. Monaga gracelessly negotiates the turn on his belly, soiling his cloak with greasy dirt and more than a few splinters.

The priest pauses kneeling, sucking in deep draughts of cool air, flexing his stiff fingers. He glances behind to see how Toki fares.

The sampan drifts seaward.

"Toss up the mooring rope, Toki!" calls the priest. "We'll tie it for you."

Toki grins broadly. He shakes his head. "I prefer a safer port, priest." His laugh is high-pitched. The grin seems to freeze, held in place by will alone. Lifting his oar, Toki pushes off against the piling.

Monaga is not very surprised. The fisherman's protests to the contrary, Toki is no willing benefactor. The nature of the suasive force is uncertain. Monaga suspects that various kami—perhaps some self-exiled from Imuri—are aiding their journey, though this does not tally well with Toki's actions. To hold the ancestral spirits in awe is only proper, but to be in terror of them? Even Buddhist converts need not fear kami who are, if anything, overly tolerant. By his words and deeds, Toki is a true follower of the Way.

Monaga rises and shrugs. Not every mystery needs to be delved. He waves farewell. "May Benten, the sea goddess, watch over you, then."

Toki shuffles uneasily, rocking the sampan under his bare feet. He puts down his oar and cups his hands about his lips. "And Amaterasu over you, priest." Lowering his hands, he murmurs, "You need divine help more than I will."

Impatient with goodbyes, and not at all surprised by the retreat of their benefactor, Hoke heads inland. He pauses to see if the priest follows. Monaga hastens to his side. Together they thread their way through crowds of Chinese sailors and native stevedores. A Chinese merchant ship discharges a shipment of silk and, Monaga notes sourly, a trio of Buddhist monks. He shuns eye-contact with the foreign missionaries, gathering Hoke closer to his side. Wooden pier soon gives way to solid ground, and they are free of the crush. Monaga halts before a broad wooden structure, wherein dwell delegates from the Korean kingdoms, year-round guests of the emperor—and hostages for the good conduct of those kingdoms.

"Why do we stop?" Hoke asks. His feet jerk up and down, like those of a shadow puppet.

"To remind my legs what land feels like," Monaga replies. He slaps his worn sandals, raising puffs of gray and yellow dust. "And to consider our next move."

"To the palace, of course, to arrange an audience with the emperor."

The boy's audacity no longer startles Monaga; it is merely wearisome. "The emperor has many palaces, Hoke. He could spend the day at any of them. There is also the matter of protocol. Our emperor has made many changes in the past five years, many of them based on foreign ideas." Distaste flits across his face. His eyes drift to the monks on the dock. They seem unaware of his scrutiny. Monaga returns to the boy. "He has, for instance, established a custom of naming nengo, or eras, starting with that of his own ascension. Without learning the new etiquette, we risk being barred at the very gate."

"More delays," Hoke grumbles. He kicks at a pebble.

"Which is better, to stumble through the forest blindly or to discover a path?"

Hoke disregards the priest's sharp tone. "You know of a path?"

"I believe so. Unless there have been new appointments in last year or so, a man named Taro tends a shrine in the city's southeast quarter. Taro and I were apprentices together. We call on him first."

As a welcome change, Hoke does not argue.

They meet an apprentice at the torii. Yes, this shrine is still in Taro's charge. No, he is not in attendance, and not likely to be for many days. Where, then? Emperor Kotoku is still Nihon's religious leader, regardless of his Buddhist leanings. By imperial order, Taro is removed to Meiko's workshop. No one knows why. Who is Meiko? Only the greatest living swordmaker in Naniwa ... and therefore in all of Nihon.

"Not a very straight path," Hoke mutters as they traverse narrow streets on the way to the workshop.

Monaga's feet hurt, and the boy's carping is tiring. He responds testily. "Can't you see good fortune when it lands on you? Taro has received an imperial mandate. That gives him influence, enough at least to gain us a hearing. Isn't that what you want?"

Hoke nods sullenly.

As they soon discover, Taro possesses more than court influence; he has news for the travelers that renders an audience superfluous. A scheme is in progress for dealing with the demonic lord, and Taro is a key figure.

Shiminawa stretch along the workshop's boundaries. Wands hung with strips of folded paper—the gohei—dangle over the forge. Purification rites are observed throughout the process, which can take several days. These are normal spiritual adjuncts to sword-making, a craft conducted in a semi-religious atmosphere. The additional presence of a high-placed priest in full ceremonial robes offering frequent prayers to Amaterasu, Inari, and a host of lesser gods, transforms this occasion into a ritual transcending all but the holiest festivals.

Monaga's staff of priesthood, attested to by Taro, gains the pair entry, but not before the Naniwa priest completes a complicated invocation.

"Meiko is upset with me," Taro confesses as soon as

introductions are made. He is a rotund imp of a man, a head taller than Hoke. A silky fringe of colorless hair ornaments his polished skull.

The brawny swordsmith looks up from his anvil, hammer in hand. He shakes the wide, brightly colored silk sleeves of his own robe, and scowls at Taro, broadly, for the newcomers' benefit.

"A cast-iron sword is a useless prop, too heavy for real war. You need tempered steel for a proper edge." Meiko rattles the blade on the anvil, though not too vehemently. This is his second attempt to meet Taro's specifications. The first was spoiled by a too-powerful blow that twisted a freshly-welded bar of iron and ruined six days' work.

"Don't expect sympathy from these two," Taro warns him. "They look to this weapon for their province's salvation." He turns to Monaga. "Vague rumors had reached us from Imuri, but few here in the capital took them seriously until a runner brought your village's petition. I still find it difficult to credit. Oni can have earth-bound interests, but their basic selfishness precludes the sense of responsibility required to govern effectively."

Monaga leans heavily on his staff. "Lord Uto is a special case. Men reincarnated as demons usually experience a gap between death and rebirth: physically, over the months it takes a corpse to disintegrate, or psychologically when a violent end causes the body's immediate destruction. Their ties to our world are consequently weakened." The priest's voice grows harsh. "Uto tricked me into eliminating that gap for him."

Taro rests a hand on Monaga's hunched shoulder. "Do not blame yourself for a small ignorance. Not even the kami can consider everything. When the emperor asked my advice, I had to consult dozens of crumbling, ancient scrolls, most of them borrowed from Buddhist temples, to outline a practical course of action."

"Pity you didn't find one," growls Meiko. He positions the blade on the anvil and delivers a single hammerstroke. His scowl deepens as he considers the next blow. According to Taro, too good a weapon would be as useless as a poor one. This delicate balancing act goes against the swordmaker's grain.

"Do you still question the emperor's judgment?" Taro's tone is flat, but not accusatory. The two men have argued so often over the past fortnight that no heat remains in the dispute. The presence of Imuri refugees rekindles a faint spark at the bottom of the ash-heap, no more.

Gesturing with his hammer, the sweating Meiko appeals to Monaga.

"It isn't enough this priest wants an iron blade. The tsuga must also be iron rather than carved wood. Even the peg, the mekugi, that holds the tang in place, is iron. My apprentice finished those pieces"—he hesitates, reluctant to admit having spoiled the first blade—"days ago, while I concentrated on the tricky part here. I hope my lad doesn't pick up bad work habits from this job."

Hoke adjusts the shifting weight of the pack strapped to his back. His breathing grows shallow. During Meiko's speech, the hammer seems to point at him. No; past him. He turns and sees a low shelf, level with his forehead, to his left. Reaching up blindly, the boy curls cramped fingers around a flat, hollow object of dull black metal. It feels warmer than its distance from the heat of the forge should permit. He turns it in his hand. His little finger pokes slightly into an opening at one end. The object is undecorated except for the crude menuke ornamentation meant to conceal the blade-fixing peg by incorporating the mekugi into the design.

Monaga notices that the boy has moved from his side.

"Hoke. Leave it be."

The boy appears not to hear.

Meiko grins. "No harm in touching a hilt, priest. It's not bad workmanship, for what it is. The seams are as good as I've ever seen for a casting, but don't tell my apprentice that when he returns from his lunch break."

"The gods aid our efforts," Taro adds.

The swordsmith does not contradict him.

Hoke's thumb pushes at the protruding iron peg. It pops loose into his left palm. He raises the tsuga and peers through the pegholes, the mekugi ana, set a third of the length from the opening for the tang.

"An iron mekugi does seem extreme, Taro," Monaga comments. "The usual bamboo peg would seem sufficient."

"I thought caution best."

"Caution!" Meiko's grin vanishes. "This sword won't last a single battle. My cheapest regular blade could slice it in two. The man who wields this will be half-defeated just by its weight!"

Taro's shoulders sag. His eyelids lower wearily. He has explained the matter to Meiko seven times in as many days, and to his tongue it feels like seven hundred. "Steel *is* best … in normal warfare. No one disputes that. But demons take a different kind of killing. Iron, being more elemental, can disperse demon-flesh more readily than steel. It draws out the oni's life-force, enervates him."

"Have you ever seen this happen?"

"The scrolls say …"

"Scrolls! I trust my own experience and the revelations of the gods, and nothing else. I only hope Iniro does not abandon me for so perverting the swordsmith's art." Meiko glances wistfully at his forge thickly hung with gohei, white paper strips cut in angular bunches in symbolic offering. His heavy lips move in silent prayer to the rice-god who, having blown the bellows for the famous swordsmith Kokaji in ancient times, acts as protector of his craft.

Taro turns from the swordmaker in exasperation. "The weapon's substance is only part of the plan, of course," he tells Monaga. "Else I would not be here. All things have kami, a spiritual force, to some degree. My prayers and rituals, joined to Meiko's, are intended to induce the kami of Nihon itself to add some of their power to the sword's natural kami. Naniwa, as the seat of imperial power, is an ideal place for this."

Monaga leans back, in awe of his childhood friend. All priests of the Way have the potential to employ such powerful magic, but few have the temperament. The strain of manipulating unseen energies leaves one more vulnerable, less prepared, in dealing with the material world.

"You have done this, Taro?"

The fat priest shrugs. "I believe so. I hope so. We cannot be sure until the sword is used. You must understand: for their

power to take hold, the kami have to commit themselves wholly.
Until the sword completes its task, they will be bound to it. This
is a lot to ask."

Monaga nods and strokes his chin. "The oni is a Buddhist
demon. Why do I see no practitioners of that foreign religion
here?"

"Pah! They claim the natural order restores itself, regardless
of intervention. They freely advise me on doctrinal points, but
refuse further aid. I believe they hope that the Way will fail,
though they avow tolerance of our beliefs."

"Generous of them," Monaga observes wryly.

"Even if we succeed," Taro continues, "and I am certain we
will, the Buddhist influence is widespread. In the long run, the
best our order can hope for is consolidation."

"I cannot accept that," Monaga replies. "The people will not
stand for it."

Hoke glances up from the tsuga. He licks his lips. "Would a
room of iron walls protect me from the oni?"

Taro's eyes widen. He'd assumed the boy was mute. Hoke's
bearing does not indicate that his unnatural silence is a signal
of politeness.

"It seems likely," he replies. "Of course, you could not
remain there forever."

Hoke nods soberly and lowers his gaze to the hilt again.

Monaga dismisses the boy's interruption. "Someone must
wield this iron sword. Has the emperor chosen a champion?"

Taro shakes his head. "Prince Naka is the perfect candidate,
but he suspects his uncle's motives. The prince's affair with
Empress Hashihito has grown more open. This puts a strain on
the prince's relationship with the emperor."

"What!" Monaga's chagrin betrays his provincialism. "His
own half-sister?"

"This is neither place nor time for court gossip," Taro adds
hastily. The Imuri priest has enough worries, he thinks, without
adding the pecadilloes of the imperial family to the load.

"The blade won't be ready for another two days," Meiko
intrudes. "There's no need to rush."

"You think not? I grow impatient!"

This new voice, harsh and sinister, seems to fill the workshop. The gohei over the forge twirl rapidly in the still air.

Three men turn as one to face Hoke, for the voice comes from the boy's direction, if not his lips. Something like a giant red beetle crawls from the boy's pack and down his right arm, leaping to the dirt floor. This thing swells rapidly until the horns atop the head touch rafters supporting the thatch roof. The workshop feels suddenly colder than the winter day beyond its walls. The forge flames are nearly quenched. Perspiration on Meiko's brow turns to ice, crackles, and tears free. Hoke shivers mightily, teeth chattering behind blue lips.

Monaga staggers in dismay, pulling loose a strand of shimenawa as he grasps for a support. "Lord Uto!"

Pointed teeth gleam as the demon grins. "Again you served me well, priest. A boy Hoke's age, traveling alone from Imuri to the capital, would have excited immediate suspicion unless he had a protector—especially one like you. Everyone knows that priests are fond of small boys. I could have made the trip openly, of course, but would certainly face a rebellion on my return to Imuri. Better to let the fools there think I sulk in my den, and save the bother." He wipes a steaming strand of spittle from his mottled lips. "Yes, you've been of great value to me, priest, but now it is time to dispense with your services permanently."

Meiko pries his left hand from the chilled tang to shield his eyes from the apparition. "This cannot be!"

"It can," the oni contradicts. "It is."

Meiko drops the free hand and points with his hammer in defiance. "I refuse to believe this nonsense!"

"You dare?" the demon roars.

"Take care, Meiko," Monaga warns.

The swordsmith takes no heed. If he can bait and distract the monster, he thinks, the priest and boy may be able to escape.

"You are an hallucination, fiend, conjured up by these priests, who toy with me for expressing perfectly healthy doubts about the wisdom of this enterprise." He glares at Taro and Monaga, who are too amazed to protest the charge. "You see, I know your secrets. Enough childishness! I will complete this useless sword because the Son of Heaven wills it. Not because of your mind tricks."

Uto's crimson face darkens until nearly black. His skull-sized fist plummets to smash apart the deity shelf. While icons spill on the hard dirt floor, the oni grasps a handful of shattered bamboo rods. They form a crude club.

"You die first! Then we shall see who is the illusion!"

"Master!" Hoke cries. "Must you kill them? It is not enough to fill their hearts with terror?"

Lord Uto snarls at his pillow boy. Hoke cringes before the baleful ebon glower and those bared yellow fangs.

"I am not so fond of you, peasant's whelp, that you may presume to question me! A chigo like you is easily replaced. These three lives are forfeit. This one must die, if only because he admits to forging a weapon exclusively to end my own existence."

With an angry shake of his horned head, Lord Uto cuts short the boy's objections. He closes on the three men gathered about the anvil. The hard-packed dirt floor shudders beneath his tread.

Meiko stands as stolid as his anvil. He holds the hammer level with his heart. How quickly the demon moves! The priests' chances to escape seem slim indeed against such speed. Still, slim is better than none. Meiko expects to die in the next few moments. He has no complaints. He asks only that he be allowed to strike a blow against his emperor's foe. The dryness in his mouth, the pounding of blood in his ears, the hollow sensation at the pit of his stomach—these things deter him not at all.

Taro is most shaken by the sudden appearance of the oni. Compared to Monaga, he is softened by life in Naniwa, and his mental defenses are weak after days of magic-weaving. The smith can deal with horror through hard-nosed practicality; Taro needs time to adjust. Time he does not have. He leans forward, knees braced against the anvil. Where are the guards posted by Emperor Kotoku at either end of the street beyond? Are the demon's gloating roars really no louder than Meiko's rhythmic hammering? Even so, a shout should bring them. But

Taro's voice is as weak as his limbs.

Lord Uto smiles his unpleasant smile. The broken shelf crackles in a three-fingered fist.

"You are all dead men. The only question is one of method. Shall I roast you over your own forge, swordmaker? You, you fat old man, shall I stain your priestly robes a deeper red?" The ebon eyes settle on grim Monaga. "Something special for my old acquaintance. I'll save you for last."

The Imuri priest stands by his colleague, apparently unmoved by the oni's threats. His drab traveling clothes, soiled and frayed though they are, seem invested by his bearing with no less majesty than the elaborate costumes of the others. Monaga hardly spares Lord Uto a glance. He fixes on Hoke with a silent rebuke.

The boy will not meet his eyes.

With a scavenger's instinct, Lord Uto starts with the weakest. The shelf-club descends, its shrill keening slicing the still air, to smash across Taro's left cheek. Soundlessly, Emperor Kotoku's chosen sinks to the ground. And stays there.

"Hai!" gloats Lord Uto. "If all Naniwa is as soft, perhaps I will seize the imperial throne today!"

Monaga kneels to aid Taro. Meiko hurls himself forward, shouting, "By Iniro's sweat, you'll pay for that cowardly act!"

The hammer swings at a red, scabrous kneecap. The oni dodges the clumsy attack. His club strikes the off-balance swordmaker across the shoulder. The blow's force spins Meiko around. He staggers toward the forge, jabbing one elbow painfully against the stone as he tumbles to the floor alongside. A pair of tongs clatters from an overhead peg and bounces off his skull.

"Taro!" Monaga whispers as he tears his robe to bind the bleeding welts. "Can you hear me?"

Taro's eyes focus slowly. The right side of his mouth smiles. "I still live, Monaga."

"That can be remedied," snarls Lord Uto. He grasps a trough of cool water, used to quench freshly-heated blades, and overturns it on the hapless Meiko. "In a few more heartbeats, it shall be."

"It shall not!" Monaga screams. He grips the anvil and pulls himself erect. His fingers touch the uncompleted blade, and wrap around the tang. The edge is dull, yet it stings as his grip tightens. A thread of blood runs unnoticed down his right wrist. "Your evil is to be endured no longer!"

"Ridiculous old man!" Lord Uto spits into the forge. Flames spurt high, singeing paper gohei. "You expect to succeed where my own guards failed?"

Monaga steps around the anvil to stand unobstructed before the towering monster. The priest is human, and has known rage—but never so fiercely burning, and never so determinedly channeled as now. New strength flows into his thin, weary limbs. His feet spread in an attack stance. He feels as if the sword is holding him, rather than the reverse.

He realizes suddenly that it is. His resolve has helped accomplish Taro's ends.

"This weapon makes the difference, Lord Uto. Kami have bound themselves to it. And they will remain bound until their task is accomplished—your destruction!"

For a moment, the workshop is quiet save for the scrabbling Meiko as he crawls from beneath the trough. Then the rafters shake with the oni's laughter.

"Have you forgotten, priest? I drove the kami from Imuri! *They* fear me, too!"

Monaga's face darkens. "Liar! Not every kami fled, and those who did had done so out of revulsion, not terror!"

Once more, the great horned head tosses back on massive shoulders. Again, hollow crackling rolls forth, mocking Monaga, kami, the Way, the Emperor of Nihon …

With an agility thought lost years ago, Monaga springs forward. The blade sinks deep into the fleshy left thigh. The priest withdraws as quickly, out of reach of that club. Black ichor steams thickly from the wound. Lord Uto seems suddenly diminished, as if slightly deflated.

The oni's mirth turns into a screech of outraged agony. In the blink of an eye, he loses the complacence of invincibility. Monaga demonstrates a power that unsettles the inhuman creature. With his makeshift club, Lord Uto could crack the priest's skull or hurl his aged form through the workshop's fragile walls ... but that weapon is all but forgotten in his right hand. The searing in his leg occupies his entire limited intellect. This cannot be! He is Lord Uto, an oni, the oni of all oni! He cannot be slain by an old man with an unfinished sword!

He needs time to think, a chance to plan his counterattack. Oh, for the burrow beneath his bedchamber in Imuri! His ebon eyes dart from one corner of the workshop to the next, seeking refuge. Panic seizes his mind. Lord Uto pictures himself in the last moments of his former incarnation, lying helpless on his deathbed.

Monaga reads his expression easily. "There is no place you can go, Lord Uto," he intones, startling himself with the thick menace of his words. "Nowhere that I will not follow, now that I hold the means of ending your foul, unnatural existence. I have stood by, impotent, far too long. No more, I promise you. No more."

Again the priest attacks. Lord Uto stumbles back, narrowly avoiding the ichor-smeared tip. He nearly trips over Hoke, whose existence is as forgotten as that of his club. Instinct takes over. The massive left hand encircles the boy's body and lifts him off the floor.

The oni has a shield.

Monaga halts, blade poised. He studies the boy's face. It is unreadable. Hoke is untrustworthy, traitorous, heartlessly cynical ... but still only a boy, under the influence of a demon that was once his human lord. The priest hesitates to harm him.

Shouts echo in the street outside the workshop. Sandals clatter on stone paving.

The oni tilts his head and frowns.

"Imperial guards, Lord Uto," explains Meiko. He steps forward stiffly, still gripping his hammer, raising it in menace. "Your own screams bring them."

"They will enter from behind you," adds Monaga. "They will drive you onto my blade. Your hostage cannot save you." But the guards might save him, Monaga realizes, if Uto thinks to use the confusion to elude the iron blade. The priest exchanges a glance with Meiko. The swordmaker has reached the same conclusion.

"No," the oni mutters. "It cannot end like this. I can destroy you, priest. I *will* destroy you!"

"No respite for you, friend!" Monaga slashes out. The bamboo club in Uto's monstrous grip is halved. The oni throws down the broken sticks and uses both hands to grip Hoke.

"Master!" cries the struggling boy.

"Be still or I'll throttle you!" Lord Uto growls.

Hoke frees his right hand and raises it over his head, into the oni's line of sight. He still holds the ornamental tsuga.

"Your sanctuary, master! In my hand! You can shrink down and..."

"And be trapped, easy prey for your friend, the priest!"

"No! Safe! See! The same metal as in the sword! Forged under the same rituals! Once you are within, the blade cannot touch you!"

Monaga sobs in anguish. "Hoke, you young idiot! If Uto escapes us now, he will destroy all Nihon, you included!"

Lord Uto gapes wide-eyed at this hostage. The infamous smile twists his lips, exposing the fangs. "What a clever boy! Isn't he bright, priest? He played you for a fool for more than a month, although I admit that is hardly a difficult task!"

Monaga dashes at the oni, blade thrust forward. Not because Lord Uto's words sting—which they do—but because this is the last chance to strike. The oni swings Hoke into the sword's path. Its edge veers off at the last moment, as Monaga leaps back. The priest curses himself for his unwillingness to spill the silly child's blood. If Lord Uto conquers the Eight Islands, Monaga feels he will be as much to blame, for his scruples, as Hoke for his betrayal.

The oni dwindles faster than the eyes can follow. In a heartbeat, he is Hoke's height; another, no larger than a cat. The rapid conversion of the oni's mass into energy ends any hope Monaga has of launching a further attack at a smaller, more vulnerable shape. Waves of heated air ripple through the shop, warping wooden wall-planks and forcing the priest to retreat. Monaga's buttocks press against the stones of the forge, which by comparison feel cool.

Hoke is spared even that much relief. The left shoulder of

his kimono falls away, scorched. Beneath is a brilliant three-fingered welt where Lord Uto's grip held him from running in the first phases of shrinking. The wound is layered, severest in the center, an artifact of the diminution of the hand. Hoke's skin becomes almost as red as Uto's. The left side of his face, which is nearest the oni, swells with blisters that force one eye fully closed and the other half shut. The rest of the kimono starts to smoulder. Yet Hoke does not flee, not even when Lord Uto is too small to hold him physically in place.

Too frightened, thinks Monaga. Or in too much pain.

Then the boy moves. He bows on one knee before the oni and lays his right hand palm up on the dirt floor. His thumb holds the tsuga firmly. Lord Uto leaps onto the hand. His footsteps raise tiny blisters. By this time the heat he radiates is considerably lessened. He marches to the open end of the swordhilt. He hesitates at the lip.

Dismay is plain on all three men's faces.

The workshop door is torn down by the leading imperial guards. Lord Uto crawls up into the slit, skittering rapidly towards the safety of the sealed end. He pauses at the peg hole to peer out mockingly at his enemies.

Hoke suddenly whips the tsuga upward. The oni tumbles to the closed end, with a fearsome, muffled curse. The boy opens his left hand to allow the mekuji in his palm to roll down to his fingers. He jams it into the hole, and keeps it clamped tight with his left hand. He races to the anvil, eluding the startled guardsmen pouring into the room. He slams the tsuga onto the anvil with a clang, and holds it there firmly. The hilt rattles on the flat metal. Youthful muscle stands out along Hoke's seared arm.

"Now, swordmaker!" the boy cries. "Strike now!"

Meiko is already beside the anvil, the first to fathom the boy's plan. He raises the hammer and holds it there a moment, waiting.

Metal scrapes metal. Hoke's sweaty grip is weakening.

"Hurry!" he shouts.

"First move your fingers, lad. I can flatten the end of the mekuji to seal Lord Uto within, but your hand is in the way!"

Hoke's breathing grows shallow and rigid. Perspiration soaks what remains of his clothing. His fingers ache with the strain of containing the oni's rage. He shakes his head.

"The moment I let go, he escapes. He moves too quickly. You must seal it first!"

Meiko licks his lips. The hardness in Hoke's pleading eyes precludes further protest. "A brave boy," he mutters. He shifts to a two-handed grip and swings.

"No!" Monaga screams. He throws down the blade and stumbles toward the anvil.

Not in time.

Bones crunch under the hammer's thick head. Enough impact is transmitted to flatten one end of the plug. It will not readily come free, no matter Lord Uto's strength.

Hoke's mouth opens, but no sound issues. His agony transcends verbalization. He falls back on the hard dirt floor, his ruined left hand trailing thick, bright blood down the side of the anvil. Even so, he forces his half-open eye to stay on Meiko as the swordsmith flips the hilt over and hammers down the opposite end of the peg.

Monaga cannot recall seeing Hoke smile before.

Blackness envelops the boy then, allowing barely enough time for a last, consoling thought:

Walls of iron now hold Lord Uto prisoner.

NEW YORK CITY

THURSDAY, DECEMBER 30, 1982

CHAPTER 35

Creeping daylight washed the last dim stars from the sky, and caused photosensitized cells to switch off the sodium vapor streetlamps along Riverside Drive. A nippy dawn promised colder temperatures than the city had so far experienced this winter, but the sun was blindingly intense.

At this hour there was little traffic on the Drive, or even on the highway that sliced Riverside Park lengthwise. Mrs. Ruggio took no chances. She crossed the street with her terrier hugged to her bosom, streaking her white rabbit's fur jacket with the pet's dark gray hairs. They were several paces inside the park when she allowed the animal to stand on his own four feet, relatively safe from canine-hating drivers.

Neighbors speculated on whether Mrs. Ruggio had been widowed, divorced, or deserted ... speculation she unconsciously fostered by giving out different stories at different times ... except for the truth that she'd never been married. This hint of mystery was her sole claim to character. When her building's superintendent referred to her, colloquially and out of her earshot, as "the loud fat blonde on the second floor," he implied more personality than she possessed. She, naturally, was unaware of her lack.

As his paws touched solid ground, the terrier let loose a full dozen high-pitched barks.

"That's a good Bootsie," Mrs. Ruggio cooed. She performed a three-hundred-and-sixty-degree scan. No one was watching. The woman slipped Bootsie's leash from his collar, allowing the animal to scamper due west, through the denuded shrubs that lined the path.

Mrs. Ruggio rolled up the leash and thrust it in her jacket pocket. No stranger could connect her with the free-running dog. She considered New York City's leash laws a silly nuisance, when she thought about them at all. Almost as foolish as the more recent law that required owners to clean up after their pets. What was she paying taxes for, if she had to do the sanitation department's job? Anyway, Bootsie wasn't dirtying the street. This was a public park. What good were parks, if Bootsie couldn't have his freedom there? A red-bearded hippie once dared to complain because, he claimed, children played here. She'd told him off! It was the parent's responsibility to see that their children didn't play in filth! Not hers!

Mrs. Ruggio strolled jerkily down the twisting asphalt path, taking her time, giving the terrier plenty of opportunity to do his business decorously, out of her sight, as she'd trained him to do. What she didn't see, she couldn't be made to clean up or get a ticket for. Shortly, though, Mrs. Ruggio picked up the pace. A frown deepened the scowl lines etched like canyons in her plump face. Bootsie ought to have frisked back to her by now.

She hoped he wasn't constipated again.

"Bootsie!" she called. "Here, Bootsie! Kiss kiss!"

Three sharp barks sounded from the next turn in the path. Mrs. Ruggio clapped her hands in summons. She listened for the familiar scuttering of unclipped toenails on the hardtop.

She did not hear it.

That Bootsie! He'd probably found another wino to badger. So cute, the way the little gray dog nipped and clawed at the merest sliver of exposed flesh, preferring the ankles, until he drove the indigent from park bench or doorway. Of course, Mrs. Ruggio knew she shouldn't let him do it. No telling what disease or parasites Bootsie might pick up.

"Just as I thought!" she scolded as she made the turn.

Bootsie was hopping like a frog, yapping away, thoroughly pleased with himself. Sniffing first here, then there, he circled a black man lying face down at the edge of the path. The man did not move a muscle. Must've gotten a snootful last night, mused Mrs. Ruggio. And such disgusting rags! Falling off his body! He could at least get a decent suit! Then maybe he could find a job!

She stopped short, gasping. The man's buttocks were completely exposed! He must have passed out trying to go to the bathroom! And people had the nerve to complain about her little Bootsie! She ought to call a policeman and have the drunken slob put away for good! Not that one could expect any better behavior from a schwartzer!

Bootsie raised a hind leg to mark his find—not for the first time.

"Stop that, Bootsie! Come here. Come to Momma. Kiss kiss."

The dog yipped and lowered the leg. He took two steps toward his owner, and stopped. He sniffed ground he hadn't sniffed before. A deep growl vibrated in his throat.

"Come on, Bootsie. Kiss kiss."

Reluctantly, the terrier took three more steps before halting again to look back at the unmoving man. A pink tongue dangled under the animal's snout. He panted white clouds.

Exasperated, Mrs. Ruggio closed the gap in five long strides, pulling the leash from her pocket. "Bad dog!" she scolded, grasping Bootsie's collar. "Making Momma come near this vile creature. Just for that, you're getting a bath today whether you ..."

The sentence died in her throat. The terrier yelped as the leash's clip snagged on curly gray fur. Mrs. Ruggio slapped his muzzle absently. Bending to fasten the leash brought her close enough to see that the black man's face rested in a pool of dark blood. Another stream of blood, mixed with excrement and freshly diluted by Bootsie's marking, smeared the ground around his buttocks.

The wind had been blowing toward the river. It reversed direction.

Pale-faced, holding her breath, Mrs. Ruggio scooped up Bootsie. His muzzle pressed tightly against the fur jacket. The terrier gave a frightened cry. Mrs. Ruggio loosened her grip enough for the animal to breathe.

She saw no one as she hurried from the park. No one saw her, she hoped. Her heartbeat did not slow to normal until she'd crossed Riverside Drive and gotten halfway to West End Avenue.

She'd narrowly avoided an unpleasant experience, but she was safe now. She wouldn't have to talk to the police about dead bodies.

"Tonight, Bootsie," she whispered to the shaking gray ball in her arms, "we take our walk in Central Park."

Bootsie growled.

Twenty minutes later, Richard Alexander Jones's corpse was rediscovered by a middle-aged man in a powder-blue jogging suit. He was looking for a phone booth when he saw a pair of oddly matched uniformed patrolmen enter the park.

"Officers!" he called. "Thank God I don't have to go through the 911 number!"

The patrolmen halted, exchanging glances. "You the one found the body?" asked the tall one.

"Just now. How did you know? This way."

"Wait a minute," snapped the short one. "That's north. The dispatcher said the old man was near the river."

"Old man? He's practically a kid."

"Didn't you call in about an old man found dead in a thicket along the river path?"

"My God." The jogger's face was ashen. "No. I was looking for a phone when I saw you two. I just found the kid a minute ago."

No further time was wasted then on questions.

CHAPTER 36

The cashier at the Seventy-Seventh Street entrance to the American Museum of Natural History had developed an automatic routine: collect the 'suggested donation' in one hand and hand over that day's color-Goded admission button with the other, in a single smooth motion. Questions were answered with a copy of the museum's floor plan.

But the plan showed only those areas open to the general public. Francine Cooper had to repeat her request.

The cashier jerked her head, annoyed. Her momentum was broken. "What name?" she asked.

"I don't have the name. Whoever the police spoke to yesterday regarding some, ah, artifacts that were found at a crime scene. *Whomever.*" Cooper didn't know how much information Amos Foster had leaked, or wanted leaked, and she didn't want to undermine his official investigation if she could help it. She might need the detective's cooperation at some point, if only to see that the record was set straight.

"*Your* name?"

Cooper told her.

The cashier reached for the intercom phone under her cash register. Cooper stepped back from the cubicle so that a troupe of pre-adolescents could march through the turnstile while a sour-faced surrogate mother fumbled with her purse. The children's high-pitched chatter prevented Cooper from overhearing the cashier.

A uniformed museum guard approached the booth. He was a tall, thin, taciturn man with a pitted and inexpressive face. The hairline moustache, far from adding character, increased the hint of anonymity in his bearing.

"The guard will escort you," the cashier announced.

The last child on line grabbed a fistful of buttons.

Wordlessly, the guard led Cooper to a bank of elevators near the museum shop. He chose a fat, stubby key from the clattering ring at his belt and inserted it in the panel beside the furthest elevator. A sign above the panel read: STAFF ONLY.

Doors whooshed open. The guard inclined his head. Cooper got on.

The ride up was silent. His glazed eyes stayed fixed on the overhead floor indicator. Cooper had nothing to say to the guard, and both of them knew it.

At the fifth floor the car jerked to a stop and the doors slid open. Cooper stepped out into a somber hallway. Her low heels clacked on floor tiles. She was met by a woman who, although her hair was silvery, looked much closer to Lynda's age than Cooper's.

"Mrs. Cooper?" The woman was rubbing her hands together, dislodging clouds of dust. She wore faded jeans, a denim shirt, and no make-up.

Cooper conceded the obvious.

The silver-haired woman dismissed the guard with a wave of her hand. Cooper heard the doors thud behind her, and the soft whir of cable as the elevator started back down.

"My name's Allison Zebar. Please excuse the informal attire, and my not offering to shake hands. I've been plowing through a century of records for several hours, along with my too-small staff and anyone I can dragoon. Bill Collins is handling routine public relations for me, but I was told that you specifically asked for me?"

Cooper liked Zebar's efficient tone. "Not exactly, Miss Zebar. Or do you prefer … ?"

"I sign business letters Ms. Zebar, but in conversation that makes me sound like a character out of Uncle Remus. You can call me Allison or, if it's easier to remember, the one the cops talked to. My office is down this corridor."

Cooper had to hurry through the twisting hallways to keep up with sneaker-shod Allison. The latter did not glance back until she came to a full stop before the open door of her office. The room had just enough space for a small desk, two chairs, and a filing cabinet. Homey touches included stray bits of museum property, including fossilized conch shells and a black metal sword. The windowsill doubled as a bookshelf, and thick filaments of ivy obscured the outside world. In summer, Cooper mused, exterior greenery would completely block the view.

"I don't want to get off on the wrong foot ..." Cooper began.

"This won't take long enough for that to matter." Zebar scooped yellowing file folders from the visitor's chair and dropped them on the floor beside it. She settled back in her own chair, propping her feet on the desk. Stuck to the sole of her right sneaker was a brown-and-gray feather. "I'm sure there's little I can tell you. You're related to Lynda Cooper, I take it?"

"Her mother." Cooper tore her gaze from the feather and sat down. Her beige wool skirt itched. She'd hoped to buy more comfortable clothes that morning, but the only nearby boutique that opened before the museum did had very little stock to choose from. Just finding the right size was a victory, though she considered her build average. "Did you know Lynda?"

"Not at all, as I told Lieutenant Foster, whom you should be talking to." She coughed. "However, I'll use any excuse to give my dust-filled lungs a break. I'm sorry I can't be of help, Mrs. Cooper ..."

"Francine. Fran, if you like. Fair is fair, Allison."

Zebar clicked her tongue against the roof of her mouth. Francine Cooper knew how to get things. She'd have to be alert.

"Fran, then. I'd never heard of your daughter until Lieutenant Foster mentioned her name."

"You knew Gary Cross, though."

Zebar shifted her buttocks on the hardwood seat. The foot with the feather dropped to rest on the edge of a partly-open drawer. She frowned.

"You're not related to him, too, are you? A secret marriage the police haven't uncovered, or something?"

"Nothing so tangible."

"Personnel records are confidential, if that's what you're after."

Cooper leaned forward, cradling her purse in her lap. "Allison, all I know from Foster is that Cross sold illicit drugs. He dismissed Lynda as a client or accomplice. The police don't care about her true status. I do."

"What are you getting at?"

Cooper sighed. "I don't know. I'm just collecting data, trying to make sense out of my daughter's murder."

Despite her own wariness, Zebar liked the older woman. "Murder never makes sense, Fran. I know platitudes aren't very helpful, but that one's true. You'll only wear yourself down."

"It's my way of coping with the loss."

Zebar stifled a sneeze. She brushed a cloud of dust from her denim shirt. "I still can't help you."

"I've already filled in some blanks on Cross. I know that he was a janitor here between May and July, and that he has not worked since. Nor did he apply for unemployment insurance, since he was ineligible. In 1978 he was involved in a scheme to defraud the state unemployment office."

"My God." Zebar's liking became tinged with awe. "How did you learn all that? I'll bet Foster doesn't have half those details."

Cooper hesitated a fraction of a second. Her occupation had so far only made it more difficult to persuade people that her interest was personal. However, she wanted Zebar's confidence. To gain that, she had to show her hand.

"I'm a professional researcher, Allison. A few minutes at a library and a couple of telephone calls to the right people. That's all it took."

Allison found a mechanical pencil in the clutter on her desk. She twirled it slowly between two fingers, a miniature baton. "I relish this less and less."

"Before you jump down my throat, I am *not* gathering background for an insider's view of the killing. The idea disgusts me."

The pencil clattered on the floor. Zebar ignored it. "I hadn't thought of that. Of course, such an unasked-for denial immediately excites my suspicions."

"I have to take that chance, if I expect you to take a chance on me."

"I believe you, but I still can't tell you anything. Let me show you back downstairs, Fran. I've got a shitload of files to wade through. I'll be clocking overtime through the New Year's holiday as it is, and the museum can't afford my overtime."

Cooper flattened a hand palm down on the smooth desktop. Blue veins stood out in sharp relief.

"I'll strike a bargain, Allison. Talk to me about Gary Cross, and I'll lend you my researching expertise."

Zebar moistened her lips. She'd been begging for *any* kind of aid for the past twenty-four hours. An offer of professional help was more temptation than she should be subjected to.

"Assure me again. This *really* isn't for publication?"

"Word of honor."

Son of a bitch, Zebar thought. I do believe her! "Ask."

After five minutes, Cooper decided that Cross's only redeeming features were passably good looks and a superficial sophistication. Allison Zebar had discouraged more than one attempt of his to pick her up, and Cooper thought the public relations woman's tastes were likely similar to Lynda's. The two shared a common-sense attitude and responsible maturity. Perhaps Lynda simply drank too much that night, or there was an external factor yet to be uncovered. Possibly both. Cooper hoped the external factor wasn't the same one Amos Foster had postulated, but she was beginning to despair of ever pinning it down.

Zebar described Cross's clumsy effort to seduce an apprentice modeler beneath the stuffed elephants in the Hall of Africa.

"Is that why he was dismissed?" Cooper asked.

Zebar laughed. "I would have fired him then, but that's not my department. The last straw ... well, it's not exactly a secret, but we'd prefer it didn't get around. Bad publicity, and embarrassing as hell."

"Rape?"

"Nothing so violent. Cross was stealing from the basement inventory. We never knew how much until yesterday. A night guard had caught him with a brontosaurus skull under his jacket."

Cooper sat upright. "A what?"

"Actually, it was an intrinsically worthless plaster cast. Not even accurate. You may have heard of the recent flap when paleontologists determined that for decades the wrong skull has been attributed to the thunder lizard. Naturally, the things are being replaced throughout the world's museums as fast as casts from a known authentic skull can be made. Our old skull was put into storage. Cross took a fancy to it."

"Why, if it was worthless ... ?"

"Intrinsically worthless, Fran. It still represents an investment of time and materials, and it's a footnote to paleontological history. There's also the principle of the thing— can't have employees walking off with museum property—and the fear that Cross may have been making a dry run. If he'd been able to lift an awkward piece of junk, he might try for something more valuable, such as a few pieces from our gem collection."

"Which someone did manage over the Labor Day weekend," Cooper interrupted.

Zebar nodded. "The police tried to tie Cross to that, but he had an alibi, I forget what. Of course, we know now that the skull wasn't his first theft."

"Then the artifacts found on his houseboat belong to the museum."

Zebar ran a hand through her silver-blond hair. "We're fairly certain. One of our anthropologists identified a West Indian doll he'd purchased in 1968. That was luck. There's a hell of a lot of stuff in our basement, and more in various storage rooms. It's hard to tell what's missing without an exhaustive search of inventory records."

"The project you're grousing about," Cooper observed.

Zebar grinned. "Am I that obvious? Yes, we're going over records of expeditions and acquisitions back to the founding of the museum, even to when we didn't have a museum and everything was stored downtown at Brown Brothers."

Cooper worried her lower lip. "The police are holding the objects as evidence, aren't they? How can you match them up?"

"They sent us photographs." Zebar reached across her desk

to grasp the topmost of the stack of manila envelopes, and skimmed it to Cooper. "You'd better have a set of prints if you're helping us look."

Cooper bent back the clasp, slid the glossies out and spread them flat on the desk. Zebar lowered her feet to the floor. "Ready?" she asked, starting to rise.

Cooper shook her head. "I have to talk to a couple of Cross's earlier employers."

Zebar slumped back in her chair, disappointed but resigned. She couldn't force Francine Cooper to honor her promise, and she had to admit the information on Cross was worth little. Although she'd warned the older woman that would be the case!

"Beggars can't be choosers. I'll leave word with the guards to admit you when you return." Her tone said if, not when. Cooper could not miss that.

To reassure the young woman, Cooper said, "Can we go over the photographs quickly before I leave? That'll give my subconscious something to work on."

Zebar blinked. She couldn't refuse a token of good faith. "Sure." She tapped the first photograph with an unpolished nail. "That Mayan stone pot is probably the most valuable of Cross's collection, worth about a grand to the right collector, yet it's so common and in such poor condition we never missed it. Not suitable for public display."

"Why steal such things?"

Zebar grimaced. Good faith! The older woman was still trying to understand Gary Cross, or at least what it was about the former janitor that might have attracted her daughter. Zebar had walked into the trap with eyes open wide. Might as well go through with it.

"Abnormal psychology is not my field. Possibly Cross swiped more than was found on his boat, and kept what he couldn't sell."

"No discretion."

"No brains, which is why I never really believed he had anything to do with the Labor Day robbery." Her fingers moved. "This one here is a bitch and a half. A trilobite fossil. No way to prove that's one of ours. A chip is missing where our Gode number would have been. The police may give us the benefit of the doubt. Those Siberian sleigh bells appear to be from our last great Russian expedition at the end of the nineteenth century. I've got two staffers re-reading the handwritten diaries and comparing them to inventory lists. This blobby thing is, or was, a Japanese tsuga—a swordhilt. It's in terrible condition, but interesting because it's over a thousand years old and forged in cast iron, rather than carved from wood or ivory. This was the only item in Cross's collection to show extensive recent damage. Seems to have been pried open. I suppose he could have used it for hiding drugs, but you can't fit much in that narrow hollow."

The photograph captured Cooper's attention. One side of the tsuga was etched with Japanese characters. Cooper spoke little Japanese and read none, but the calligraphy conveyed an uneasy air of menace. She shivered. An eddy of air stirred below her knees.

Zebar paused, eyes narrowing. "Are you all right, Fran?"

Cooper nodded. She took a deep breath. "Just a draft."

"I felt nothing. Close the door behind you, if you like."

Cooper did not move to the door. Her gaze focused on the dark object that leaned against the wall, under the windowsill. She looked at the last photograph again.

"I see why you're so sure about this hilt. It looks like a spare for that blade."

Zebar turned to follow Cooper's line of sight. She frowned. "That's odd. I don't remember bringing that up here. Yes, I do. I think." She waved a disparaging hand. "We stumbled across the sword yesterday, but the hilt had already been identified. A senior administrator remembered it. The museum had been threatened with a lawsuit over a group of objects that included the tsuga … and that sword. That was only about twenty years ago, so the documentation had been duplicated in a more accessible area." She glared at the sword again, wrinkling her nose. Her fingers moved to the next photograph. "Now, this fragment...

"Stop a moment, Allison. This bothers me." Cooper picked up the tsuga photograph and turned it in her hands. Light shimmered from the glossy coating. She resisted an impulse to reach for the sword itself. "Doesn't it seem strange to you that the only museum piece damaged on Cross's boat was part of a recent lawsuit?"

"Twenty years ago isn't that recent," Zebar protested, "and the suit never reached the courts."

"Unlikely connections sometimes bear interesting fruit. What was the lawsuit about?"

Zebar sighed. Compliance would take less time than argument. She flipped through pages on her desk until she came to a yellowed file folder. Its tag was in smudged pencil. She opened it flat in the center of the desk and scanned the brittle contents.

"A Japanese-American," she began, "named Matthew Kura claimed the museum had illegally obtained certainly family heirlooms that were his by right of inheritance." She looked up, meeting Cooper's cool gaze. "Since it's my job, I feel obliged to justify the museum's position. I won't say there weren't a lot of shady deals involving museums a century ago. At least as many as there are today in spite of modern safeguards. However, this particular purchase was completely legal, even if the museum's representative took unfair advantage of the chaos following the Meiji Restoration to pick up swords and art objects at bargain prices. Samurai families were struggling for daily food. Kura claimed a dozen items all together, including some exquisite netsuke, a lacquer cabinet, a samurai court costume, two fine swords, and that iron weapon you keep staring at, which was likely reserved for ceremonial functions. It's totally useless for battle."

Cooper nodded thoughtfully. "How was the case resolved?"

"The museum's lawyers were negotiating an amicable out-of-court settlement with Mr. Kura when the old man died. He'd suffered poor health since World War II, which he spent in a relocation camp in Idaho. Not one of our government's better ideas. His only survivor, a son, let it drop. Oh, I didn't notice that before." Zebar unfolded a crackling, legal-sized sheet of thin paper.

Cooper leaned forward. "What is it?"

"The son's release. It isn't signed. Ah, I see. Young Kura was just under the legal age for signing contracts. No guardian was appointed by the father's will. Looks like we forgot to follow up."

"The son's name?"

"Andrew Kura."

"The commercial photographer?"

Zebar lifted an eyebrow. "I've no idea. Do you know him?"

"I've come across the name. My work often involves permissions and reproduction rights. How solid was Matthew Kura's case?"

Zebar skimmed the rest of the file. "Solid enough for the museum to prefer a settlement. Aha! Here's a genealogy going back to the middle of the Tokugawa shogunate era. More than adequate for Kura's purposes. Hmm. The family name was originally Akuragawa. No doubt shortened by some immigration clerk when Matthew arrived in San Francisco in the thirties. Quotas were rough then, too."

"Any indication why the son dropped the case?"

Zebar shook her head. "I can guess. Ancestor worship is slowly dying out, even in Japan."

"Too bad."

Zebar shrugged.

Cooper reached for the brittle release form, handling it delicately. "Without his signature on this, Andrew Kura could reinstate the suit, couldn't he?"

"If he cares to."

Cooper was suddenly tired of sitting. She sprang to her feet. "My first contribution will be to get that signature."

Zebar groaned. "You know, Fran, these other problems are much more, er, problematic."

"It won't take long. If he *is* the photographer, the Japan Society will have an address. They keep tabs on celebrities of Japanese descent. I know one of the higher-ups, and even if he's not in New York his name will open doors. I'll bet Kura lives here in the city. His father lived here, didn't he? Wouldn't he have had to establish residency for the lawsuit?"

Sighing, Zebar bent to retrieve her mechanical pencil from

the floor. She tapped its blunt end on her desk. "This has no relevance to my inventory search … or to your daughter's murder."

"Likely not," Cooper agreed buoyantly. "Hunches don't always pan out. But sometimes they do, and that's too often for me to ignore my instincts. I must talk to this young man."

"Young? He must be nearing forty."

"Younger than I am, anyway." Cooper folded the release into her handbag and shuffled the photographs back in their envelope, which she tucked under her arm.

"You'll come back?" asked Zebar, with little hope.

"I promised, didn't I?" Then she was gone.

Zebar twisted in her chair and stared at the entwined, leafless vines outside her window. She felt certain she'd been taken advantage of and half convinced she would never see Mrs. Cooper again. Yet she still couldn't help liking the handsome woman, and Cooper *seemed* sincere. You didn't make a freelance living with a record of broken promises. What Allison Zebar did not understand was Mrs. Cooper's sudden compulsion to track down an obscure photographer whose connection with both their objectives seemed tenuous.

Francine Cooper did not understand it, either. Then.

CHAPTER 37

Sunlight glared on the Hudson River, reflecting into Lieutenant Amos Foster's bleary eyes. The detective blinked, eyes tearing in the wind. The sluggish-flowing water looked exceptionally cold and gray to him this morning.

Foster stepped back from the railing at the rocky shore. He crossed the asphalt path and entered the sharply-defined shadow of a leafless elm. Deceived by spring-like weather over the past few days, the tree had put forth tentative buds. These would freeze and blacken before the year was out.

Foster added a line to the observations in his black loose-leaf notebook. He slipped his ballpoint pen under the wire loops, clipping it to the cover, and returned the whole thing to his left breast pocket. His eyes drifted to the chalk outline at the path's eastern lip. Where an old man had bled away the few years of life remaining, another man half his age now knelt gingerly, scraping up further samples of blood and tissue and soil and anything else the Forensic Lab might find remotely useful. Specimens were placed in individual plastine envelopes and meticulously labeled. Another field specialist moved through defoliated underbrush as if she were stalking a gun-shy doe. Periodically she, too, stopped to fill envelopes.

Foster wished that Ed Bailey was on the scene, but this morning Ed was autopsying Gary Cross. As soon as the lieutenant heard from Doctor Asprin about the fatal blood clot, he insisted Bailey handle the official inquiry. By now, though, an ambulance bearing two more corpses for Bailey's urgent attention should be arriving at the Medical Examiner's building. Just in time to spoil the doctor's lunch plans. Foster pictured

Bailey's reaction and permitted himself a tight smile.

Sometimes even this part of the job had compensations.

Worn leather scuffed black asphalt. Sergeant Joseph Evans, his raincoat unbuttoned and flapping in the cold breeze, joined his partner. Evans had been supervising a similar scene to the northeast. His victim was a much younger man named Richard Alexander Jones.

Foster looked at him incuriously.

"Officer Gottfried said you wanted to see me," Evans began.

Foster nodded. He rubbed his eyes. "I'm almost through here, Joe. You?"

"The same. These are good people picking over the scene. Did you tag the old man?"

"Found his wallet. Norman Wilding. Born 1899. Current address, Wilton Hotel."

"That's an S.R.O. east of Broadway," Evans observed with a grimace. Single Room Occupancy hotels on the Upper West Side of Manhattan were too often the best accommodations elderly people on limited incomes could afford, and they grew scarcer as one by one they were being transformed into high-priced condominiums. The Wilton was better than most of the survivors. Only a handful of rooms were reserved on an hourly basis for the neighborhood hookers, and other illegal dealings were confined to the lower floors to permit more and faster escape routes.

"I know," said Foster. "No next of kin indicated, though. Gottfried was to check out the room after he delivered my message. He might find something among Wilding's personal effects, a letter with a return address or something."

Evans wiped his mouth with the knuckles of his right hand. "Eighty-three years old," he mused aloud. "Seventeen years short of a century. The things Norm Wilding's seen! Two world wars, mass-produced automobiles, the electric light ... and it ends like this."

Any reply Foster could make would seem trite. The sergeant's father, who lived alone in a Brooklyn brownstone on which he'd paid up the mortgage a quarter-century ago, was entering his ninetieth year. A rift between father and son had not completely healed, but they got along well enough. With each birthday celebrated by the elder Evans, Joe seemed to find new things to respect in his old man. Longevity carried a mystique transcending differences of opinion.

Sergeant Evans shook off his reflective mood. "I guess this clinches your rival drug gang theory, Amos. Jones was holding about half an ounce of weed. The regular beat man remembers warning him recently when he'd tried pushing joints near a playground. I'll pull his yellow sheet, of course, but it seems Jones rarely carried enough junk to qualify for more than a misdemeanor. No hard stuff the beat man knows about. What's wrong with it, Amos?"

Foster started shaking his head halfway through Evans's speech.

"That theory's in the toilet, Joe. Mr. Wilding put it there. Why kill *him?*"

"Possible witness?"

"You know better, Joe. The bodies were too far apart. If Wilding was near enough to see the Jones assault, he couldn't have gotten this far at his age. The killer could have caught him earlier. And Wilding would have headed for the street, where there was a chance of getting help, rather than go along the river."

Evans licked his lips, reluctant to accuse the late Norman Wilding of criminal intent. "Try this on," he said at last. "Suppose Wilding is a steady customer for Jones. Lots of old folks go for the milder street drugs, if they can't get the treatment they think they need legally. Maryjane is considered helpful by some for arthritis pain and cataracts ..."

Foster stroked his chin. "That angle hadn't occurred to me, Joe. I like it because it saves my hypothesis, but that's not a good enough reason. Wilding wasn't coming back from a buy because there was no marijuana on him, and he wasn't on his way to meet Jones because he didn't have enough cash even for a nickel bag. He did have a couple of bucks in the wallet, so he wasn't robbed, either."

Evans turned narrowed eyes to the river. A barge piled high with garbage was being towed south, to be dumped in the

Atlantic Ocean. The scenic view. "There could be some other connection we don't know about."

"There could be, Joe, but we can't work on what we don't know. In hindsight, I see how thin the gang war theory is. Gary Cross is—was—small potatoes on the drug scene. Anyone with enough clout to have him hit is too powerful to work up a sweat over him. And there's the really damning point: our best suspects on that angle were either in custody for questioning or under surveillance last night."

"There's always the possibility of new talent."

Foster sighed. "I'd like to believe that, Joe. I'd like to believe that there's a reasonable pattern to these brutal killings, and a little hard-nosed detective work will nail the bastard, and no one else will be taken down." He clasped his hands behind his back and stared at the towering apartment buildings dotting the cliffs of the New Jersey Palisades. "No one new, Joe. I went over that a dozen times last night, with Narcotics. The only thing new on the streets was our own manhunt for Cross and his possible assailants. That activity alone would have persuaded fresh talent to pull in its horns rather than strike again."

Evans nodded, unsurprised. He'd seen where Foster was leading, but he also knew the lieutenant had to talk it out, perhaps not for the first time, before admitting it to himself. Still Foster hesitated to pin the label on. So Evans did it.

"We're looking for a psychopathic killer, then."

Foster's lips thinned. His face paled slightly, as if a drop of cream had been added to already light coffee. The insane ones were the most difficult to run to ground. There was no discernible motive, no useful pattern, no way to predict where or when he would kill again. The police could possess clues aplenty, but these would be meaningless unless they got lucky. Until then, they could only collect more clues—which meant more victims.

"Lieutenant!" called the detective in the bushes. "I've found something you ought to see."

Welcoming a break from his musings, Foster waddled over, followed by his partner. Leaving the asphalt, both men took care to step only in the forensic detective's footprints, but their ᴄ were larger than the woman's and inevitably disturbed more ᴄound.

When Foster stood in the last pair of footprints, save those the detective herself occupied, she pointed out an even larger print in a small, clear spot ahead of them. Broken twigs were scattered at the outline.

"This guy is a size eighteen, easy," she said.

"Missing a couple of toes, too," Foster observed. "No gaps, though. Maybe a birth defect. The size, however … no one could be that big. You're sure it isn't a freak natural deformation?"

She looked up at Foster with cool hazel eyes. "I've seen footprints in melting snow look overlarge, but this is simply moist soil. Not even as plastic as mud. Nothing indigenous to the City of New York leaves a track like this." She wiped a dirty hand on her slacks and pulled a tape measure from her shirt pocket.

"A hoax," Foster offered. "Kids fooling around."

"Hoaxers would want it to be discovered," the woman replied, as she unraveled the tape. "They would've picked a more obvious spot. Also it was done *after* last night's rain. The track is well-defined, barely weathered."

Foster licked dry lips. "In which case they should have spotted the body and reported it … or at least taken the wallet."

Evans cleared his throat. "There's something else, Amos. I found two similar prints near an overpass just west of Jones's body."

"You didn't mention that."

"It'll be in my report. Like yourself, I didn't think it immediately relevant. Until now."

"You had them photographed anyway, didn't you?"

Evans nodded. "And casts made. When it doubt, check it out. First rule for detectives."

Foster turned back to the woman from Forensics. "Then we'll do the same here, Detective … ah, I'm sorry, I didn't catch your name and rank?"

The woman glanced up through a tangle of jet-black hair. "Sergeant Maria Barracas. I was transferred last week from Staten Island. And you may have noticed that I'm already setting up for photos."

Foster evaded her eyes as he made the entry in his notebook. "Sergeant Barracas. I'll remember it now. You're in charge of the wrap-up here. I want a full report by four this afternoon."

"You'll have it by three, Lieutenant, if you and your friend will let my partner through with the camera."

Foster and Evans eased back the way they had come, retracing their steps except when they stepped around the approaching photographer. Thorns clung abundantly to Foster's sweater and jacket as he stepped clear of the brush. Evans's free-hanging raincoat escaped such nuisances almost completely.

"Touchy lady," Evans observed.

"Edgy," Foster corrected. He plucked at his clothing, trying not to get scratched. "Her first big case."

"I guess."

Foster cursed and sucked a punctured thumb.

"Let's walk south along the river."

"Do you want to see my footprints?"

"No. It's enough that they exist. I hope they can give us an angle on the killer's psychological makeup. I have to assume he's making these tracks with modified boots or shoes. Even if he's just kicking up dust, we can start a profile on him."

Evans grinned. "I see the headlines now. 'Bigfoot Baffles Cops.'"

Foster stiffened to a halt. "The papers don't have this yet, do they?"

"Bits and pieces. Only a matter of time."

The lieutenant relaxed and began walking again. "We'll use that time while we can. We've got reliable people on the spot here. Nothing more you and I can do until they get some lab results. Why don't you go home to Liz and get some shut-eye? I want you fresh tonight."

"Stake-out?"

"Of course."

Evans studied his senior partner's sagging face. "You're the one who ought to be in bed. You look shagged out."

"I'll head for my place as soon as I clear the stake-out duty with Captain Matherson."

Evans swiveled his head eastward. Dark green pines and

their leafless fellow trees cast deep shadows in the winter sunlight. Manhattan was a hell of a place for an enchanted forest.

"Do you really think," the sergeant said, "he'll hit the same area three nights in a row?"

"No," answered Foster, not looking at his partner. "No more than I'd've thought he'd hit it two nights running. But it's the only pattern we've got. Have you a better idea?"

Evans hadn't.

CHAPTER 38

Jiro Nakato's office, on the third floor of Japan House, was conveniently narrow and arbitrarily dark. Bookshelves lined its eastern wall, crammed with methodically-arranged and necessarily thick volumes. Opposite stood a five-tiered display case with a credenza for a pedestal, guarded by a pair of the ordinary straight-backed wooden chairs used by students in the language classes that the Japan Society continually offered. The case's dusty glass protected a dozen well-spaced, exquisitely-carved ivory netsuke, a traditional artform that had sprung from the desire, centuries before, for decorative toggles with which to seal one's containers, for traveling the Japanese countryside.

Other Society offices looked out on broad East Forty-Seventh Street, or across First Avenue to the United Nations Plaza, or on the small but soothing bamboo garden partially enclosed by the building. Nakato could have asked for one of these, but divined no reason why he should deprive someone better able to enjoy the view. A breeze from the airshaft between Japan House and its northern neighbor on First Avenue ruffled curtains drawn before the single, partly-open window.

Mr. Nakato sat placidly at his desk, undisturbed by the draught at his back. He wore a dark gray three-piece suit, with the vest buttoned but the jacket open, and his thin blue tie boasted an impeccable knot. His face was shrouded in shadow, his eyes concealed by the smoked lenses of his aviator-style glasses. He turned his head slightly as the door creaked open, so that he seemed to be staring at a murky corner rather than his visitor.

"Nakato-san," greeted Francine Cooper, inclining her head.

The Japanese term of familiar respect had seemed awkward on her tongue ten years earlier. Then the two had met daily for more than a fortnight, collaborating on a catalog for an exhibition of Edo-era netsuke at Boston's Fine Arts Museum. Now it seemed so natural that Cooper hadn't realized she was going to use it until she had.

She paused in the doorway, letting her eyes adjust from the fluorescent glare in the corridor.

"Mrs. Cooper." Nakato smiled, flashing strong teeth. Interpreting her hesitation, he reached across his desk for the knob on the shaded sea-shell lamp. The room brightened at a twist. Just as smoothly, Nakato was out of his chair, negotiating the space between desk and bookcase with balletic grace, grazing neither. He met Cooper halfway, following the clack of her low heels on the uncarpeted floor. "Francine."

The woman grasped Nakato's outstretched hands and raised them to her face. She smiled for his fingers, as they traced her cheekbones. His touch was as light as a butterfly's wings. When Nakato lowered his hands, his grin had broadened. Cooper reached out herself, removed his dark glasses, and slipped them into the case in his jacket's breast pocket.

Nakato accepted the liberty with guarded approval. Cooper was one of a handful of people outside of his immediate family with whom he could unselfconsciously expose the shriveled sockets. When he was eight years old, his eyes had been burned out by the same blast that flattened his home city of Nagasaki.

"Please excuse me for greeting you with such Stygian illumination." Nakato spoke without an accent. He had a keen ear for language.

"Not so Stygian," Cooper replied. "Back in 1972, you insisted on writing up your part of the catalog in a hotel room that was darker than the inside of a black cat."

Nakato chuckled. That had been a pet phrase of his. "Such a show-off, wasn't I? Lately, though, I find I like a bit of light in a room, for its warmth. It takes little to satisfy that whim. Ten years makes a difference. Nearly eleven years, now." Unerringly, Nakato dragged one of the straight-backed chairs nearer his desk, and reclaimed his own seat.

"Eleven years since we last met," Cooper mused, taking her seat. She placed her purse and manila envelope on the floor. "You haven't aged a day, Jiro."

Nakato ran a thin, paste-white hand through his wiry crewcut. He acknowledged the compliment with a slight head-bow. "A felicitous heritage. Our reunion might have been delayed several more years, had you come three hours later. I leave this evening for my homeland on a year's sabbatical. I have some long-overdue research to do with original sources. Fate has smiled upon us."

"A happy coincidence, at least."

Nakato pursed his lips. "There are no coincidences, Francine, merely connections that we do not perceive. An example. I did not know you would come here today, but I tried to telephone you in Boston yesterday."

"Oh?"

Nakato clasped his hands before him on the desk. "Francine, you did not have to force a smile for my sake."

Cooper shifted uneasily, and stopped on realizing that each creak of her chair's joints was further confirmation to the man's ears. "Am I so obvious?"

"Your facial muscles were tense. Your voice is strained. I should have known something was wrong even had I not heard of your daughter's passing. I had called to extend my sympathies. Lynda was a delightful and exasperating little girl. Do you remember the weekend I visited your home, and you were called away for an hour?"

"Vaguely."

"She immediately invited two friends over and insisted we play blind-man's buff until you returned."

"She didn't!" Cooper reddened. "I'm terribly sorry, Jiro. If I'd known ..."

"Precisely why I did not tell you. Now I have another reason to be glad I held my tongue. In your time of bereavement, I am able to offer you this small part of Lynda that you did not know."

Cooper reached under her chair and drew a package of tissues from her purse. She had thought herself cried out the day before but the thin paper soon grew soggy. Nakato waited, his scarred face impassive. Cooper took several deep breaths to recover her voice.

"Thank you, Nakato-san. I cannot repay this debt."

The eyeless man again bowed his head. "Between friends, it is not necessary. Now," he continued firmly, "forgive my brusqueness, but I have spent too much time in this city for its attitudes not to have worn off onto me. What information do you require?"

Cooper sat erect, startled. "What?"

Nakato ticked off his points on his bloodless fingers. "This is no social visit, or you would have telephoned first to be certain I was available. It is not in response to my call, for I left no message on your recorder; what I had to say was better said directly or not at all. So you have come to the Japan society for information."

Her grief temporarily purged again, Cooper felt a more natural smile cross her lips. "If you had eyes, no secrets would be safe. You're right, of course, Jiro. Last year, the Society exhibited the work of several prominent Japanese-American photographers."

Nakato leaned back. His fingers forms a steeple over his top vest button. The curtain rustled behind him.

"I recall the event, Francine. I was not personally involved. Photography is an artform that eludes my appreciation. I can enjoy a painting when I'm permitted to touch the canvas, feel the texture of the oils, the varying warmths of the colors ... yes, I like that very much. The Society has assembled an exhibition of old shop-signs to run through this coming Spring, which I regret I'll miss. Unfortunately, one sheet of chemically-treated paper feels like another. We have catalogs left, if you wish one."

"I'm interested in one photographer. Andrew Kura."

"Kura? Kura." Nakato tugged his lower lip. "Ah. Not exactly the star attraction, as I recall the reviews."

"I need his address."

"Done." Nakato reached for his telephone. His longer fingers jabbed three buttons before Cooper could blink. In a moment, he followed this with a burst of rapid-fire Japanese.

Cooper allowed her gaze to wander over Nakato's library. Dozens of hand-bound Braille translations of rare and valuable research material occupied the middle, most-used, shelves. Many of these books were one-of-a-kind, painstakingly copied by Nakato himself from an assistant's dictation.

The receiver returned to its cradle with a sure click. "I did not mean to exclude you, Francine. The clerk I spoke to is not a Japanese native. I like to keep their language skills honed. Had I gotten a native speaker, I'd have used English."

"No explanations are necessary, Nakato-san."

"Keep it Jiro. I also took the liberty of ordering a pot of green tea and some pastries. You will join me in a light lunch?"

"Have I a choice?"

"None whatsoever. Is it permitted to ask why you require this man's address?"

Cooper bit her lower lip. "It's a sort of favor for someone at the American Museum of Natural History."

Nakato raised a patchy eyebrow. "I did not know it was that institution's policy to recruit errand-runners from the ranks of out-of-town bereaved parents."

Cooper lowered her head, ashamed that she should hold back anything from this man, after the great gift he had just given her. As if Nakato would somehow betray her! As if he *could* when, in a few hours, he would be on an airplane headed halfway around the world! She'd only had to say "No" and Nakato would respect her privacy, but he deserved better than half-truths and evasions..

"It's a favor for myself as well, Nakato-san. Jiro. I am probably on a wild goose chase. The fewer people who know about it, the less embarrassed I'll feel when it comes to nothing."

"Then we shall speak of other matters."

"I appreciate your understanding."

The silence that followed was long and awkward. Jiro Nakato was patient. Cooper suddenly leaned forward, resting both palms flat on the desk. "Here's the meat of it: I cannot reconcile the circumstances of Lynda's death with what I know of her habits."

Nakato permitted a tiny twitch to the corner of his mouth. "People change. Also, there may be motives that are unknown … and unknowable."

Cooper sighed. She sat back in her chair. "That has not escaped me."

"The trail, then, leads to Andrew Kura?"

Cooper shrugged; even with the scar tissue over the eyesockets in full view, it was easy to forget Nakato could not see the gesture. "A side-trail, anyway. I don't know. I'm floundering, reaching out for any connection that the police seem uninterested in. There's no point in my duplicating their efforts, since they're better equipped to investigate murders than I am. I'm just hoping I'll get lucky."

Nakato smiled thin-lipped. "A moment ago you belittled fate."

Cooper offered no reply.

"Is there any other way I can help you?" asked Nakato. "However, as you say, tenuously?"

Cooper shook her head. "I'm afraid not, Jiro. Believe me, I would not hesitate if … wait. Perhaps there is." She scooped the manila envelope from the floor and undid the clasp.

"What is it?" Nakato said suddenly, pitching his voice louder and swiveling his head back and forth. "Who is there?"

Cooper paused, contents of the envelope half removed. "Jiro? Is something wrong?"

Nakato raised his index finger for silence. "Do you feel a draught?" he whispered. "Hear voices?"

Cooper felt her spine tense and the skin on her arms tighten. There was a rush of air, not unlike the one she'd sensed in Allison Zebar's office. It did not quite touch her flesh.

She laughed abruptly. "The window is open. There's your draught!"

Nakato shook his head slowly.

"I don't hear any voices, though," she continued. "What are they saying?"

"I don't know. It is only a faint susurration. Something about the tone hints of power. And *giri*."

"Giri?"

"One's duty." Nakato clicked his tongue. "Tcha! It's gone now."

"It was probably someone in another office standing too

near an airshaft window. You're closer than I am, and your ears are certainly keener."

Nakato brushed the top of his head with a damp palm. "Yes, perhaps. Where were we?"

Cooper singled out a photograph and carried it to Nakato's side of the desk. Her skirt brushed a shelf; she was not clumsy, but could not match his grace. She placed the picture flat on the desk before him.

"I should have thought of this downstairs, when they told me you were in. You're an expert on ancient Japanese lore. If anyone can translate this inscription, it's you."

Nakato spread his hands humbly. "I can at least try."

"This is a photograph of a mangled sword hilt. The damage distorts the characters somewhat. So does the angle at which the picture was taken. The text is almost certain irrelevant to what I want to know. Still..."

"We may get lucky?" finished Nakato.

"Fate may smile on us again," Cooper admitted, smiling herself.

"It is the hilt alone? No blade?" Nakato inquired, as Cooper took his pale right hand in hers.

"Yes. I see what you're getting at. No, no inscriptions on the blade, not even a swordmaker's mark. Just an ordinary straight sword."

"Ah. If it is not curved, it must be quite old, indeed. Proceed."

Slowly, gently. Cooper guided Nakato's long, thin index finger along the strokes that made up the characters. "This is a fairly thick line," she commented, "tapering off right there. Yes. This hairline crosses it midway ... so ..."

"There should be another line to its left."

Cooper squinted at the picture, all but touching it with her nose as she leaned forward. The bright desk lamp reflected off the glossy coating.

"Hard to tell, Jiro. If so, it's very faint, likely well-worn. Whoever took this picture was not going for legibility of graven characters."

Again the fingers traced the image, as Cooper described the relative thickness of each stroke. Nakato merely nodded, memorizing the shapes. Whenever she paused, he bid her to continue.

In the middle of the final character Nakato jerked his hand away as if burnt. Cooper withdrew her own hand in reaction. The photograph skittered across the desk and fluttered to the polished wood floor.

"What's the matter, Jiro?" Cooper asked as she retrieved the picture. "What does it say?"

Nakato moistened his lips. The scar tissue covering his eye-sockets began to pulse, an indicator of stress. The cause of the stress was not tangible, not even definable. He turned in his chair, stretched his right arm to its fullest, and shut the airshaft window.

The office seemed no less chilly.

A small warm circle on the back of his left hand. Francine Cooper's touch.

"Are you all right, Jiro?"

Nakato squeezed Cooper's palm. The woman wanted distraction, needed it, but the vague disquiet that tightened his bowels was, he felt, not what she was looking for.

"Anticipation of my flight." He shrugged. "At my age, excitement must be taken in small doses."

Cooper returned to her own chair and slid the photograph back into its envelope. "Can you say anything about the inscription?"

Nakato nodded, steepling his index fingers under his chin. "Very old and, as you observed, badly worn. I cannot give you a literal translation. The overall impression is cautionary, but this is so ambiguous that the object itself could be the subject of the warning. One of the characters is a protective rune, combined with a plea to the kami—the ancestral spirits. Perfectly normal for a talisman, which this seems to be. That object may have been created as a sword hilt, but I doubt it ever served that function."

Cooper toyed with the reclosed envelope, running a finger along its edges. "The blade it supposedly belongs to was fitted with another, less elaborate, hilt."

Nakato clapped his hands. "There. It was not then fashionable to change tsuga, hilts, as one would change one's sash." His voice became somber. "The symbols also convey a strong suggestion of … forgive the dramatic turn of phrase … unutterable evil."

Cooper tugged at the collar of her blouse. The cotton fabric clung to her back. "The police found this … talisman … near Lynda's body. Could that be the source of your impression?"

Nakato laughed. "Such an idea from the rational Mrs. Cooper!"

"I don't disdain irrationality, when it fits the facts. I prefer to have it explained, of course."

The man sighed. "I may seem something of a mystic at times, Francine, but I will not insult your intelligence by claiming psychic powers. It is the shape of the characters, the nature of the strokes, that suggests this evil. Whoever etched these figures was in a state of terror."

"You stopped before we'd finished the last one."

"Yes. I apologize. That was clear enough, anyway. The thing is a charm against oni; possibly a specific oni. Again, I can't be certain."

Cooper's brow furrowed. "Oni? Isn't that the Buddhist term for demons?"

Nakato nodded to the right. "In the showcase behind you, on your left, there's an excellent netsuke image of an oni about to attack. Second shelf. Between the badger-priest and the monkey scholar."

Cooper's chair scraped the hardwood floor as she rose. Standing in front of the case, she bent her knees for an eye-level view and tapped the glass with a fingernail.

"May I hold it?"

"That was my intention. You sighted people usually miss the best qualities of a piece of art. I examine the netsuke frequently. Meditating on the craftsman's skill is one of my fondest pleasures, perhaps a vice. At times I fear I am destroying the very thing I admire, as my fingers slowly wear away the intricate carved details. Then I will not touch them for weeks, until I remember that the plucked flower soon shrivels. Nothing lasts forever."

Gingerly, Cooper drew forth the squat, stocky figure, as tall

as her thumb. The subtlety of its lines, even with so vulgar a
subject, was truly marvelous. Fingers and toes, three digits to
each appendage, even bore tiny cuticles. Bulges at the joints,
more felt than seen, showed where skin folded and doubled
on itself. The head was too large for the body, in keeping with
legendary appearance, and the horns on the skull tapered to
needle sharpness. Teeth were individually limned within their
rows; their points indicated the creature could use caps.

Even the gnarled club held aloft by the right arm had whorls
to represent wood grain.

The grotesque face was nearly split in two by a grin of
awesome malice.

"Lovely work," Cooper said. "Ugly brute. Seems to enjoy his
work, though." She returned the carving to its former position,
defined by a ring of dust.

"That they do," Nakato replied absently. He leaned back,
hands clasped behind his head. "Actually, except for murdering
the occasional traveler, oni led fairly dull lives. They stayed in
their caves most of the time, and liked it. Not unlike some of
your countrymen. There's something to be said for the sluggish
minds demons possessed."

"I thought devils like this were supposed to be clever,
tricking people out of their souls and so forth." Sitting, Cooper
began to play with the manila envelope again.

"You're thinking of occidental demons. Not to mention an
occidental concept of the soul, though that metaphysical can
of worms is better left until we both have more time. A better
European analogy to the oni is the ogre." He pursed his lips.
"Now that I've had a moment to reflect, Francine, I believe
the calligraphic style on that tsuga must be seventh or eighth
century, certainly no later than tenth century. Not many demon
legends date back that far. Chinese Buddhists had to convert a
score or so of emperors before their religion really took hold. The
most ancient story I know of, in which an oni plays a major part,
is the tale of Akuragawa."

The manila envelope slipped from Cooper's fingers and
slapped against the desk with no more sound than that of a cat's
tread.

"Akuragawa," she said, eyes widening, "is Andrew Kura's family's original name."

A smile flickered on Nakato's lips. In his best Warner Oland impersonation, he said, "The similarity of nomenclature had not eluded me." He reached one-handed for the aviator glasses in his jacket pocket, unfolded the earpieces, and slipped them on. "Excuse this, please, Francine. Some of the staff find my unconcealed appearance disturbing. That clatter in the corridor is no doubt the tea I had ordered so long ago. With luck it may still be tepid."

Now that her attention was drawn to it, Cooper became aware of clinking, clacking, rattling sounds beyond the door that she'd closed behind her on entering. A drunken samurai in full armor could not be more conspicuous.

"The Akuragawa story," Nakato continued, "possesses a number of interesting aspects. It even has a certain Arabian Nights flavor which may cause you to doubt its authenticity. You realize, of course, that there is no point in my being one of the few people to know of the legend if I cannot show off my knowledge."

The door opened slowly inward at that point. Nakato fell silent as a young man with rolled-up shirt sleeves entered. The newcomer was clearly unused to balancing such a laden tray, and Cooper could not let him suffer. As she moved to lend a hand, she looked back at Nakato and said, "Jiro, you don't dare *not* tell the story now."

CHAPTER 39

The fitted sheet clung for a moment to Amos Foster's chest and abdomen, peeling free as he rolled onto his back. The linen was beige, as close to his own skin color as Adrianne, his last ladyfriend, could find. A good detective was inconspicuous at all times, she'd said. That seemed amusing on her lips. Foster wouldn't have stood it from anyone else, not even Joe Evans. Well, maybe Joe. But his partner, though addicted to wisecracks, never made racial jokes.

His eyelids fell open. Sunlight, filtering through Venetian blinds, cast bright stripes on the bedroom wall. Because of its southern exposure, this room was comfortably warm in freezing weather and overheated every other season, even with the window air conditioner chugging away in August. Topsheet and bedspread were heaped at the foot of the bed. Foster lay exposed, stripped to his shorts, feeling drops of sweat trickle along or evaporate from his skin.

He knew he'd slept, because the last time he'd noticed the sun-stripes they were halfway across the room. That was good detective work. Unless he just hadn't been paying attention. His head throbbed. Thoughts had been whipping through his brain all afternoon. Not one of them slowed enough for him to grasp. He wasn't sure he wanted to grasp any, at least not just yet.

Eyes fixed on the ceiling, Foster stretched out his left arm. His knuckles scraped the lip of the night table. He raised the hand and hooked the metal ring atop his wind-up alarm clock. Foster distrusted electric clocks. They lulled you into a false sense of security, and then a wire shorted out or a power failure struck while you were asleep. He usually woke before the alarm went off, though.

His elbow bent until the clock face dangled above his broad, flat nose.

Almost two hours before he was due back at the station. Not enough time to risk further sleep. He'd been shortchanging himself, and could plumb somnolent depths that even the alarm's harsh jangle might not penetrate. On the other hand, two hours was too long to be sitting alone doing nothing.

Joe Evans wasn't having this problem. Foster would stake his life on that. Joe could nod off at a moment's notice, even in a squad car, and waken fully in even less time. He never brought his work home with him, at least not so anyone would notice. Not so his wife Elizabeth would notice.

Too lazy to return the clock to the nightstand, Foster laid it on the pillow, beside his ear. The ticking was loud and strong. A gust of air escaped his lips. He sat up, feeling the strain where he'd pulled a back muscle the week before, and the faint, ever-present throb in his leg. The linoleum floor was cool to his bare, callused soles. His toes searched for his red felt slippers. He slid them on without bending over.

Crumpled on the floor by the night table was his bathrobe, which also approximated his skin tone. Adrianne had bought the set for his birthday. It was sexy, she insisted; he looked almost naked even though the robe reached halfway down his calves. He picked it up, grunting. Foster hadn't seen Adrianne since the weekend before Thanksgiving, hadn't spoken to her since the Friday after that holiday when he'd tried explaining over the telephone why he couldn't join the turkey dinner at her parents' home. In the short time they'd been together, Adrianne had heard about too many last-minute shift rotations. Foster had never lied. She knew that. That was what hurt, on both sides. It had not been the first time he'd let her down, but apparently it was the last time she'd allow him to do so.

He draped the robe over his broad shoulders, trying not to think of its origin. Foster was accustomed to such break-ups. He bounced back fairly easily. The difficult part was getting himself to try again. Apart from the handicap of his profession, he found that many women—black, white, whatever—simply did not want to get involved with a man of mixed race. Perhaps he should give up looking. He was getting too old for that sort of thing. Or maybe he was bored with the roller coaster.

A shower would feel good now, Foster decided. A long, hot shower. A two-hour shower. Better yet: a bath.

He sniffed and rubbed his nose. It was plugged with dry mucous, due to the room's aridity. He rose heavily to his feet.

His living room was unfurnished, save for an oversized table and half a score of folding chairs. Here he held infrequent poker parties for his colleagues, mostly. He knew few people outside of the Department. Most of his at-home time was spent in the bedroom, with the television, or the kitchen when he got hungry enough. A narrow door next to the kitchen sink led to the bathroom.

Even through the terrycloth robe, which sagged open in front, the toilet seat cover felt cold and hard. Foster leaned forward and spun the faucets. Water gushed unsteadily, spattering his knees. He captured a cupped handful before it got too hot and splashed it on his face, briskly rubbing cheeks and forehead to complete the waking-up process.

With elbows on knees, he tried to concentrate solely on watching the tub fill. He failed.

No matter how much detective experience you had, Foster mused, occasionally a case got its claws into your emotions and wouldn't let go. You might be struck by the possibility that the victim could have been your mother, or a friend's child, or just someone you'd liked to have known. Or the circumstances were too close to an incident in your own past. Sometimes it simply felt wrong, and you didn't know why.

Foster had never seriously figured Gary Cross for the murder of Lynda Cooper, not even when he'd seen the dead girl's battered corpse amid the splinters of the houseboat's bunk and Cross was the only logical suspect. No one would leave a body where he lived! Foster was so certain that rival drug gangs were involved that he'd ignored loose ends that didn't fit, especially when Cross turned up dying to vindicate himself. A detective's most fundamental error.

The lieutenant's hands knotted into fists, unnoticed.

Because Foster was sure. Homicide had wasted twenty to thirty hours and four were dead instead of two. Five if you counted Eric Fuchsia, who wouldn't have gone off a rooftop if Foster hadn't asked Evans to bring him in. Of course, Captain Matherson offered neither criticism nor encouragement, and would not until the case was solved—or taken away from Foster.

The pounding in his head grew worse. He should take some aspirin. The medicine cabinet was two steps away. He remained seated.

Foster realized that he shouldn't blame himself. Police work consisted mainly of eliminating possibilities. He'd made his best guess, given the information available. He'd not been unresponsive to other probabilities; he lacked the manpower to investigate every one, and had to make a choice. He'd chosen wrong before. A couple of times, people had died because he hadn't hit on the right track earlier. He'd reconciled himself to such situations. He was not omniscient. He was no television cop, saving the world and solving each case in forty-nine minutes (not including commercial breaks). He *knew* better.

Still his head ached, his stomach churned. It wasn't enough this time to tell himself he wasn't negligent. Someone else had to drive that point home. Someone whose opinion he respected, and who did not lie.

Foster was tempted to call Joe Evans at home, right now. Liz would have a fit. Anyway, where was the urgency? He'd see Joe in a couple of hours, and then all night. On stake-out.

Foster yelped and jerked his foot away from the tub. Steaming hot water cascaded over the rim. He quickly shut off the flow. Limping to the sink, he moistened a face towel with cold tap water and held it to the bright red streak on his instep.

At least the steam had unclogged his nostrils.

CHAPTER 48

Bare yellow lightbulbs, one to a landing, cast just enough glow in the gritty, sour-smelling stairwell for Francine Cooper to locate the next bannister. She relied on the scraping of her soles on splintering steps, and the groaning of wood under her weight, for clues to her progress. Gravity itself might be untrustworthy in this gloomy former cotton mill half a block west of lower Broadway. Cooper would not have been greatly surprised to suddenly find herself at any turn facing the street again. Only the lessening traffic sounds seemed to belie this impression.

A bitter, cold updraught accompanied her. She thrust her free hand deeper into the coat pocket.

Cooper had hesitated entering the gray brick building for fear of startling some wino or other drug-besotted derelict. The reputation of the nearby Bowery reached much further than Boston. Now she decided that no one desperate or foolish enough to take refuge in this inhospitable corridor could be much of a threat, if she stayed reasonably alert. It was better than wasting another half hour ringing for the freight elevator while truck drivers and warehousemen alternately cursed each other and made passes at her. Either the bell did not work or Kura was not at home. After all she'd gone through to find the place, she could at least leave a note at his door.

The address in the Japan Society's files was easily found, but a choreographer now occupied that studio. The American Photographers' Institute had been sending his "late dues" notices to a post office box at the Canal Street station. The box was reassigned in October. Cooper called on half a dozen model agencies before she found a woman who had posed for Andrew Kura in mid-November. Fifty Dollars—half of what the model claimed Kura still owned her for the session—was her price for this address.

Having come this close to her goal, Francine Cooper would not quit now.

As she reached the third landing, Cooper became aware of a steady thrumming that rose from the wooden stairboards up through her feet. Earthquakes were not a feature of New York City, but the word flashed through her mind anyway. She froze, fingers whitening on the creaking bannister.

The stairs did not collapse.

This time.

She continued up, slower.

Street sounds were soon overwhelmed by an arhythmic thunk, thunk, ka-thunk from above, joined at frequent but unpredictable intervals by a high-pitched, wavering squeal. Making the turn on the fourth landing, Cooper realized the source of the sound was electronic. When she reached the sixth and last landing to face a sloppy, gothic "K" painted in orange on a sheet metal door, the noise was deafening, and obviously a record or tape of some rock group played at a volume far beyond the capacity of the speaker system. A mere elevator bell could make no impression.

Cooper rapped on the door, and hurt her knuckles. She pounded with a cupped palm. The door flew inward. She stumbled after.

The cavernous loft vibrated with driving rock. Sunlight angled through an overhead skylight, but the row of south-facing windows was covered by cardboard squares held in place by thick strips of black electrical tape. Activity was concentrated in a corner that would have been suffocated in shadow except for a blinding triad of kleig lights arranged to cancel out each others' shadows.

The intense beams focused on a thin young woman with sharp features and shoulder-length red hair. Despite the cooling weather, she wore a minuscule bikini, and danced in jerky, exaggerated movements on a broad, knee-high platform. The backdrop was a turquoise curtain stretched taut on a curved frame along two sides of the platform.

Cooper crossed the empty loft space, shivering inwardly for the model's sake. With those lights in her eyes, the redhead could not see her, and of course could not hear anything as subtle as low-heeled shoes on a bare wooden floor in that aural atmosphere.

Kura popped up suddenly, like one of the birdlike tengu Nakato had mentioned to Cooper over lunch. Instead of a long nose or beak, however, Kura's face was obscured by his camera and the hands that held it. The lens made a satisfactory substitute. A cigarette that was half gray ash dangled beneath the camera, presumably from his lips. His hair was cropped short and stuck up in stiff bristles. He, too, was nearly naked, wearing only a pair of dark green swim trunks. Abdominal flab partly hid the waistband. He'd been lying on the floor for a worm's eye photo series, and flakes of grit stuck to his back. These flew loose as he hopped around the platform, shouting encouragements that Cooper could not make out.

The researcher continued forward until she stood just beyond the circle of white light. She knew then why the pair were not blue with cold. The heat of the lamps was sweltering. Cooper slipped off her heavy cloth coat and folded it over her arm.

Kura backed into her then. Cooper shifted her weight. Her shoulder jolted Kura's, saving them both from a comic spill.

The photographer turned on the intruder. His face twisted in a snarl. Cooper stepped into the light. A sarcastic remark died on Kura's thick lips.

"It's about goddamned time someone at an agency listened to my specs!" Kura draped his camera's strap on a hook on one of the light poles. He backed toward the platform, gesturing Cooper along with both hands. He might have been giving directions for parking a car.

"Come on, let's have a proper look at you. You can't be shy in this business. That's the girl!"

Cooper seethed silently under Kura's gaze, drawing her head out of the stream of his tobacco smoke. He leapt back and forth before her, a mad elf, his glazed eyes roving her body with an offensively detached obscenity. Cooper could not reply at the moment. She was fighting an impulse to make him eat his camera.

"Looks like they had to go back a ways," Kura went on. "No offense meant. Age has not withered you, not where it counts. I can soften the lighting, airbrush the prints. Easy enough to take out a few wrinkles and firm up those tits by shooting from the right angles. What I can't do is add what nature didn't provide in the first place!" He jerked his head at the redhead, who stood stiffly in the center of the platform, hands on hips, hard green eyes glittering as they studied the newcomer.

"You've made a mistake, Mr. Kura," Cooper began.

"Andy. When we're working together, you'll have to call me Andy. I can't get your best work if you don't feel at home, eh?" He cocked his head to one side. "Hey, nice ass, too." He patted it for emphasis.

Cooper grasped the bony wrist and pulled the hand away. She turned sideways, giving the arm a half twist. She didn't need to use the knowledge from her self-defense course often, but when she did she was glad to have it.

Kura yelped. If she applied proper leverage, Cooper could dislocate his shoulder. His cigarette fell to smolder on the rough wood floor. Cooper stamped it out.

"Touch me again," she said, "and you'll have to flick shutters with your left hand."

"All right, all right!"

He stumbled as she let go. Rubbing the wrenched muscles of his arm, Kura stepped back hurriedly, eyes wary. The resounding rock stopped abruptly. Kura's lower lip stuck out.

"Kee-rist!" he exclaimed. "What's with you, anyway? I didn't mean anything. I'm a professional. Like a doctor. You must have been in this business long enough to know that. Hey, Jenny! Put on another tape and get me a fresh cig …"

The platform was empty.

"Jen?"

"She went behind the curtain." Then, because even the Andrew Kuras of the world have feelings, she added, "I don't think she saw your … accident."

Kura grunted gracelessly. "Probably touching up her make-up. She needs it, too. I'll put on more music."

"Don't. I resent having to shout."

"Then don't talk. Just look gorgeous."

"Mr. Kura, I am not your new model."

"Oh."

"Yes. Oh."

Kura's neck seemed to vanish. His tone grew respectful, almost servile. "Cripes. That's why you got pissed. Why didn't you say so? Of course. I should have realized who you were. I didn't expect you so soon."

"You expected me?"

"I know I promised your agency I'd have sprinklers in by the end of the year, but you can't find a plumber over the holidays. I bought new bulbs for the hallway and I'll put them in this weekend ..."

Cooper raised her hand for silence. Kura flinched.

"Nor am I a city inspector, Mr. Kura. My name is Francine Cooper. I'm a professional researcher on a special project for the American Museum of Natural History. Museum ownership of certain artifacts seems to be in doubt. You can assist us by signing this." She drew a yellowing sheet from her purse. Brittle fragments snowed from the folds as she opened it.

Kura perched chunky buttocks on the platform edge. His bleary eyes took in Cooper anew. He did not reach for the document.

"What the hell are you talking about?"

Cooper sat, placing the coat between the photographer and herself. She laid the release form atop the coat, facing him.

"Before his death, your father was negotiating with the museum for the return of certain relics purchased from your family a century earlier."

"That? I'd forgotten. Load of junk. I was glad to get rid of it." Kura yawned, neither covering his mouth nor turning his head.

"You're not rid of it. You didn't sign the release."

"I must've. I didn't want the stuff."

"So you said at the time. However, you were a few weeks underage and had no legal guardian to handle the matter for you. The museum failed to follow up. Legally, you can still claim the relics. It's the sort of loose end that makes administrators nervous. I'm sure you'll help update our files."

Kura picked up the document gingerly. He scowled as he read it. A bead of sweat dripped from the tip of his nose to stain the paper. He looked at Cooper.

"Why now?"

Cooper shrugged. "We just found it. If you'll sign?"

Kura patted his stomach and fleshy hips. "My pen is in my other suit."

"Here. Use mine."

Kura did not reach for it.

"Mind if I smoke?"

"Actually, yes."

He stopped looking for his pack.

"I've had a lousy year, you know."

"I didn't know."

"Yeah. Lost an invasion of privacy suit." He smiled. "How much is this stuff worth?"

Cooper's shoulders sagged. I've blown it, she thought. Came on too strong. Let my instant dislike for Kura cloud my judgment.

"I'm not an expert in this field."

"Put it this way: how much would the museum pay me to sign this and not make any waves? Ever since *Shogun* was on television, Japanese antiques have been hot. I'll bet I could get a good price up around Twelfth Street."

"I'm not empowered to negotiate." Cooper struggled to conceal her dismay. Allison Zebar would give her a well-deserved tongue-lashing. Fortunately, Cooper had spent so much of the afternoon tracking down Kura that it was too late today to return to the museum. She wouldn't have to face the silver-haired woman until morning.

That damned paper! It wasn't even the real purpose of her visit, only an excuse. Cooper was beginning to wonder exactly what that real purpose was.

She wanted to drop the subject. Instead, she found herself saying, "There's a legend tied to some of those relics."

Kura shrugged. "Something about a demon and an iron sword. My old man never really went into it."

"The demon was supposedly imprisoned by your ancestor, thirteen hundred years ago." Briefly, Cooper outlined the tale that Nakato had told her, concluding. "The iron sword was crafted specifically to slay the oni. Your family was entrusted with guardianship of both weapon and prison."

"You know more about it than I." Kura slid back on the platform and sat cross-legged. "My old man wouldn't talk about the past. Or the future, for that matter. At his funeral, a friend of his told me how he'd spent World War II in an American relocation camp. From that time on, he only spoke of the immediate present."

"Yet a few months before his death, he was ready to go to court to reclaim these ancestral goods."

Kura scratched his ear. "Yeah, I thought that was weird at the time."

"Perhaps he knew he was dying. This was his last chance to make amends to his ancestors." Let it go, Francine, she told herself. Why don't you let it go?

Kura nodded. "Maybe that's it. I know a few old Nisei like that. Like the line about there being no atheists in foxholes?"

"I've never been convinced of that," Cooper replied.

The photographer refolded the release and skimmed it to the rear of the platform. "Tell you what, Franny. Give me your phone number and I'll let you know. Okay?"

Cooper's lips thinned to invisibility. "No one calls me Franny, ever. It's Francine. Sometimes Fran. In your case, Mrs. Cooper will do."

Kura leered and tugged at the waistband of his trunks, pulling the suit up over the roll of flesh. The bulge at his groin grew more pronounced.

"That's almost a challenge, Mrs. Cooper."

"You scumbag!" Jennifer screamed as she stepped in front of the curtain. Her mint-green down jacket billowed over matching ski pants and sweater. She struggled to get her knapsack's straps over her shoulders, snagging a strand of red hair.

Kura turned, face sagging. Cooper noted the deep hollows around his eyes.

"Hey, Jen, come on. I'm just kidding around."

"That's all you ever do, Andy."

"Where are you going? The session's not over yet."

"My session with you is over, for good. It's not enough for you that I pass up paying jobs to pose gratis so you can build up a new portfolio, or that I have to nurse you through screaming nightmares and watch you gulp uppers by the handful and choke on your lousy nicotine habit and put up with your constant pawing! You have to grope this bimbo right in front of me! After you insult me to her, like I wasn't even standing here. I'm not deaf, Andy, though you're making a good try at that with your tapes at full volume."

"I need that music to create."

"Bullshit. You need it to blot out the real world, when you would be better off having your nose rubbed in it!"

Jenny adjusted the knapsack and strode in long steps to the huge double doors of the freight elevator. She yanked the bar aside, cursing when she broke a fingernail. The doors flew apart with a vibrant clang. Cold air rushed up through the gap, penetrating even the circle of light, cooling the sweat on Kura's neck and back. He leapt from the platform and started after her. The chill slowed him down.

Jenny glared at the stocky photographer and pointedly threw a switch. The elevator groaned and jerked into motion.

"My tits are too small?" she shouted up the shaft. "Go fuck a cow!"

Kura reached the double doors. He glared down, spat, and slammed them shut.

"Temperamental bitch," he muttered. "Damn! I'll have to walk down."

Cooper had slipped her coat back on and was buttoning it. "Tact is not your strong point, is it, Mr. Kura?" She picked up her purse and manila envelope.

"Not when I can't think straight." His eyes narrowed. He owed this woman no explanations. "Are you leaving, too?"

"I don't see what I'd gain by staying."

"The least you can do is fill in for Jen for the next hour. It's your fault she ran out." A corner of his mouth curled upwards. "I don't know if you can squeeze into her bikini, but I'd like to see you try."

"I'm sure you would, you dirty little boy," Cooper said, fully aware the man was no more than five years her junior. "I have more important tasks than providing you with wet-dream material."

"Damn it, you owe me. I won't let you leave." Kura moved toward her, arms and legs spread widely, a parody of a sumo wrestler.

Cooper raised an eyebrow. "How's the wrist feel?"

Kura glanced at his right arm. The muscles still ached dully. Cooper passed within arm's length of him and then through the door to the ill-lit stairwell. He did not lift a finger.

On the landing, framed in the open doorway, Cooper turned.

"By the way. Do you still have the documentary proof your father used to establish ownership?"

Kura shook his head, eyes fogging. "I burned them. I like to travel light."

Cooper chuckled. He seemed to have managed to do that quite well in the intelligence department. "In that case, I won't be bothering you again, Mr. Kura. I doubt we'll need that release, after all."

That bluff ought to deflate his balloon a bit, Cooper thought smugly. She descended as quickly as caution and dignity permitted. A genealogy could be reconstructed, and in a legal test the museum would have to yield its copy, but Andrew Kura might not realize that.

Considering that Francine Cooper had apparently wasted the entire day running around New York, had committed herself to several hours of unpaid research of the dreariest sort, and was about to battle her way through early rush hour crowds to reach the room on West Seventieth Street, she felt curiously at ease with the world. The paralyzing numbness that had infected her for most of the previous day had been purged from her system, and her talk with old friend Jiro Nakato helped put things into perspective.

Cooper began to realize that her attempt to "clear" her daughter was an excuse for busy work, something to occupy her conscious mind while her subconscious dealt with the shock of her grief. It was the same trick she'd used when her husband had been killed in a guerilla raid in Southeast Asia, more than a decade ago. She'd kept pressing for details, reports, every scrap of information she could dig up until, finally, she'd done all she could, and the pain became bearable. Cooper's mother had never had that knack of coping; she'd carried the death of Cooper's father, in the last days of World War II, like a cross, and when her only child also became a wartime widow, the flood of memories killed her. The fatal stroke must have seemed quite a convenience to her.

Cooper had done all she could to find out about Lynda's death, and she was glad to be free of the burden. She was also glad that she didn't have to spend any more time on Andrew Kura, the has-been photographer.

As she stepped out onto the narrow sidewalk, it did not seem that she could possibly be mistaken.

CHAPTER 41

An unmarked patrol car stood facing south along the park side of Riverside Drive. In the front passenger seat. Lieutenant Amos Foster gazed sourly out the side window. Beyond the web of naked branches and the lights of the elevated Henry Hudson Parkway that sliced the park lengthwise, behind the Palisades on the opposite shore of the river, the last dull glow of daylight was fading.

A raw wind blew off the Hudson River, carrying muted sounds of parkway traffic as it seeped around the car and through the partially rolled-down window on the driver's side. With it came the dry odor usually associated with an impending snowfall. Foster rubbed his gloveless hands together and blew on them for warmth. The car heater, beneath the dashboard, roasted his kneecaps.

He turned to the windshield. Half a block down, a medium-sized, unremarkable-looking man stood by an entrance to the park, apparently walking his German shepherd. His long gray overcoat flapped around his shins. The dog did not pull at his leash, but patiently awaited the man's decision to move. Only the man's left hand, with the end of the leash wrapped around it, was visible. The right hand sat deep in a wide coat pocket. Too deep. Foster knew there was no lining to that pocket. The coat hung loosely to mask the shotgun clutched beneath it.

Nightfall.

Foster caught the waiting man's eye and nodded once. Without outwardly acknowledging the gesture, the man in gray tugged on his leash. Dog and man started into the park. They were soon swallowed in gloom.

That was the cue for others to begin their patrols. Each man and woman carried a walkie-talkie, but Riverside Park was riddled with radio dead spots. It was safer to use signals whenever possible rather than grow too dependent on a device that might fail at a crucial moment.

In addition to the uniformed officers normally assigned to cover this park, a score of plainclothes-men stalked asphalt paths between West Ninety-First Street and the park's southern boundary at West Seventy-Second. Most were volunteers from the Street Crime Unit. They all could well be wasting their time. The killer might not strike again tonight. If he did, he might strike north of the stakeout area, or outside of the park altogether. But they had to start somewhere. Foster had only a sketchy, two-day pattern to go on, until something new turned up.

Something new meant another murder.

"Let him try it tonight," Foster muttered through stiff lips. "We're ready for him."

The door on the driver's side clicked and swung open. Foster turned his head. His hand darted beneath his coat to touch the .38 revolver in its shoulder holster.

"Talking to yourself again, Amos?" A ruddy, horse-faced man slid onto the cold leather seat. He hugged a plain brown bag to his chest.

Foster grunted. "I meet a better class of people." He took his hand out, empty, and thrust it toward Sergeant Evans. "Give."

"Don't spill it on your foot."

"Can't tell you anything, can I?"

Steaming warmth helped thaw his fingers.

"Goddamn." Evans screwed up his face when he peeled off the lid of his own coffee container. "I asked for two black. They put cream in yours, too?"

"Doesn't matter. Think I'll just hold it. You called the hospital?"

"Can't tell you anything, either. Yeah, I called. They're pretty sure now that they can save Carver's sight. Eyes heal fast. Of course, it'll be months before the Department puts him on a beat again."

Foster smiled. "Good. The rookie gets a vacation, and I get a partner who can concentrate on tonight's stake-out instead of blaming himself for something that isn't his fault. Right?"

"That cuts two ways." Evans took a noisy sip. "Faugh! Sugar, too!" He swallowed half of the beige liquid at a gulp. "Did I miss anything?"

"Sun went down. Troops are moving."

"I noticed. Got some bad news for you. I ran into Diehl at the counter."

"Ouch." Foster rubbed his forehead, although his afternoon headache had vanished as soon as he'd come on duty. "Damned reporters. Well, somebody besides us had to connect the murders, no matter how tightly we screwed on the lid. Anyone else?"

"A photographer I don't know. Must be new on the staff. That's all. Of course, the night is young."

"Last chance for the 1982 Pulitzer. Think they know anything hot?"

"I didn't ask. That would have clinched it for them."

Foster stifled a yawn. "Probably doesn't make any difference. The rag Diehl works for, if they can't find a story to sensationalize, they'll invent one."

"Maybe we'll get lucky and grab this nut tonight before New York even knows he's running loose, eh? Make your mayor look real good!"

"I hope so, Joe, and not just to give the man in Gracie Mansion another crack at the governorship." Foster snapped off the lid on his coffee, sipped, pursed his lips and sealed the container again. Holding it on his lap with both hands, he stared moodily into the deepening shadows of Riverside Park. "I hope so."

He woke puzzled and dissatisfied. For the second day in a row, unbidden sleep had overcome him. The terror he'd inflicted these past two nights should have strengthened him, just as hatred had nourished him through his thirteen-hundred-year confinement. He did, in fact, feel much more vital than when he'd first broken free. No one would crawl away from one of his blows now! He was master!

Still, the spells of narcotism could not be shrugged off. They might bode ill for his plans of conquest.

His mind was not a subtle one. The fact that thirteen and a third centuries of total darkness might have left him leery of direct daylight did not occur to him, although he well knew of his kind's natural affinity for cave-dwelling. The possibility that refusing even to acknowledge this state could erect a psychological block in his primitive brain driving him to retire well before dawn—he would consider this laughable, were it not beyond his comprehension. Instead, he thought the fault might lie with the release of his sexual passions, draining him, sating him. He had grown unused to such excesses.

Easy enough to find out! After more than a thousand years of celibacy, he would manage a few nights by way of experiment.

He leapt from his hiding place. His size was tripled before his three-toed feet touched the ground, and did not slacken its rate of increase. Thin white frost rimed the stone walls on either side of the underpass. Tonight he set himself a task beyond mere exploration: a search for a more suitable dwelling place. These caves near the river were wide open on either end, and most were barely deep enough for their own shadows. He'd noticed some smaller, better insulated caves with open pits for entrances, but rushing water gurgled through these. He could not drown, but suddenly to be dragged out to sea by an underground stream would be inconvenient.

He turned away from the river. The east held more promise for his quest. Woe to the fisherfolk who crossed his path this chilly winter night!

The German shepherd stopped in the center of the path. Limbs stiffened. Flanks heaved. Ears flattened against the skull. There was a wrongness here, an odor so elementally aberrant that it undermined the animal's training. Discipline called for silent tracking. The dog's growling was low, from deep in the throat— low, but audible.

"What is it, boy?" whispered the man in the gray coat. His only reply was an increasing uneasiness. The rapport between man and beast, so useful in normal investigations, now only fostered mutual disquietude.

The detective's fingers tightened on the shotgun's trigger guard.

In the shadows ahead, a few paces before the parkway underpass, dead brush rustled.

The weapon rose beneath the coat until its barrel protruded from a gap between two buttons, even with the man's navel.

He snapped off an elm branch as thick as an ordinary man's leg. Swinging it, he shattered several lesser branches. A serviceable club. He returned to the asphalt. Pathways meant little to him, but they meant a great deal to the peasantry on whom he wished to test his new weapon.

He glanced up. For the first time, he had a view due east unobstructed by highway underpasses or thick clumps of nearby trees.

His brutal eyes widened in amazement. Mountains glimpsed dimly through drizzle the night before were not mountains at all. Squares of light dotted their tall, regular shapes, lights in the hundreds, the thousands! So bright they might consist of every candle in the empire! More extraordinary—within the glaring squares, occasional shadows moved. Familiar shapes. People!

The mountains were artificial constructs designed for habitation!

No simple fishing village boasted so many imposing castles. He had to be in the very capital of the empire … perhaps of the world!

Here were lodgings worthy of his rank. To start, he need oust but one clan and intimidate the retainers to do his bidding. He would have a readymade headquarters. He felt a niggling reluctance to tie himself to a surface dwelling, but he paid it no need. Once his rule was firmly established, he could live where he pleased.

His three-toed feet scraped along the hard, black asphalt.

Suddenly there was a man barring his way, and some sort of animal as well. A dog, apparently, though he'd never seen one quite that large. He roared challenge, rushing forward. He also added a few hand's-breadths to his considerable height, to be sure.

A thunderclap ripped the air. His side burned. As his free hand grasped at the hole from which black ichor slowly leaked, animal fangs tore at his left calf.

He forgot the wound and roared again, exulting in the promise of battle. His own weapon came into play.

Amos Foster pushed open the car door far enough to dump his nearly full cup of coffee into the gutter. Evans tossed his own container out the half-opened window. A second report shattered the night.

"Both barrels," Evans observed, wrapping his hands around the steering wheel.

"Move it!" Foster barked.

The unmarked patrol car came to life, headlights blazing. Evans turned sharply and jolted over the curb. Tires squealed protests. Foster flipped on the siren and slapped a switch to start the rotating red beacon on the roof. As they sped down twisting, narrow paths, the flashing crimson light played eerily on leafless elms and denuded underbrush, giving the illusion of a forest fire.

The lieutenant patted his .38 in its shoulder holster. The car swerved. He braced one hand on the dashboard and reached under the seat with the other for his own shotgun in its special hidden rack. Shells were in his jacket pocket. He loaded quickly.

Men and women raced between trees and other patches of dead brown grass. Mostly civilians. The plainclothes officers wore bright yellow headbands for identification. No one wanted to be shot by a fellow cop.

Flashlight beams stabbed out. Shouts filled the winter night. Foster's eyes stayed fixed dead ahead. His partner concentrated on not hitting any trees or colleagues.

A dark form suddenly huddled in the center of the path. Evans slowed and swerved to avoid it. Headlights focused on a long gray overcoat. A shattered gun stock lay across the man's spine. His feet were lost in a tangle of brush beside the path. The head was unrecognizable pulp.

In the beacon's blood-red glare, the killer loomed behind the corpse.

Foster goggled.

Twice a man's height, thrice a man's breadth, a humanoid thing hissed at them through rows of pointed, gleaming teeth. Scarlet skin glistened as the advancing form stepped into the headlight glow. The bulging loin-cloth affirmed its sex. The savage murders were well within this creature's capacity.

Black pebbling on the left flank marked where one shotgun blast had hit. His right hand waved a thick, bloodied branch, while the left circled the throat of a limp German shepherd. Entrails dangled from the dog's torn belly.

"We'll need extra-large handcuffs, Amos."

Neither man smiled. Evans's face was drained of color. The slowing car braked to a halt beside the murdered plainclothesman.

Foster flung open his door. Kneeling on asphalt, with the door as a shield, he aimed the shotgun and fired pointblank.

The monster moved quickly for his bulk. He dodged the blast, catching only a slight peppering—again on his left side.

"Read him his rights!" Evans shouted from behind the steering wheel.

Foster swung his barrel up and around, trying for a better scatter pattern. Close range hindered him; a high-powered rifle would have been more useful. He saw an opening, but before he could discharge the second barrel the creature leapt in front of the car.

"Hai-eee!" screamed the thing. The hood crumpled under his club, exposing the motor. He kicked the front bumper. The car's front section rose into the air and crashed down hard.

"It's not for sale!" Evans shouted with a bitten tongue.

Three toes slid under the front end and kicked up. The car jounced high, like a bucking horse. Foster was exposed.

Clutching the gun to his chest, the detective rolled into the same dry brush that concealed his dead colleague's feet. His scraped, stiffened fingers fumbled for more shotgun cartridges. Revolvers cracked behind him. Metal shrieked. Glass shattered.

Foster finished reloading. Only then did he look to see what had happened to his cover.

The unmarked car had flipped over. Its rear wheels spun

like the kicking of a dying insect's legs. The creature was no longer in sight.

"Joe!"

The car rocked, creaking sourly. No other sound issued from it.

Foster rolled onto his side and glanced toward the gunplay behind him. A line of officers, in and out of uniform, made a human blockade across the path. The red-skinned monster stood between them and Foster. The lieutenant aimed his shotgun, but did not pull the trigger. Shooting low, from the ground, he might hit some of the men and women beyond.

Before Foster could stand, the thing broke through the blockade. A man in blue was hurtled over a lamppost to land with a series of crackling snaps in dark underbrush. His scream came to a sudden end.

The remaining officers scattered, but re-formed immediately to give chase. The creature bounded east towards Riverside Drive … and its hundreds of apartment dwellers.

Unable to get a clear shot, Foster lowered the gun and scrambled on hands and knees to the overturned car. The passenger door still hung open. He crawled inside.

Sergeant Evans lay crumpled against the interior roof. One leg pointed straight up, its foot tangled in the steering wheel. Blood matted his hair in thick clumps, flowing sluggishly, already congealing. An unfired .38 was still clutched in his hand.

"Come on, Joe. This is no time to screw around."

Evans, for once, had no come-back. His neck was twisted at too sharp an angle not to be broken. Foster sobbed a curse and grabbed the radio mike from the dashboard.

"This is Foster. That riot squad on stand-by. Send 'em in."

The receiver crackled. "Details?"

"Three dead cops, so far. That enough detail?"

Foster dropped the mike. Without thinking, he freed Evans's foot from the steering wheel. Shouldn't touch the body at a crime scene. Wait for the investigation. Fuck that. Joe deserved this much dignity.

The detective backed out of the ruined car. Using the right

front tire for support, he struggled to his feet. The hubcap jarred loose with a clatter.

Foster had neither time nor inclination to satisfy some nosey radio squad man. Anyway, he didn't dare try to describe what had happened. They might refuse to send in the back-up.

He picked up his shotgun and hurried east.

Foster caught up to the monster at the edge of the park. Three squads trapped the thing in a handgun crossfire. Bullets dented the horn-hard crimson skin, but they did not draw what passed for blood. Huge, black, pupil-less eyes glared at the attackers. The squads fell back.

"Hee-yah!"

Swinging tree-limb club and canine corpse, the thing smashed through a cordon of patrol cars. High-powered rifles fired at face and gut. They had no more effect than a swarm of mosquitoes. The monster seemed more distressed by the flashbulbs of newspaper cameramen, who retreated into doorways as he approached.

A patrol car each blocked north and southbound lanes of Riverside Drive, at Seventy-Second and Eighty-Sixth Streets respectively. One-man vehicles sealed off westbound one-way streets. The devil-creature charged across the trafficless Drive and down Seventy-Eighth Street. The stake-out had been well-manned. Overmanned, Foster would have said ten minutes earlier.

Police couldn't be everywhere, though, and West End Avenue was alive with cars and vans—more than usual, as it absorbed the detoured Riverside Drive traffic.

The creature slowed as he neared West End. The speeding machines were new to him in such numbers, but he knew they were connected to his persecutors. Shouts and sharp cracks told him his pursuers were catching up. Under the streetlamps, he posed too good a target. He turned ninety degrees and plunged into relative darkness.

Panting, Foster joined a score of officers at an alley entrance on the north side of West Seventy-Eighth. An officer in uniform saw the shotgun and shouted a challenge.

"I'm a cop!" Foster gasped. He glanced down and saw that

his lapel had twisted around. He laid the weapon on the curb and with slow, obvious moves turned back the lapel to show his shield. "Foster," he added. "Homicide. I organized this surprise party."

The uniform lowered his .38 but did not holster it. He smiled sheepishly. "Sorry, Lieutenant. I recognize you now."

Foster nodded. He couldn't blame the man for being keyed up.

"What happened to that big red fucker?" he asked.

"We've got him bottled up, Lieutenant. This alley is a dead end. There's no other way out."

Foster took deep breaths. He retrieved his loaded shotgun. "Good. Let's move in."

The group of officers shuffled reluctantly. The one who'd challenged Foster said, "If it's all the same, Lieutenant, we'd like to wait for reinforcements."

"Preferably a tank division," added a woman in plain clothes. Her yellow headband had slipped down to cover one ear.

Foster could order these men and women into the alley. He was ranking officer, and this was his case. Common sense prevailed. They were ill-equipped for such an assault. Foster would not even have suggested it if he wasn't upset over Evans.

He looked down at his hands, noticing for the first time how badly they shook. His grip tightened on the shotgun as he fought the reaction. From his left came a screech of tires as two police vans turned onto the sidestreet. They were the prettiest things he'd ever seen, their insides packed with specially-trained reinforcements, tear gas canisters, and heavy artillery. Who said Christmas was over?

"Heiei!"

Foster spun at the sound. The monster lunged from alley darkness and plowed through the waiting officers. The lead van swerved onto the sidewalk to avoid the sudden rush into the street. Skulls cracked, bones crunched, as the tree branch rose and fell. The dead dog had been discarded.

Foster let go with both barrels.

Roaring, the thing threw his club at the detective. Foster

ducked, not fast enough. It struck his right shoulder, numbing the arm. He almost dropped the gun. Almost.

The Special Tactics vans followed as the monster turned east to stagger across West End Avenue. Car horns honked. Brakes squealed. A Ford Falcon ran onto the sidewalk, smashing into a canopy brace. A Beetle-style Volkswagen spun completely around and stopped in the center of the intersection. The police vans had to stop, but the creature continued down Seventy-Eighth toward the brilliant lights on the next north-south street.

Upper Broadway.

Foster scrambled through the tangle of vehicles, taking the lead. At this hour, Broadway's sidewalks were densely crowded. The potential for havoc and death was staggering. Foster tried not to think of it, or the fiery shooting pains in his leg, or the shallow gasping that brought too little oxygen into his lungs.

At the corner, the thing pushed over a newsstand and swung north. Fenders crumpled as brakes cried out. Shoppers and moviegoers scattered, shrieking in terror. Foster pumped his legs harder.

The lieutenant took the corner at a wide turn, leaping over stacks of magazines and morning editions. He glanced back, without slowing, at the ragged formation of surviving officers. Rearmost were a dozen men in thick-padded bullet-proof jackets. They held weapons that made Foster's shotgun look like a peashooter. The special vans had discharged their cargo.

Civilians ran in every direction, without thought. Some people raced in front of the police, forcing the latter to zigzag. Others actually charged toward the monster, who paused on the median at Seventy-Ninth Street to glare hatred at the armed pursuers. Foster glanced down for three seconds, to load two more shotgun cartridges.

When he looked up again, the monster was gone.

"No!" Foster screamed. He stumbled against the iron rail of the median. He clung as though his life depended on it, and sucked great rasping gulps of frigid air. Tears streaked his face. His ears buzzed. The lining of his jacket was soaking wet at the back and armpits.

A woman said, "I wouldn't have believed it if I hadn't seen it."

Foster turned to the speaker as her blue-clad arm shot forward to assist the detective. He accepted the aid without embarrassment.

"I still don't believe it," he gasped.

Broadway traffic was at a standstill as police on foot flooded the intersection. Civilians, since they could do nothing to help, drifted back to clog the sidewalks. The wail of an ambulance went unheeded.

Foster finally shrugged off the helping hand, with a nod of thanks. He jogged past the planted section of the median to where he'd last seen the creature. A subway grating's metal bars had bent under the superhuman mass, but they'd held in place, and could still support Foster's weight. He scowled at the dark under his feet, then glared up at the equally black starless sky. The grating rattled as he stepped off to sit heavily on a slatted wood bench. He looked around. A knee-high concrete barrier, the leafless trees in the center of the median, a wire trash can full of sour-smelling garbage; these afforded no hiding place for a thing that huge. Still, Foster could not believe that the monster had moved from this spot.

For the rest of the night, in cars and on foot, every available man and woman covered the Upper West Side for a mile north and south of Seventy-Ninth Street, and as far east as Central Park. Rooftops were stormed across, basements ransacked. Low-flying helicopters kept apartment-dwellers on upper floors awake with brilliant floodlights and the whup-whup-whup of their blades. Forty-six homeless indigents were roused and sent to various shelters. Precinct-house holding cells became crammed with startled burglars, participants in assorted now-aborted shady deals, and hookers who didn't bother with hotel rooms.

There wasn't a horned red-skinned giant among them.

His path from Riverside Park to Broadway was marked by broken trees, bloodied corpses, cracked pavements and twisted traffic signs. After Broadway and West Seventy-Ninth Street, however, the creature might never have existed.

But he had existed. He'd killed Joe Evans—Amos Foster's partner and only real friend—and more than half a dozen other officers. He'd been seen by scores of police and hundreds of civilians. His picture would be plastered across the front page of every morning paper in the city, and later editions of the major out-of-town papers as well.

As if the world needed fresh nightmares.

CHAPTER 42

He hurt.

It was only a minor sting that no real warrior would begin to notice, but that he felt it at all disturbed him. Since his transformation, hundreds of years earlier, only one thing had been able to harm him. This village obviously possessed a magic unknown to the priests of his time.

They could not kill him, of course. Not him! Yet he considered delaying his conquest a day or two longer, until he learned more about their sorcery. He might be able to use it himself.

His blunt fingers pinched together the torn flesh of his left side, where shreds of crimson skin dangled after viscous black blood ceased running. When he released the grip, his wounds were all but healed. Not even a scar would remain. Except, of course, the hideous scars this body had borne from its creation.

Otherwise, he thought the night's activities had gone well. The battle was a welcome diversion. A new and better cave had been serendipitously found, one in which he could stretch out full length—though it were best to keep to the alcoves that lined its unnaturally even sides. Huge black dragons rushed back and forth in these caves, at incredible speeds. They ignored him, intent on mysterious missions, but their passage created frequent localized earthquakes. Well, he was accustomed to earthquakes, and the great worms might prove helpful allies. Not that *he* needed allies, but he would let them alone for the time being, provided they did likewise.

Then drowsiness returned, puzzling him. He had refrained from the fleshly delights of the previous outings. Why, then?

Ah! He *had* satisfied another desire. He did not need mortal food, no more than he needed sexual release, but he still found pleasure in it, and he'd always had a special fondness for one particular dish. Indeed, fresh, raw meat was even tastier than when it was roasted. He wished he'd discovered that thirteen hundred years ago.

If, however, eating, like sex, acted as a soporific, he supposed he must also put that sensual pleasure aside.

For the time being.

NIHON (ANCIENT JAPAN)

650 A.D.

CHAPTER 43

Second month. Tenth day.

Hoke occupies the most luxurious room in the Imperial Palace, saving that of the Emperor Kotoku himself. Buddhist prayers mention him. Offerings are made to the kami in his name. The emperor's personal physicians, including a specialist from Cathay, tend his ruined hand with acupuncture, herb poultices, and burning moxa. The bones are crushed beyond proper healing and the fingers will never grasp again, but the experts can at least make it resemble a human hand more than the pulped lump of flesh that had lain on Meiko's anvil.

Hoke finds all this attention disquieting.

"Everyone talks of how brave I am," he complains to Monaga during the priest's daily visit.

"You are," Monaga affirms.

"I did no more than I had to do. Doesn't anyone understand? I had no choice. I was almost petrified with fright when I realized what opportunity the gods had placed in my hands in Meiko's workshop. I could do it only because I was more frightened by what would happen if I did not."

Monaga nods. "That is a fine definition of courage, Hoke. Not to lack fear, but to overcome it; to do what is right in spite of it."

Hoke's head drops back onto his silk-padded wooden pillow. The boy is thin from privation and illness, but after several days of lavish care his stomach no longer forms a hollow almost to his spine when he lies flat. "That sounds too easy."

"It isn't. If it were, would the emperor honor you in his palace?"

"I do not belong here. A rude peasant boy ..."

Monaga gently pats Hoke's good right hand. "The emperor's only son, Prince Arima, is about your age, Hoke. As for status, the ceremony five days hence will take care of that."

The boy sits up abruptly, spilling silk sheets into his lap. Sudden movement brings a twinge of pain to his bandaged hand. He winces, but more important things concern him.

"What ceremony?"

"The adoption I told you of yesterday ... ah, that's right. You fell asleep before I got to it."

"I'm awake now."

Monaga smiles. "So you are. Well. You must first understand that, for political reasons, the emperor does not wish to publicize the story of Lord Uto."

"That much I remember. There is already too much opposition to his governmental policies. His opponents would use the oni as an evil omen. Lord Uto's name has been stricken from the official chronicles. Imuri will be divided among its neighbors, and its people compensated and relocated."

Monaga stifles a yawn, which becomes a grin. "No wonder you fell asleep. To continue, then. Yesterday the provincial governor of Anato presented to the emperor a white pheasant, which everyone agrees is a very good omen. On the fifteenth day of this month, when the doctors say you'll be well enough to attend, the emperor will declare a new nengo—the era of the white pheasant. Only a handful of us, sworn to secrecy, know that this nengo really honors your defeat of Lord Uto. The subsequent adoption ceremony will seem one of many beneficent acts celebrating the occasion, along with a general amnesty, presents to nobles, and special concessions to the province of Anato."

Hoke leans forward in exasperation. It seems as if Monaga was far more likely to speak to the point when doing so might cost him his life. "*What* adoption ceremony?"

The priest rubs his forehead, abashed. "Oh. Yes. You will be adopted by Lord Akuragawa. He is an old soldier with no living sons. You shall carry on his lineage."

Hoke's eyes brighten with excitement despite his dour mood. "Akuragawa? One of the emperor's personal guards?"

"Exactly. You will officially be a noble warrior."

Hoke stares at the folds in the sheets about his knees. "What of my real parents?"

"That is up to you. Send them money. Have them live with you if you wish. Brothers and sisters, too. Nobles have wealth and influence. Lord Akuragawa will teach you to use both wisely."

Hoke raises his bandaged hand. The pain there is no longer sharp enough to make his eyes water, but he will never be free from the dull ache.

"Who can be a warrior with but one hand?"

Monaga sighs. He does not want to say more until the lad is better ... say, in another day or two. He dreads the next revelation. Yet, the boy asks. He deserves to know it all. He earned that right, if anyone has.

"Hoke, the emperor wants you to assume a responsibility graver than that of any soldier, even his personal guard. Once you are adopted and made noble, the sealed tsuga containing the demon Lord Uto is to be placed in your care ... and the care of your descendants."

Hoke's face is a blank. His small body shivers. "I thought the hilt had been thrown in the sea."

"Meiko stopped that. He realized that sea water would corrode the iron, allowing Uto to escape but leaving the kami forever bound to the lost object. The thing must be guarded. Along with this ... object ... comes the iron sword, now fitted with a new hilt, and with its spirits still bound to it by oath. This is also to be passed down the generations. If Uto breaks free, your son or grandson or great-great-grandson must put an end to him."

Bile rises in Hoke's throat.

"I do not wish this honor, priest."

Monaga nods, patting the good hand once more.

"Nor need you accept it. The emperor is a kindly man, though misguided in religious matters. He will understand.

You sacrificed much already for the safety of the Eight Islands. More must not be expected."

Hoke looks away from Monaga. The old man removes his fingers. The boy suddenly grips his bony wrist.

"I do not wish this honor," Hoke repeats, "but I accept it. The emperor is right. I lived through Lord Uto's reign. I know his evil intimately. I appreciate the gravity of this charge as few others can ... and will impress it on my family to come." Hoke frowns. "You said that Prince Arima wished to play with me when I recovered. I think I have forgotten how to play, and it is too late for me to re-learn. I should not meet him. My descendants must avoid political entanglements that might threaten the line's continuity."

Monaga touches his forehead to the floorboards beside Hoke's sleeping mat. "And you disclaimed bravery!"

"I still do," Hoke replies, lying back on his pillow. "But it must be done."

He rolls onto his right side and pretends to sleep until he hears the priest shuffle from the room and the door slide gently shut behind him. Then the boy opens his eyes again. He sees a robe of red silk, one of several tailored for him at the command of the emperor. The gold dragon embroidered thereon has no more choice of where it is than Hoke, unless the threads come loose, and then they are no more a dragon, but a shapeless heap.

Unworthy he feels, and fearful, but he must follow the pattern. It is the Way.

NEW YORK CITY

FRIDAY, DECEMBER 31, 1982

CHAPTER 44

Stephanie de Lint stretched her stubby hands high above the brown curls topping her head, and grasped the knob of the vestibule's inner door. She'd only gained the height for this maneuver around Thanksgiving and was not yet jaded by the achievement. Still, it took every bit of strength in her five-year-old body to pull the heavy door open. Her tongue pushed against the inside of her cheek as she strained. She tasted the metal key clenched in her teeth—the key she'd quietly taken from its kitchen peg. Stephanie was a bright girl, and had planned this caper carefully. She knew she could not hold the inner vestibule door open and at the same time pick up the newspaper that had been delivered that morning. Greg, the paper boy, always left it just inside the front door, and Stephanie's arms could not reach that far. Even Mommy's arms couldn't reach that far. Maybe Daddy's could, but he was in Chicago on a business trip. Besides, Stephanie wanted to surprise her mother, who would soon be getting up to fix breakfast.

With heartfelt groans, Stephanie wedged her slippered foot in the narrow gap and tugged at the edge of the door with both hands until the opening was wide enough to slip through. She squeezed around. Getting back in would be easier: she could lean against the door and push instead of all this pulling.

The door closed behind her faster than she'd expected. It bumped her rudely, just like Uncle Jake sometimes did. Stephanie was propelled into the vestibule. She scrabbled at the stained wall tiles, below the mailboxes, to keep from falling. The key flew out of her mouth, clattering in a shadowy corner.

There was the paper, all right, lying flush against the

threshold. Stephanie bent her knees and grasped a corner in each hand. Slowly she dragged it to the inner door. The vestibule was too dim for her to read the headlines, not even the short, easy words, but she noticed the funny picture on the front page. It looked like one of the balloons from last month's Macy's parade, sort of. Maybe it was a new one, for next year. She'd have to ask Mommy to help her read the story.

When she'd gotten the paper where she wanted it, her little hands were smeared gray with newsprint. She wiped them on her Kliban cat pajamas, then went back to search for the key. The floor tiles felt like squares of ice as she felt around on hands and knees, for cold air seeped past the outer door where it did not quite set snugly in its frame. In the dull pre-dawn light, Stephanie imagined herself exploring a glacial cave.

Her fingers found and curled around hard, cool metal. She shivered, and scrambled to her feet. That was when the other hand touched something bristly. She pulled back from it, then bent forward, squinting.

That corner of the vestibule was too dark. Putting the key in her pajama pocket—why hadn't she thought of that to start with?—the child reached out boldly and pulled the bristly thing into the faint streetlamp glow that came through the fanlight over the outer door.

It was brown and stiff and sticky. Stephanie couldn't recognize it at first. Not until she felt the hard pads at one end did she realize what it should have been attached to.

Then she screamed.

Stephanie was still screaming when Mrs. de Lint found her. It took the mother several minutes to pry her terrified daughter's tiny fingers from the dog's hind leg.

CHAPTER 45

Across the hall from Mrs. Barclay's apartment was a front parlor with grimly functional furnishings. Three plastic-covered armchairs and a battered sofa were ranged around a coffee table cluttered with month-old magazines and three days' worth of newspapers. One of the table's legs had mysteriously shrunk over the years; an old *TV Guide* made up the deficit. The lamp table was a low cabinet, with a lock, that housed a black dial telephone that had been installed without the phone company's knowledge by the late Mr. Barclay, in the days when such an act was liable to prosecution. This instrument, for the tenants' use, was reserved for only the direst emergencies.

Inhabitants of the rooms above were expected to entertain guests—if any—in a decorous fashion in this parlor. Room visits were not explicitly forbidden, but they were frowned upon. Mrs. Barclay was a champion frowner. Naturally, the notion of an overnight guest was beneath consideration. Little wonder that Lynda Cooper had always insisted on meeting her mother at the latter's hotel when she came to New York to visit.

Francine Cooper walked downstairs that morning thoroughly refreshed. She'd had a light dinner in a Japanese restaurant on Columbus Avenue—though normally she was not fond of sushi—then gone to bed early and slept deep, letting her subconscious grapple with the reality that there were facets of Lynda that she would never know or understand, even if her daughter were not dead. Cooper's attempts to investigate Lynda's recent past were singularly and, for her, uncharacteristically inept. She had overreacted. Lieutenant Foster was right to that extent. Lynda was a victim of circumstances. If the New York

Police did not care whether Lynda was involved with drugs or not, and their speculations went no further than departmental files and, perhaps, a few sleazy local news articles, what difference did it make? Lynda was just as dead.

Today Cooper planned to have a big breakfast, make good her promise to Allison Zebar, and catch an evening shuttle home. She could be back in Boston before the year was out. Familiar surroundings and associates, *real* work to do; she felt better just thinking of such things. The futile, scattergun interviews of the past two days couldn't have accomplished less if she'd been deliberately steered aside.

The hour was early. Even Mrs. Barclay appeared not to be stirring. The morning paper stood on end in the vestibule. Cooper carried it back to the hall table for her first good deed of the day.

She could not miss the four-column photograph on the front page.

It was a picture of something very like the netsuke carving she'd handled in Mr. Nakato's office at Japan House. Nakato had even named it for her.

Oni.

Standing as though paralyzed, Cooper read the article through twice, absorbing the words with difficulty. She was starting it for the third time when a raspy voice cut through her mental fog.

"I get the paper first. House rules."

Cooper turned to face Mrs. Barclay. It was hard to tell whose complexion was paler at that moment. The concierge slid the newspaper from the researcher's numbing fingers.

"You're not coming down with somethin', are you?" The doughy woman glanced at the paper suspiciously. "I don't want any of your germs."

Cooper spoke in a harsh whisper. "Phone."

"What?"

"A telephone. I have to make a call, Mrs. Barclay."

"At seven in the morning? Come to think of it, you looked awfully bright-eyed last night." Mrs. Barclay's eyes narrowed. "Let's smell your breath."

"Goddamn it. I'm not a child!" Cooper snatched the paper back and dangled the front page in front of the concierge's nose. "A dozen people were murdered by this … creature … last night."

Emerald eyes grew round and wide.

"Jesus Mary! What's *that* supposed to be?"

"An oni. An ancient Japanese demon. The thing that killed Lynda!"

Mrs. Barclay gave ground before Cooper's vehemence. She bumped the hall table. The vase of plastic flowers wobbled.

"I still need a telephone," Cooper reminded her.

The concierge licked her lips. She'd let this woman use her own, private telephone two days earlier, as an act of charity. She didn't want Cooper in her apartment now, though. Not in such a state.

"The parlor." She pointed. "Phone in there's for tenants. I'll get the key for the cabinet."

Thirty seconds later, with her coat still buttoned, Cooper perched on the edge of a chair, receiver pressed to her right ear, fingernails drumming an irregular staccato on the scarred top of the coffee table. Each time she shifted her weight, the plastic cover creaked.

Mrs. Barclay stood behind the couch, face as enigmatic as ever. Cooper forgot that she was there and listening to a one-sided conversation.

"May I speak to Lieutenant Foster?

"No, I prefer to talk to him.

"Yes, he knows me. Francine Cooper. We met the day before yesterday. It's very important. Are you sure he can't be reached?

"Of course I know that. I've just seen the paper. That's why I'm calling.

"I suppose I'll have to. Can I have your name?

"I have information about the creature from Riverside Park. No, I haven't seen it, Officer Chelli, just the newspaper photograph, but I can identify it. It's called an oni."

"Fine, you know that. Do you also know that oni can change their size? This one was trapped in the hollow of an ancient sword hilt, which isn't much more spacious than the inside of a thimble.

"I can't help how it sounds. That's the legend.

"It's staring you right in the face. The reporters missed it, too, even though the story mentions the twisted grating.

"That's exactly why I'm telling you.

"*You* don't have to believe me. Just pass it on to Lieutenant Foster. Let him decide how much credence to give my story."

She hung up and sat back, sighing. "I hope." Awake less than half an hour, Cooper already felt exhausted. Her eyes met Mrs. Barclay's. "Officer Chelli thinks I'm another crank. They've been fielding nut calls since this edition hit the newsstand."

The concierge nodded warily.

Cooper found a twenty-dollar bill in her purse and dropped it on top of the November issue of *Good Housekeeping.* "A few more calls," she explained. "All local. That'll more than cover the cost."

Two puffy fingers snagged a corner of the crumpled bill and reeled it in. Mrs. Barclay deposited it in her bathrobe pocket as if it were a record trout for her creel. She was having second thoughts about the misguided sympathy that led her to accept the researcher's tenancy for a few trying days, to begin with. Lynda Cooper had been a quiet, stable young woman, if anything a little too shy. Who would have expected that her mother would be driven by grief to the opposite extreme?

Cooper lifted the receiver.

Mrs. Barclay backed out of the room. She'd heard enough gibberish in the last five minutes to last her for all of the forthcoming year. She had work of her own to do. For example, a graceful way of expelling the Boston woman had to be devised.

Now alone in the parlor, Cooper dialed information. She hadn't used this most obvious method of tracing Andrew Kura yesterday because it sounded too common a name, and frankly she enjoyed using resources most people didn't know existed. She was surprised to learn that no one named Kura was listed in the Manhattan directories, white or yellow pages. The latter contained three photographers with similar last names, but none of them had a SoHo address. She frowned. A professional photographer ought to have a telephone, or at least an answering service. If Andrew Kura relied exclusively on agencies for assignments, it was little wonder he'd fallen on hard times. Certainly his studio was not designed to impress walk-in clientele.

Maybe it was better this way. Calling to prepare Andrew Kura was a courtesy the photographer would certainly abuse. Approaching him cold might be the best method, under the circumstances.

Who else? A few moments ago, it had seemed to her there were scores of people she ought to call, and now she could not think of anyone else.

Jiro Nakato. He'd recounted the legend of the iron sword to pass the time, just how coincidental was that? He was currently somewhere over the Pacific Ocean.

Allison Zebar. The American Museum of Natural History opened at ten, but Zebar might be in early. She'd spoken about working overtime. And Zebar was expecting to hear from Cooper.

She picked up the receiver, then cradled it without dialing. The Museum was a ten to fifteen minute walk north, and Cooper suddenly had a lot of nervous energy to discharge.

In the overcast dawn, low heels clattered on the sandstone steps in front of Mrs. Barclay's building. They struck the pavement and turned east.

Unobserved, a puffy, paste-white face with glittering emerald eyes pressed against window glass, smearing it, until Cooper was out of sight.

CHAPTER 46

The chair seat pressed hard against Amos Foster's rump, and the back slats jabbed his shoulder blades. They were so spaced that it was impossible for any normal human being to sit back comfortably. The lieutenant leaned back anyway. His arms crossed over his chest. He glared at the other two men who'd invaded his cramped office. Perhaps it was natural that he should resent Captain Matherson's usurping the padded desk chair that he, Foster, had fought to requisition for four years, but that did not bother him half as much as what the burly, steel-haired captain was saying.

"It isn't that we lack confidence in you, Lieutenant. This case is simply too big for one squad to handle. Lieutenant Rogan here is more experienced with large-scale operations than you are."

Foster glanced at the tall, thin black man who rested one buttock on the edge of his desk. He'd exchanged professional courtesies with Bill Rogan in the past, but didn't really know the man.

"That's not the point," Foster returned. He bent forward to flatten a palm on the desk top. "I don't object to working with Rogan, under his orders if that's what you want. Hell, call in the National Guard! I'd do as much myself. But you're doing more than that ... you're pulling me completely off the case!"

"In view of your partner's death," Matherson answered smoothly, "we feel you're too close to this case, too emotionally involved ..."

"Bullshit. I've handled emotional situations."

"Not in a command position," the captain snapped. "I checked your record."

Lieutenant Rogan added, softly, "You *did* lose track of a creature ten feet tall, in the middle of upper Broadway. Are you sure, Lieutenant, your judgment is completely unclouded?"

"We're getting to the meat of it now, aren't we?" Foster stood to tower over the desk. His knuckles pressed whitely on the scarred surface. "Last night was a fiasco. I admit it. I'm not ashamed to admit it. No one could have anticipated those events." He drew a sharp breath. "So what is it? The department has to look good for the press? You need a scapegoat? Sure ... typecasting for yellow trash!"

Captain Matherson's lips tightened to a thin line. He rubbed his neck, which was starting to ache from looking up at Foster. "No one said that, Lieutenant."

"No one would. Not in public. I've been on the outside all my life, Captain. That doesn't mean I'm ignorant. I make blacks and whites alike uncomfortable. I can't belong to either community, not fully."

Rogan's eyes met his. "Is that why you joined the force, Foster? To belong?" His tone was sincere, not mocking.

Upset though he was, Foster perceived his fellow lieutenant was touched by his words. He hadn't meant to reveal that much. Foster couldn't dislike Rogan; his beef wasn't with the choice of replacement. Still, he didn't want Rogan's pity, either.

"That might have been part of it," Foster admitted. "Wasn't it, for you?"

Matherson interrupted impatiently. "If I needed further proof that you're too overwrought to stay on this case, Foster, you've just handed it to me. Listen to me. I am *not* throwing you to the wolves. If anything, this will protect you from them. You don't see that now, but you will. In the meantime, if that ludicrous accusation of racial prejudice leaves this room, you'll be suspended indefinitely."

"If I needed further proof of what I said," Foster growled, "*you've* just handed it to me."

When he was angry, Captain Matherson could make his bulk loom without moving a muscle. It loomed now.

"Do yourself a favor, Lieutenant. Shut up. I've been making allowances for the strain you're under. Another outburst like that, however, and I'll have to ask you for your gun and shield."

Foster sat stiffly. He glanced from Matherson to the discomfited Lieutenant Rogan, and back to his superior. He closed his eyes and swallowed hard before he could force out the expected words.

"My apologies, Captain."

Nonetheless, as Galileo said, the earth *does*.

Matherson nodded. He knew the lieutenant could be pushed no further, and in good conscience the captain would not have cared to do so. It was unfortunate, but Foster was probably very near the truth. Matherson had considered the same possibility when the orders came from One Police Plaza to make the change. After all, the lieutenant had been doing as well as any cop could in a difficult and unusual situation. Suspicion alone, though, did not prove discrimination.

"Accepted, Lieutenant. I've already forgotten what you're apologizing for." He hauled himself out of Foster's chair and lumbered toward the door. "Lieutenant Rogan will need a full report on last night's ... incident ... as soon as possible."

Foster nodded, not trusting himself to speak.

"After that, take the afternoon off." The captain's smile offered a weak sort of camaraderie, but it was the best he was capable of. "You look like shit."

Right, thought Foster. Yellow shit.

CHAPTER 47

With a tattered, knee-length bathrobe draped over his unclad torso, Andrew Kura sat on the edge of his cot. One hand held a magnifying glass, the other a stack of glossy photographic prints. Periodically he flicked his wrist and the print on top slid onto the cot, its shiny surface reflecting the exposed lightbulb overhead.

Kura was in his private space, between an exposed brick wall and the backdrop screen. The heater's glow gave his toes a disturbing reddish tinge. Blankets and pillows formed a tangled mountain at the foot of the cot. Kura had found no sleep here for three nights running. Last night he'd even been denied the comfort of a warm body next to him.

The last picture slipped from his fingers. He looked up. A hairline streak of sun oozed around the cardboard taped over the window panes and crossed the mortar between bricks at an angle. Yet another kind of intrusion. This area was Kura's bedroom, his models' changing room, and a modest retreat from the outside world.

The outside world did not take the hint.

Kura tossed the magnifying glass onto the mountain of bedclothes and reshaped the glossies into a less ragged pile. Their edges were sharp against his bare knees. He rose stiffly and knotted the cloth belt to hold the robe closed. His mouth was cottony. His scalp itched. He rubbed his face, sighed, picked up the photos and walked in front of the backdrop.

Cooper was still waiting. Too bad. Kura'd hoped she'd have left, though he hadn't expected her to. She sat on the platform in the full glare of the klieg light he'd flicked on for warmth.

Her coat was neatly folded behind her. The pants suit could not disguise her full figure. She turned to him and he took care not to ogle. His wrist remembered the previous afternoon, or so he imagined. Another futile desire. Mrs. Cooper would not go in front of his lenses, let alone anything more intimate.

Her eyes held an unspoken question.

Kura slapped the glossies on the platform and sat alongside her. Grimy dust spattered and quickly resettled. He rubbed his bleary eyes.

"I can't detect any air-brushing, double exposure, or darkroom gimmickry in these prints," Kura admitted.

"You're convinced they're genuine, then?"

"I wouldn't swear to it in court, not without seeing the negatives. Maybe not then. Off the record, yes, I'd say what was photographed was really there."

Cooper nodded impatiently, resenting the need to treat Kura like a child.

"Now do you believe this creature tore through the Upper West Side last night?"

Kura licked his lips. Dryness made his mouth ache, and water wasn't enough to satisfy. "These prints are more persuasive than the muddy reproductions in the newspapers you brought. That doesn't rule out a hoax. Could be a trick of perspective, some clown in a rubber suit …"

"There were too many witnesses, Mr. Kura. At least two zoologists who've examined these shots are not prepared to categorically reject them."

The photographer shrugged. "Not my specialty. Where did you get these, anyway?"

"The police subpoenaed them from the newspaper. Copies were given to various scientific advisers. Mine came from an associate who works at the Museum of Natural History."

Kura's eyes narrowed. He wasn't *that* dull. "You said that *you* worked for the museum when you wanted me to sign that release."

Cooper shook her head. "I said I represented the museum. In that particular matter."

Kura scowled. "Why come to me? Other photographers are

better qualified to make this sort of verification." He toyed with the knot of his robe's belt and raised an eyebrow. "Unless you changed your mind about something else?"

Cooper hissed in annoyance. "You can't be that stupid, Kura. Look at those shots again. You know what that thing is, of course."

"I told you what I think: a man in a rubber suit."

"It's an oni!"

"A what?"

"A demon, from the legends of ancient Japan. You *must* have seen paintings and carvings of them. I saw one myself yesterday, at Japan House. I know you've been there, because you attended the opening reception when the Society displayed some of your photographs."

Kura pursed his lips and shook his head. "I never left the party, except to visit the john."

"You *really* don't know the story of the iron sword?"

"We went through this yesterday. No. I don't."

"Then I'll tell you. The sword was made over a thousand years ago, with the aid of a shinto priest, to slay a demon. It was never used. A boy tricked the oni into the hollow iron hilt, and sealed the demon within."

The photographer snorted. "The same demon now making headlines?"

"Don't you think I realize how insane this sounds? But it's true! The creature first struck three days ago. Near the first victim, the police found the mangled remains of the iron hilt."

A whispering current of air suddenly eddied about the pair on the platform. It did not displace a strand of Cooper's thick brown hair, or dry a drop of perspiration on Kura's brow. Neither of them mentioned it, but both sensed the presence.

Kura tensed, bare soles pressing flat on the rough wooden floor. "I have a splitting headache, Mrs. Cooper, and you're not making it better. I want you to leave. Now."

The researcher did not move. "That hilt was part of the collection your father wanted back from the museum. It had been stolen from storage."

"Proving my old man was right to ask for it."

Cooper ignored this. "According to legend, the boy hero went on to found the samurai family Akuragawa ... the original name of *your* family, Mr. Kura!"

The photographer sprang to his feet. He jabbed a shaking finger at the woman. His eyes glittered.

"Who are you, lady? Why badger me?"

Cooper's voice faltered. "My daughter was this creature's first victim. That's whom I am. As to the second question, you're the only person who can kill the oni."

"Tchah! That's ridiculous. I ..." Kura's face turned ashen. He staggered as though struck, and dropped back heavily onto the platform. His hands covered his face. "No. Oh no."

This sudden change alarmed Cooper. Her hand reached out, but stopped short of the photographer's shoulder. She didn't quite trust him. "Are you going to be sick?"

"Yes. No." Kura rubbed his face briskly with his palms. Blood rushed to his cheeks, giving him an even ghastlier countenance. "I don't know. This thing first showed on Tuesday night?"

"To the best of my knowledge."

"About midnight?"

Cooper nodded. "That's close to Lynda's ... to when it happened."

Kura's breathing grew ragged. He turned to Cooper with red-rimmed eyes.

"At that same time I was woken by a woman's screams. My body dripped sweat. My heart felt like it was being squeezed. I screamed myself." He took a deep breath. "Jenny said she'd heard only my outcry."

Cooper smoothed a crease in her slacks. "Interesting."

"The thing is, I haven't been able to sleep since. Whenever I drop off, I hear that scream, and each time more screams join it."

"The dead cry out for vengeance." Cooper shook her head to clear it. Where did *those* words come from? One of Nakato's stories, perhaps.

"I don't understand," said Kura.

"I'm a rationalist, Mr. Kura. I can't blame you for having a hard time accepting this. I wouldn't credit it myself, without those pictures."

"Why me? Why do I alone hear the torments?"

Cooper met his pain-filled eyes squarely. "Because you are the last of the Akuragawa line. The hilt and the sword were entrusted to your ancestors for just this reason. You are the demon's appointed guardian, Andrew Kura. You are the only man who can destroy it!"

Kura stared at his knees. "No."

"Yes. If this demon can survive for a millennium, why not the kami who have pledged themselves to the sword's purpose? Why not the spirits of your ancestors? It is they who bring the screams to your ears. They want you to face your destiny."

"No!"

The denial echoed in the huge, empty loft space, and clung to wooden beams. Even the imperceptible draught seemed to shrink back from such vehemence. Kura bent forward, face buried in his hands, shivering despite the hot light and his heavy bathrobe. He did not look like the end result of generations of proud soldiers.

"I'm sorry, for your sake," Cooper said softly, "but you must pull yourself together. There's little time."

His head shot up. He glared at her. His lip trembled. "This is absurd. I'm not chasing monsters on your say-so."

Cooper sighed. "Try to understand, Andrew, it's not my decision. Given a choice, I wouldn't be here. Thousands of people in this city would make better champions. I know a bartender uptown who'd be happy to help. Unfortunately, the obligation is yours."

"I renounce it."

"You can't."

"I can. I do. You're so fucking eager, you can go after him. I put it on your shoulders."

The draught seemed to close in again. Almost, Cooper felt it touch her cheek, stroke her hair. Almost. She glanced at her folded coat, but did not reach for it. She wasn't really cold. Not that kind of chill.

"I'm tempted to accept. I doubt it works that way, though."

"Just get the fuck out of here!"

Cooper shook her head. "I can't leave, not until you agree to do what you must. My own obligation is different but no less binding."

"I'll leave town. Move to San Francisco where my old man lived before the war."

"That won't do any good, Andrew. The kami will follow. You'll never know a good night's sleep."

Kura shut his eyes tight, trying to escape her words. Death cries of more than a dozen people swelled in his brain. He writhed, sharing their anguished final moments again and again. His face grew damp. He groaned and fell forward, sobbing.

Cooper caught his hand in her lap. She rubbed his shoulders and patted his back and head. Eventually, Kura calmed.

The loft was very still.

Kura whispered something.

"What was that?"

"I'll do it." His eyes opened. "On one condition."

Cooper breathed a sigh of relief. "Which is?"

His hand crept under her suit jacket and cupped a breast.

Cooper pushed him away and stood. Kura had to scrabble to avoid rolling off the platform onto the floor.

"No," she said.

Kura sat up. His eyes shone with anger. "You want me to risk my life. What I want from you is comparatively little."

"If you need it, I'll pay for a prostitute."

Kura smiled. "I don't just want sex. I want you, the proud, upright lady who knows what's best for everyone! I want to use you, Frannie, before I let you use me."

"Of all the petty, degrading...

Kura shrugged. "Otherwise, you'll have to find someone else to lug that iron sword around."

Reaching for her coat, Cooper gripped the edge of the platform as she fought to keep her temper. Her fingernails left deep gouges in the wood.

"This is not something one barters, Mr. Kura. If you won't undertake the task to fulfill your family obligations or save

some lives, what about freeing yourself from your nightmares?"
The photographer wiped his chin on the collar of his robe.
"I can survive another sleepless night or two. Next week I
might be desperate enough to modify my terms. However, each
additional death in the meantime will be on your head, not
mine. You'll be sharing my nightmares."

Standing with her coat over one arm, Cooper took a slip of
paper from her purse and scribbled Mrs. Barclay's number on it.
She dropped it on the platform.

"I can be reached at that telephone number, Mr. Kura, the
minute you change your mind."

He ignored it. "I'm out of dimes. I'll wait for you."

Cooper stalked to the door of the loft. Halfway there, she
looked back. Kura sat smugly, legs crossed, eyes glazed with
uninhibited lust, confident that she wouldn't risk breaking his
wrist now. If Cooper held the iron sword at that moment, with a
choice between the oni and the photographer, her decision as to
which one to kill would be very close. Very close.

Something new had been added to the inside of the loft
door: a 1983 pin-up calendar from a local garage. Miss January
wore the traditional garb of the symbolic New Year's baby,
though hardly the traditional pose. It reminded Cooper of
another tradition: the crowds that gathered in Times Square
on New Year's Eve to watch the glowing red apple descend at
midnight. If she was right about the oni's whereabouts—and
she was sure she was—and if the monster followed the path
of least resistance, as it seemed inclined to do, the celebration
would be a bloody one. A massacre of thousands.

Cooper stalked back to the platform. She threw down her
coat, slipped off the suit jacket. Fingers trembling with rage, she
began unbuttoning her blouse.

"Let's get this over with," she said grimly. "We have to stop
at the museum for the sword."

Kura's eyes dilated victoriously. "How, ah, how do we obtain
this magical weapon? Let me help with that."

"No. You'll tear it!" She did not want his hands on her flesh
a moment more than necessary.

"Legally, the sword is still yours. I've spoken to Allison Zebar in their public relations department. I'm sure the museum will cooperate, in exchange for your signed release." Slacks pooled around her ankles. She freed her feet and stood, shivering, in her underwear. "Can you at least stop staring long enough to find a blanket? This platform's full of splinters."

Kura grinned and pointed behind the backdrop screen. His robe fell open.

Cooper tasted bile.

CHAPTER 48

"I thought you'd gone for the day, Lieutenant."

Foster turned to the swarthy man standing hunched over an open file drawer.

"I did, Chelli. Then I decided to clean my gun and remembered I'd left it in my locker."

Frank Chelli was the newest addition to Foster's squad, assigned to Homicide on the first day of autumn. That was long enough for him to know that Lieutenant Foster didn't forget things. It was even long enough for Chelli to know better than to mention that fact. He nodded and continued filing.

Foster tapped a thick folder in a wire basket atop the cabinet. "This the file on that oni creature?"

"Some of it."

"Rogan has copies of all the reports?"

"Yes, sir. Even transcripts of crank calls. Suspect has been positively identified as the Antichrist. Someone claimed it escaped from Three Mile Island. Also it's part of a Communist plot, and an excuse by Washington for the President to declare martial law."

"I like that last one." Foster chuckled. Serves the case-stealing bastard right. No, strike that thought. It wasn't Rogan's fault. "Speaking of phone calls, Chelli, I tried returning Mrs. Cooper's call this morning, when I got your note. Had to leave word on her recording. If she calls again, put her on to Rogan, but if she insists, you can give her my home number. I don't expect to be partying tonight."

Chelli's eyes narrowed. "You really want to encourage that one, Lieutenant?"

"If she's willing to call long distance from Boston. Why?"
Chelli grinned. "I took that call myself. She talked pretty
wild, about this creature changing size and stuff like that. Said
it was hiding in a subway tunnel." His grin widened. "Nothing
is so weird that some people won't try to top it, eh, Lieutenant?"
Foster did not share Chelli's amusement. Francine
Cooper had impressed him as sane and competent, though
understandably distraught. She wasn't the type to bother police
with bizarre theories; and if she were, why wait two days to start
when her connection with the case, and subsequent influence,
was less strong?

"You're sure you're talking about the Cooper call from this
morning? Francine Cooper? Mother of Lynda Cooper?"

"Yes, sir. Around seven thirty. Do you want the exact time
it came in?"

Foster felt a twinge in his game leg that had nothing to do
with the weather. "I wonder how the Boston papers got the story
that early. Unless ... that call *did* come from Massachusetts?"

Chelli put down his armful of folders. "I'll check the log
downstairs."

"Don't bother. I'm thinking aloud. No, it had to be a local
call. She's here in New York. That's the only way she could have
figured the subway angle so quickly."

Chelli goggled. He'd seen that same look, almost a glow, on
Foster's face three weeks ago, just before the lieutenant solved a
porno-king slaying. "You think she's on the level?"

The New York City subway system, Foster recalled, possessed
more than seven hundred track miles, all interconnected. "I'm
afraid she is. Do you know if Rogan's still in my office?"

"As far as I know, Lieutenant."

Without another word, Foster limped away in search of his
replacement. He hoped his earlier words, spoken in bitter anger,
hadn't estranged Lieutenant Rogan completely. Foster needed
one hell of a favor.

CHAPTER 49

Obtaining the iron sword was as easy as twisting a baby's arm. Cooper expected more of a fight from Allison Zebar. The silver-haired woman practically thrust the relic on Kura and herself. It felt right, Zebar explained. She only wanted to clear up loose ends, not create more complications. Andrew Kura signed the release for his family heirlooms, muttering something about borrowing the sword to use as a prop in a photo session. That was all Zebar needed, or wanted, to know. She shrugged off Kura's opinions on the genuine quality of the oni pictures. The museum's experts reached the same conclusion *before* Zebar lent Cooper the prints. The photographs merely gave Cooper an excuse to talk to Kura again—regarding the release, Cooper had told Zebar.

Fortunately, there was no one at the museum at that late hour to countermand Zebar's authorization. Most of the higher echelon staff had taken an early start on the holiday weekend. Police photographs could be studied as well, or better, at home.

Now the last of the Akuragawa clan walked alongside the woman from Boston, west on Seventy-Ninth Street, under clouding night skies. A raw wind screamed across from the Hudson River to tear at their faces. Cheek and nose and ear were stung crimson. A smattering of tiny hard flakes bit their skin.

Kura wore a heavy, dark blue coat purchased for him by Cooper at an Army surplus store near his loft. One sleeve hung empty. Beneath the coat, Kura clutched the hilt of his ancestors' blade. The iron's cold penetrated his leather gloves, seeping up past his wrist, numbing the arm.

Cooper ignored his whining moans.

At the corner of Broadway, Kura turned to the nearest subway entrance. Cooper had been clutching his arm, using him as an anchor against the icy blasts. She tightened her grip. He drew up short, stumbling.

"This is the Uptown side," Cooper explained. "We want Downtown."

"So what? We're not taking it anywhere!"

"At this hour more people will be headed toward Times Square than the Bronx. There will be fewer people on the opposite platform to notice what we do after we let the Downtown Local pass."

The traffic light changed before Kura could protest further. He was half-led, half-dragged across Broadway. When they were halfway, crossing the median, the "Don't Walk" sign began to flash. Cooper plunged on. They left the crosswalk to go around a cab that blocked their way and saved a trip around the sprawling corner newsstand. Traffic began moving south as they clambered over the curb and down a flight of concrete steps.

The wind seemed to follow them, reaching icily up Kura's pants legs. Cooper paused at the bulletproof change booth to purchase fare tokens. Once the two were past the turnstile and on the station platform, they were enveloped by lesser but fouler air currents, created mostly by Express trains rushing along the center tracks.

Cooper's nose wrinkled at the sickly sweet odor of urine. "Some people never heard of bathrooms," she muttered.

Kura smiled. "You're lucky it isn't summer." His free hand reached for the armrest of a wooden bench, the slats of which were clogged with thick blue paint, not quite as dark as his coat.

Cooper jerked him onward, to the station's south end. The bathroom smell grew stronger.

"This isn't the way I'd planned to spend New Year's Eve," Kura observed.

"Nor would I willingly choose your company, Mr. Kura." Her tone was more frigid than the breeze.

"Still mad about this afternoon?"

Cooper looked at the photographer as if he were a new and not very interesting species of cockroach. "Until the oni is slain, I can't afford the luxury of despising you."

"You loved it. You just won't admit it."

Cooper's free hand shot up. She forced herself to lower it. Her lips thinned. Her face paled. The fingers of her other hand unconsciously tightened on Kura's arm. When he yelped a complaint, she eased the vise of her grip, not without regret. Kura needed both hands to wield the heavy weapon.

Express trains rumbled through in both directions before a Downtown Local pulled into the station. Cooper watched silently. The lead car screeched to a stop within arm's length. Waiting passengers shoved rudely on or off, and sometimes both if they were not alert. The doors wheezed shut. The train jerked forward again. Cooper moved to the yellow line marking the edge of the platform and stared down the tunnel. The red lights of the rear car stopped at the Seventy-Second Street station.

"Looks clear," she said. She tugged Kura's elbow.

The photographer balked. "Those three kids who just got off are still fooling around on the platform."

"They're not watching us. They're busy adding bon mots to the billboard ads. That couple on the Uptown side aren't interested in us, either."

"I didn't see them." His eyes widened. "Is she doing what I think she's doing?"

"Why do you think they're standing behind that trash can?" Cooper snapped. "Don't tell me you're shocked."

"I wish I'd brought a camera."

Cooper pushed Kura toward the narrow lip at the platform's south end. His free hand shot out for support. It slid along the grimy tunnel wall. He staggered down the short steps leading to the trackbed, and paused. Surely this commotion would attract attention! If it did, however, it was a passive sort of attention.

Cooper followed quietly in rubber-soled loafers.

They crept forward, staying near the tunnel wall to avoid the electrified third rails. In the darkness it would be too easy to stumble into that deadly voltage, despite the raised wooden covers intended to prevent workers from doing just that. In addition, Cooper reasoned that the oni would probably hide in one of the wall recesses. The creature's full-sized bulk would interfere with subway operations anywhere else, whereas shrunken he'd find the tunnel's center to be uncomfortably draughty and hazardous.

Kura unbuttoned his coat and changed sword hands, in order to slip his arm in the empty sleeve. He swung the weapon out over the tracks as he walked. It cut the air with a fine, whispery echo, but its weight made him limp.

He nudged Cooper. "You don't have to come, you know." His words bounced back and forth between steel stanchions.

Cooper whispered her answer, setting the volume for the conversation. "The hell I don't. If I left you alone for two seconds, you'd crawl into some sidestreet bar and hide out in the back room."

Of course he would, Kura silently admitted. "What's the big rush, anyway? Even if this sword is the only thing that can kill the demon, and I'm the only one who can use it—and I'm still not a hundred percent sold on either premise—couldn't we get some police backup, or something?"

Cooper wiped moist hands on her coat. She left greasy streaks on the dark fabric.

"I called Lieutenant Foster of Homicide. He's in charge of the case, and he knows me. I'd half hoped we'd run into him here with a squad or two. Maybe he didn't get my message. Maybe it was twisted around. Maybe he doesn't buy the size-changing. If I'd been able to talk to the lieutenant personally ..."

"The oni's vanishing over a subway grating should be persuasive evidence," Kura said, startling himself. Was he *really* getting caught up in this insanity?

"Well, we can't take the time to look for him. We may already be too late."

Kura raised his eyebrows.

"Too late for what?"

"The creature seems to be nocturnal. Tonight is New Year's Eve. Two miles down these tracks lies Times Square."

"So?"

"Do you need everything spelled out for you? Imagine the

havoc if that monster pops up in the middle of that crowd!"

Kura sniffed. "Small loss, I'd say."

Cooper laughed sharply. The echo was almost metallic, and went apparently unnoticed by anyone on the platform at Seventy-Second and Seventy-Ninth Streets.

"Yes," she whispered, "I daresay ninety percent of the population could perish tomorrow, to good effect. Who cares if Andrew Kura is crushed like an insect?"

Kura stopped walking. "No need to get personal."

"An individual has but one life. No one else should have the right to determine who forfeits theirs."

"I've got you there. What about the oni's life?"

"He's had more than his share. Move."

The photographer started forward at her push. His heavy boots crunched gravel. Periodically he touched the rough, soot-coated wall, to be sure he was not drifting too far from it, although his eyes were adjusting well to the gloom.

"There's another contradiction," he said.

"What is it?" Cooper asked impatiently.

"You claim that this oni is the reincarnation of a Lord Uto, who died in the seventh century. You also said the kami who've been haunting my dreams are spirits of my ancestors. Doesn't that imply life after death?"

Cooper sighed. She hadn't been giving much thought to the philosophical implications of these bizarre circumstances. She'd been more concerned with dealing with them on a practical level.

"I don't have *all* the answers, Mr. Kura. I know what the kami are supposed to represent, and who the oni is believed to be. Legends don't come with footnotes. Prior to today, I never saw a scrap of real evidence for an afterlife. I'm still not sure I have. There may be explanations for Uto's incarnation that we can't imagine, but which nevertheless avoid the supernatural. There's no guarantee that the story Mr. Nakato told me has *any* basis in fact. All I know is that so far everything seems to fit the legend, and all I can do is act as if it were real until I discover something to the contrary."

"For a skeptic, Mrs. Cooper, you're certainly sold on this

fantasy."

Cooper searched for the mockery in Kura's expression, but even with her eyes now accustomed to the tunnel's murk she saw only shadow above his collar. She could have pulled out her flashlight for a look, but she didn't want to give him that satisfaction. His own eyes would have had to readjust, besides, and the oni might choose that moment to attack. If he really was near.

"I may reserve judgment," she replied slowly, "but I will not deny a fact just because its explanation isn't yet clear to me. The oni is certainly too big a fact to ignore. Now shut up and keep moving. If you must speak, lower your voice. We don't need an audience."

CHAPTER 58

Because Captain Matherson had thrust him into an awkward situation, sitting behind Amos Foster's desk while the detective he'd replaced paced before him, Lieutenant Rogan was inclined to hear his colleague out. His patience, however, had its limits. When Foster grew strident, Rogan got to his feet.

"You're not supposed to be here anyway, Foster, let alone dictate how I should handle the case. You're out of it. Go home. Listen to Guy Lombardo."

"He's dead. Damn it, Rogan, I'm not grandstanding! This lead is worth following up!"

The two men were practically touching noses across the desk. Their muffled shouts reached beyond the closed door and into the squad room. Rogan backed off and lowered his voice.

"Based on what?"

"My experience on the case. The reliability of the source."

Lieutenant Rogan glanced at his watch. His car was waiting to take him on the rounds. "I haven't time for a wild goose chase, Foster. Every unit I can scrounge up is covering Riverside Park tonight. They're nowhere near enough, as you damn well know; less than half the manpower you had last night."

"The park is ancient history now." Foster slapped open palms to his own chest. "Let me check the subway out. Under your command. Lend me a couple of uniforms."

"You're not listening. I don't *have* a spare couple of uniforms. Nearly every other cop in the city is on crowd control in Times Square."

"It's not midnight yet. You can borrow a unit off that detail for an hour. Come on, Rogan. I lost the fucking creature. Give me a chance to find it again." Foster swallowed hard. Tension tightened every muscle in his body. His leg throbbed. He wasn't used to begging. It hurt.

Rogan saw that hurt. He sat down heavily and stared at the wood grain of the desk top for a long moment before replying. "All right, Foster. One hour. Keep a low profile, though, or Matherson will hang us both."

Foster slapped a meaty hand on his colleague's shoulder. "Call me Amos. Suddenly I don't hate you half as much as I did this afternoon."

Rogan shrugged as he reached for a copy of the duty roster. "Try to keep the feeling mutual, will you, Amos?"

CHAPTER 51

With her eyes fully adjusted to the gloom, Cooper was surprised to realize how well-lit this section of tunnel actually was. She wouldn't have tried reading the New York Times by the dull yellow work lights, but neither did she seem to need the heavy-duty flashlight in her coat pocket. In addition, there were few solid walls among the old-fashioned angled struts to block the glow of lights from the Seventy-Second Street platforms.

Nonetheless, the underground atmosphere was oppressive. Rats as large as kittens scurried over the toes of her loafers, making her wish she'd worn her high boots even though the latter were too heavy for the running she might have to do, and did not have rubber soles. An acrid scent of burnt paper hung in the dank air. Soot and metal dust clustered on exposed flesh; her hands and face itched. Wary of loose gravel, splintery wooden ties, crumbling concrete and other signs of neglected maintenance, she tested every step.

Kura was muttering to himself again. As long as he kept it low, she could not bring herself to curse him quiet. Despicable he might be, but Kura was risking his life, and at her urging. Cooper could not forgive him for what he'd demanded in payment for this service, but she thought she understood his need to humiliate her. It could have been worse.

You can train an ape to flap his arms, but don't expect him to fly very far.

Each time a train roared through, they leapt to the tunnel wall and huddled in the nearest recess. Only their eyes moved as car after car rumbled past, dragging soot and steel dust and old newspapers in the wake. With their collars turned up, the two demon-hunters were almost completely enveloped in dark folds of clothing, resembling the ninja spies of medieval Japan. No ninja, though, had had to remain invisible within a headlight's beam. If they hadn't been spotted so far, Cooper thought, it was due entirely to luck and, possibly, the fact that the average motorman was not looking for track-walkers here at this time. That couldn't last for long. The train wouldn't stop, but the conductor would radio the dispatcher, who in turn would call the Transit Police at their Columbus Circle headquarters, less than three stops south. So far, however, there were no signs of pursuit.

Cooper's left foot brushed a rail. She felt it vibrating and glanced back to confirm her deduction. A Downtown Local approached Seventy-Ninth, the first since they'd started down the tracks. Cooper threw herself flat against the tunnel wall, pulling Kura with her, to dodge the bright beams of the lead car.

The photographer's cheek smashed the grimy wall as he struggled to keep his balance. He tasted blood; the impact had caused him to bite his tongue. At least his monologue had been interrupted, and Cooper hissed a warning for him to remain silent.

Together, they slid over the shifting gravel by the roadbed. They found and clambered into a recess as the train screeched to a halt. The two waited for it to start again.

When it finally did, it passed near enough that Kura could have raised sparks on its metal side with his sword point. No sooner did the last car go by than air brakes squealed once more for the Seventy-Second Street stop.

We *must* have been spotted then, Cooper thought. She licked her lips. Kura opened his mouth to speak. She waved it shut again until the Local pulled out and its rear lights vanished around the curve of the tunnel.

"What is it now?" she finally whispered. "You don't have to go to the bathroom again, do you?"

Kura winced, wishing she hadn't reminded him. No, he was all right. His kidneys must be squeezed dry after all the time he spent in the men's room of the museum.

"I only wanted to know your next step." Kura pointed. "Up onto *that* platform and down the other side, all the way to Times Square?"

Cooper shook her head. "Not on an Express stop. Too many people. Anyway, we're not finished with this section of tunnel. The demon *has* to be hiding between these two stops. He entered through a ventilation grate on the south side of Seventy-Ninth. If he'd gone uptown towards Eighty-Sixth Street he'd have passed through the station, and someone would have seen him. Since this western wall seems to be clear, we'll have to check the east."

"Unless he got bored and left."

"According to Jiro Nakato, oni love caves. He's here."

"He might've hopped a ride to Prospect Park."

Cooper shrugged. "Or the Bronx Zoo. If he did, there's no way we can trace him until he shows himself."

"Let's wait at my place."

"No. We go by what little we know, not what obstacles we can imagine." She leaned out of the recess. "No trains coming. Let's cross over. Watch out for the third rail."

"I know that much!" Kura muttered, following as Cooper leapt to the roadbed and started briskly across. He scrambled to take the lead, and turned his head to flash a grin at the woman as he passed. His right foot rose higher than necessary, and then came down too soon. His sole scraped the wooden safety cover.

Cooper plunged forward to grasp the sword and lift it away from the humming rail. Her fingers tingled from the contact. The blade seemed to possess its own electricity.

"Kura, you ass! Don't drag the sword like a damned pull-toy!"

Kura swallowed a thick clot that had formed in his throat. He did not reply. He was too shaken by his sudden, narrow escape.

Sticky warmth oozed onto Cooper's left palm.

She brought it to her lips. The blood had a sharp, acrid taste. An eyebrow fluttered in mild surprise. When she'd hefted the iron sword under Allison Zebar's cool gaze, the edge looked anything but keen, barely capable of cutting butter. Cooper would never have considered it a feasible weapon, but the legend insisted on its inherent power. She wasn't sure what that meant; bolts of energy, she'd supposed, like something out of *Star Wars.* Yet now the edge was sharp enough to slice her hand at a touch. She sucked at the wound, hoping her saliva would counteract any disease-bearing bacteria that might be harbored in the tunnel sludge staining her hands.

The sword was preparing for the realization of its thousand-year-old destiny.

They'd reached the Uptown Local tracks and Kura was already creeping north.

"Kura!" she whispered. "He's near. He *must* be."

She reached for his elbow. He drew his arm away so that she could not feel his trembling.

"Why suddenly so sure?"

Cooper had no chance to explain. The wall came to life in front of the photographer. The tunnel floor shook with a vibration unlike that of any passing subway train. A shadowy mass came between them and the lights of the Seventy-Ninth Street platform.

Their search was over.

Again he'd overslept! Though not without reason. He'd battled fiercely and eaten well the night before. Much of his old confidence had returned as he grew used to surprise. He feared these villagers less with each encounter. Feared? Never!

He'd just been sizing up his opponents, as any good warrior would do.

They had thrown their best at him. Their methods were unusual, but that wasn't good enough. He'd been more startled than harmed by, for example, those lead pellets.

He was impatient now. Tonight began his conquest in earnest. Tonight he hunted.

He had barely made his decision when harsh whispers reached his pointed ears. The infamously unpleasant grin twisted his lips. He would not have to seek far for his first prey. They were coming to him: foolish, would-be heroes, no doubt.

If they were so eager to die, of course, he saw no harm in obliging them.

Cooper reached into the left-hand pocket of her coat for the heavy black flashlight. Blood from her cut made the casing slippery. She shifted it to her right hand and flicked it on. The barrel end prevented the beam from diffusing.

Spotlighted in the sudden glare, the oni blinked but otherwise did not flinch. The creature's grin revealed dark-stained fangs. The horns atop the hairless skull scraped the roof of the tunnel, and the temperature seemed to take a sudden drop.

"My God," moaned Kura. "My God!"

Though Cooper, too, was shaken, her companion's whimpering strengthened her own resolve. "Lift the blade, Kura! It's the only thing that can kill him! Can't you feel the power in your grip? The sword *wants* this conflict! Defend yourself, you idiot!"

Kura couldn't understand her words. Panic overrode his senses. He heard only the blood rushing through his arteries, felt only an all-enveloping cold, saw only the great three-fingered hand reaching for his throat. Despite this paralysis, he was raising the blade.

When it leveled parallel to the tracks, Kura stumbled forward, less attacking than dragged into conflict.

The demon's mouth writhed. Guttural syllables spewed forth. The ebon eyes blazed with loathing as they fell upon the iron sword.

His previous glimpse had been fleeting, a moment or two, more than a dozen centuries ago, but that had been sufficient. Its image was branded in his mind. Meiko's workmanship was undeniable. He'd brooded on the memory of it for a millennium.

The weapon clove the thick air between its wielder and himself, singing his doom.

His doom? Pah! He feared no man.

He gave challenge.

Cooper's free hand covered her left ear, matting her hair with blood and cutting the volume not a decibel. The monster's roar echoed from the recessed walls, bounced off metal struts, to throb against her eardrums. When it finally faded, it was replaced by a swelling babble from somewhere behind her. Subway riders at the north end of the Seventy-Second Street station could hardly have failed to hear that outcry. Many of them jockeyed along the platform's lip for better views.

Kura tightened his grip on the hilt with both hands. The swordtip wavered, but it did not lower.

Straining to keep silent, Cooper bit her tongue. She concentrated on holding the flashlight steady.

No verbal encouragement could counter that awesome sight and would only distract the photographer ... likely with fatal results.

The demon's hand shot forward.

Kura dodged to the right, swinging the blade. It missed the oni and clanged along the tunnel wall. The iron reverberated in anguished frustration.

The demon moved quickly. He would corner his assailant before Kura recovered from the misstep.

Kura spun to the left, letting the weapon's weight drag him along. He realized that his best chance was to let the sword have its way. It knew better than he how to fight.

The blade's edge sliced a thin line on the oni's right thigh, level with Kura's chin. Ichor welled thick and black as pitch.

The oni shrieked, backing rapidly away. Cooper had to trot to keep her circle of light focused on the red-skinned giant. It seemed to her that there was suddenly more clearance between the monster's horns and the tunnel roof. Was the creature simply crouching as he ran ... or did he plan to escape by shrinking down?

He mustn't be allowed to escape.

"Follow through!" Cooper called to the reluctant champion.

Moving through the gloom at the edge of Cooper's lightbeam, Kura closed in. His flannel shirt stuck to his back. He was already overheated from exertion. He licked dry lips. With one eye on his quarry, the Akuragawa heir shifted the weapon from hand to hand in order to shrug off his overcoat. The garment fell, forgotten, into the greasy filth between the tracks.

The oni moaned.

He, Andrew Kura, was winning! At least, he'd hurt the thing. That was more than New York's Finest had done, according to the newspapers. The sword really was blessed, and the hilt tingled in his hands. A mere scratch caused the oni unutterable agony, to judge by his screams. Of course, the monster could be faking, trying to lure him in, but something told Kura that this was no act.

Something which might have been the kami of the sword.

Cooper's advice was sound, he thought. Press your advantage.

Kura ran forward, swinging the sword in an arc above his head.

An impressive charge. Not a practical one. The demon, who had vastly more battle experience, mirrored it. The gap between them narrowed faster than Kura thought possible.

The photographer wasn't prepared for this. He tried to slow and turn aside. The eager sword defied him. Kura skidded on roadbed gravel and stubbed his toe on a crosstie. He tumbled to land sprawling at the oni's feet.

The creature chuckled and reached down.

Kura rolled between those massive legs. Talons raked his back. The sword clanged on a rail, the impact jarring his arm to the elbow, but he managed to hold onto it.

The oni spun to face him.

Kura struggled erect. He stood waiting, feet apart, knees bent slightly, sword angled protectively before him. As a novice, he could only guess at the best defensive posture for the situation. The demon's counterattack was swift. Even an experienced samurai might have been slow to make the proper move.

The three-fingered hand circled both of Kura's wrists at once. Bones ground against bones. The oni jerked him off the tunnel floor. The photographer's left shoulder tore out of its socket with a wet pop. His cries ripped through the darkness.

The iron sword fell from nerveless fingers. It clattered dully on the ties.

A rush of air struck Cooper's left cheek, tugging at her hair.

She turned her face into it expectantly. This could be a kamikaze, a divine wind such as that which miraculously saved Japan from the Mongol invasion. They needed a miracle now!

Miracles didn't happen that easily.

A Downtown Express hurtled along the tracks. The oni held Kura suspended between the Uptown Local and Express tracks. The motorman did not yet see the monster. Safety lights on his route were green; he expected no obstacles. The cars barreled down the straightaway, for this was the best section of track in the whole system for feeling the speed these cars were capable of, as any subway buff would attest. The oni's body blocked the beam of Cooper's flashlight, denying the driver even that much hint that something was not right.

Kura dangled like a puppet. Suddenly, his right shoulder also dislocated. A gurgling scream escaped his lips, and his world was a ball of red pain.

The oni grinned.

Cooper followed, ashen-faced, as the oni moved northward with his prize. What else could she do? There was a chance, however small, that the creature would get bored or distracted, allowing her to drag Kura free.

There was a much better chance of getting herself killed.

The Express whipped past the Seventy-Ninth Street station. Its rumble drowned the faint scrape of Cooper's loafers on the awkwardly-spaced ties.

The oni stopped and twirled Kura about his horned skull. The man's ankle smashed against a steel strut. Kura screamed in fresh agony. The oni released him.

The photographer thudded onto the Express tracks, in the center of the lead car's headlight beams.

Brakes groaned. Passengers slid along hard plastic seats, piling up on one another. Standees grappled with straps or sprawled on laps or floors.

Cooper stared in wide-eyed horror. The train obviously would not stop in time.

Metal wheels sliced and crushed. Blood spattered stanchions on either side of the track. Skin tore like tissue paper. Bones split.

It was over very quickly.

Bile burned Cooper's throat. I killed him, she thought. As surely as if I'd pushed him in front of that train myself. I browbeat Andrew Kura into performing heroics he was clearly unsuited for, and now ...

...now the last survivor of the Akuragawa clan was dead. No one remained to halt the oni's terror. Oh, ordinary mortals might succeed—with weapons undreamt of in the creature's time, such as the one that had defeated Japan almost forty years earlier—but not without other kinds of horror.

Three cars rolled over the photographer's corpse before the train halted. Cooper fought the urge to vomit. Her palms were damp, almost too damp to hold the flashlight. Her face felt fevered. Yet she would not give in to the creeping weakness. She *could* not!

Ignoring her, the oni strode to the lead car. Inside, riders cringed against the opposite side as his grotesque features appeared by the windows. The oni sneered. He would get to them later. He reached the front of the train and peered through the motorman's window—the serpent's eye.

Serpent! Contrivance, rather!

His bloodlust whetted, enraged at this trickery, the oni smashed his three-fingered fist through that window. The driver's compartment was small. The man had no room to duck. His head was crushed flat against the back panel.

The Dead Man switch locked the brakes. The train, with its eight cars full of eager New Year's Eve celebrants, could not now continue downtown. Passengers in the rearmost cars were unaware of the danger, but the public address system was working. No one was reassured by the broadcasting of the motorman's death gurgle. They were all at the demon's mercy.

And oni have no mercy.

CHAPTER 52

Lieutenant Amos Foster knelt at the yellow line marking the lip of the Seventy-Nine Street Uptown platform. His lips were a thin, straight line. He watched a huge, shadowy figure prod the stalled Express train as a child might molest an unfamiliar caterpillar. His revolver was heavy in his hand. A handgun would not harm the thing even if he were in range, but the sound of a shot might distract the creature's attention from the trainload of civilians.

Sergeant Dorothy Brunner trotted up behind him. She was a uniformed officer with eleven years' experience. "The clerk in the token booth confirms all traffic on the Seventh Avenue Line has been halted in both directions, Lieutenant."

Foster nodded, eyes still fixed on the oni. "Any chance of moving that train?"

"Negative. The conductor radioed the Control Center. The driver's been killed, or so it sounded to him. He might've just had a heart attack."

"Either way is murder." Foster's bad leg, the one he was kneeling on, throbbed. "Can the conductor move the train from his post?"

"Apparently not. He's in a car with faulty wiring; only the emergency lights work. If he changes cars he'll be exposed, and the movement would probably attract the creature. He wants to avoid that."

"Can't say I blame him. We'll have to get another driver, slip him into the last car before the oni notices, and have him bring the train uptown. The important thing is to get enough distance from that monster to evacuate the passengers safely."

Brunner frowned. "If that thing lets us."

"We'll keep him entertained. Afterwards, when we have a clear field, we'll cut the electricity and surround that demon."

Brunner glanced uneasily over her shoulder at the empty platform. "The back-up Rogan promised isn't here yet."

"It will be." Foster spared the sergeant a glance. "You're taking this pretty much in stride. Were you in on last night's fiasco?"

"No, sir, but I talked to some who were."

"Ever consider trying out for detective? I need a new partner."

"I don't know, Lieutenant. I'm not very good at tests, and I'm used to working alone on my beat."

"Think about it. We'll talk later."

Sick guilt all but overwhelmed Francine Cooper. By pressuring an unready Andrew Kura, she'd doomed the middle-aged photographer along with a few hundred subway passengers … and those were only the immediate consequences. She should have waited. She shouldn't have insisted they act now, tonight, immediately. A crash course in swordsmanship for the last of the Akuragawa line might have tipped the balance.

Cooper half wished that another train would rumble up the tracks on which she stood. She did not think that she would step aside.

As if acting on her suicidal impulse, Cooper walked slowly toward the oni. An eerie calm pervaded her being, driving off debilitating thoughts. Although she courted death with each step, she felt that she was actually affirming life. Her eyes locked on her goal: the red-skinned giant who now rocked the huge metal worm on its rails. His odious grin widened. Muffled shrieks of terror reverberated in the cavernous tunnel.

Cooper's shoe touched hard metal where a rail had no place to be. She lowered her flashlight beam.

The iron sword shone ebony in the light.

Unthinking, Cooper picked up the weapon with her injured hand. The dull ache of her slashed palm subsided, receding in response to the cold metal. She closed her eyes. Her memory replayed a conversation so vividly she might have been reliving it. Kura's whining voice renounced his obligation, thrust it on her. You can't do that, she'd insisted.

But she didn't know for sure that he could not.

The hilt fit perfectly in her bloodied hand. It seemed designed for her grip. She raised the weapon easily, an extension of her arm, while recalling how cumbrous it felt when Allison Zebar handed it to her less than two hours ago.

Less than a lifetime ago.

An unearthly current eddied about Cooper, tugging at the fringes of her thick cloth coat and loose, flowing hair. She sensed, rather than felt, that wind's inherent warmth.

The Akuragawa kami were gathering in support.

Cooper hurled her flashlight away. It crashed against a stanchion to vanish in darkness as the bulb shattered. The woman raised the sword overhead in a two-handed grip. Her rubber shoes thudded heavily alongside the tracks without a single false step. A scream she'd never screamed outside of her self-defense class tore from her lips.

"Hai-yah!"

Sergeant Brunner's heels thudded on the grimy concrete platform as she again hurried from the token booth to join the detective in charge. Communications liaison was a task she'd normally assign to one of the officers in her command, but they were needed to cordon off the subway entrances.

"A train was stopped north of Eighty-Sixth Street, Lieutenant," she retorted. "Passengers being discharged now. As soon as they're all above ground, a squad car will bring the motorman down here."

Foster took a deep breath. "He understands the risk?"

Brunner nodded. "And volunteered."

"Good for him. When he gets here, I'll take a couple of officers and move in to distract the oni. As soon as we draw him off, you get that driver aboard and … what the fuck?"

Lieutenant Foster leapt from the platform, landing heavily in the center of the tracks. His bad leg almost folded beneath him but, though he wobbled, he did not fall. Still holding his revolver, he squinted down the murky tunnel.

"What's wrong, Lieutenant?"

"Who's cowboying down there?"

Brunner eased herself down and stood beside Foster for a clearer view. "No one from my unit, that's for sure. Out of uniform. From the stride, I'd guess she's female."

Foster moved to the Express tracks, nearer the center of the tunnel, stepping gingerly over the humming third rail. The woman neared the stalled train. Light from the car windows illuminated her features.

Foster's jaw sagged. "That's Mrs. Cooper!"

"Who?" asked Brunner.

Foster did not reply. What did that crazy bitch think she was doing? He started forward.

Sergeant Brunner moved to follow the lieutenant. Foster waved her back.

"Call in your unit, Sergeant. If the back-up shows now, fine, show them in. If not, we move in without them. Weapons ready, but no shooting until I say so. Someone might hit the woman."

The oni expected no attack and was too startled to dodge. Cooper's first blow cut him to the bone. Thick, oily fluid seeped down the scarlet calf of his left leg.

Cooper retreated, not waiting for the counterblow. She was pleased to note that her earlier impression, that Kura's attack had diminished the creature, had *not* been an illusion. With this wound, her foe became dramatically smaller. The horned forehead was now level with the subway car roof.

Which still meant that the oni towered over her.

Cooper rushed forward, thrusting again. The creature leapt out of the blade's path. His crimson bulk slammed into a car, almost derailing it. It rocked unsteadily, shaking the attached cars as well. Screams of panic rose anew.

The uptown end of the tunnel suddenly echoed with footsteps. Cooper dared not turn to look. If her eyes left the demon for a single second, he could shrink to hide in the sooty gravel of the roadbed. While she watched, however, that strategy could leave the oni momentarily more vulnerable. The proof of this was that he made no such attempt.

The showdown had to come here and now. This was her best, likely her only, opportunity. The oni was still befuddled by pain and the fact that his opponent was a round-eyed woman. Cooper stalked the brick-red giant as it backed slowly southward.

More footfalls, a herd of them, came from behind Cooper. The woman hoped no fool would grab or otherwise distract her. Not only would the oni escape, but she and the sword, both frustrated, might cut down the misguided rescuer.

Over the thundering heels, and the oni's agonized roars, came a familiar voice.

"Mrs. Cooper! Francine! Move aside!"

She neither turned nor slowed as she replied. "Lieutenant Foster? You got my message?"

"Yes! Now move! You're in our line of fire!"

"Bullets won't harm an oni. Lieutenant. Didn't you learn that last night?" Shouting made Cooper's throat raw. Her eyes began to water. She rubbed the lids, one at a time, with a bloodied hand.

The demon's too-bright ebon eyes looked past Cooper to the blue-clad warriors, obviously members of the same clan he'd fought the night before. Then his gaze returned, fascinated, to the iron sword held by his nemesis.

"You're interfering with police business, Mrs. Cooper!" Foster shouted. "I order you to leave the scene!"

"No, Lieutenant. This is *giri* ... duty!"

A word! An isolated word, out of all the gibberish that passed for speech in this time and place! He stopped to study the woman warrior more carefully.

She did not stop.

Could she understand him? Might she be persuaded to share an overlordship with him?

He made the offer.

The woman must have understood, if only from his tone. A thin smile curled her lips. Still she advanced.

He'd seen such determination before:

In his traitorous bodyguard, Ashika.

In the peasant who'd died under torture, after first biting through his own tongue so that he could not speak.

In the eyes of a frail and aged priest.

In the expressionless face of a preadolescent pillow boy whom he'd thought he'd thoroughly cowed.

Then the woman did something that sent a shudder of pure fear through his body.

She invoked his name.

"Uto! You've lived too long!"

The snarling tone of the unexpected words startled Cooper as she spoke them. She did not talk in this manner. Yet doing so felt appropriate.

The oni stopped. A triad of thick fingers grasped the wooden plank that shielded the third rail and tore it free. A flying bolt ricocheted off a stanchion to strike the exposed rail, raising blue sparks. The oni waved the makeshift club triumphantly. His favorite weapon could easily keep the woman more than a sword's length from him.

Cooper's heart sank as she realized this. She was sure to lose a contest of stamina, kami or no. She knew her limitations.

The plank smashed the flat of her blade. Her two-handed grip retained the sword, barely. Her fingers tingled with numbness.

Cooper retreated, moving to her left. If she lured the oni into a confined space, such as one of the recesses along the tunnel wall, he wouldn't have room enough to swing the plank. Close-quarter fighting had another risk, though. If the oni actually got his hands on Cooper, she was good as dead. She would not mind, if she could take him with her.

Her sidestep left a clear path between the oni and the police. Foster ordered the squad to fire.

Bullets glanced off rock-hard skin. One ricochet gouged Cooper's right cheek. She ducked between two subway cars, realizing the gunplay would be directed away from the train. There she muttered blistering opinions of New York's Finest.

The demon forgot her. His ebon eyes glowed preternaturally.

Spittle foamed over crusty red lips. Titanic limbs trembled with bloodlust. He spread his arms wide, threatening, and advanced on his latest foes.

It was an opening Cooper could not afford to ignore. She plunged for safety, keeping low to avoid the hail of bullets.

"Cease fire!" Foster ordered.

Most of their guns needed reloading, anyway.

The force of Cooper's charge drove the sword point into the oni's stomach and out his back, unfortunately missing the spine. A roar of agony tore at her eardrums, but Cooper clung to the hilt, pushing upward until the guard prevented further movement. The oni's club whistled through the fetid air, but Cooper was too near the creature for a clean strike. The wood splintered across her shoulders, not unlike a hearty slap.

The oni gnashed his fangs. His free hand wrapped around Cooper's throat, throttling her as he tried to shake her off. She tightened her own grip, hands already white with strain, fingerbones crackling. She fought to ignore her body's growing need for air, and the increasing dread of a sudden snap that would mean a broken neck. Photons streaked through her eyes, blurring vision.

The blade twisted sideways, opening a wide gash in the belly. The demon howled and released the woman's neck to clutch at his wound.

Intestines like huge black snakes spilled steaming from the cut. The stench from the creature's bowels overwhelmed the half-suffocated Cooper. She staggered back, gasping for fresher air. The hilt slipped from her fingers, but the blade remained buried in the oni's gut. It *wanted* to stay there.

Cooper stumbled northward, nursing her sore neck, gulping to relieve her burning lungs. She'd gone almost the length of the stalled train when her legs rebelled. She toppled.

By then, Lieutenant Foster had run forward. He caught her with an arm about her waist. The right side of her coat was wet and sticky. His cease-fire order hadn't come fast enough. He half-carried the woman to a spot behind the officers stretched in a thin line for the width of the tunnel.

Cooper recovered her wits. She dug in her heels and turned

her head to look, with widening eyes, at her nemesis.

The oni stood less than a man's height now, and was still slowly diminishing. He wavered on the crossties, tossing the shattered plank aside. Black, gelatinous blood spilled down his crotch and legs to pool thickly about three-toed feet. The creature's hands grasped the hilt of the iron sword and tugged.

Cooper gasped in horror. The blade began to slide free.

"No!" she screamed. She struggled forward. Foster reached from behind to pin her arms to her sides. She kicked at him. He smacked her ankle painfully with a sharp heel.

"None of that, Mrs. Cooper."

"You don't understand," she said, pleading. "If he pulls that sword out, he'll get away!"

Foster jerked his head toward the ceiling of the tunnel. Overhead, upper Broadway was filled with wailing sirens.

"He won't get far." The promise sounded hollow even as Foster made it. He was tempted to trust her judgment and let her go back. Training overcame instinct. He couldn't risk the lives of civilians on a whim, not even on a civilian's own whim.

Cooper tensed to break free and became abruptly aware of the searing in her right side. The pain made her sag limply into Foster's arms. She could only watch the oni's struggle with resigned horror. Emotion was leached from her voice.

"Too late," she said.

The sword was easing free, though slowly, hindered by the viscous blood. The hilt bounced dully on a wooden tie. By this time the oni was too small to allow the blade to slip straight down, but he only had to step back. Gravity would finish the task.

The oni looked north along the tunnel. His eyes fixed on Cooper. His scabrous lips twisted in that infamous grin, solely for her benefit. He'd lost this skirmish, but the war was barely begun.

The callused sole of a three-toed foot rasped on the discarded wooden plank. The board cracked under his weight. The oni turned to check his footing. It would not do to slip and fall in the middle of his victory. Dignity must be preserved.

The sword swung as he turned. It scraped the tunnel floor.

And touched the exposed section of the third rail.

Sparks flew, filling the tunnel with light for a blinding instant. Ozone scorched the air. The oni's skin shone blue-white.

And started to run like melting wax.

The tunnel plunged into total darkness. Signal lights, work lights, even the bulbs on the station platforms blinked out. Miles away, subway controllers had been informed of the planned evacuation of trapped passengers. They shut off the current at the first sign of a short. Some idiot had obviously stumbled into the third rail. Two questions hovered in the minds of the men at the master control:

How many were dead?

Who would catch hell for this?

The hour-long seconds that followed were filled only by soft sobs from the stalled train, heavy breathing from the line of police officers, and a muffled curse from the Seventy-Second Street platform, where a bag lady had evaded the evacuation team.

Sergeant Brunner clicked her service flashlight on, its beam focused where the oni had stood.

Kura's ancestral blade lay by the third rail, scorched and twisted almost beyond recognition. Cooper didn't know how she would explain that to Allison Zebar, much less how Zebar would explain it to *her* supervisors.

All that remained of the oni was a formless puddle, dark red, sticky, and malodorous. This evaporated even as Cooper and the police watched. It would never be reconstituted.

Warm, intangible breezes circled Cooper for the last time, unfelt by Foster and the other police. The kami of the sword, and of the Akuragawa family, were free to pursue other destinies— or no destiny at all, if they so desired. The obligation had been met. Even Andrew Kura, she sensed, forgave her. He, too, was now kami, a god in his own right.

Then the warmth was gone.

And Cooper knew that, although Kura might forgive her, she would never quite forgive herself.

Wetness splotched her cheek over the drying blood from the ricocheted bullet wound. Cooper glanced up. She stood beneath an open air grating. Because it was bent downwards, she knew it was the same one the oni had used to enter the subway tunnel. A brilliant moon poked a round edge through a gap in the cloud cover. More police flashlights clicked on. In the criss-crossing beams, Cooper saw a white crystal flake drift down through a gap in the grate.

She turned to Lieutenant Foster, who still supported her. "It's snowing," she said.

Foster looked up at the night sky. "A light flurry." He gave her a reassuring squeeze. Cooper gasped, reminding him of the sticky feel of her coat. "Sorry. Take it easy. You've been shot."

"Damn," Cooper said. "No wonder it hurts." She closed her eyes and rested her head against the lieutenant's shoulder. She was asleep on her feet.

Fifteen minutes later, Francine Cooper was being treated in the same Emergency Room that Gary Cross had stumbled into half a week earlier. It was there, in the waiting room, that Foster made the telephone call that explained to him what had happened to Rogan's back-up. Bombings by terrorists had rocked police and federal buildings in lower Manhattan and Brooklyn.

An ancient terror had been laid to rest, leaving room for the modern ones to continue.

ABOUT THE AUTHOR

Gordon Linzner is founder and former editor/publisher of
Space and Time Magazine. He is the author of the novels
The Spy Who Drank Blood, The Oni, and The Troupe, as well as
dozens of short stories appearing in Fantasy & Science Fiction,
Twilight Zone, Sherlock Holmes Mystery Magazine, and numer-
ous other magazines and anthologies.

Curious about other Crossroad Press books?
Stop by our site:
http://store.crossroadpress.com
We offer quality writing
in digital, audio, and print formats.

Enter the code FIRSTBOOK
to get 20% off your first order from our store!
Stop by today!

Made in the USA
Las Vegas, NV
27 May 2024